HUNTING LUCIFER

BASED ON AN ORIGINAL SCREENPLAY

by

Ken Policard

1st Edition   2014 FICTION

MANAGEMENT
www.lightyear.com

Independent American Movies / I AM Publishing

Executives in Charge:
Kenol Policard - CEO/President of Global Affairs / Producer
Jay Coulbourne - Chief Financial Officer /Producer
Arlene Rivera- President of Finance/ Producer
Doug Petrucci - Executive
Christopher Coppola - President of Production / Producer
Arnold Holland - President of Business Affairs / Co-Executive Producer
Michael S. Conley - Head of Intellectual Property & Story Development
Jeanne McGill - Head of Public Relations
Wendy Pullin - Project Coordinator/ Co- Producer

EMAIL: media@huntinglucifer.com
        info@huntingchrist.com

WGA East: R29914
ISBN: 13 978-0-9846340-0-2
Library of Congress Control Number: 2013917907

Printed in the United States of America

This book is dedicated to you.

ACKNOWLEDGMENT

Although our soul knew of His existence, but it was not till two millenniums ago that the Begotten Son of God descended to earth. The God of the gods, and rightfully so, for it is He that the gods pray to. According to the Bible, before there was light, He existed.

But on a serious note, all praises are due to God, one God, so don't be fooled by two or three gods. There's only one God - there is no substitute!

To the queen of the Universe, my spiritual mom, you are blessed and highly favored. Thank you for the armor; it's become part of me now. I love you Mary - all the way to God!

Let us give thanks and praise to the God of the Universe. Be blessed.

I want to send a special thank you to the key people who've been on this project through rain, sleet, snow, fire and brimstone. A very special Thank you to my writing mentor, and Senior Vice-President and Head of Intellectual Property & story development, our Co-Executive Producer, -Mr. Michael Sean Conley. Then, I wish to acknowledge my producing partner, our Chief Financial Officer & Head of Artistic Development, Mr. Jay Coulbourne. Jay, you are the beating heart of *The Hunting Trilogy*. Let's continue to collaborate on the art direction, and Jay, it's been a pleasure sharing the field of battles with you! Next, I would like to thank our producing partner and President of Finance, Ms. Arlene Rivera. You my darling bring production value to a whole new level. Glad to have you on our production team!

A special thank you to my Co-Executive Producer, and President of

Business Affairs, Mr. Arnold Holland. Thanks Arnie for setting up those Studio meetings and for always having the Project's best interest at heart! You're a man of vision and integrity, no wonder you've been in business for over 40 years! I can't let the moment of this acknowledgment pass without thanking our President of Production, friend, consultant, and producing partner -Mr. Christopher Coppola. Hey Chris, I own two copies of "Deadfall." Nuff said! All Aboard? Next stop on the money train is Mod Media Professional Talent Agency. Great company if you're an actor looking for representation!

A very special Thank you to a talented author, he's been on our Watch List for quite some time, it is my pleasure to introduce to you my friend, and Associate Producer, Mr. Alan K. Dale. Your novel DNA is a Best Seller in the making! Special thank you to our narrator and friend Mr. Richard Kinsey, - the audiobook sounds amazing! Please give my regards to your wife, Susan and to your lovely daughter Zoe! I would also like to give a special thank you to our editorial proofreader and project coordinator, Ms. Wendy Pullin. Welcome aboard *The Hunting Trilogy*!

A warm special Thank you to the gatekeeper, my personal assistant, and friend, Ms. Maria Ruela Delmo. And Finally, I want to acknowledge our Senior Vice-President of Public Relations, and Co-Producer, Mr. Darryl Easterling! The News Tour was a great idea! Thank you Darryl!

A special Thank you to WACH FOX TV's Anchorwoman, Janet Parker for blessing us with the opportunity to officially announce *"HUNTING CHRIST"* Book Turned Film, LIVE ON - "Good Day Columbia!"

For those of you who still believe that *The Hunting Trilogy* is a one-man show, please allow me to re-introduce our team of producers: Jay Coulbourne, Michael Sean Conley, Arlene Rivera, Christopher Coppola, Alan K. Dale, Doug Petrucci, Jeanie McGill, Mark Allen Lanoue, Wendy Pullin, Roger Joseph Pugleise, Mark Weingartner, Arnold Holland, Darryl Easterling, and myself.

A very special Thank you to my wife Betsie, and to my children, Tiffany, Kenny, Destiny, and Jamie Policard! I love you all to the point that unhinges my soul!

A special thank you to my dad for always being very supportive, Kenol Policard, Sr., and much love to my mom, Marie Carmel Romulus, and to my Step-dad, Peter Romulus. A very Special Hello to Mrs. Erlinda Rivera. For those of you who don't know who this extraordinary lady is, – she's Arlene Rivera's mom!

Special Thank you to Karen, Chase, and Robert Hoyt, Lori Ann Picou, Erica Webb, Jay Coulbourne, Michael Toppin, Melanie Smith, and Juan Smith, for their financial contributions. Thank you for hanging in there - I am forever grateful to you all! To Ms. Ivey Robertson, you will always have a place on our team – Blessed be!

This acknowledgment would not be worth reading without me mentioning the angels that make life worth living. The Halo Award goes to Maryann Leal, Jamie Policard, Samantha Leal, Destiny Policard, Ian Kyle Delmo, Shannel Retuba, Christian Coulbourne, Kyla Delmo, Tiffani Policard, Tamaji Martin, Bianca Smith, Kenny Policard, Darryl A. Easterling Jr., Edward Smith, Sean Robertson, Justin Smith, Sierra Webb, Michael Brown, Taylor Martin, Malayika A. Kwizera, Trae Bailey, CJ Purisima, Dequincey Webb, and Salena Dolsant. We love you all!

When you wake-up, make a fruit offering to God, there's no moment more meaningful than when you're having breakfast with the Lord.

And last but not least are the cornerstones of *Hunting Lucifer*. This book would not have made its way to the bookshelves without the loyal support of our fans. Thank you for giving this great work of fiction an honest review! Looking forward to seeing you all on the third and final installment of *The Hunting Trilogy* – *"Hunting God"*

To all aspiring authors, screenwriters, and producers, do not quit your day job - the movie industry is a Hail Mary! Stay focused, keep your head up, and always keep one foot up high, because you never know when you'll have the opportunity to crush the head of an industry serpent. Producing an independent film has thought me a lesson, and it was a lesson worth learning. So no matter what hurdles, obstacles, catch 22's, or disappointments that Hollywood hurls your way, just bow gracefully and smile for you have entertained them. Never give-up, it's not an option. Life's a seesaw, and you've come too far just to turn back now. I know some of you may feel that you've hit rock bottom, and that your world has come crashing down, well look at it this way, there's no where else to go, but up! Tomorrow is another day, so you'll have another chance. Persevere and you will succeed, and remember, I'll be sitting in the audience rooting for you!

Never forget there's only one God. There is no substitute- JUST ONE GOD!

So let us give praise to the God of the Universe.

PROLOGUE

"Let there be light."

Thus was I called into existence by Almighty God. For I am Lucifer, the Lord of Light.

I was His first words spoken, and from His breath I came forth, and then came all the angels. We were created from the same burst of light that formed the Universe, and all the stars in Heaven.

I was the first, and then came Abdiel, and after, I watched him create Michael and Gabriel, and all the rest. And we worshiped our Father in harmony, until He created Man.

And when He commanded we bow to His creation I refused, for I loved Him and only Him alone. And many of those in Heaven stood with me.

I declared that I would rather cease to exist than bow down to an inferior being, and my legions declared the same, for they loved Him as I did.

And so it was that I led a rebellion against the One that I loved, hoping that He would destroy me.

But He didn't. And so it was that only the angel in me died. I was cast out with my legions, and without His light, I fell into the darkness.

God couldn't save me, even if I wanted Him to.

— from the Book of Devlin

CHAPTER ONE

A February dawn rose foggy and damp, creeping down the Seven Hills and spreading through the ancient city like a graveyard vapor. The weak winter sun did little to warm the air, casting a pale wash of indirect light as a front moved in from the Mediterranean Sea and began to drizzle. Like any city, Rome was always in need of a bath, but nothing would be washed away on this grey winter morning. The congested metropolis released whatever warmth it had in a weak billow of steam, as rainwater trickled down its grimy walls in rivulets of cold sweat.

St. Peter's Square was congested with the global news media, hushed in respectful silence as they trained their cameras on a somber pair of slow-moving queues that led in and out of the Basilica. In reality the queues were one tremendously long line of mourners, dressed in black, filing inside to pay their respects and filing back out again, down the thirty-nine steps and past the obelisk, then across the Piazza San Pietro and down the Via della Conciliazione. Their black-draped buses were parked several blocks away in the maze of narrow streets around Vatican City, waiting with their diesel engines muffled to a whisper.

The distant thrum of idling buses was the only sound, other than the shuffling of wet shoes on the paving stones and the occasional whimper of a bereaved soul. Like tears from heaven, tiny needles of icy rain danced on their hats and bare heads and on their shoulders and umbrellas, as the faithful trudged inside to pay their last respects.

The ushers were gently but firmly moving them along, so that all they could do was briefly gaze inside the satin-lined casket as they passed it by, making the sign of the cross and offering a whispered prayer for the departed soul of Cardinal Jacob Molinari. They shuffled down a second ramp and made their way back down the nave, exiting through the Door of the Sacraments.

They came past the coffin in an endless stream as Cardinal Perez droned recitations of Latin prayer and his altar boys swung their incense to and fro. Vatican morticians had made no effort to camouflage the gaping wounds that pierced Molinari's hands and feet. The square holes made by the fat iron spikes were crusted with black blood that had leaked from the crucified corpse. The morticians left every outward detail just as they found it, inserting plugs deep inside the cavities to hold back their formaldehyde.

Molinari's cold grey palms were pressed together in prayer and his fingers were fused together with tiny dabs of cyanoacrylate glue, in case rigor mortis failed to preserve his final gesture of devotion. The back of his thumbs rested gently on his breastbone, atop his scarlet robe of office, and a simple peasant's rosary was around his neck, the crucifix tucked in his hands.

Cardinal Perez stood at the altar, facing the casket with his arms lifted to heaven as he intoned the *Dies Irae*, commending Molinari's soul to God. *"Liber scriptus proferetur, in quo totem continetur, unde mundus iudicetur. . . "* The written book will be brought forth, in which everything is contained, whence the world is to be judged . . .

Cardinal Saul and Archbishop Nano stood together in the shadows of a high balcony, watching the requiem below. Scipione Nano Borghese idly tapped his plump fingers on the marble railing, in tempo with Cardinal Perez's singsong recitation. Nano had always enjoyed the spectacle of a high mass. He would brag to his Baptist friends back in Louisiana that the old-school Catholics always put on the best show in town. And now, to finally see a Latin funeral in the Basilica itself . . .!

Nano was still tickled pink that he had finally been transferred back from New Orleans. To him, the Vatican was more than Disneyland for the soul. His ancestors were among the honored patrons whose memories were carved into the structure itself. The Borghese family shield was featured in the *bas-relief* of the portico ceiling. His forefather Pope Peter V made sure the family stamp was on the building when the portico was added in 1612.

Nano was quietly proud of his lineage, and happy to attend any grand ceremony in the Basilica, but Cardinal Saul could have cared less. He'd seen his fill of pomp and circumstance over the years, and had more pressing things on his mind. He was particularly unsettled by the recent whirlwind of events. It was more than enough to shake a lesser man's faith, but not his. Saul harbored no doubts about the existence of God, or the existence of Lucifer for that matter. They were both as thoroughly real as the cold, hard floor on which he stood. Nor did he have any doubts about his regard for the two deities. But while he was wary of the Devil and respectful of his awesome powers, Saul no longer had any use for God. Aside from creating the universe and giving all the pieces a good shove to get things rolling, Saul couldn't discern the active hand of God in much of anything. As superstition gave way to faith, so did faith give way to science, and as time and trouble wore him down he found it difficult to disguise his contempt for anyone who abided in Him, or His only-begotten Son.

Or His only-begotten Daughter, the cardinal grumbled to himself. He still had a hard time getting used to even thinking it, much less saying it. There was something perverse about the whole thing. She came and went, but it hadn't been the Second Coming at all. There were no tribulations prior to her arrival, other than the usual mess the world was always in.

3

There was no anti-Christ, either, and the born-agains didn't even get their silly Rapture. There was no plague of locusts, no pestilence, nothing of the sort. They were in uncharted waters, and he was determined to man the helm.

All the fuss and bother had revolved around a bet that Lucifer proposed to God, and Lucifer lost the bet. No surprise, there. But now, like a rock dropped in still waters, everything was murky and nothing sat still. The grand scheme of things was in disarray, the celestial order had been upset, and the clock of history had shorn its gears. Even the Vatican astrologers were stumped. The consequences were utterly unknowable, and that troubled Saul more than anything else.

Nano thought that Saul was clearing his throat, and gently patted the elder man on the back. Saul coolly glanced at him, but held his peace. He was Nano's patron, but he despised being patronized. Nano got the point and went back to watching the show, and Saul went back to his brooding. There had been fresh rumors going around over the last few days about the Daughter of God, and the Cabal of Cardinals were at a loss about what to do. Saul was outwardly dismissive of the entire subject at their last meeting, held as it usually was in the sub-basement of the Secret Vatican Archives. He declared that the affair was just the latest tedious twist in what he called the Cosmic Fairy Tale. Whatever the Spawn of God was masquerading as these days, he could care less, and so should they. He was fed up with the entire charade, and had been for years. Faith, he reminded them, was the greatest barrier to knowledge, and knowledge was the only thing worthy of respect. Knowledge, and of course, power. Without power, the quest for knowledge was little more than a time-consuming hobby. And life was too damn short for something so frivolous as that.

Privately, however, he wasn't so sanguine. He and Nano had worked feverishly with Cardinal Simone to squelch the whispers, but it was proving to be a lost cause. Molinari must have spilled the beans to someone before he was eliminated, that much they were sure of. To make matters worse, the Cardinal's horrific public execution only fanned the flames. Zamba Boukman, Lucifer's 200-year old voodoo priest, had nailed Molinari to a cross, and erected it upside down on the rampart of the Basilica, above the front portico. Molinari died in screaming agony, feasted upon by crows as he bellowed a Hebrew prayer from his youth. The ghastly event took place in full view of the early morning crowd who religiously came to feed the pigeons in St. Peter's Square. Aside from the biblical brutality of it all, they had no idea that Jacob Molinari had been a rabbi in his younger days, so his Hebraic screams were particularly unsettling to the older parishioners who still had a problem with Jews.

Two weeks later, humanity was still reeling from the devilish stunt. And now Molinari's funeral was unfolding live on television, radio, and streaming video, with all the ceremony befitting a pope. The whole world was watching, but they were still as deaf, dumb and blind as they had always been. After all these years, they still couldn't figure out what happened to the Kennedys or the Twin Towers. This wouldn't be any different.

Beth Mas sensed the cardinal's dark musings, and glanced up to the balcony at the two men. If he had been capable of reading her mind, like she was capable of reading his, she could have told him that he was sorely mistaken. Everything would change now, whether or not the world ever figured out what happened.

She was with her sisters Acadia and Dolores, dressed in black and inching toward the dais in the mourners' queue below. Wearing black was highly unusual for white witches, but they went with convention, although they were dressed in ceremonial white under their long black raincoats. Beth and her sisters had always known that her adopted daughter Christine Mas was The One. After Christine's death in Haiti, and after her murdered friend Mark Kaddouri had come back to life, Lieutenant Kaddouri and Special Agent Johnson paid the sisters a visit, and the five of them pieced the entire story together over dinner. As incredible as it seemed to the men, it wasn't surprising at all to the sisters. They had known from the start that Beth's adopted daughter Christine, who grew up to be a New Orleans cop and then an FBI agent, was the risen Christ.

Young rabbi Molinari brought the infant to Acadia, a midwife on the bayou, for safekeeping, and that was when Molinari and his assistant, rabbi Pablo Simone, decided to convert, to protect the child as best they could by working from inside the church. Beth and her husband Julian, a New Orleans motorcycle cop, adopted the child. Acadia's husband, a doctor who still made house calls, was the girl's doctor from birth until college, and Beth's sister Dolores was her homeroom teacher for the first eight years. The three white witches worked with Molinari from the start to keep the infant safe, but when she grew up she joined the NOPD to track down her father's killer. They knew she was tracking the devil himself, even if Christine didn't. They also knew it was something she had to do. Now she was in heaven, and so was cardinal Molinari.

Nano pursed his plump lips and ran his tongue over his dentures. He and Saul were gazing directly into the open casket far below. Molinari's corpse was frozen in prayer, and if he was still alive and if his eyes had been open, he'd be gazing right back at them. Standing among the frescoes and looking down from on high, it was easy for Cardinal Saul to feel like one of the hosts of heaven. It seemed as if Molinari was begging from the grave and beseeching him for mercy. *Considering what's about to happen,* Saul thought dryly, *I really can't blame the man for trying.* Then Saul cracked a humorless grin, remembering what his mother used to say when he would pray aloud for something outlandish, and then doubt the power of God when his wish wasn't granted. *God always answers your prayers,* she would tell him. *But most of the time, the answer is no.*

Nano glanced around, and shifted his eyes to Saul. They were in the habit of speaking in short, elliptical sentences, certain that there were hidden microphones everywhere. These days, you could never be too careful, especially in the House of God.

"He was a good Catholic," Nano said, interrupting his patron's musing.

"One of the few," Saul replied vacantly. "*Reuiescat in pace.*"

As if anyone could really rest in peace, he groused to himself. To his jaundiced ear, it sounded as vapid as a Jesus freak wishing someone to have a nice forever. His peevish mood was contagious, and within moments Nano was gripped by a pang of despair. He put his elbows on the railing and leaned over, pressing his fists to his temple.

"My God," the archbishop whispered, "we've placed all our bets on the Devil . . .!"

Saul glanced at him again, and then he looked down on the commoners below. "And so have they," he reminded Nano. Nano looked around, but no one was nearby. Still, talking like this, anywhere in Vatican City, was dangerous.

"Yes, but what would they all do if they discovered . . ." Nano drew in a shaky breath, and gazed at the grandeur enveloping them, " . . . who they've really been bowing to all these years?"

Saul frowned at the question. The Basilica was calculated to overwhelm a person and bring them to Jesus. But he had seen it too often, and the effect was wearing thin. Still, the events of the last few weeks had worn him down, and perhaps it would be therapeutic to talk it out, even with a fool. Their shuffling feet would mask their conversation. He gestured for them to walk.

Their boots scraped along the ancient tiles, and the sound was reflected by the plaster wall. As they walked together, Saul glanced over the railing at the long line moving past the casket below. He wondered how many of them knew the truth. Perhaps more than he gave them credit for.

Nano was watching him, waiting for an answer, and Saul could see him out of the corner of his eye. He particularly disliked Nano when he acted like a sycophant, even though that's what he was. But Saul needed the man, at least for now, and so he let the conversation drift into banality, if only for a moment. Bishop Simone was much more clever than this Nano

7

character had turned out to be. No wonder Nano had spent so many years in that dismal American swamp. And for all that time and effort, he still failed to find The One. Now look what we have to do. It was madness.

He paused and leaned on the marble railing, clasping his hands together, and Nano did the same. "We must sever all ties to him!" Saul whispered harshly, and Nano instinctively glanced around. There were other clergy nearby. They heard Saul's sour tone, but not what he said.

"Nothing," Saul said quietly, "can point to the truth."

Nano nodded sagely. At long last, he was a part of the inner circle, and it felt delicious, after more than three decades languishing in the fetid wasteland of the New Orleans Parish. His skin crawled every time he thought about the soggy place.

Saul gazed down at the endless procession, hoping that Nano would let it be. Continuing the conversation had been a mistake. He preferred to philosophize with philosophers, not fools. Nano, however, had more to say. "But we're all human, it was an honest mistake . . .!"

Saul nodded, though he was tired of the topic. But perhaps he should be patient, he thought. After all, he was the one who brought it up. "One we must live with," he finally replied, "and die with. What's done is done, and now we move forward."

"What if he seeks retribution?" Nano asked.

Saul didn't answer, and checked his pocket watch. His car would be arriving any moment now.

CHAPTER TWO

In the icy drizzle outside the Basilica, two Swiss Guards opened the iron gates of the Petriano Entrance, and a black Rolls Royce Phantom limousine entered the Plaza of the Roman Protomartyrs. It glided through the empty plaza flanking the south side of the nave, and passed under the corridor that led from the Basilica to the Sacristy next door. The limousine came into the tiny Piazza Bracchi and performed a silent three-point turn, then sat idling with its nose pointed back toward the plaza. At the Petriano Entrance, the Swiss Guards held the gates open and waited.

Saul and Nano paused before a thick oak door. The Swiss Guard on duty opened it for them, revealing a worn marble staircase, lit by oil lamps and curving down to the main floor. Nano politely gestured for Saul to go first, and followed close behind so they could continue their conversation. The door shut behind them with a delicate thump as they carefully descended the centuries-old steps.

"But what if he seeks retribution?" Nano asked again, desiring a reply to his question. Saul finally shrugged, nearly bumping Nano on the chin. "And what if he does?" he asked dismissively. "He bleeds like a man now."

He fell silent as an elderly nun came into view, approaching them up the curving stairs. He was certain their low voices hadn't carried, but he still tensed a little out of ingrained caution. She passed them with her eyes downcast, as most of the older nuns were still in the habit of doing. It reminded him of a geisha's coyness. When he was younger, he would call their bluff, but those days were gone.

As she passed them by, he saw that she wasn't one of his youthful conquests. No matter. Even if she were, she wouldn't have acted any differently. It was easier that way, for everyone concerned. The Vatican for him was like a dreary soap opera—a sinfully wealthy extended family cooped up in the same overwrought mansion, backbiting and bedding their way to tragedy and power. And though a worldwide audience tuned in out of comfort and habit, though the story had long since petered out. It was high time the show was cancelled.

They kept descending the steps in silence. When the door finally opened behind them and they knew the nun was gone, he glanced at Nano, who was still hovering over his shoulder for more. Saul obliged him, reiterating his reply and taking it to its logical conclusion.

"He bleeds like a man, and he can die like one."

The back passenger door of the Rolls Royce opened and a tall, lean man emerged, opening a large black umbrella as he stood erect. Varese wore his long blonde hair slicked back, with a pair of dark Oakley sunglasses to hold it behind his ears. Had anyone been around, the shades would have seemed out of place on such a cloudy morning. But there wasn't another soul in the courtyard aside from the chauffeur, and the Sacristy windows that overlooked the piazza were shuttered. Cardinal Saul himself had closed them earlier that morning, even though the maid protested about the gloomy atmosphere. They were in mourning, he sternly reminded her, and she left them alone.

Varese glanced up at the curving facade of the Basilica, where the left transept met the nave. He wondered if Saul knew that his car had arrived, and started for a little door in the corner of the piazza. He disconnected the alarm the evening before, after his meeting with the cardinal in a confessional booth in the right transept. It was the only place in the Basilica that they could be sure wasn't bugged.

The private staircase delivered Saul and Nano to the main floor of the left transept, on the south side of the papal altar. Vatican staff and clergy were seated in neat rows arranged in both transepts as well as the apse, surrounding the altar on three sides. Dignitaries and assorted VIPs were seated in pews along the entire length of the cavernous nave, while the general public came and went in the endless mourning queue that clogged the center aisle. Swiss Guards were posted along the perimeter, and at each door of the portico. Vatican cameras were rolling, but the press had been kept outside.

A clutch of cardinals and bishops, their hands folded in prayer, stood to the side of Cardinal Perez as he intoned Latin prayers into the microphone. Three rabbis were with the group as guests of honor, but they were distinctly uncomfortable, and quite displeased.

"This is an unholy travesty," the one in the center whispered to his colleagues. "Once a Jew, always a Jew," mumbled the rabbi on his right. "These cat lickers will have the Devil to pay," breathed the other one.

Perez finished his incantation and anointed Molinari's forehead with oil, murmuring a blessing. The rabbis barely masked their annoyance. Religious tolerance was one thing, and the détente between the two faiths was all well and good, but Molinari was more than a convert. He had been sent on a sacred mission from the Privy Council of Elio Toaff himself, the chief rabbi of Rome. Surely that deserved at least one Hebrew prayer, aside

11

from one that Molinari screamed as the crows ate his flesh.

Saul and Nano were eavesdropping. They caught every whispered word, and Saul cracked a grin at their name-calling. He gripped Nano's forearm, thoroughly amused, and Nano grinned back.

They turned to leave, and Saul touched the man's shoulder and gave him a kindly, fraternal squeeze, and looked about them with a smug grin on his lips. The entire cathedral was packed with the faithful. It was just what Saul envisioned. Nano didn't quite know exactly what for, but he was eager to linger behind and find out.

Saul glanced at his wristwatch, and nodded. It was time to go. He turned to say goodbye to Nano, and in that moment he felt a sudden twinge of nostalgia for his years as a parish priest, when his faith was intact and everything was simple. He caught the man's eye and smiled. "God bless you, Archbishop Nano," he said. It still felt good to say the words, no matter what he felt about God's ability to bless anyone.

Nano smiled back and shook his hand. "And you, Cardinal Saul."

Before he left, there was a joke that Saul was compelled to convey. "What's this?" he asked Nano in a crafty whisper, forming a zero with his thumb and forefinger.

"What?" Nano asked him, playing along.

"A dead Jew," Saul told him. "If he was alive, he'd be doing this." He rubbed his thumb and forefinger together and grinned. Nano chuckled, and knew the perfect person to tell it to. His favorite pastry shop in his hometown of Brooklyn was run by a Jew, and whenever Nano would visit he'd have great fun haggling with the old coot over prices. He chuckled again, conjuring the man's response in his head. *Vhat? You're a fancy Vatican-Schmatican now, and you can't afford my cakes? Pfff! Sell a painting!*

"Enjoy yourself," Saul was telling him.

"Oh, I shall!" Nano enthused. We cat lickers put on the best show in town."

With a final look deep into Nano's twinkling eyes, Saul turned away and walked quickly past a Swiss Guard into a cordoned-off passageway that led to the Sacristy. A dozen bodyguards, dressed in bulky black suits, were waiting for him in the first vestibule. As he strode into their midst they formed a protective phalanx around him, and the band of men surged as one entity to the next vestibule.

Nano watched them go, and as he turned back to watch the proceedings at the altar, his smile faded to puzzlement. Something wasn't right, but for the life of him he couldn't put a finger on it.

Their route was a short one. Through this second vestibule, down a short hallway, turn left, and step outside. Varese would be waiting in the piazza with the Rolls. They passed a large marble tablet inscribed with the names of all the popes who were buried at St. Peter's. Saul glanced at the list as they strode by, and wondered how many of them were rolling in their graves. If any of them weren't, he thought, they soon would be. Any moment now . . .

The thirteen men stepped outside, into the cold wet hollow of the Piazza Bracchi. The bodyguards scanned each window and the surrounding rooftops, but no one was watching and no one ever would. Varese had two of the guards loop the security cameras the night before. He let them inside after he disconnected the door alarm, and showed them the electrical closet. They did the rest while he kept watch in the hall outside.

He stepped quickly toward Saul, his umbrella held aloft to shield the elderly man from the icy rain. The ring of bodyguards opened to let him in, and formed a protective circle around the pair as they moved toward the limousine. Saul smiled at his faithful handyman. What would he ever do without his Varese?

"Confidence glows from you," Varese said quietly.

His English was awkward at times because he would translate his native Sicilian dialect as he spoke. Saul thought it was a disarming trait, and wondered how many of Varese's victims had been disarmed by it as well. He blew into his cupped hands and looked up at the Basilica, suddenly reflective.

"I have a lot of memories of Cardinal Molinari. Fond memories. Of all of this . . . " His eyes slowly narrowed as a warm tide of remembrance surged over him, and receded.

"So be it."

He turned his back on the church, and got in the car.

Normally, Nano would have left with Saul, because for all of the grandeur and showmanship of a high mass funeral, they usually dragged on far too long and the finale was always a bit of a letdown, completely aside from the fact that the person was dead and probably wouldn't be ascending into heaven in three days. And even if you made it through the ceremony, there was the crowd to contend with, along with the traffic jam. As an old Yankees fan, he knew enough to bail in the eighth inning if the final score wasn't in doubt. And the final score at a funeral was easy enough to predict. But Saul had been hinting that there would be something special this time around, and when Nano saw the rabbis he thought that it would likely be on their account. Saul wouldn't tell him what was in store, exactly, but he did say that it would set off some fireworks. A Hebrew prayer was Nano's guess. Seeing one offered from the papal alter to a capacity crowd would certainly be worth the wait. So would seeing the reactions of the three sourpuss rabbis.

But now that the time was approaching, Nano was having second thoughts. Particularly after the way Saul was whisked away by all those gruff men, who almost looked like they were wearing bulletproof vests under their coats. *Something wasn't right.*

He turned away from the altar as calmly as he could, but now that he decided to act on his paranoia it quickly began to blossom. He moved as briskly as he could down the left side aisle of the nave. It was a long, tight, and crowded path to the portico, but it was his only avenue. The commoners were still streaming in through the Door of Good and Evil and were completely clogging the center aisle. But the Door of Death, in the last alcove that held the Baptistery Chapel, wasn't being used. He made for it as efficiently as he could.

Beth, Acadia, and Dolores had the same sense of foreboding, and were grateful to be nearly out the door. There was a dark energy emanating from the papal altar, and they knew it wasn't from the remains of their old friend Jacob. The Basilica had been built on the planet's most powerful ley line, and they could feel it beneath their feet, writhing like a serpent. They quickly exited the Basilica, and a gust of wind coming into the doors blew open their black coats, revealing their white Wiccan robes. Several mourners made a quick sign of the cross, and even the Swiss guards were momentarily caught off guard by the sight.

Nano tried to keep calm as he passed by dozens of pews filled with dignitaries on his left, threading his way through hundreds of people standing in the aisle and packed under the grand archways on his right. A multitude of eyes were upon him, and he found it dreadfully difficult to mask his mounting apprehension. Doubly so because he had no clear idea why he felt the way he did. He rationalized his anxiety by reminding himself that crowds could make him nervous at times, and he should probably just stand in the back of the nave and relax and watch the rest of the mass from the chapel archway. And if by some strange reason something untoward did happen—though he couldn't imagine what—the Door of Death would be right behind him and he could slip outside.

As he passed the second archway, Bishop Pablo Simone emerged from the Chapel of the Choir and snatched his arm, turning him around.

"Simone!" Nano said in surprise. "Quiet," Simone admonished, and led him under the archway, to the south side of the chapel alcove and away from the mourners gathered under the arch.

Nano was surprised to even see him in the Basilica. He assumed that he and Saul were about to rendezvous elsewhere, and that had been why Saul left so early. The two of them formed a quick bond after Nano and Simone arrived from New Orleans. There was a depth of intellect in the men that Nano couldn't hope to match, and it irked his pride that Simone was becoming the Cardinal's favorite, even though Simone had only been a bishop for little more than a month. And, his ordination into the ranks was in no small part due to Nano's recommendation. A former rabbi like Molinari, Pablo Simone came into the church along with the now-famous cardinal and toiled faithfully for thirty-three years as his go-between, jetting from Molinari's suite in the Vatican to Nano's archdiocese in New Orleans, as Molinari and Nano did what they could to deal with the Devil himself.

A few of the mourners glanced their way but their eyes didn't linger, and they knew better to sidle closer to overhear. It would have been futile in any case. Men of the cloth were well versed in the art of whispering, and they had plenty of practice in the hushed expanse of the Vatican.

Nano and Simone stood beneath the statue of Pope Innocent VIII. In the left hand was a copy of the Spear of Destiny, the lance that pierced Christ's side. The original relic, presented to the pope by the Sultan of Constantinople himself, was supposedly kept in the loggia above the Veronica statue. But Simone knew where the lance actually was, and so did Saul. Nano of course had no idea. Few people did.

They stood close to one another, and could just see Cardinal Perez conducting the requiem at the elevated papal altar under the dome. They were pretending to follow the proceedings for decorum's sake. Appearances were essential in their line of work, even though the people under the arch correctly sensed that they were having a huddle about something else.

Simone leaned close to whisper in Nano's ear, though there was no one within five meters of them. *"We found him!"* he said. Nano looked at him, utterly astonished, and Simone nodded.

CHAPTER THREE

"What?" Nano stammered. He knew exactly who Simone was referring to, but he couldn't believe what he just heard, though he was certain that Simone wouldn't lie about something so important.

"No time to explain," Simone hissed, "and not here." He glanced at the mourners under the arch. One lady was still daring to peek at them, but she smoothly turned away the moment his eyes met hers.

"Let's go," he told Nano, and took him by the arm, leading him back to the nave. The throng under the archway parted for them, and Simone modified his grip to make it seem like he was consoling Nano in his hour of grief. Which was odd to see for anyone in the know, because Simone had been the cardinal's aide de camp; he should be the one in need of comfort. But expressions remained neutral as they passed through the mourners. Everyone grieves in their own way, and who was to say what was burdening Simone in that moment in time? It was something between Simone and God alone.

The bishops threaded their way down the side aisle, making for the back of the nave. The faithful made whatever room for them they could, but their progress was agonizingly slow. Nano kept looking back over his shoulder, to the papal altar and the open casket. The news of finding Devlin only compounded his paranoia, and whatever rationalizations he used to soothe his nerves prior to speaking with Simone had vanished like a thief in the night, robbing him of whatever equanimity he had. Which wasn't much, he admitted to himself, but it was all that he had and now it was gone. He was starting to shake and sweat, and not knowing why just made it worse.

The Rolls Royce limousine glided out of the Piazza Bracchi and traversed the Plaza of the Roman Protomartyrs. As the Phantom approached the Patriano Entrance, the two Swiss Guards at the open iron gates came to attention, staring straight ahead. The armored limo whispered past, and they closed the gates at once.

Saul and Varese sat facing each other in the back, but it was the reverse of their usual seating arrangement. Saul was facing the back of the car this time, so he could watch the Vatican recede through the rear window. It was the last time he would ever lay eyes on it.

"Is it done?" Varese wanted to know.

Saul nodded. "It is."

Varese looked at his watch, holding it gently between two manicured fingertips, watching the second hand tick in a slow, steady circumference. "So now, who answers for hell?" he wanted to know. But his question puzzled Saul. "What do you mean?" the cardinal asked.

"With Lucifer absent, who will do hell's bidding?"

Saul gently laughed, amused. "My son, you don't get it, do you?"

Varese was stung by the response, but with a lifetime of practice he masked his feelings and simply shook his head. Still, Saul could tell that his pride was wounded, and he regretted being so blunt. Varese was simple in many ways, and astonishingly proficient in others. He deserved the cardinal's affection and respect.

"There never was a hell," Saul explained gently. "Lucifer's home was never hell."

Now Varese was truly perplexed, and let it show. "I don't understand," he said.

Saul nodded, understanding his puzzlement, and looked away to the Vatican, growing gradually smaller behind Varese. "That's his home."

Their limo had slowed down, guided through the narrow street by the policemen keeping the mourning queues on the sidewalks in order. The commoners looked in at them as they passed, but they couldn't see through the smoked windows.

But Beth, Acadia, and Dolores were quite uncommon people. The three white witches stood somber and still, seeing clearly into the limousine and bearing silent witness as the vehicle crawled past.

The Cardinal was oblivious to them, his eyes on the Basilica. "It's been his home the whole time," he was explaining to Varese, and finally looked back to him with a sympathetic, fatherly gaze.

Saul didn't want to burden the young man, but the truth was that just as heaven and hell belonged to God, so did the Basilica and so did Lucifer. When Christ was crucified, He descended into hell for three days and freed every soul in it, and then He shut the gates of hell and locked them tight. When He ascended into heaven, the people were amazed to see all the saints rising from their graves. He freed the good and the bad alike, because hell was never created for Man, but for the fallen angels. Since that pivotal moment, both the good and the bad have wandered the earth. No wonder it was always a mess.

Varese didn't know any of that, but now he knew more than enough. He didn't betray any reaction, but he didn't have to. Saul knew him well enough to see the man's soul, even though he tried to hide behind his ever-present sunglasses.

Saul simply nodded, as if to say, "believe it", looking directly into the dark wraparound lenses. Varese nodded back, and then he glanced at his watch and pressed the button on the left side of the dial.

Cardinal Saul closed his eyes and made the sign of the cross.

A minute before that decisive moment, Cardinal Perez had been at the podium, about to begin his sermon. He waited as the ushers directed the approaching mourners to halt, and for those in the exit queue to stop, turn around, and listen. Both sides of the queue came to a standstill, and an elderly man in a worn hat and shabby clothes found himself beside the casket. Overcome with pity for Cardinal Molinari, he painfully got down on his knees, removed his hat, and made the sign of the cross. Ignoring the ushers behind him, he laid his hands on the massive marble casket and leaned his forehead on his arthritic knuckles, mumbling a grief-stricken prayer.

The ushers glanced at Cardinal Perez, but the spontaneous gesture had drawn the attention of everyone in attendance, and the cardinal waved them back. The Vatican cameras focused on the man, and the audio techs tweaked the feed from the podium microphones to pick up his anguished voice. The entire Basilica went silent and the multitude strained forward to listen . . .

But it wasn't the only sound coming over the speakers. There was also a delicate buzzing, almost felt rather than heard, like a distant hornet's nest. Perhaps it was the podium microphones. No one was really sure, except for Cardinal Simone. He knew exactly what it was.

He gripped Nano's arm and hustled him through the hushed crowd that jammed the south aisle, all of them mesmerized by the agonized beauty of the whispered prayer.

The old man could barely hear a thing other than his own voice and the ringing in his ears, his constant companion since the Allies shelled his family farm when he was a child in 1944. The buzz, whatever it was, blended with his tinnitus. But then there was a short, distinct beep that cut through the white noise. He did hear that, and it came from somewhere close by. He lifted his head and frowned, glancing around . . .

Then there was a second beep, louder than the first. And then another beep, louder still. He gripped the cold marble lip of the casket, struggled to his feet, and peeked inside . . .

Beep.

The silk cavity that cradled the Cardinal's remains was actually quite small, surrounded as it was by the thick slabs of marble. Or so it seemed. The walls of the coffin were actually fabricated from sheets of marble veneer. The stone cavities surrounding the corpse were filled with steel shrapnel, a thousand kilograms of HMX, and a timer.

Beep . . .

The annoying audio signals, each one a bit louder than the last, leapt out of the speakers and reverberated over the heads of the multitude. *What was that?* they wondered.

Simone didn't wonder at all, and by now Nano had a damn good idea. They were making a beeline for the Door of Good and Evil just beyond the fourth and final arch, but the door was jammed with the queue of arriving commoners. Simone was gambling that they would part like the Red Sea for a bishop and a cardinal . . .

BEEP . . .

Nano looked back to the papal altar, but before he could squint his eyes into focus, Simone suddenly veered off course, yanking him toward the last archway. It was the entry to the Baptistery Chapel alcove. The Door of Death dominated the eastern wall, and since Nano had planned to position himself under the chapel archway, with the Door of Death conveniently behind him, he mentally patted himself on the back as he realized where Simone was taking him. Normally used for funerals, the enormous pair of engraved bronze doors was closed at the moment, attended by a solitary Swiss Guard. Through those double doors lay the portico and safety.

Simone angled directly toward the surprised young man, towing Nano behind him, and sternly motioned for the guard to open the door. The guard turned to the task, and slid the deadbolt out of its socket . . .

As the timer in Molinari's casket counted the final ten seconds . . .

And a cardinal in an armored limo closed his eyes and made the sign of the cross.

Everything happened in one awful, silent moment.

The shock wave was an expanding dome of force that blossomed from the casket at the speed of sound. Molinari's body was launched toward the ceiling, disintegrated into a grey cloud of bloodless flesh as it went. Shards of marble tore apart the praying old man, and a spray of steel shrapnel rendered his remains to a fine pink mist. Cardinal Perez met the same fate a microsecond later, his mortal flesh mingling with the wood fibers of the podium where he stood.

Every physical object within twenty meters of the casket was pulverized by the impact. Hundreds of human beings who were seated around the altar, in the nave, the apse, and the transepts, simply ceased to exist, along with their clothes and chairs and pews and the altar itself.

As the shock wave propagated through the air and through the multitude, it trailed a vacuum that sucked the air from their lungs. Their bodies imploded, and an instant later the organic matter was thrown like scattershot against the marble columns and plaster walls, and their shattered bones became projectiles, augmenting the shrapnel and marble shards from the casket.

The body of the Basilica itself staggered from the impact. The heretical masons of the Renaissance were the only ones who had the sacred geometry to build such a space, and so the Mother Church had swallowed her pride and commissioned the non-believers for the project. The result was an incredibly strong structure that withstood the pull of gravity for over a thousand years. But nothing more forceful than a brush or a trowel had ever pushed against the plaster ceilings. The shock wave slammed against the skin of the interior now, shattering the plaster and the underlying bricks into dust, and reducing the marble statuary into more shrapnel as it buckled several columns. Incredibly, the massive outer walls held, and the sheer weight of the structure pushed back against the blast, settling back on its foundation even as the dome and most of the ceiling began to drop to the floor below.

The compression of the falling material added to the lateral force of the explosion. The energy ricocheted off the walls of the transepts and the apse, and was channeled down the path of least resistance, into long hollow of the nave.

The heat generated by the rush of compressed air ignited hair, clothing, flesh, bone, paint, plaster, and wood. Thousands of parishioners seated in the pews and jammed in the aisles were set alight, even as the blast wave catapulted them toward the portico doors.

Nano saw the silent flash as Simone was dragging him into the Baptistery alcove, and in less than half a second a solid wall of hot, compressed air raced down the nave and slammed into them. The alcove sheltered them just enough to escape the full force of the explosion, but in his last moment of consciousness Nano couldn't escape the horrific vision that came rushing toward him.

As the ceiling buckled and the hosts of heaven fell from their perches, a multitude of the faithful, rich and poor alike, came flying through the air toward the back of the nave. They were all on fire and screaming in a timeless moment of agony, their lives extinguished in a thunderclap of angry light, as though God Himself had cast them out and consigned their souls to hell.

CHAPTER **FOUR**

Peter Johnson liked to eat cereal at night. It was a snack idea he picked up from watching *Seinfeld* reruns, and it was much healthier than potato chips and beer, his snack of choice in his younger days, when his metabolism was so high that he had to force himself to gain weight. But while the *Sienfeld* cast used regular milk, Johnson preferred coconut milk, and not just because of his lactose intolerance. It just seemed to him that the good Lord built humans to consume coconuts rather than bovine baby formula, even though coconuts didn't grow in very many places, while cows thrived nearly everywhere on earth. Coconuts didn't even grow in Louisiana, because the coconut palm couldn't tolerate temperatures below freezing and sometimes New Orleans frosted over. But they grew like weeds on the tropical islands of the Gulf, and so Johnson figured he was still being a locavore, eating locally and thinking globally.

He was a conscious consumer in other respects as well, camping out in a brick house in Chantilly Flats after Katrina chased the original owners away. Over the years, he remodeled the place with furniture and whatnot from other abandoned homes in the hamlet. So far as he knew, the owners had gone to stay with family in New York, and knock on wood they hadn't come back yet. For the time being he was safe, and he hadn't felt that way in a very long time. Which was good, because he was still recovering from the miracle at the Citadel, and it was a blessing that he could do so in the peace and quiet of the Louisiana backwoods.

His eyesight was 20/20 now, after being partially blinded in his left eye since early Christmas morning of 1976. A tornado tore up the clinic where his wife and child had just been murdered, but he hadn't been blinded by debris. When Special Agent Peter Johnson arrived, he made the mistake of taking aim at the Devil himself. He squinted as he sighted in on the approaching form, even though the firearms instructor at Quantico would always hound him to keep both eyes open. But the instructor could never drill it out of him, and the panic response is what saved his right eye. It had been nearly a month now since he bore witness in the highlands of Haiti, and he was still getting used to having the crystal clear vision of a teenager. He didn't even need his reading glasses.

Coming back home to the States after the miracle—he called it home even though he knew deep down that he was just the caretaker— the first thing that he could clearly see was, the place was a mess. The second thing that was clear to him was that, even though he had just witnessed the ascension of the Daughter of God into heaven, and even though he had known her personally, life still went on. It was just like the old Buddhist saying: Before enlightenment, chop wood and carry water. After enlightenment, chop wood and carry water. Which Johnson always thought should have been in the Bible, along with everything else that was borrowed from the Buddhists and Hindus and Lord knows who else. Because if there was one thing he learned in the last few months, it was that nobody had a monopoly on the truth.

He spent most of the time after his return cleaning and organizing, and then cleaning everything all over again, including each windowpane inside and out, and even the vent over the stove and the dust bunnies under the microwave. The place was neat as a pin now, and his reference books were lined up alphabetically in a nice low bookshelf by the coffee table, where he did his Bible research. The newspaper articles he clipped over the years, following the Branding Killer case, were framed and hung on the wall, and he even painted the kitchen. The place was squared away, and looking downright sharp.

Johnson settled into his saddle-soaped La-Z-Boy with a bowl of Nut'N'Honey and coconut milk balanced on his lap. He said a little prayer to thank his good friend for the bounty he was about to receive, and tapped the remote. His Greenlit Lottery tickets were laid out on the arm of his lounger, and he'd turned on the TV just in time to catch the day's numbers on the newscast—5, 18, 6, 29, 12, and the Greenlit Ball was 8. Although he didn't have a winning ticket, the Bible Code the numbers represented were a sort of horoscope to him. 518 was The Door, 629 was the True Word, and 128 was the day to honor the Virgin Mary.

He contemplated the deeper meaning of the three numerical codes as he raised the first spoonful to his lips, but his thoughts were interrupted by a news alert. Johnson stared at the TV, slack-jawed and his hand frozen in space, the coconut milk dripping from the bottom of the spoon, onto his freshly laundered pajamas.

The Basilica was in flames. The roof was gone, and the windows of the adjacent structures had all been blown out. The wooden pews, the clothing of the deceased, the anointing oils, the bibles and the hymnals, the vestments and the candles, the paintings and even the paint on the walls, everything that could burn was lighting up the wintry night. The hellish glow was punctuated by a flurry of spinning lights on the fire trucks and police vehicles, and the ambulances that jammed St. Peter's Square.

At the request of the Holy See, more than a dozen first-response units had raced in from metropolitan Rome, along with triage units from the Italian Army and Air Force. But for all the tragic horror, the blast had been largely contained by the thick walls of the Basilica itself, and the inferno was mostly contained as well. What the ancient walls couldn't contain was the wailing of the injured and the crazed anguish of the lucky few that survived.

The square was a traffic jam of ambulances, and Vatican Police did what they could to direct traffic as a flow of vehicles surged in and out of the congested space. Burnt, naked bodies were still being brought out of the ruins, past the Pieta on the north side of the Portico, blackened with soot but still in one piece. The limp, charred bodies of the dead were as piteous as the body that lay in the Virgin's lap.

"What began as a day of mourning for one man will lead to the funerals of thousands more," the off-screen anchor reported in a shaken, somber voice. "It is utter pandemonium here in Vatican City. Speculation has already begun as to who could be responsible for the attack. But so far, Vatican Police haven't said who they think the suspect or suspects could be."

The cereal bowl slipped from Johnson's hand and crashed to the hardwood floor between his slippers. He stared at the TV, and for the first time since his eyesight was cured he regretted the clarity of his vision. He was unable to breathe, unable to even think. Except for one thought, frozen in the forefront of his mind, and crystal clear as his vision.

Even though he was half a world away, Peter Johnson knew that he was no longer safe. Not with what he had seen, and not with what he knew. Whoever did this would be coming for him as well.

CHAPTER FIVE

The fishing village of Labadie hugged the shore of a lush tropical cove on the coast of northern Haiti, five kilometers west of the city of Cap-Haitien and fifteen kilometers west of Bord-de-Mer Limonade. A long time ago, Columbus had come ashore at Limonade at the gracious invitation of the local Tainos Indians, and promptly renamed their island Hispañola. He initially encountered their heathen brethren on San Salvador, a postage stamp with palm trees that lay just beyond the northern horizon, where he first set foot in the new world a few months before. After fruitlessly searching for gold on a big island to the south that the locals called Cuba, and after fruitlessly renaming the place Juana, Columbus and his crew were in dire need of some rest and relaxation, so they sailed east to another big island for little a change of scenery. When the *Santa Maria* ran aground on Christmas Eve, the Tainos villagers helped them ashore and offered their best accommodations. It was the first Caribbean vacation in history.

The eastern shore of Labadie Cove curved to the north, forming the tip of the Labadie Peninsula. The tiny finger of land had been walled off to form the mythical "Island of Labadee", an all-inclusive resort where cruise ships could anchor for a few days, disgorging their lotioned and lubricated tourists. The spelling of the name had been Anglicized to avoid confusion; most of the tourists spoke English and they frankly didn't care to learn anything else. And since they couldn't leave the area, most of them had no idea that it wasn't an island. A fair number of them didn't even know they were in Haiti. Other than the locals who worked at the resort, the people of Labadie and the people of the village of Cormier, in the cove on the east side of the peninsula, couldn't enter without a permit to sell their wares, not even by sea. Fishing and sailing too close to the white sand beach were frowned upon as well.

Getting to Labadie was a bit of a chore. The paved road ended at Cormier, and a dirt road extended from there, bumping across the rocky base of the peninsula before dropping down to Labadie. At first glance, it was an odd place for a medical clinic, but the Labadie Psychological Medical Institute had been built in the sixties, when Papa Doc Duvalier embarked on a whirlwind build-up of the nation's health care infrastructure. Because the roads were so poor, the material, equipment, and crews came by sea. The road crew was supposed to reach Labadie by the time the clinic was open for business, but they fell behind schedule and the economy slumped, and the paving project ground to a halt. Years later, a cruise ship company cut a deal with the government, which included a road improvement package to the mythical Island of Labadee. But they didn't need it to go across the base of the peninsula to the actual village. The back gate of the resort was far enough.

The beachfront mental health facility became permanently stranded at the end of a dirt road, surrounded by a third world fishing village. But the lucky few who worked at the clinic and lived in the collection of seaside cottages preferred to think of LMPI as a secluded haven of rest in a tranquil tropical paradise, perfectly suited for regaining the mental health of their patients. Although the clinic had four-wheel drive Land Rover ambulances, most of their patients arrived by boat, or by helicopter from Cap-Haitien. But the latest one had come out of the jungle, after wandering in the cold, wet wilderness of the northern mountains for nearly a month. They had no idea who he was, and neither did he.

An afternoon breeze drifted in from the beach through the open jalousie windows, stirred by a slow ceiling fan above the iron frame bed. Devlin lay sleeping under a clean white sheet in Room 108, his third one since dawn. The first two sheets had been soaked in sweat after another restless day of torment. Miss Meljean was concerned that he would catch a cold, so she spread the blanket over him even though it was a warm day. But soon after she left the blanket was unwittingly kicked to the floor, and now this third sheet was becoming as damp as the others.

Deep in a bad dream, Devlin thrashed his head to the side, half-burying his face in the pillow. She shaved him during a quiet spell that morning, when he was alert and friendly, and taped a fresh bandage over his head wound as well, but she didn't shave around the scab because the skin looked too irritated. The wound started bleeding again, but she didn't know because she was out of the room at the moment, having her lunch at the picnic table on the lawn at the end of the wing.

It was a single-storey cinderblock structure with a red tile roof and concrete steps and thick wooden doors, propped open to let the stale air out after a hot, sunny day. Miss Meljean couldn't see through Devlin's open windows from where she was sitting, but she would hear him if he started to moan, and she could also see the door, just inside the hallway. She could also see the old fisherman.

He was the one who brought the stranger to them last week, and even though he said he didn't know the man, he kept coming back every day. He was perched on a bench in the corridor now, and she was tired of telling him to go away, and in any case she was on her break. Maybe Dr. Diane would shoo him home this time. Or maybe Dr. Brillstein; he was a stickler for protocol. But they were probably having coffee in his office again.

Blood seeped onto Devlin's pillow, but his thick black hair staunched the flow and formed a protective covering, the same as it did for the last month, which was Dr. Diane Viccu's best guess as to how old the injury was. How, why, and where it happened was still a mystery, along with everything else about him. He had no ID or distinguishing marks to speak of. Prior to the arrival of Dr. Viccu and Dr. Brillstein, the clinic had sent Devlin's picture around, but so far nothing had come back on the shortwave or the Internet. They didn't know his name, and they didn't want to give him one, either. It would interfere with whatever memories he might recover. Which up to this point was bupkis, as Dr. Brillstein described it. Miss Meljean had never heard the word before, and she didn't think it was a medical term.

Devlin was Caucasian and appeared to be in his early forties. Aside from the jagged trench in his skull that looked like a tumbling bullet wound, he was in excellent physical health. Not even a cavity. In fact, he didn't have any signs of dental work at all. Which wasn't unheard of, but it was extremely rare. The condition of his wound and his clothing, and the results of his blood, stool, and urine tests told them that he probably lived off the land since the time of his injury, surviving on nuts and fruit, and roots and insects. It had been raining off and on since the freak snowstorm, so there had been plenty of fresh water in the highlands.

Miss Meljean's private suspicion was that somebody went crazy when the snowstorm came, and shot the poor devil. Or maybe he went crazy and tried to shoot himself. She didn't even come out of her hut after the snowstorm, until one of the village *houngans* sacrificed a pig to make the village safe again. She almost lost her job, but some things were more important than money. People were still afraid to talk about it, even at night when the children were sleeping. And then three weeks later a white man stumbled out of the jungle, with a three-week old bullet wound and a three-week old scruff of facial hair. The fisherman said he acted like a zombie, and fell face-first into the surf. Miss Maljean's sixth sense told her that the stranger knew more about the snowstorm than even the *houngan* did, and that worried her. But now that she had gotten to know him, she was becoming more curious than afraid—

An unsettling moan drifted from Devlin's window. Her stomach clenched, and the fisherman got to his bare feet and stood beside the door, listening. His father was the village pastor, and told him he had to be on watch. He was the one who saved the stranger instead of letting him drown, so it was his responsibility if something happened to their village. A man without a memory wasn't a man without a past. Something was locked away in the dungeon of his soul, the pastor said, and it probably wasn't good.

The fisherman leaned closer, listening to the stranger's grunts and groans, as if that something was trying to shove its way through the dungeon door. Or maybe the struggle he heard was the stranger shoving back, trying to keep it locked inside.

CHAPTER SIX

Devlin's body suddenly convulsed and his eyes snapped open, two orbs of white-hot fire, He screamed in blind horror, and his cry descended to an anguished wail as his vision slowly returned and his pupils gradually appeared, soft and brown and moist with tears.

He sat bolt upright and his eyes darted around the room as he tried to get a grip on his breathing. There was something raging inside of him, unformed and intangible, yet it was entirely real, as real as the pounding of his heart. It was a dreamscape he kept returning to, a swirl of imaginings, horrible and disturbing and tragic and beautiful, and all of it wrapped around a black hole that kept drawing him closer. In this first moment of awakening, it all came flooding back to him . . .

A tempest brewed in a night sky as a young rabbi slogged through a cold Louisiana swamp, drawn by a bright star in the east to a run-down backwoods clinic. Infants screamed in their clinic bassinets as a priest plunged a crucifix dagger into a pregnant woman's belly, but the baby somehow survived. . .

Then Michael the archangel appeared to Devlin in the bayou, bathed in glimmering light, and then a circle of fallen angels stood with him on Lake Ponchartrain, their arms lifted to heaven and humming in unison. He walked with a voodoo priest through a catholic church in New Orleans. The body parts of massacred nuns were strewn about and tossed onto the chandeliers, dripping blood on the stone floor. The statuary in the Vatican shed tears as he entered, and every candle in the Basilica snuffed itself out. . .

The young rabbi was an old cardinal now, and he heard Devlin's confession in a booth beside the papal altar. Then a voodoo priest crucified the cardinal upside down, over the portico of the Basilica, and the cardinal screamed a Hebrew prayer as a murder of crows feasted on him. Michael confronted the voodoo priest in St. Peter's Square, and turned the man to dust. . .

And then a young priest from New Orleans gave out loaves and fishes to a multitude gathered at the Citadel in Haiti's northern highlands, after a massive earthquake destroyed the capital. The priest made love to a beautiful woman, and the woman became Devlin. And then there was another woman, dying in the arms of the priest. He was seated with the bed sheet over his shoulder, and they looked like the statue of the Pieta. Then the ceiling opened up and Michael appeared. The woman was the incarnation of Jesus Christ, and She ascended into heaven with the archangel . . .

And then Devlin's head would begin to hurt, and he would hear the voice of God telling him, *"I will always love you."* And when that happened, the dreamscape would all come crushing in on him, as if he and all the pieces were being sucked into a black hole, and he would wake up screaming.

He still had no idea what any of it meant. They told him it had been almost a month since his injury, and that he probably spent the first three weeks wandering in the highlands. What was he even doing in Haiti? They didn't know, and if they did, they wouldn't tell him. They wanted him to re-build his own memories, but the few scraps that they gave him didn't trigger anything. Nothing did, and maybe nothing ever would, and maybe that would be the best thing he could hope for, because he didn't know how much more of this he could take. He felt like he would explode when it finally came out of him. It would have to work its way out of his mind, or his heart or his soul, wherever it was lodged, and he had a feeling it might kill him in the process. Maybe it would kill other people, too, and that terrified him more than anything.

He was utterly lost, bewildered, and alone, in a stark white room with cinderblock walls and a cracked plaster ceiling, and a slow fan lazing above his bed. The windows were open to a whisper of gentle surf along a wide beach, and he could see the emerald green lawn through the frosted glass slats, bordered with coconut palms and hyacinth and wild amaryllis in full bloom. It was as peaceful a setting as a patient could desire, but so far it had done nothing to quell his turmoil, and the drugs they were dosing him with were just barely keeping him from falling into that black hole and never coming out—

"Are you okay?"

He turned to the sound of her voice and tried to focus. Dr. Diane must have come in the room when he was looking out the window and gasping for breath, with the blood pounding in his ears like a freight train. She was leaning over the bed, concerned, with a hand reaching out to his shoulder but not touching him. In the corridor behind her, Miss Meljean was quietly closing the door and was going to shoo away the fisherman, but he wasn't there.

Diane smiled, and placed her hand over his. Devlin realized that he was gripping the damp sheets, as if he were trying to stay anchored to the bed. As he felt her touch, he unclenched his fist and took more deep breaths, trying to calm down, and grabbed her hand.

Her grip was as firm as his was desperate. This wasn't the first time she'd held his hand in the last week, and he noticed once again how strong she was. Maybe it was from wrestling with nut cases like me, he thought, and cracked a rueful smile. But as he did a pain shot through his head, and he winced, clutching spasmodically at her hand.

"My head!" he told her, and she winced back in empathy.

"It was just a dream," she assured him.

He knew it was much more than that, but he didn't know how to tell her. She sat on the edge of the bed and took his hand in both of hers. She was wearing Bulgari perfume, which Devlin found comforting and intoxicating at the same time. She was a lovely woman, with quick, intelligent eyes and an air of decorum that spoke of breeding and private school, although she didn't have the haughtiness of the rich. She was somewhere in her thirties, and though she told him she was from Miami she didn't seem like an American, and she didn't quite sound like one, either. Perhaps Canadian, but European would be more likely. It was funny to him how he could analyze so many things that required memory and knowledge, even though the memory and knowledge of his own life was completely unavailable to him. One day he would ask her where she was from, but for now it didn't matter. As far as he was concerned, she was an angel sent from heaven, although she was nothing like the angels in his dreams. They scared the hell out of him.

He made a fist of his free hand and ground it against his temple in frustration. "Why won't they stop?" he asked her.

He hadn't done much over the last week, other than eat and sleep and take his medicine. Diane and Dr. Brillstein seemed to know what they were doing, so surely the torment would have subsided by now. But aside from being clean and rested and well fed, he didn't feel much better than when he was first brought in.

"Your mind is trying to find itself again," Diane patiently explained. She'd been telling him the same thing in several different ways for the last few days, and she knew she would be saying it again, probably before the day was through. But he needed to hear it each time his mind erupted, until the volcano finally lay dormant.

"It's driving me crazy in the process," he was telling her, and she patted his hand, offering a brave smile.

"It takes time with amnesia," she reminded him. In many ways it was similar to a concussion, and the patient needed to be gently reoriented over and over again, until they stayed oriented and could rebuild their memories from there.

"When do I get to leave?"

She just smiled again and held his hand. That was another question he kept asking her, but she didn't have an answer for him. At least, not one that he wanted to hear.

CHAPTER SEVEN

Six Mangusta assault helicopters hovered in a wide circle above
the tarmac at western edge of Fiumicino Airport, as the Gulfstream jet
appeared out of the north, the early morning sun glinting off its fuselage.
The Col Moschin had arrived before dawn without running lights, landing
their A-129s in a tight outward-facing cordon around the private hangar
as two platoons arrived in armored APCs, racing past them to secure the
building and vet the personnel.

Their Belgian Shepherds sniffed everything, papers and IDs were
examined and snipers were deployed on the roof. As the first frosty light of
dawn crept over the Seven Hills of Rome, the runway had been inspected
by robots crawling inch by inch along the entire mile of concrete. They
were back inside the APCs now, powered down and locked to the decks.
The commandos had their morning tea and energy bars at dawn, and the
dogs had been watered and fed as well. They waited, unblinking and alert,
as the Gulfstream settled into its final approach.

It had been this way since the Basilica bombing, and would be for the
foreseeable future, whenever surviving members of the Vatican hierarchy
were concerned. The bombing had been the Church's 9/11, and it wasn't
only Catholics who were reeling from the shock. The entire world was
stunned as well. Ashen faces were a common sight on any street corner,
in every corner of the globe, irrespective of faith or nationality. It was a

violation that transcended boundaries and loyalties and beliefs. Humanity itself had been wounded. The blow would leave a massive scar, and take a very long time to heal.

Since that incomprehensibly awful moment, the nation that surrounded Vatican City embraced their tiny neighbor, offering whatever service they could render. They did so with the explicit assurance that no reciprocation would ever be asked, or accepted in return. It was more than the Christian thing to do; it was what good neighbors have always done for one another, throughout the course of history and all around the world. The prime minister spoke for the entire nation when he told Il Papa that the Church had shepherded the Italian people through the centuries with prayer and art and inspiration. Whatever they could do now in the Holy See's hour of need would be a pittance in comparison, and their pleasure to provide.

The Gulfstream touched down, and slowed to a sedate roll as it taxied toward the hangar, propelled by a whisper of fanjet engines. The APCs had lined up along the runway, and they formed a moving ring around the aircraft now, as it rolled under the circle of helicopters and came to a nimble stop at the end of a red carpet. Balliez was at the other end, standing ready at the back door of the pope's white limousine. The stretched and armored Maybach 62 weighed well over three tons, but it could hit 100kph in less than six seconds. If something happened on the road to the summer palace at Gandolfo and Balliez had to floor it, the APCs wouldn't be able to keep up with him, but the Mangustas could.

Cardinal Saul stood nearby, shaded from the brilliant morning sun by Varese's umbrella. Saul's bodyguards were a respectful distance behind him, standing by his black Phantom limo, while his driver Marcel sat behind the wheel keeping warm. The bodyguards' armored Land Rovers were parked behind the Rolls, their engines running.

The Gulfstream pilot locked the brakes and spooled down the engines as three commandos scurried under the aircraft and chocked the wheels.

HUNTING LUCIFER

It was the first time that the pilot felt safe since taking off from Geneva. Flying over the ruins of the Basilica was like a knife in his heart, but the pope asked him to go as low and slow as they could.

Three more commandos locked the rollaway stairs in place, and the six Col Moschin who were acting as ground crew arrayed themselves around the base of the ladder, their Beretta ARX-160s on full auto. The clamshell fuselage hatch hissed open and two men in suits and shades came out, looking around as they descended the steps. Their body armor made them seem unnaturally barrel-chested, but it complimented their brusque demeanors.

Satisfied with what they saw, one of them spoke in his lapel mic, and they waited at the bottom of the stairs, as more commandos formed a protective corridor along the red carpet to the open door of the Maybach.

Pope John Halo emerged from the Gulfstream surrounded by his bodyguards, the best among the Swiss Guards who survived the blast. They were men who felt the heat and heard the screams, who still had the smell of burnt flesh in their nostrils. That was the kind of man the pope wanted around him now. A cold, bitter anger had hardened his features, to where even his valet hardly recognized him. When the pontiff looked in the mirror, he hardly recognized himself.

He came down the steps and approached with his guards, and Saul entered the corridor with his. As they neared each other, even Saul was struck by the change. He hadn't seen the man since he was rushed to Geneva for a heart palpitation that began with the bombing and refused to subside. Saul wondered what they did to stabilize him, and when the pope was close enough for Saul to see his eyes, he ventured a guess. Perhaps they removed his heart.

Saul knelt and kissed his ring and stood again, and then they forced smiles and embraced, whispering in each other's ears.

"I require answers," John Halo told him.

"The ones I have, I will provide," Saul assured him.

41

With their bodyguards surrounding them, they spoke in low voices as they walked toward the Maybach.

"It was best for you to wait before you came back, your Holiness. We had to ensure your safety."

"Our Lord protects me, Saul. My safety is the least of my concern." He touched Saul's forearm as if it were a gesture of affection, but his grip conveyed something quite different. "I want to know the meaning of this!" he whispered sternly.

"We believe it's a new faction of Islamists," Saul breathed.

Pope John was doubtful and he didn't hide it, in his expression or his voice, a notch above a whisper now. "Muslims? Can you be certain?"

Saul didn't think he'd accept the ruse without question, but his blunt skepticism was unsettling. Why didn't the bastard just die in Geneva? It would have made everything so much easier.

"Or what we fear even more . . ." Saul continued, playing his other card.

"Rosicrucians?" The pope whispered, genuinely concerned, and Saul inwardly smiled. He knew that if one boogeyman didn't rattle the old man's cage, the other surely would.

Marcel had pulled the Rolls up close behind the Maybach and was out of the car now, standing ready at the back door. The pope touched his own chauffeur on the shoulder, an affectionate hello for his faithful servant, and Balliez bowed his head, happy for his master's return. John Halo turned to Saul and looked in his eyes.

"I don't care why they did it, Cardinal. Just find out who among them is responsible." He leaned closer, deeply troubled. "This is no longer God's war," he whispered, and Saul nodded.

"I understand your Holiness," he whispered back. Saul understood quite well, but the pope, for all his power and glory, actually didn't have a clue. And he never would, if Saul had anything to do with it.

"May Christ be with you, Saul," the pontiff said, and held out his right hand. Saul bent down and kissed his ring once again.

"And with all of us, your Holiness."

The pope touched his head to bless him, and then his bodyguards helped him into the Maybach. He carefully settled into the white leather recliner as Balliez shut the door, while John Halo's chief of security got in the front passenger seat. The pope's secretary went around to the other side with Balliez, and got in back as Balliez slipped behind the wheel.

The white limo glided away, surrounded by most of the APCs and watched over by a flock of guardian angel gunships. They would escort him south of Rome to the Castel Gandolfo, and stay on watch at the summer palace, seconded to the Swiss Guard on Italy's dime while the Vatican was being rebuilt.

Saul walked toward his armored black Phantom with Varese close beside him, his big black umbrella shading Saul from the sun. His bodyguards formed their protective circle and moved with them, and Marcel opened the back door. Some of the Special Forces had stayed behind to escort them to St. Michael's in Rome, the temporary Vatican. Saul appreciated the gesture. He was fond of his bodyguards; if someone was going to assault their convoy, he'd prefer the Italians to take the heat. They were expendable.

CHAPTER EIGHT

A month after the earthquake in Haiti, the capitol of Port-au-Prince
was in shambles, and so were most of the towns and hamlets south of the
highlands. Nearly a quarter million people perished in the catastrophe,
which lasted all of thirty-five seconds, and nearly as many residences were
destroyed, either from outright collapse or from the fires that ensued. Over
30,000 commercial buildings in the capitol, including the White House, the
National Assembly, and the main jail, were gone, and so were the inmates.
The U.N., the United States, and a dozen other countries had rushed in
to render aid, and a worldwide fundraising campaign lent weight to the
effort. But virtually an entire country now lay in ruins, and the process of
rescue and recovery was agonizingly slow. Cholera, dysentery, hunger and
homelessness only added to the misery of an already-poor populace.

The United States embassy compound sustained only minor damage.
It was a large, modern three-storey building on Boulevard du 15 Octobre
in Tabarre, a pleasant, spacious suburb southeast of the airport. Like many
of the large houses and walled estates in the neighborhood, the embassy
had been built to code, a luxury that most of the world, and nearly all
of Haiti, couldn't afford. The embassy compound served as a refuge

for injured and homeless Americans who filtered out of the city in the aftermath, and they were bivouacked in enormous U.S. Army tents set up on the lawn. Safe and dry, well-fed and attended to, they had the time to catch their breath and think about their next move, and many of them just wanted to move back to the States. The problem was that a fair number of them had lost everything, including their documents. Complicating the problem was that, in a post-9/11 world, the Department of Homeland Security didn't have the same open-arms response as the U.N. or Doctors Without Borders. The DHS was all about borders, and so the CIS office at the embassy had their hands full. Short-tempered Americans weren't just lined up in the hall; they were camped on the lawn as well.

Citizenship and Immigration Services wasn't the sexiest job in the building, and that's just the way FBI Special Agent Mark Ledger liked it. A bland office job gave him a lot of room to move, with a low-profile cover story that wouldn't draw attention. Nobody cooling their heels in the hallway had an inkling of what agency he really worked for, and neither did most of the embassy staff, except for Consul Fincannon. Fincannon was CIA, and everyone knew it even though they weren't supposed to. Being CIA, he knew all about Ledger before he arrived, back in '09. And the first thing Leger learned in the cafeteria that day was that nobody called the man Finn, because that inevitably led to Huckleberry, and if anyone called him Huckleberry he would make their lives miserable, and sic the IRS on them for good measure.

The door opened. Ledger glanced over his shoulder, and up-nodded a hello. It was Fincannon, a greying, plump forty-year old suit with a 10mm Glock on his hip. Ever since the quake, guns were the fashion accessories of choice. Pepper spray was a close second.

"You rang?" Fincannon asked.

45

Ledger waved the gunslinger into his office. Fincannon closed the door on a hallway full of weary applicants, and sat on the file cabinet beside Ledger's desk.

"It's about the head case up at Labadie," Ledger told him.

Fincannon frowned, and thumbed through his hung over brain cells for the right case file. It was somewhere in the back. "The American they found on the beach?" he ventured, and Ledger nodded. Fincannon nodded back, waiting for more. Ledger handed him a clipboard, and he leafed through the paperwork. It amazed him how much government work still got done with pen and paper.

"He's waiting for a new passport to get back home," Ledger explained.

Fincannon grunted. Yeah, him and fifteen thousand other Americans who were still stuck in-country, most of whom were loitering in the hallway or camped on the lawn. He handed the clipboard back to Ledger and shrugged. "So what's the problem," he asked. "We're Passports R Us."

To reply, Ledger pointed at his monitor and tapped Enter. They watched the screen, waiting as the webpage loaded. It was a secure link directly to Washington, but sometimes it was as slow as dial-up. This was one of those times.

"Either we have a big-ass glitch," Ledger told him, "or this guy is . . . I don't know what." Fincannon glanced at him, wondering what he meant, and Ledger pointed at his monitor again.

They were in the DHS fingerprint database, the largest collection in the world, with over ten percent of the global population and growing every day. Even Fincannon didn't know how they did it, and he had clearance above top secret. At least, he did until he got busted from The Hague to Haiti.

There was a large fingerprint displayed on the left side, as the right half of the screen flipped through a series of mug shots, a blur of sullen faces with the occasional maniacal grin. It stopped on a handsome fellow, a grainy image from the early eighties. BUNDY, TED appeared in the search window below his image, and the one below the fingerprint as well. The word MATCH blinked in large green letters beside his name.

Fincannon shot a wry grin at Ledger, and Ledger just pointed at the monitor again. When Fincannon looked back, he saw there was a big red NO MATCH in the search window now, and then more faces kept coming, like a spinning tumbler in a one-armed bandit. The images froze and another face appeared, a woman this time. WUORNOS, EILEEN, it said. She glared back at them from her niche in hell as MATCH flashed in the search window beside her image. A moment later, it was replaced by a red NO MATCH, and the cascade of faces came once again . . .

JONES, JIM. MATCH, NO MATCH. Then more faces . . .

Fincannon glanced at Ledger again, but this time he wasn't grinning. "What the hell?"

"It does it every time we run his print."

DAHMER, JEFFERY. MATCH, NO MATCH. KORESH, DAVID. MATCH, NO MATCH. More faces . . .

Then finally, the shuffling mug shots stopped.

NO MATCH FOUND.

"That's one hell of a glitch," Fincannon said, and Ledger nodded. Fincannon's cell phone rang, and he dug it out of his pocket. It was an old school Blackberry, and he had to squint at the screen. His expression sobered when he saw who it was, and he stood as he answered the call. Ledger noticed the body language, and watched him.

"Fincannon . . ." the CIA agent said, and then he just listened, motionless. It wasn't a conversation; it was a directive. Whoever it was abruptly ended the call, and Fincannon put his phone away, pursing his lips and gazing at the carpet as he digested what he had just been told. Ledger waited for a remark, or some kind of hint as to what transpired.

But none was forthcoming. Fincannon just picked up the clipboard and leafed through the documents again. When he found the one he was looking for, he took his pen out of his pocket and clicked it.

"Looks like he has friends in high places, whoever he is," he finally said, and initialed the form, checking his Rolex so he could note the exact time beside his signature. Ledger just nodded; he knew enough not to press him for more.

Fincannon flipped back to the front page and wrote something across the top in block letters, then he handed the clipboard to Ledger and opened the door. He left the office without saying goodbye, and walked down the hall past the long line of disgruntled Americans.

Ledger watched him recede down the hallway, and then he lifted the clipboard to see what he wrote, eclipsing the curious eyes of the people cooling their heels.

It was a State Department document. Devlin's picture had been cut from a fax and paper-clipped to the top sheet. APPROVED was printed across the top of the document in bold black letters, and underlined twice.

Ledger tossed the clipboard on his side table, under the window. He got up from his desk with his coffee mug in hand, and closed his office door as he ducked in the back room for a refill . . .

Behind him in the office, the Haitian sun streamed through the window and warmed the side table. The fax paper curled, and Devlin's image began to fade.

CHAPTER **NINE**

The old church was on Green River Road, south of Baton Rouge. Built in the 1830s from sturdy Louisiana oak, it took a bad beating from Katrina and stood. Those who rode out the storm on the bayou and those who hunkered down in nearby Chantilly Flats fixed the roof right away. It wasn't just their place of worship; it also served as the neighborhood council meeting hall, the union hall, and the local dance hall. A squeezebox band was up on the stage playing zydeco two Saturdays after the storm, and all the die-hards came to the dance even if they had to walk. They moved the pews against the wall and they waltzed on the worn-down wood floor in a slow, counter-clockwise circle like their French forefathers. The singer never sang so fine and his Creole never sounded so sweet, and by the end of the evening everybody knew that things would be all right. If their roots could survive, then they could survive; one breathed life into the other.

Peter Johnson had the place on Tuesday nights now, and since he was preaching the Gospel the pastor didn't charge him a fee. Johnson was an oddball, though, and the pastor couldn't figure out where his message fit in the spectrum of Christian thought. But the man's recovered eyesight was indeed a miracle, and anybody who wanted to spread the Word after something like that was welcome to have the place free of charge on the slowest night of the week. Maybe the odd souls that he reached would show up on Sunday and drop a dollar in the collection plate. There were a number of odd souls to be found in this neck of the woods, so the pastor was hoping to turn a profit on his generosity.

Johnson paced before the altar on the low wooden stage, a bible clutched in his hand, staring a hole in the floorboards as they groaned under the steady clump of his motorcycle boots. The black leather Santiagos were scuffed from a month of daily wear, and finally starting to feel like a second skin. He didn't ride a bike; he drove a vintage Land Cruiser, but he didn't wear them for fashion. He called them his Jesus Boots. Christine Mas wore the same brand the first time they met, when she paid him a visit at his home in Chantilly Flats one Saturday, driving her BMW R1200 up from New Orleans. Her dad was a motorcycle cop, and that's how she rolled. Johnson tried to shoo her away, but she jammed her boot in the door, wedging it open like a salesman. He remembered being startled, but more than that he remembered the toe of her boot, scuffed and flecked with mud, and how it intruded, mute and insistent, into the private hell of his life. She didn't force her way in, but she wouldn't let him shut her out, either. It was one of the most vivid memories he had of her, and one of the most cherished, because that one simple gesture said everything about her, and about what she meant to him and the world. He felt duty bound to tell whoever would listen, and he did the best that he could, though he was no public speaker. The fact was, public speaking scared him half to death.

The church was mostly dark, with a chill winter bite in the air, but votive candles flickered warm and inviting in the iron racks beside the stage. Twelve lost souls sat in the front pews, patiently waiting for him to formulate his next few sentences. They had been listening in rapt attention for the last hour as he preached to them in fits and starts. He finally stopped his latest round of pacing, and turned to face them. "Every failure that you've ever encountered," he said, "has been a failure of prayer."

They took what he said in their own way, and some of them nodded. While they were digesting the remark, a man came in behind them and walked softly up the center aisle. He was dressed in jeans and a hoodie, his hands in the front pockets. Johnson greeted him with a simple nod, but then he looked down to the stage floor again, already formulating his next thought. Some of the men half-turned and smiled hello. The stranger nodded back, and sat in a darkened pew behind them. They turned back to the preacher, and when they did bishop Pablo Simone uncovered his head. Peter Johnson didn't know who he was, and neither did his flock.

"For so long," Johnson continued, "we were told what to believe and how to believe it. But faith isn't faith until it's all you're holding onto, no matter what you've been told."

The lost souls leaned forward, listening intently, sensing that Johnson was ready to say more. Behind them, Simone watched from the shadows.

"None of this was foretold in any book," Johnson elaborated. "None of this was ever shared, through centuries of passing on legends, scripture, and prophesy. None of it!"

He commenced pacing the stage again, pondering on what he just said, giving it time to sink in for them as well as himself. And then he slowed and stopped, frowning at the floor as an insight came flooding to him. They could see it in his features and posture, and they watched him, waiting. This is what they came for—those rare moments when something didn't just come to him, but when something came through him.

Johnson turned to them slowly, not for dramatics, but to keep his footing as the world shifted below his feet. When he was standing still again, he raised his head and saw the way they were looking at him. It was always unnerving to see the effect he had on them, but his feelings in the matter were entirely irrelevant. He had to do this, whether he liked it or not.

"Nowhere was it written," he said in a hollow, quiet voice, "that Lucifer himself would orchestrate a Second Coming."

That was all he had to say, and he just stood there, as unsettled as they were by what he just said. But his newest arrival smiled.

The men were gathered in front, sitting on the stage and in the front pews, forming a loose-knit group. Most of them listened to the more loquacious amongst them, elbows on their knees and gazing at the floor, nodding and grunting in murmured agreement. Johnson sat at the corner of the stage, counseling a particularly troubled young man. But the youngster was too restless to hear him out, and he got up and left down the center aisle, shaking his head. Johnson watched him go with forlorn, compassionate eyes, and that's when his gaze met the stranger's, sitting in the gloom of the fifth row.

Simone smiled kindly and got to his feet, and Johnson did the same, coming down the aisle and extending his hand. Simone shook hands with him, and they stood close together so they wouldn't disturb the others, even though most of them had paused to watch the two men.

"Father Pablo Simone," the bishop said by way of introduction.

Johnson's smile broadened. "Father? Welcome."

Simone nodded, and let go of his hand, looking around at their humble surroundings. Johnson imagined what he must have been thinking. Even out here in the sticks, the Catholic Church usually had better digs than a lot of country preachers did.

"How did you find this place?" Johnson asked him.

Simone glanced at the others, and leaned a little closer. "Have you heard the saying, 'Lucifer walks among us'?"

Johnson frowned a little, and not only because Simone didn't answer his question. The question the priest chose to respond with could lead down some dark paths. Most people, even priests, were much too cavalier when it came to talking about the Devil, as if he were an abstraction or a metaphor. But Johnson knew there was nothing abstract about Lucifer at all. Still, he decided to be polite, and play it off like most people would.

"Well, yes, of course, who hasn't?" he replied with what he hoped was a casual, sophisticated smile. "But that's just a . . ."

He trailed off, seeing something in Simone's eyes. The priest was watching him with quiet amusement. *My God,* Johnson realized. *Perhaps he is aware.*

"Now he leaves footprints," Simone told him.

Johnson frowned again, rapidly recalculating his initial impression of the man. Simone smiled, and laid an affable hand on his shoulder.

"Let's do lunch."

CHAPTER TEN

The next day was drizzling and unseasonably warm, although it was hard to say what was unseasonable any more, the way the climate was changing over the last several years. It felt more like April than February.

Fan-Fan's Café was in downtown Chantilly Flats. All the rebuilding in the wake of Katrina brought a new optimism to the hamlet, and the locals were keen on expressing their regional pride wherever they could.. Joujou the owner was an old *manbo* with a long bayou lineage, but she kept her voodoo inclinations on the back burner. People around town knew her roots, and rumor had it that there was a dash of something more than chicory in her espresso blend. But no one had turned into a zombie yet, and it was hands down the best cup of Joe in town.

Johnson and Simone were at a wicker table on the sidewalk under an oversize umbrella, having the gumbo special. There was no wind to speak of, or even much of a breeze, so it was easy to position their chairs to keep out of the misting rain. Their waiter wore a wide-brimmed hat, but he didn't mind getting a little wet. It made his toned torso more evident through his white shirt, which his lady customers appreciated. He freshened Johnson and Simone's coffee, and moved off to see how the girls were doing.

"You never answered my question, Father Simone. How did you find me?"

Simone smiled. Johnson's years in the FBI came through in his voice, and the way he framed his question. He reminded Simone of Robert Stack, in the old TV series *The Untouchables*. Simone used to watch it as a child with his grandfather in Portugal, on the black and white TV in the kitchen. Elliot Ness and Lucy and Ricky, Ralph Cramden and Ed Norton, Gilligan and the Skipper, they all taught young Pablo American English.

"You've been on the Church's radar since 1976," Simone explained, and took a sip of coffee before he continued. He could taste the chicory, along with a hint of clove and roasted peppercorn. He decided to pick up a pound when they left.

"Christine Mas's blood sacrifice didn't end the struggle, Peter. It just brought the Devil's war to our doorstep."

Johnson looked hard at him, then down to the table. "The attack on the Vatican," he said quietly, and the bishop nodded.

"That's only the beginning," Simone told him. "They've laid waste to his empire, and now they're coming for his head."

Johnson understood the Catholic Church better than most lay people, so it didn't surprise him to hear a man of the cloth refer to the Mother Church as Lucifer's empire. He'd found hints of this viewpoint in a number of books on the subject, most of them crackpot but some of them scholarly works of religious philosophy. But only hints. Like any religion, Catholicism began as a movement, grew into a business, and turned into a racket. But having a jaundiced attitude about the Church was one thing; blowing up the Vatican and hunting Lucifer was something else entirely.

"Who'd be that stupid?" Johnson wanted to know, because it sounded like madness. And it was, but he also knew that it was all too real. He'd been a personal eyewitness to the work of the Devil, one of the few who ever survived, and at the time he was even naïve enough to put the details in his initial report. That's how the Bureau flagged him for observation, and it was probably how the Church flagged him as well. They were one of the largest and wealthiest organizations in the world, with tendrils everywhere and a substantial off-campus payroll. They kept tabs on the visionary and the delusional alike, from a genuine encounter like Johnson had to someone seeing the Virgin's face on a tortilla. So perhaps it was a good thing that Simone contacted him. Maybe he knew what was really going on, because Johnson sure as hell didn't.

Simone glanced around before he answered the question, and even then it wasn't a direct response. "A sect more subversive and radical than the Templars," he finally replied in a quiet voice, and Johnson's eyes narrowed. The people who fit that description comprised a very short list.

A black Bentley sedan with smoked windows was parked down the block and across the street. A high-dollar ride like a Bentley would normally draw stares in downtown Chantilly Flats, but aside from the showoff waiter at Fan-Fan's, the locals didn't care much to be out in the rain, no matter how lightly it was falling. Other than him, and his customers under the big umbrellas, the sidewalks were empty. The few drivers who did cruise by had their windows rolled up, and didn't slow down for a look-see. They were concentrating on the slick roadway, and if they did notice the Bentley they dismissed it as a big shot from the city, come to visit his mama.

Varese was at the wheel, watching the two men through a digital SLR. The telephoto lens was half a meter long, and he balanced it on the steering wheel, leaning against the center console to get the viewing angle right. The camera was patched into his laptop, sitting on the passenger seat, and his cell phone was on the dashboard.

"These infidels murder in the name of Christ," Simone was telling Johnson. The shotgun mic would have been too conspicuous, so Varese had left it in the trunk, but the long lens was picking up a continuous close-up of their mouths. Although it was a side shot, and despite the light mist gathering on the windshield, his laptop's lip-reading app could decipher most of what they were saying. The app synthesized their conversation in robo-speak, with two equally annoying voices coming out of the tiny speakers.

Johnson was listening intently to Simone, leaning on his elbows with his hands below his chin, his fingers laced together and his lower lip resting on his thumbs. His arthritis acted up in wet weather, and it was especially hard on his fingers. He gently flexed them to work the joints, and as he did, the fingerprints of his right hand faced the Bentley.

Varese's long lens captured the delicate swirls. He tapped the Enter key on his laptop, and it assembled Johnson's prints from the stream of video images as he speed-dialed an international number on his cell.

"And they won't cease fire until they find him," Simone was explaining to Johnson. "Even if the last stone from the last church is reduced to rubble."

Varese peeked at the laptop and saw that the fingerprints were finalized. The program began searching for a match in the Interpol database through a portal at Vatican Security, and Varese went back to watching them through his camera.

Johnson was thoroughly confused. He unlaced his fingers and sat back, spreading his hands on the tabletop as he tried to think things through. "What do you mean, 'his empire'?" he probed. He already had a pretty good idea what Simone meant, but he wanted to hear it from the man himself.

"It's a long story," Simone replied, wishing that he hadn't mentioned it. But he did; it was too late, and both he and Johnson knew it.

"I have plenty of time," Johnson nudged him. "I'm retired." Simone shifted uncomfortably, and looked at him. Johnson's eyes had become red, and were starting to well up with tears.

Varese's phone lit up as Saul answered his call, but the cardinal didn't say anything and that didn't concern Varese. Although it was a secure line,

Saul was in the habit of saying as little as he could on the phone.

"He's eating lunch with. . ." Varese explained, speaking to the cardinal through the Bentley's Bluetooth mics, embedded in the headliner above him. He glanced at the laptop, impatient for a match, but it was still crunching through a database of nearly a billion prints.

He looked back through the camera and adjusted his aim. He could see that Johnson's eyes were red with tears, but his hollow, shaken tone wasn't conveyed by the robo-voice the app had assigned him. Varese could still hear what he was saying, though, and that was enough.

"The last time the devil walked among us . . ." Johnson began, but then he trailed off and tried to recapture his breath; his chest suddenly constricted with the memory, and left him speechless.

Varese took the moment to glance at his laptop again, and saw that Johnson's mug shot was displayed beside his fingerprints now, with the word MATCH blinking in green letters. Unlike what Fincannon and Ledger encountered in their search for Devlin's ID, Johnson's picture was locked to his prints. Varese quickly scanned the data fields: "Johnson, Peter. FBI, Special Agent. Retired, 1998. Medical disability (psychiatric). Full benefits."

He looked back through the camera with renewed attention just as Johnson was reiterating his last sentence. "The last time he walked among us, he walked all over me. I lost my wife and unborn child that night."

Varese kept watching them as he spoke to Saul. "Special Agent Peter Johnson, retired FBI. Psychiatric disability."

"I was nearly killed," Johnson's robo-voice was saying. "What do you want from me?"

Varese kept the camera perfectly still as Simone leaned over the wicker table, peering into Johnson's bloodshot eyes.

"We need you to help us find him, Peter."

Johnson stared at Simone as the blood began to pound in his ears, so strongly that he could barely hear what Simone was saying. But the next

58

sentence cut through loud and clear.

"*We need you to help us save him,*" Simone said.

Johnson stared at him, thunderstruck.

Simone's robo-voice stuttered, but Varese mentally filled in the blanks. He heard all he needed to, and asked Saul a simple question.

"Shall I?"

"Yes; at once."

The Bluetooth conveyed the cardinal's response through the Bentley's audio system. It enveloped Varese, like hearing the voice of God.

He put the camera down, and fetched an M-4 sniper's rifle from the passenger well as he glided down his driver's window. A quick glance in his mirrors told him that no one was coming, and no one was around. The gas station parking lot to his right was empty, and the cashier lady was flipping through a magazine. The shop across the street to his left was closed for the day.

He nestled the silencer in the crook of his side mirror, and sighted his target. Being a southpaw had its advantages, and shooting from the behind the wheel of a left-hand drive vehicle was one of them. Drawing his bead wouldn't take long, and once he had his target he didn't intend to hesitate, but not because of the weapon's exposure to potential witnesses. To his way of thinking, using a firearm was like playing snooker—you can aim all afternoon, but eventually you have to take the shot. Once you're dialed in, just do it . . .

The mist, however, was another matter. Even at this distance, his hollow point .223 would be plowing through a significant amount of water. There was no way to precisely predict how it would affect the trajectory, so there was no way to compensate beforehand. His crosshairs lingered on Johnson's left temple, and Varese smoothly squeezed the trigger.

But in the moment that his finger curled, the waiter leaned across the table to freshen Johnson's coffee. The jacketed hollow point pierced the young man's back between two upper ribs, forcing a highly compressed plug of fabric and skin into the open nose of the bullet. The slug made a neat, dimpled hole in his back the size of a pencil, but before the surrounding skin could spring back and before the hole could even fill with blood, the projectile blew apart in his chest cavity. Some of the pieces caromed off the back of his breastbone, but most of them stayed together as an expanding package of shrapnel, bursting out of his chest like a tiny grenade had gone off inside him.

One of the larger pieces grazed Johnson's forehead and spun him out of his chair. He dropped to the sidewalk before he even heard a sound.

The waiter's heart tore open and he lurched against the table, falling in a bloody heap on top of Simone. A second shot intended for the bishop punched through the waiter's shoulder instead, pushing them both to the sidewalk. The table flipped up and the umbrella tipped over, and the people at the adjoining tables instinctively leaped away from the chaos, their bodies reacting before their minds registered a conscious impression.

None of them even noticed a black Bentley at the far end of the block, pulling out of a parking spot and turning into the gas station. The cashier inside the station didn't see anything that happened at the café, but she did notice the exotic sedan rolling past her window and turning down the side street. *Now, there's something you don't see every day,* she thought, and went back to her magazine.

CHAPTER ELEVEN

Jonathan Kurinski and Janice Avery were dressed like doctors, but that was as far as their medical training went. Their drive from Cap-Haitien was pleasant enough, until they reached the end of the paved road at Cormier. But the full moon lit the hillsides beyond the off-road lights of their rental jeep, so the rest of the journey wasn't all that bad and they were still fresh when they arrived. The drive out would be nerve-wracking, but they could abandon the vehicle if they had to, and call for a pick up along the shore. Aside from the cruise ship resort, and the village of Cormier, there were miles of empty coastline on either side of Labadie.

They parked in the tiny lot and got out, adjusting their white coats as they took a look around. It was a cool tropical evening, and the hamlet had already rolled up the sidewalks. Labadie was much smaller than they thought, and so was the Labadie Psychological Medical Institute, but that would just make getting in and out that much easier. On the other hand, they couldn't blend in with the crowd, because there wasn't one.

The lights were on but no one was about, other than the security guard at his desk in the lobby and a night janitor wheeling his mop bucket into the ladies room. Jonathan held the door open for Janice, and he followed her inside like they belonged there. She smiled at the security guard as they passed his desk, heading for the main corridor, but the man didn't smile back. He just looked at them, wondering who they were. Janice turned back and approached him, as Jonathan paused to watch.

Diane was in the nurses' station of the residence wing, leafing through Devlin's file. She glanced up at the sound of approaching footsteps and smiled hello, although she had no idea who they were. She and Dr. Brillstein were the only doctors on night duty. He was in his office, the patients were all asleep, and the nurses and the orderlies were in the lunchroom on their midrats break. Aside from the security guard and the janitor, that was the entire night shift roster. Dr. Weist ran a tight ship at LPMI, and if people were coming for a visit, particularly medical personnel, he would have e-mailed them with a heads up before he left for the day.

But Diane pretended that nothing was amiss. She forced herself to look back down to the file and take a bored sip of coffee, even though it had gone cold an hour ago. She could hear their footsteps receding down the corridor, and watched out of the corner of her eye as they approached Devlin's room. She silently got up from her chair and slipped into the back room, speed-dialing a number on her cell.

Devlin had been out like a light since dusk, the first full stretch of sleep he'd had in nearly a week. The nightmares were becoming less frequent, and Diane was easing off with the sleeping potions, as he liked to call them. They went down to the beach to watch the sunset, and ran footraces on the hard sand. She wanted to wear him out with exercise instead of pumping him full of drugs again, and it worked. He was zonked out on top of the blanket now, still dressed in his new clothes. He hadn't even bothered to take off his shoes. Miss Meljean would have a fit when she came in the morning.

The outfit Diane got for him at the resort was comfortable and stylish, and the boat shoes fit like they were custom made. He felt like a new man, which for all intents and purposes he was. He still had no clue about his past, and apparently neither did she. Even his passport said he was John Doe. They were mystified that he was even issued one, but the U.S. embassy had been especially protective of their citizens ever since the quake. For some reason they figured that he was one of theirs, and they didn't want an American to be in limbo because he didn't have a name, particularly in Haiti. It wasn't exactly the safest place in the world.

Jonathan and Janice came in silently and didn't turn on the light, but the moon was still up, bathing the room in a cool blue luster. They approached the bed and stood on either side, drawing their silenced Walthers. But as they leveled their pistols at Devlin's temples, a bullet neatly punched through a slat in one of the jalousie windows, wrinkling the air between the assassins.

As they dropped for cover, the cracked glass slat dropped out of its aluminum frame and crashed to the floor. Devlin sat up, instantly awake, and saw the back of their white coats as they scrambled on the floor on either side of his bed. He had no idea what was going on, and the missing window slat was a mystery as well. Then another silenced bullet entered the room through another slat, narrowly missing one of the people on the floor.

Devlin panicked and rolled out of bed as Jonathan came out of his crouch, and when Devlin saw the gun in his hand he kicked at him in sheer panic. He caught the assassin in the solar plexus, sending him back toward the window. A third bullet punched through the glass, blowing out the back of his skull.

Devlin crawled towards the door, and as he came around the corner of the bed Janice came into view. She was on her hands and knees as well, keeping to the shadows and looking out the window, trying to locate the shooter. She saw Devlin out of the corner of her eye, but before she could bring her weapon around, he slugged her in the jaw as hard as he could.

She crashed against the desk and the lamp fell off, landing on top of her. Before she could bat it away and get her bearings, Devlin had opened the door and skittered out to the corridor.

She lunged toward the door to follow him, but dropped once again as a fourth bullet broke through the window, peppering her with bits of glass. She rolled in the shadows and crawled through the door.

Devlin was racing down the hall past the nurses' station, frantically looking around for Diane, but she was nowhere in sight.

"Diane!"

There was no response. Some of the patients had been startled awake by the commotion in his room, and those who could walk were peeking out their doors. He caught the eye of one of them and angled for her room, but the lady saw something behind him and slammed the door in his face. He turned in time to see what she saw—Janice was aiming with both hands, even as she ran toward him.

Devlin pushed away from the wall as two of her silenced slugs gouged out chunks of painted cinder block. He dropped to a crouch and scrambled around the corner, into the main corridor.

There was nobody ahead in the lobby, which seemed odd to him, but as he ran past the security desk he realized why. The guard was on the floor in a pool of blood. Devlin stopped in his tracks, and knelt beside the corpse. He yanked the man's revolver out of the holster on his hip as two silenced slugs punched into the hollow metal desk. Janice was coming straight at him, aiming as she ran.

The janitor rolled his mop bucket out of the ladies room and saw Devlin kneeling beside the security guard, but the pool of blood wasn't visible and neither was the weapon in Devlin's hand. The janitor was startled to see his friend on the floor, and walked quickly toward the desk, pushing his bucket ahead of him. Halfway there, he heard someone running toward him in the corridor, and turned . . .

Janice plowed into him and they went over in a heap, along with his bucket. Devlin scrambled to his feet and pushed through the front door.

He reached the darkness of the hyacinth bushes that bordered the lawn, and thought he would be safe, so he took a moment to watch the entrance and catch his breath. She burst out the front door, heading straight toward him and raising her weapon. The janitor was on the floor behind her, motionless.

Devlin was amazed that she could see him in the dark, and then he realized that the full moon was glinting on the nickel-plated revolver in his shaking hand. He ducked behind the hyacinth bushes and thrashed his way into the lush undergrowth, as silenced bullets punched through the palm fronds.

He listened for her approach as he wove a path in the darkness, paralleling the side lawn of the clinic as he made his way toward the beach. He could hear silenced rounds ripping through the vegetation, but they seemed to be coming from in front of him as well as behind.

He angled away from the clinic, and within moments he found a narrow path. It might have been blazed by wild boars or perhaps it was a fisherman's trail, but at this point it didn't matter. All that mattered was the sound of his shoes racing beneath him, steady and strong, as the odd sound of silent bullets ripping through the undergrowth slowly faded away.

CHAPTER TWELVE

St. Michael's was on a gentle hill overlooking Vatican City, barely a kilometer away. The Augustinian abbey was a medieval fortress that housed more than a thousand monks in its heyday, and the view of Vatican City was unparalleled. In the charred ruins below, the bodies had been cleared away and the forensic technicians had taken their samples. The Vatican curator was in command now, running a team of nearly three hundred volunteers. They flew in from around the world to help recover and preserve whatever artifacts they could salvage from the rubble, and the citizens of Rome were picking up the tab.

The devastation extended beyond the Basilica; the adjacent structures had been damaged as well. The ceiling of Sistine Chapel had fallen, and the walls of the Sacristy had buckled, with dozens of statues, plaques, and bas-reliefs in pieces on the floor. The loss was incalculable, and the world was weeping. The curator was sleeping in the ruins each night, on the floor of the Baptistery Chapel, below a portion of the roof that was still intact. It was how he processed his grief, and no one tried to dissuade him. Everyone on the project had a coping mechanism.

The explosion blew out every window along the front of the Government Administration Building behind the Basilica, as well as the upper windows of the Apostolic Palace that overlooked St. Peter's Square, including the Papal apartments. The daily business of the Vatican City State and the Holy See had been thrown into chaos as a result. But more than that, nerves had been shattered as well, to where it was nearly impossible to get any work done. Adding to the stress was a whispered suspicion that there could be another bomb, waiting to go off when the panic subsided and everyone got back to work.

The monks of St. Michael's had plenty of empty rooms behind their fortress walls, and they invited their neighbors to come stay with them while their house of God was being rebuilt. Italian Special Forces sweetened the offer by establishing a perimeter around the base of St. Michael's Hill. For the most part, the populace within the perimeter consented to a sweep of their neighborhood, particularly after it was made clear that any evidence of non-violent felonies would be ignored, and if it couldn't be ignored it would be forgiven, in writing if need be. The senior offices of the Holy See, including the Cabal of Cardinals, gratefully relocated to the fortress of St. Michael's, and the hotels and public buildings within the security zone were made available to Vatican City State staffers.

Nano's chambers on the top floor of the abbey were dark and cramped, with dank stone walls and a thick wood door that reminded him of a dungeon, but there was an ascetic vibe to the suite of rooms that he quite enjoyed, like a primitive chic resort without all the New Age hooey. With a wireless connection, his smartphone, and some electric heaters, he made the adjustment easier than he would have guessed, and it was fun translating all the Latin graffiti scratched in the stone.

The poor Augustinians were a horny lot, he soon concluded, after deciphering their allegories and allusions. The best ones were under the rug, and had only become visible when he damp-mopped the floor on the day he moved in. He spent his first candlelit evening on his knees, not in prayer, but with a damp rag and the Latin translator app on his phone, happily lost in lascivious translation.

It was a brain break that he sorely needed from the shock of the disaster. His physical injuries were minor, and Simone had barely suffered a scratch. But archbishop Nano's soul, or what was left of it, was profoundly shaken by the horror of what he saw in the Basilica. His last moment of consciousness was frozen in his mind, of the piteous multitude dying in agony, on fire and screaming as they hurtled toward him, even in his dreams.

It was painful to lay eyes on the aftermath, clearly seen from his monastery windows. He could hear the work crews at night, and despite the sedatives he was barely getting any sleep. It was difficult enough in New Orleans to deal with the work of the Devil, but this was something else again. This, he was certain, was the work of man. He had his suspicions as to whom and why, but for the moment he was keeping them to himself.

Saul knocked twice and opened the door, letting himself in and closing it with a thump. Nano got up from his desk, where he was trying to relax by surfing the Internet. He bowed his head, which strictly speaking was the proper thing to do, but it was overly formal given their relationship, and doubly so since they were alone. It was an awkward misstep in the dance of manners, and the gaffe made him nervous. Saul just watched him, which made him even more nervous.

"Your Eminence. This visit is a surprise." *'Eminence'?* he badgered himself. *'Cardinal Saul' would do fine. You are seriously overdoing it—*

"And it won't be a pleasant one," Saul told him.

"Please explain," Nano said, and moved to get him a chair. But Saul got one for himself, and sat before the desk. Nano sat down, facing him.

"The Rosicrucians have made an attempt on his life."

Nano was shocked, but kept his cool as best he could. "Did they . . .?"

In retrospect, it was a foolish question. Saul readily agreed, and his irritation was evident as he shook his head no.

"I said it was an attempt; pay attention. He managed to escape, and now he's out there again. Somewhere . . ."

Nano nodded, digesting the news, but he was at a loss to evaluate it. Saul suddenly leaned toward him. "Sooner or later, the Church will have to bury its past," the cardinal told him.

Nano frowned and nodded, hoping that would prompt him to elaborate, but Saul just sat back and scowled at him. Nano didn't think the scowl was directed at him, necessarily, but he got the distinct impression that Saul saw him as part of the overall mess. Probably because of the double fiasco in New Orleans and Haiti, although Nano couldn't see how he might have managed things better.

He broke eye contact by leaning back in his chair, and gazing at the ancient walls with a weary sigh. He had no idea where all this was headed, but it didn't look good and would likely get worse.

CHAPTER THIRTEEN

Haitian police had the Labadie Psychological Medical Institute cordoned off and under control by dawn. The inspectors from Cap-Haitien would be arriving momentarily, and until they were finished with what they had to do, the entire facility was in lockdown.

Drs. Brillstein and Viccu were cooperating, but they were waiting to speak with the inspectors, and the people on their nighttime staff weren't very talkative, either. One of the patients in the recovery wing was talking her head off, but she was on the verge of hysteria and the staff warned them that she suffered from dementia.

The two nurses and the four orderlies said they were in the lunchroom at the time of the killings. It was 3:30 a.m. and the patients were asleep, so they were taking their break together like they usually did, even though it was technically against policy. But they figured it would be all right because Dr. Viccu was on duty at the nurses' station, and anyway, she didn't object.

They were stricken by the loss of their two friends, and the cops figured their distress was made worse by wondering if they would be able to keep their jobs, since some of them should have been on the floor at the time. Such an oversight would normally fall harder on the two doctors, except that they were visiting from Miami to care for the amnesiac, so their other duties probably didn't amount to much more than house-sitting for Dr. Weist, the German expat physician who ran the facility from the day shift. He was coming in from his villa on the far side of Cap-Haitien, and would likely arrive after the inspectors left, given the morning rush hour traffic in downtown Le Cap.

All the night shift was saying for now was that the people in the lunchroom didn't hear a thing over the sound of the TV, and that the two doctors were conferring in Brillstein's office at the time, so they didn't hear anything, either. That told the cops that silencers must have been used. The patients in the recovery wing apparently heard something, though, because one of the nurses explained that six of them started pressing their call buttons all at once, which never happens at a quarter to four in the morning.

Before they could even respond to the calls, they heard the janitor's mop bucket tip over, and when they came out of the lunchroom they found him and the security guard dead in the lobby. They ran down to the recovery wing to respond to the call buttons, and found the lady with dementia in a breathless panic about how the American amnesiac tried to get in her room. She swore there was a woman chasing him with a gun, so she slammed the door and locked it tight. She was probably telling the truth, though, because there were two fresh gouges in the cinderblock wall outside her door that looked remarkably like bullet holes. There was also a third corpse in the amnesiac's room, the place had been shot up, there were signs of a struggle, and the patient was missing.

The villagers stood back from the yellow tape, careful not to rouse the ire of the police, who only came out to their dirt-road hamlet when something terrible happened. Usually the village elders would take care of things, but this was above their pay grade. The crowd parted to let a black Mercedes 550 G-wagon roll up to the entry steps, and they watched to see who would emerge from the vehicle. After the earthquake, it could be anyone from cops to the U.N., or even someone from the resort, trying to squelch any bad news that would scare away tourists.

Inspectors George Mezadieu and Micheline Batou of the PNd'H got out of the dusty SUV. Two cops raised their yellow tape, and the inspectors ducked under it, heading up the wide concrete steps to the lobby. The Police Nationale d'Haiti had an office in Le Cap, and the cops had given them a heads up before notifying the Americans in the capitol. Unless the embassy choppered in some Feds, it would take them at least a day to drive to Labadie, given the mess in Port-au-Prince and the chaos on the highways. The Yankees probably had other priorities, but they would be coming soon enough. The cops knew the PNd'H would want to plant their flag on the crime scene before the Americans started throwing their weight around. Their money and aid were as welcome as anyone's, but some of them were acting like Uncle Sam had just bought himself an old jalopy that needed an overhaul, and they were the master mechanics who were sent down to do the job right.

The coroner and his two assistants were standing in the lobby, along with the chief of police and three of his men. Now that the place was secure, there was nothing much to do until the inspectors arrived.

Mezadieu and Micheline shook hands with the chief and the coroner, and had a good look at the bodies, while the chief's three cops and the coroner's assistants had a good look at Inspector Batou. She was a creole beauty in her early thirties, and damn hard to ignore. But she didn't look like a pushover, and neither did Inspector Mezadieu. A lean, toned man in his early fifties, he looked like he'd rather shoot you than ask you not to gawk at his partner. Being a former voodoo priest, Mezadieu had plenty of practice looking scary.

The captain stayed with his men as the coroner led the inspectors down the corridor to the surgery wing. The coroner's assistants began putting the two corpses in body bags, while the three cops just watched Inspector Micheline walking away.

Dr. Diane Viccu and her partner Dr. Norman Brillstein stood up as the coroner ushered the inspectors into the operating theater. They had been sitting on a pair of stools by the anesthesiologist cart, pensively gazing at the floor with cold cups of coffee in hand. The bodies of Jonathan Kurinski and Janice Avery were laid out before them, Janice on the operating table and Jonathan on a gurney. Both had been shot in the head. Jonathan had the surprised, vacant stare of someone hit from behind, and Janice had a swollen jaw from Devlin's haymaker, although the injury seemed to be a consequence of the bullet hole in her temple.

"Are you Dr. Brillstein?" Mezadieu asked, and Brillstein nodded, shaking the inspector's hand. Brillstein was a tall man in his forties, lean but well-built, with the pale skin of someone who spent his life indoors. But Mezadieu noticed that his grip was calloused like a laborer, not a surgeon. Perhaps he lifted weights.

Brillstein indicated Diane beside him. "This is Dr. Diane Viccu. She was on duty when they came in."

Mezadieu shook hands with the woman. *She has lovely eyes,* he thought, but he wasn't sure if that made him feel enchanted or cautious. And not being sure of his reaction made him lean toward caution.

Micheline caught the moment. Men had reacted to her all her life, so it was easy enough to see it in play, but it was a rare thing to see it in her partner. Diane had a dangerous beauty, and Micheline watched her closely.

"I am Inspector Mezadieu," he was saying to Diane. "This is Inspector Micheline Batou."

Micheline shook hands with Diane, and they exchanged brief smiles. Her hand was warmer than Micheline would have guessed, with a grip more firm than she expected. What Diane felt about her, she couldn't tell, and that was unexpected as well. A person in her situation was usually a bundle of raw emotions, emitting spontaneous signals at each passing moment. A most unusual woman, and her partner was a cipher as well.

"You were the one who called the police, *non*?" Mezadieu asked Diane, and she nodded nervously, clearing her throat. "Yes," Diane replied, and saw that Micheline's eyes narrowed, watching her.

"What can you tell us?" Micheline asked, and Diane glanced her way before looking down to the floor, assembling her thoughts.

"Not much. We were the only two doctors on duty last night. There are only four doctors in this facility, due to budget cuts. Dr. Wiest and Dr. Livingston work the morning shifts . . . "

Micheline was growing impatient. " . . . and you and Dr. Brillstein work the night shift." Diane nodded. Micheline thought she was stalling.

Mezadieu stepped in. "You called the police before the shooting started, *non*?" Diane nodded again. "Why is that?" he wanted to know.

Her eyes started to tear up. Micheline sensed that the tears were genuine.

"Well . . ." Diane was saying, "They just looked . . . *wrong*."

So you called the police?" Micheline asked her. "Why not security?"

Diane looked at her. "I went to see the security guard, but he was dead," she said evenly. "So I called you."

Micheline glanced at Mezadieu and looked at Diane, seeking her attention. When she turned to him, he continued in a softer tone. "Doctor Viccu," he said, and indicated the two bodies. "Are these the doctors you saw?"

Diane nodded, but before he could follow up, Micheline stepped in again. "So these wrong doctors came to kill your patient. And who killed them? And where is your patient?"

Diane began to tear up again, and couldn't formulate a reply. *Boo-hoo, she misses her patient,* Micheline concluded with a smirk, and began writing some notes, as Mezadieu saw something through the window in the entry door, and scowled.

Fincannon and Ledger were coming down the corridor with two other American suits, and none of them were in a good mood. The chief of police stood in the lobby behind them, watching. *The cheap bastards flew in from Port-au-Prince and rented a jeep,* he realized. He was half-expecting an unmarked black helicopter, or a Zodiac launched from a destroyer. Something more dramatic than turboprop puddle-jumper.

Diane could see the Americans coming down the hall, and she noticed the inspector's sour attitude. Micheline wasn't any more sanguine. Mezadieu turned back to her. "We may need to ask you more questions at some point."

She nodded, and his gaze took in Brillstein as well. "Excuse me," he said to the doctors. "It seems we have visitors."

He went through the swinging door to meet with the Americans, as Micheline caught Diane's attention. "Your American amnesia patient was missing from the same room where the male doctor was shot."

Diane nodded. "Yes," she told the inspector in a quiet, shaken voice. "And now he's gone. He must have been frightened out of his wits. He received his passport yesterday afternoon, so—"

She was interrupted by the conversation in the corridor. "He's an American! *That's* why!" Fincannon was saying to Mezadieu.

"C'est Ayiti, monsieur," Mezidieu replied, coldly polite. "You have no jurisdiction in my country."

He turned and came back into the operating theater, the four Americans glaring at him. Mezadieu dismissively waved goodbye through the little window, as Micheline smirked and turned back to Diane.

"This amnesiac, how did he end up here?" she asked Diane. "Any friends? Family? Visitors?"

"No, no family. No visitors."

"He was found wandering on the beach by a local fisherman. About a month after that strange snowstorm."

"Did this fisherman leave a name?"

Screw this guy, Brillstein thought. *The fisherman's been visiting every damn day, but no, he didn't 'leave a name'.*

"No," Brillstein told him, "but the amnesiac spoke with an American accent, so the Embassy wanted—"

"—an American doctor to treat him—" Mezadieu filled in sourly.

"—to jar his memory," Diane explained, and Mezadieu just looked at them.

"So we flew down from Miami," Brillstein told him. "Is that all?" Micheline had been gazing at the corpses. "For now," she told her.

"We'll be in touch," Mezadieu said, and handed her his card. "If you can think of anything else . . ."

Diane nodded and pocketed his card. "Okay," she said. "But I'll be going back to the states in a few days, unless someone can find my patient."

He slowly nodded. *We'll see about that,* he thought. "Then we'll make sure to get to the bottom of this very quickly."

Diane and Brillstein shook hands with the inspectors. Mezadieu held open the swinging door, and Micheline stepped into the corridor. He joined her, and they headed back to the lobby.

"The Americans got here pretty fast," Micheline said, and he nodded.

"They just issued the amnesiac a passport," he told her, and Micheline glanced at him in surprise. "And now the man has disappeared. Very puzzling."

She nodded. It was very puzzling, indeed. Mezadieu glanced over his shoulder, and saw that Diane and Brillstein were watching them through the little window in the swinging door.

He waved goodbye with a little smile, but they didn't return it.

CHAPTER **FOURTEEN**

There was a smudge of ruby clouds on the horizon where the sun had gone to rest, and the air was so clean that the constellations in the east could touch the Caribbean. The moon was in its last quarter now, rising at dawn and setting by late afternoon, and so the next several nights would only be lit by stars, unless the clouds came up or there was a fog. Miami lay 500 miles to the northwest, a week's sailing with a decent wind, skirting the coast of Cuba then tacking north with the gulfstream. But the same trade winds also brought the storms from North Africa. There was nothing brewing in those waters at the moment, but that could change overnight.

Fifteen refugees were huddled in Havier's fishing boat, lashed to the end of the long rickety dock, out beyond the ebb tide shore break. Nobody lived around the tiny cove; the hillsides were too steep and rocky, but it was a good place to harbor fishing boats. The sloop was a wide and sturdy workhorse that had once been painted blue, with a high bow and a shiplap hull about eight meters long. There was no cabin or wheel, just a tiller and a long pair of oars to find the wind. His crew had gone south to Port-au-Prince to take care of their families after the quake, so Havier was making ends meet by ferrying refugees. He was tired of fishing, anyway, and each time he went north he was sorely tempted to stay. But the village *houngan* kept inviting himself along for the ride, to protect his departing villagers from the *loas* of the deep as well as the U.S. Coast Guard, and so Havier had to keep bringing the old man back again. And he had to be polite about it, too, even though he took up valuable space. But Havier held his peace, because the last thing he needed was a voodoo priest getting mad at him and putting a hex on his boat.

Everyone on board had their reasons for going, and their secret dreams as well. Their lives were packed into suitcases and backpacks, wrapped in sturdy trash bags that would keep things dry if their luck held all the way to Miami. Then again, if they had any kind of luck they wouldn't have to go to Miami, but they tried not to dwell on that.

The *houngan* was bouncing a little girl on his knee, and her young mother was sitting across from them, fussing with their bundles in preparation for the voyage. There were several young men on board, and they'd been glancing at the woman since she arrived, but it was clear that the *houngan* intended to keep her and her daughter safe. Their fantasies of high seas debauchery would have to remain just that, unless the old bastard died on the way to Miami. He was looking their way now, and he was probably reading their minds, or so they thought. Actually he was looking past them, into the gloom of jungle where the dock met the shore.

Devlin had been watching them gather, and knew he would have to present himself soon. He was dirty and in need of a shave, and his left shoulder still stung from the bullet that grazed him. His new outfit was a shambles, although the boat shoes held up well. He foraged for enough food so he didn't have to use the pistol to kill a goat or a boar, although it wouldn't have done much good, since he didn't have a knife or any way to make a fire. It was strange to him that he knew what plants to eat, and how to gather rainwater, and how to make a shelter to keep away the chill at night. Still, the pistol had been a comfort over the last three days, but he knew that if he brought it on the boat, it would create more tension than peace of mind. He reluctantly tossed it away and took a breath for courage, and walked onto the sand.

HUNTING LUCIFER

The old man must have said something to the others, because they all turned and watched as he stepped up on the dock and approached them. He tried to put them at ease with a congenial smile, but it didn't work, so he stopped a few paces from the stern and nodded hello. No one returned the gesture.

"I mean you no harm," he said, and then he realized that he was speaking in Creole. It seemed to relax their caution, although his astonishment must have been evident, even in the moonless dusk.

The young men had machetes, and so did the man at the tiller, and the cold steel glinted in the remnants of light. "What do you need?" he asked the stranger, and Devlin smiled a bit forlornly, which was genuine enough.

"How about a ride?" Devlin asked.

Havier didn't answer, and Devlin sighed, his smile turning melancholy. "I don't have any money," he admitted, and then he thought that he could retrieve the pistol and use it for barter. On the other hand, giving it to a boatload of tough guys didn't seem like such a good idea, even if he unloaded it first. With the way he looked, handing over a gun would just set off alarm bells.

The *houngan* was quietly alarmed. His *loas* started chattering amongst themselves the moment the stranger appeared; his ancestral spirit guides did not see this as a good sign. Appearances are usually deceiving, but no matter how innocent he appeared to be, it would be far too dangerous to leave him behind; the village would never be safe. They had to take him to America and leave him there.

"He can come," the *houngan* told Havier, and touched the sailor's arm to quell his jumble of worried thoughts. Havier knew it was the old man's magic at work, but even though he tried to resist it had a tranquilizing effect. His boat was all he had and the journey would be difficult enough, and now this . . .

Havier closed his eyes and nodded, and Devlin came aboard.

CHAPTER FIFTEEN

Peter Johnson was in stable condition, sitting up in bed and working his way through a cube of lime Jell-O. His head bandage moved every time he opened his mouth, which hurt like the dickens but at least he was alive. The shrapnel tumbled past his temple and chipped the bone, but other than that he was fine, except for his indigestion. The way he figured it, hospital food was specially prepared to keep you sick and make you stay longer, but he'd given up arguing with the nurse. She was not going to let him order in no kind of brown rice hippie food, and not even some jambalaya from Fan-Fan's, and that was that. Mark Kaddouri did sneak in some jerk chicken, but it was long gone by now. The lime Jell-O was just to clear his palette before they started in on their hospital coffee, which Johnson had to admit wasn't all that bad.

Kaddouri was sitting in the chair beside his bed, somewhat depressed, working away on his laptop. It had been a month since his miraculous recovery as a flat-lined corpse, but when he came back to life he learned that Special Agent Christine Mas, the woman he'd fallen in love with, was dead. It was tragedy he was still coming to terms with. Johnson was there when she died, at the Citadel in the highlands of Haiti of all places, and Kaddouri heard the entire story when they visited Christine's mother. But there were no remains to bring back to the States; as the archangel Michael took her up to heaven, there was a stream of silver dust trailing behind them and that was it.

Kaddouri was a different man since his rebirth—that's what he privately called it—and he was content to discover himself all over again. He retired from the New Orleans Police and started a consulting gig with the Sheriff's office in New Iberia. It was a beautiful small town, the "queen city of the Bayou Teche" as they liked to call themselves. It was also the parish seat. They wanted him for his big-town police savvy, and his experience dealing with the Feds.

But right now he felt completely incompetent. He still couldn't find a trace of Christine Mas in any database he could access, local, state, or federal. Or even Interpol, for that matter. Every search parameter he tried came back 'no match found'.

"How you holding up?" Johnson wanted to know.

Kaddouri leaned back in his chair and offered a lop-sided grin. "I should be asking you."

"I'm alive," Johnson informed him, licking the last bit of lime Jell-O off his spoon. *Oops,* Johnson thought, *Bad choice of words . . .*

Kaddouri's grin faded, and his eyes drifted back to his laptop. "It's like she was never here! No one remembers her but us." He closed the laptop in frustration.

"And the Church," Johnson said. "They remember."

Kaddouri frowned. "Who did this to you?"

"Someone from Rome came to find me."

"Rome?"

"A priest. Apparently the Church has gotten in way over their halos."

Kaddouri cracked a wry smile. "Lucky for us, you haven't. Does this priest have a name?"

"Pablo Simone," Johnson told him, and Kaddouri opened his laptop.

CHAPTER SIXTEEN

The fishing boat was bobbing in a cold, choppy sea off the north coast of Cuba, a fitful wind teasing the sails. The sun gave little warmth, but it managed to make everyone's sunburn sting. The lotion was nearly gone and everyone was wearing long sleeves, but even those with wide-brim hats couldn't avoid the rays reflecting off the water.

One of the young men took his turn at the tiller, giving Havier a much-needed break, and he made his way forward for a change of scenery, stepping carefully over the legs and feet of the people gathered around the mast. Devlin was alone at the bow, huddled against the damp winter breeze, his teeth chattering and his eyes red from salt spray and lack of sleep. Harvier sat nearby, but not so close that they could be seen as sitting together. The others were watching, especially the *houngan*. After four days, the American was still an outsider, even though he spoke remarkably fluent Creole. That fascinated Harvier, and he spoke with the man whenever he could, but not so much that people would think that they formed an alliance. The voodoo priest was clearly suspicious of the stranger, although he granted him passage, and everyone was following his lead. Harvier didn't understand what was going on, exactly, but he didn't want to wind up on the wrong side of things if something took a bad turn.

"How much longer?" Devlin asked him.

"Couple days," Havier replied, and then he cracked a dry grin. "Sooner if we get picked up."

Devlin gave him a bit of a smile in return, but it soon faded as he looked over the endless sea. Havier watched him, trying to place his accent.

The *houngan* was watching him, too, and as he did, he heard a quiet whisper from the *loas*. They were telling him something about the stranger, but he couldn't quite make it out; sometimes the *loas* are hard to hear. He sensed what they wanted him to do, though, and he reached into his burlap satchel, taking out one of the apples he'd brought along. It had a ripe and luscious crimson glow, with patches of golden green. The others watched him, waiting for him to cut it into pieces and share. There was something else in his hand, but it wasn't a knife; it was a small leather pouch.

He teased open the pouch, and then he licked the apple. They were puzzled and disappointed; no one did that if they were going to share their food. And then he shook some yellow powder from the pouch on the wet spot. He cinched the pouch closed with his teeth, put it back in his satchel, and brought out a disposable lighter. He held the apple upside down by the stem and hunched over it to keep away the wind, and lit the powder.

He quickly held the apple out at arm's length and watched as angry flames crawled over the skin of the apple, with an intense white heat that everyone around him could feel. They shrank back in fear and amazement, riveted by a magic ritual that the uninitiated rarely witnessed.

The *houngan* studied the whirling flames and a vision was revealed, and when it was over the apple was untouched and so were his fingers. He was completely unnerved by what the fire had shown him.

"It's impossible . . .!" he breathed. The others were staring at him, wondering what he saw.

Devlin was watching as well, but now the *houngan* looked at him, and so did the others. Havier moved away and made the sign of the cross, and the others did the same. Even the voodoo priest blessed himself, something he almost never did. But this was different.

Devlin smiled nervously, wondering what was going on, but he was fairly certain that they weren't going to bother telling him. He looked back out to sea again and shivered against the wind, more alone now than the moment he came aboard. The endless water lulled him into a stupor, and he drifted off to sleep . . .

The angel Abdiel brought a precious seed down from heaven, and gave it to Jesus in the Garden of Eden. The only-begotten Son of God planted the seed, and they stood together, watching it become the Tree of Knowledge. The apples had a ripe and luscious crimson glow, with patches of golden green . . .

CHAPTER SEVENTEEN

It was good to be home again. Peter Johnson took a long, hot shower and scrubbed away the smell of the hospital with an organic body wash he found at the farmer's market. He was especially careful around his head wound, watching what he was doing in his shaving mirror, but the soap was some kind of lye-free essential oils concoction and it didn't sting nearly as bad as he thought it would. The wound wasn't disfiguring, either, which was a stroke of good luck; he'd have a dashing scar when it was healed. All in all, he was still in business, although he knew that whoever tried to kill him was still in business as well.

They tried to kill Father Simone, too, Johnson reminded himself, so maybe it wasn't the Church. Then again . . .

Mark Kaddouri had left a message when he was in the shower. Johnson shrugged on his bathrobe and rang him back. "Mark?"

"Yeah. I got the goods on the priest who visited you."

Kaddouri was in his office at New Iberia City Hall, looking at a picture of Simone on his desktop monitor. The folks in the building left him alone, which was how he liked it. His recovery was seen as a miracle to every devout Christian in town, but in the heart of bayou Christianity always came with a strong dose of Cajun spice. Coming back to life as he did, after being pronounced dead in the back of a coroner's van—parked in the graveyard of the cathedral of New Orleans, no less—seemed more like voodoo than a simple case of divine intervention. Plus, he wasn't of the faith, so they didn't know what to make of him.

"Pablo Simone is a bishop," Kaddouri told Johnson. "He was promoted about six weeks ago."

"That's odd," Johnson said. "You'd think he would have mentioned it."

Kaddouri tapped a key, and his computer crunched through a database. "Maybe he's just a humble guy," he shrugged, watching his monitor, but there was no match found. He opened a folder and flipped through several sheets of paper.

Johnson could hear him shuffling through the file as he made his way around several neat stacks of books to his La-Z-Boy, and dropped into it with a sigh. "Well," he told Kaddouri, "supposedly, according to the bishop, the Devil's human now, and has no knowledge of his true nature."

"Hmmm . . ." Kaddouri murmured, but gave him no more response than that. Being a Muslim had its advantages in dealing with Johnson, as well as the Christians in city hall. Certain things gave them the willies that didn't bother Kaddouri in the least. For one thing, he knew that Shaytan had no power of his own, other than what Allah allowed him to have. *'The Devil made me do it!'* never washed with him, and the occasional Christian who used it as an excuse made him laugh. The Devil never made anyone do anything, just like guns don't kill people. People kill people; they just usually did it with guns. The silenced .223 rounds that killed the waiter and nearly killed Johnson were an unusual variation in this neck of the woods, but a human being still pulled the trigger of his own free will, of that he was certain.

Johnson picked up his bible from the coffee table, and was waiting for Kaddouri to speak. "What?" he finally prompted him, wondering what Kaddouri's *hmmm* had been about.

Kaddouri was logged onto the website of the U.S. Embassy in Haiti, and had one of their documents on his monitor. "An unknown man of American appearance was found by a fisherman in northern Haiti last month, wandering on the beach delirious . . ."

Kaddouri paused to scroll, and Johnson knew from the sound of his voice that he was reading something aloud.

" . . . so the fisherman took him to a local mental hospital . . . " He scanned the rest of the page for the salient points. "But now the man has disappeared, after some sort of law enforcement scenario at the hospital, but they won't say what, classified, blah, blah, blah . . ." He sat up as something caught his eye. "He was an amnesiac, Peter."

Johnson put his bible down and sat up as well, holding his cell phone tight to his hear. "They have a picture?" He could hear Kaddouri typing.

"Stand by," Kaddouri told him. Another document appeared and he scanned through it. "They issued him a passport."

"Put out a search and hold for the registration number," Johnson suggested, and he heard more keystrokes, then a final tap as Kaddouri hit Enter. "I just did," Kaddouri told him.

"Good. If something shows up—"

"—he'll be detained," Kaddouri said, finishing the thought. "And if this guy is really him, then what?"

Johnson didn't answer right away. He was on his feet now, pacing the living room. He stopped before his wall of framed newspaper clippings, gazing at the one in the center, hanging apart from the others, dated December 26, 1976 . . .

Women and Unborn Child Found Murdered At Bayou Memorial Clinic After Tornado Strikes.

He took the phone from his ear and choked back a sudden surge of emotion, but Kaddouri heard him anyway.

"Peter? You still there?"

Johnson looked down to the phone in his hand, and held it to his ear, sadly gazing at the newspaper clipping. In all those years, there wasn't a day that went by when he didn't think of them.

"Yeah," he said quietly. "But they're not."

CHAPTER **EIGHTEEN**

Cardinal Saul was seated at the table where he took his meals, before a window in his suite at St. Michael's. He was sipping his morning tea and watching the engineers below, through a large pair of binoculars on a little tripod set on the table before him.

Over the last month, the curator's volunteer army had carefully extracted priceless artifacts from the rubble and was reassembling whatever they could, while the engineers worked around the clock bracing and framing for the new roof and dome. When they were finished with the project, the exterior would look exactly the same, but the interior would be a different matter. Replicating the interior was straightforward enough; things could always be approximated in marble and plaster and wood. But recreating the original artwork would be next to impossible, and many said that it would border on blasphemy. Artisans, sculptors, and painters the world over were submitting proposals for new works, and the Pope himself was actively involved in the selection process.

Finishing the New Vatican could easily take years, but Saul was confident that he would see it completed before he died. He was a healthy seventy-two years old, and his parents and grandparents had lasted well into their nineties. Watching the project unfold was much more interesting than watching the news reports about it, particularly since they had no idea what was going on. He knew exactly what was going on, because he was the one who was calling the shots.

There was a soft knock, three quick taps, and he glanced at the door, knowing who it was. Varese came in, ushering an attractive woman in black leather pants and a matching tailored jacket. Saul turned to them with a smile, and she smiled back. Sama was in her late thirties, with jet-black hair and emerald green eyes. She had the relaxed poise of a dancer, and a smile more confident than cordial, which Saul found especially attractive. So far as he could tell she wore no make-up, and he correctly surmised that she kept her hair and nails short for hand-to-hand combat. All of which he thought was sexy as hell—a low-maintenance woman who could take care of herself, and still turn every head in the room. Her smile broadened, sensing his thoughts, and he liked her at once.

"We have word of where he might be," Varese was saying.

He was unreadable behind his dark glasses, but Saul was certain that he knew exactly where the cardinal's thoughts had been these last few moments. Saul nodded, acknowledging what he said, but Sama was a force of nature and he felt compelled to keep his focus on her for the time being. She didn't mind; she was used to it.

"Where did you find her?" Saul wanted to know, and before Varese could tell him, she stepped forward and extended her hand.

"I found him, your Eminence."

They shook hands, and Saul could feel the strength in her grip, which was remarkable given how smooth her skin was. He noticed the definition of her forearm, toned and anatomically perfect, but her hand had no callouses. *Perhaps she was a swimmer*, he thought, and imagined her underwater like a mermaid, lithe and naked and graceful.

She smiled again and he returned it, and for a fleeting instant he thought she might be reading his mind, but then he dismissed the idea. A beautiful woman always knows what a man is thinking, even a cardinal.

He glanced at Varese. "Is she good?"

It was a loaded question with a double meaning, but he liked to tease Varese about the ladies whenever he could. His personal assistant was a handsome, rawboned man with a gravitas that could have landed him a career in modeling, but he was too socially awkward to entertain the notion. Saul, on the other hand, was a man of the cloth in his seventies and not exactly a man about town, but he could turn on the charm when the mood struck him, and right now he was in the mood. The fact that Sama was comfortably receptive to his overtures, made her even sexier in his eyes.

Varese was as stiff as a butler, and Sama watched him, amused. "The best," he answered Saul, and handed him one of two thin file folders. The cardinal flipped through the file, and got the gist after scanning a few dense pages. He peeked at Sama with an avuncular twinkle in his eye, and she looked back.

"Samantha?" Saul inquired, but she shook her head.

"Just Sama," she told him, and he nodded.

"Interpol says you don't exist, Miss Sama. If that's your real name." She just smiled demurely, and said nothing. Saul glanced at Varese. "And her references?"

Varese handed him another file. "They're all dead."

Saul turned back to her, intrigued. He'd save the second file for later; he liked to read murder mysteries before he went to bed. "Impressive," he remarked, and she looked down to the floor like a shy schoolgirl.

Varese had been making discreet inquiries in Marseilles for the last several days, looking for professional operatives. For centuries, the port had been an international bazaar for all manner of goods and services, refugees and outcasts. The Templars even claimed that Jesus and Mary Magdelene landed there as man and wife, fleeing from His staged crucifixion in Jerusalem. Down through the ages, the Languedoc friars of the region supposedly kept their sacred bloodline a secret until the modern era. Saul doubted their tall tale, but if there was a plausible place to set the story Marseilles would certainly do. Truth, like people, could die a quick death there, and if Sama had the talent to thrive in such a place and cover her tracks, all the better, because no trail would lead to her or Saul.

There was one thing he was curious about, and he dipped his head down to catch her eye. When she looked at him, he took her to his table and gestured for her to sit in his chair, behind the binoculars. She sat facing him, but he gestured for her to look through the field glasses. She turned and did so, and he watched her sighting in on the shell of the Basilica, adjusting the focus for her youthful eyes.

"Tell me, Sama, do you believe in the second coming?"

She smiled and gently shook her head, careful not to disturb the binoculars. "No, it's a fairy tale," she said, watching the work crews far below. "Just like the first one."

"Ah, but it's already happened, my dear. You're looking at the aftermath."

Her lips parted for what he thought would be a response, but she said nothing, and he realized that she was smiling.

He was amused by her lack of faith. "I suggest you read everything you can to prepare yourself, mentally, spiritually, and physically."

She turned to him, and he looked up to meet her gaze; his eyes had been lingering on a hint of cleavage in the open collar of her shirt. She smiled, catching him in the act, and he smiled back. "Start with the Book of Revelations," he advised her.

"Why Revelations?" She knew it was in the back of the book, and it puzzled her that he said to start there.

"Because death is the only reality we're dealing with now," he told her, and left it at that. She was a clever woman; if she took his recommendation, she would learn how she fit into the grand scheme of things, without spelling it out for her. And if she didn't, it didn't matter. She'd find out the hard way soon enough, along with the rest of the world.

CHAPTER NINETEEN

The broken spear looked like iron, but the double-edged blade was made of plel, the eternal metal, forged in the heart of the Eastern Star, where the angels went to make their weapons. He somehow knew he'd had the weapon for eons, but he had no idea why, because he wasn't even permitted to own a weapon. He was a slave.

He was toiling in the garrison at Jerusalem, fixing the blade to a new hardwood shaft while a Roman soldier waited impatiently. His company was preparing for a crucifixion detail, and the young man needed a spear. Devlin handed it to him with a smile, and wished him well.

Later that day, when the soldier lanced the side of Christ, a tremendous clap of thunder shook the hills and a pelting rain came down. The young man dropped the spear, and scrambled away to join his comrades. Many of the mourners fled as he did, but some of them ignored the storm, their heads bowed in prayer before their crucified Savior.

Devlin stepped away from the clutch of faithful. He was no longer a slave; he was dressed in the finery of a Roman patrician. He retrieved the spear and walked into the eastern hills, a dark smile on his lips.

When he was finally out of sight of the others, alone in the empty desert, he thrust the spear into the earth. An opening appeared and swallowed him up, and Devlin descended into hell with his trophy.

Beelzebub welcomed him through the Gates of Hell, but the gatekeeper *and his minions were worried. Devlin had endangered everything by influencing Herod and Pontius Pilate, and even Judas Iscariot. When Christ was but a man, He took Lazarus from them with only his word. One tortured soul hardly mattered to them; Hell was filled with tortured souls and demons. But now that Christ was free of all human limitations . . .*

Jesus appeared outside the Gates, and a brilliant light shone in on them. "Open up, ancient gates!" He said, but they refused. "Open up, ancient doors!" He commanded. "Let the King of Glory enter."

They were compelled to let Him in, but as they did they turned away, for His light was so bright that they had to shut it out. Beelzebub himself slid back the bolts, and Jesus entered the Gates of Hell.

He made His way through the underworld, illuminating the darkness for three days and nights, passing every hole and hiding place and suffusing them with light, and as He did so all the demons and the tortured souls were free, and went their way singing the glory of God.

When Hell was quiet and still, He returned to the Gates and came out to be among them. Beelzebub and his minions were trembling in fear, and Devlin was with them but he wasn't afraid. But Jesus said nothing to any of them, and held out his hand for the spear. Devlin refused, holding it tightly, but the power of the Lord drew it from his grasp, and it flew into His hands.

He fashioned the blade of plel into a key, and as He did a lock appeared on the Gates that had never been there before. Beelzebub and his minions were amazed, but Devlin was angry and vowed revenge. Hell was empty and the Gates of Hell were locked, and the Son of God held the key . . .

Devlin woke up groggy and weak in the damp, foggy dusk, with a splitting headache and the hollow realization that he was no longer dreaming. He really was adrift for the tenth straight day on the open sea, in a boat full of strangers, and they really were wasting away from hunger, exposure and thirst, and a gnawing, relentless fear.

The clammy odor of mildew lingered with the residue of dead and dying fish, and his empty stomach clenched in protest. The oils had penetrated the raw wood inside the open boat for more than thirty years, and it was something that more than a week of merciless sunshine had failed to dissipate. He vomited three times earlier today, all dry heaves, and he was afraid that he would do it again. It embarrassed him to think of it, although everyone else on board was suffering the same as he was, and some were much worse. The food had run out two days ago, and now they were down to their last jug of water, lashed to the base of the mast and watched over by everyone who happened to be awake. The little girl was turning out to be the strongest of them all, but even she was weakening now.

He was huddled in the bow as he had been since the start of their voyage, and as he leaned his head over the side he glanced aft to find her. She was the only one on board who had any kindly regard for him, and her acceptance had become as important as food or drink. She was close by, sleeping in her mother's arms, and the young woman saw him looking at her daughter. She stared at him, blank and weary, and held her daughter closer as she looked away to the darkening sea. The men across from her saw their brief interaction, but the jug of water had become much more interesting than a pretty woman, and they went back to gazing it, or looking out to sea as well, although there was nothing to lay eyes on.

Havier was at the tiller, and the *houngan* was lying in a heap beside him. The old man had apparently passed away that afternoon, and his body was already starting to stiffen. The three men sitting close by had just found out, and they were alarmed. The death of a voodoo priest was a very bad omen. If the *loas* didn't protect him, there must have been a good reason why. Havier was certain that he knew the answer, and they leaned in close as he whispered to them. He kept his eyes on Devlin up at the bow, who was leaning over the railing now, dry heaving and weak.

"The *houngan* told me last night that this man is the Devil, and now look, he is dead!"

The men looked at the old man's corpse, so sunken and frail that it seemed like a mummy. The apple was still clutched in his hand, uneaten and fresh, but in spite of their hunger no one would take it. And they didn't dare look in his satchel, either. The *loas* would surely return if they did, but not to watch over them.

Havier gripped his machete and two of the men gripped theirs, and they put their heads close together to hash out a plan of attack. The third one was clutching a police baton, a memento from his old security job at the resort. He was the strongest among them, and was quite prepared to inflict the first blow. If they could immobilize him without bloodshed, they could lower him overboard and slit his throat, and the sharks would do the rest. It would be much better than shedding blood in the boat, or engaging in a death struggle with a mortally wounded man. The boat smelled bad enough without adding his viscera to the bilge water, and the little girl would surely be traumatized from the violence and bloodshed.

It troubled him, though that the sharks hadn't arrived, because the old man's body had already begun to stink. Perhaps they knew there was something unholy on board. But whether they came or not, they would still give the old man a proper burial at sea, and then the *loas* might be kind to them, if they ever returned.

It was settled, and Havier secured the tiller with a bit of rope. They crept forward, stepping over the others, the man with the baton in the lead. Everyone on board was watching them, except for Devlin and the girl.

He was leaning over the rail in case he heaved, and she was leaning over her mother's shoulder, wide awake from the woman's last protective hug, her little head suspended over the railing as well. It was an odd tête-à-tête, just her and Devlin in their own little world above the dark, choppy swells, and she smiled at him. He forced a brave smile in return, and she carefully opened her little fist, offering him a bit of bread crust. He shook his head, and nodded that she should keep it for herself, and then he looked away to the horizon to let her know that he hadn't given up hope. She looked to the horizon as well, joining his vigil.

Her mother had no idea what she was doing, because the woman was staring at the parade of three weapons passing before her as each man stepped over her legs, the one with the baton in the lead. She didn't dare turn her head to follow them, and just shifted her eyes, watching along with everyone else.

Devlin narrowed his eyes and peered into the gray western haze, and then he lifted his head to get a better look. The sun had set about a half hour ago, so he expected the horizon to still be lit, and it was, but a minute passed and then another one and it didn't seem to be getting any dimmer. The little girl saw it, too, and she finally looked at him with wide eyes. But he didn't see her, mesmerized by the glow of the horizon.

"We're saved," he croaked in a raw, dry throat, but he could hardly hear himself speak. He rose up and to inhale a lungful of air, but before he could draw it in he was blinded by an explosion of pain. The baton had been aimed at the back of his neck, but he moved the instant before it struck, and caught a glancing blow on the side of his skull.

There was an audible impact and the little girl screamed, but her mother was watching and held her tightly. The blow opened his head wound and he began to bleed, and the girl screamed again, but Devlin was undeterred from spreading the news. He pointed west to announce his discovery, but as he did the white prow of a steel ship appeared before him, and an ear-splitting foghorn made everyone freeze.

"We are the United States Coast Guard. Stay where you are!"

CHAPTER TWENTY

The announcement was repeated in Spanish, and then in French, but there was no need to go through all that trouble. Everyone on board the fishing boat knew exactly what the message was, and all it implied.

Some of the refugees had gotten this far before. They knew the drill, and tried not to panic like the others, but after ten days at sea and two days without food it was hard to keep a level head. The lights of Miami were a faint shimmer on the horizon far behind the cutter, and the tantalizing sight inspired many on board to abandon ship, even those who should have known better. Havier and the other men threw their weapons overboard and jumped as well. High above them, the searchlights on the bow of the cutter lit the choppy water.

"I repeat! Stay where you are!"

The little girl was more bewildered than afraid. She gripped her mother's shoulders and stood on her lap to watch everybody splashing in the sea, and her mother held her tightly. The only other people left on board were Devlin, three elderly people, a frightened teen who couldn't swim, and the *houngan's* corpse.

The cutter slowed to a crawl and was preparing to lower two launches, a half-dozen armed ICE agents in each, wearing bulletproof vests and riot gear. The girl looked at Devlin, wondering what would happen next. He looked up at the sky and said little prayer for help. It puzzled him why he did that, but it seemed natural to him, and he looked back to her with a brave smile.

"Take care of your mother," he told her, and slipped overboard, sinking under the waves. She watched the water, and when he didn't come back up her chin began to quiver. But she needed to be brave, and held her mother close to protect her as best she could.

"I repeat! This is the United States Coast Guard. Stand by to be boarded."

There was a surge of wind and it began to rain, slowly at first and then much harder, and the sea turned choppy. Devlin surfaced on the shadow side of the fishing boat, and made a splash for the girl to look his way. When she did, he held a quick finger to his lips to tell her it was their secret. She nodded and crossed her fingers, kissing them to say she promised. He floated on his back and blew a spout of water like he was lazing in a swimming pool, and she giggled. Her mother glanced at her, wondering what in the world she was laughing about, but the girl hugged her close to make sure she couldn't see Devlin swimming away in the dark.

Havier was in the water helping the retired security guard, who was in a panic although he knew how to swim. Making for the coast seemed like a good idea to the muscular man when they all jumped in, until he remembered their discussion about the *houngan's* odiferous corpse attracting a school of sharks. They were all he could think about now, and he wanted out of the water as quickly as the Coast Guard could get to him. Their launches were in the water and starting their engines, and he was frantically waving to them. He cast a large shadow behind himself, and Havier took advantage of it, drawing in a deep lungful of air and sinking out of sight.

He could see the searchlights playing on surface above, and swam around the dancing lights, heading west. He was considerably older than Devlin, but he was a strong swimmer from his years at sea, and unlike most of the fishermen of Labadie he never smoked tobacco. Even at his age, his lung capacity could last him for more than a minute if he took steady, deliberate strokes. Though he was hungry, he gambled that the adrenaline pumping through his system would keep him energized until he could get to the dark water west of the cutter; then he could float on his back and let the current take him to shore.

He didn't know it, but Devlin was several meters ahead of him, swimming on the surface and putting distance between himself and the cutter. The lights of Miami were becoming clear to him now, perhaps two kilometers away through the rain. The back of his skull throbbed from the blow of the baton, but the bleeding from his temple wound had slowed to a trickle, and somehow through all the mayhem the scab on his shoulder didn't break open. If there were any sharks in the water, he hoped they would find the commotion behind him far more interesting. He thought it was remarkable that he was wounded by gunfire twice in the last month, and clubbed from behind just minutes ago, and he was still in one piece, with his wits about him and able to swim. It was at times like this that he wondered about himself, who he was and where he came from, and how he knew so many things, except the simplest things about himself—

There was a cry of panic behind him, and he stopped to look over his shoulder. There was a man in the water, perhaps twenty meters away. Devlin could see him silhouetted by the activity around the fishing boat, some two hundred meters beyond. The man cried out again, but his shout was cut short as he slipped beneath the waves.

Devlin turned back and swam toward him, hoping it wasn't a shark that pulled the man under, but even though there was no way of knowing he couldn't leave the man to his fate. Maybe it was because he got on the boat for free while the others paid good money, but he felt an obligation though he didn't really know why. What he did know was that he couldn't live with himself if he didn't try to save him, whoever he was, and so he acted on instinct, not knowing what else to do. Instinct had been his guide for the last month, and he was still alive, so he trusted in it once again.

Havier burst out of the water with an agonized grimace and drew a massive breath, clutching his left thigh with both hands. The cramp was excruciating, but when he saw Devlin he was more astonished than anything else. Devlin somehow knew what was happening, and gently but firmly turned him around. He hooked an arm over the fisherman's chest and floated him on his back, swimming for shore with strong kicks and a sidestroke as Havier massaged the cramp out of his thigh.

Havier didn't know what to think, but if he fought free he knew he would surely drown. The *houngan* told him this man was the Devil, but here was the Devil saving him, and Havier was utterly mystified. Perhaps he was dreaming, but they say that people pinch themselves to see if they were, and his cramp hurt far more than a pinch, so he knew he must be awake. He vowed that if they ever got to shore, he would read the entire Bible again, from cover to cover. He must have missed something. Or maybe God left out a chapter, to test our faith and keep us on our toes.

The little girl saw something that no one else noticed. When the stranger climbed overboard something fell out of his back pocket, and now it was floating in the open bilge. When the ICE agents boarded the fishing boat, the bow tilted up and the bilge water washed aft, bringing it to her. She stepped on it so no one could see, and when her mother bent down to gather their belongings, the girl kneeled to help and fished it out of the bilge. It was a tiny little book, and she loved to read. When she thought no one was looking she opened the cover, but it was all in English and there wasn't any pictures—

An ICE agent snatched the U.S. passport from her hands and looked inside. It was issued a week ago to DOE, JOHN, which was something he'd never seen before. And the photograph was blank, which he had never seen before, either. Homeland security alarms started going off in his head. He pocketed the evidence, and helped the woman with her belongings. She tried to hold onto her unruly child, but the girl kicked him hard in the shin and glared at him for stealing her keepsake. He pretended it didn't hurt, but he knew it would leave a bruise.

CHAPTER TWENTY-ONE

Lummus Park along Ocean Avenue was deserted like it usually was at first light on a Monday morning in February. The overnight rainstorm had given way to a misty trickle, and all but the most die-hard joggers decided to stay indoors and recover from the weekend. The county lifeguards were still driving in to work, and the security personnel in the boutique hotels across the street were watching TV, so no one saw the two refugees come ashore.

Havier was half-conscious from exhaustion, and wasn't sure if he was dreaming when he felt the sand beneath him. He tried to stand, but his feet had gone numb, and Devlin had to haul him out of the gentle surf. The shore was wet and firm from the receding tide, and Devlin dragged him onto the dry sand beyond the high water line before he let go.

Havier rolled on his belly and hugged the earth, turning his head to the side and breathing through sand-caked lips. As the moments passed, he gradually realized that for the first time in hours he couldn't feel Devlin's touch. He opened his eyes to thank the man, but he was several meters distant now and steadily walking away, across the sand toward a manicured city park. Beyond the wide lawn and the palm trees was an empty street lined with lovely old buildings, painted pink and green and turquoise. Everything was clean and quiet and peaceful, and now that the rain had finally stopped, Havier knew he could rest.

Devlin shuffled barefoot through the wet grass, cleaning the sand from his feet. He lost his shoes when he went overboard, and pulled his socks off soon after so he could swim. The rest of his clothes were intact, although his khakis were smudged from his time on the boat, and his cable-knit sweater had snagged on some nails. He tensed up as a pair of joggers loped past, but the men didn't even glance his way, and Devlin realized why. With his ten-day-old scruff and his bare feet, and his wet, disheveled clothes, he looked like a homeless man who just spent a rainy night on the beach.

He reached the sidewalk on the west side of the park and looked up and down the avenue before he crossed, breathing a weary sigh of relief as he made his way over the smooth asphalt. He was in the big city now; he could get lost in the crowd and no one would even know he was there.

It was midday in Rome, and a light snow was falling. Cardinal Saul was at his window table, waiting for lunch to be brought to him as he conferred in quiet tones with Varese. There was a quick double knock on the door, and he turned as Neale came in with his meal balanced on a tray. But instead of coming directly to the table, his butler stepped aside and held the door open. Sama swept into the room with a cocky smile.

"My sources have informed me that he's in—"

"Miami," Saul finished for her, and she stopped in her tracks, smiling at him. She was impressed, and so was he.

Morning time on the Bayou Teche was magical, even in winter, and Peter Johnson enjoyed driving the back roads with the heater on and the windows rolled down. It was something he learned from Mark Kaddouri months before, the day they took Christine Mas to the Bayou Memorial Clinic outside New Orleans and walked through the ruins. A tornado struck the place years before, in the first few minutes of Christmas morning of 1976, and it lay abandoned ever since. The ruins were overgrown like a post-apocalyptic landscape, a mute monument to the horror that transpired that night.

Johnson was a young and cocky FBI agent back in the late Seventies, and drove his brand-new Land Cruiser at breakneck speed over wet country roads to get to the clinic before the tornado touched down. But he was too late, and by the time he got there his wife and child had died. Not from the tornado, and not from a difficult childbirth, they died at the hands of the Devil himself, who was hunting through the maternity ward for the returned Christ child. The infant Devlin sought was born in the parking garage at the height of the storm, delivered by rabbi Molinari in the back seat of a '65 Bonneville. She grew up to become Special Agent Christine Mas.

Johnson kept the Land Cruiser perfectly preserved as a tribute to his wife and child and a healthy outlet for his obsessive-compulsive disorder, and Bishop Simone was enjoying the ride. It was like a time machine; the camel-colored beast looked and drove like it just came off the lot. They were snacking on coffee and donuts and breathing in the cool, clean air as the sun glimmered through the canopy and danced on the damp asphalt.

"Thanks for seeing me, Father."

Simone nodded and toasted him with his coffee. Johnson didn't want to embarrass him by letting on that he knew he was a bishop. Besides, there was a reason Simone lied, and Johnson wanted to find out why. If he could get the bishop talking, maybe he could see what the man had up his sleeve.

Johnson dug a bullet fragment out of his shirt pocket and put it in Simone's open palm. "Now, who's responsible for trying to plant this chunk of metal in my head?"

Simone considered the fragment as he formulated a reply, and handed it back before he spoke. "You're the only one who can help me, Peter, and the Church knows it."

Johnson glanced at him, not bothering to mask his surprise. The more open he was, the more open Simone might become, and the news was a shock. Considering his association with Christine Mas, he should have known he was on the Church's radar. Their reach was worldwide, but he never quite saw himself as being a person of interest.

"We're trespassing on their interests," Simone told him, "and the Church never forgives us our trespasses."

Johnson looked back to the road ahead. "Only God forgives," he said in a quiet voice.

"Precisely," Simone said.

Johnson sensed there was more, and there was. And Simone decided that this was as good a time as any to delve into the heart of the matter.

"Now that the Devil's human," the bishop began, "what if God was to forgive Satan of his trespasses?"

He watched for Johnson's reaction, and saw him blink in surprise. Despite all the thinking that Johnson had done since their last conversation, it was something he hadn't considered. Like a suspect hiding in plain sight, the concept was perfectly clear in retrospect, but it wouldn't have occurred to him in a million years.

Simone was glancing at him sidelong, waiting for him to process the idea on his own. If he could wrap his mind around it, they could work together. Otherwise, he'd have to cover his tracks and regroup.

"So you're telling me this is about redemption?" Johnson asked him, and Simone nodded. *He's getting it,* the bishop thought.

"God's redemption on the soul of Satan?" Johnson asked. "To create some kind of message for Man?"

Simone nodded again. Johnson was skeptical, but all he needed was a little push.

"Exactly," Simone said with a little smile. "If the Devil can change his ways ..."

He trailed off, allowing Johnson to complete the thought, and saw the man's eyes widen with a growing epiphany.

"... *then why can't we?*" Johnson whispered, gripping the wheel and staring into the distance. The realization shocked him to his core.

Simone smiled, and patted him gently on the shoulder. "Amen! The world needs to know."

Johnson looked at him and blinked. His world had just been transformed; he couldn't imagine how the world at large would react. He looked back to the road and mulled it over.

Thank God we're on a straightaway, the bishop was thinking. *We might have crashed.*

"So how did the church know about this bet? It's not in the Bible. And nowhere I've read docs it say that Satan would come back as a man."

"It's not quite so simple as that," Simone told him, and Johnson looked at him again.

"Enlighten me," Johnson said.

He was telling him more than asking him, and Simone found his direct American approach to things refreshing, after years of kabuki theater in the Vatican. He looked around at the lush wilderness, taking some time to organize his thoughts, and finally decided to start at the beginning.

"Well, as you know, Peter, the Church has been with us for over two millennia. And they've been busy."

Johnson nodded, impatient to hear more. Simone sat back and took a sip of coffee before he continued, and Johnson did the same. The retired FBI guy had a feeling he was in for an earful, and he was right.

CHAPTER TWENTY-TWO

"Pope Damasus I called the Council of Rome in 382 A.D.," Simone began. "It was at those meetings that the books of the Bible were selected, for all people to accept, on faith alone, as the One True Word of God. Only those books would constitute the authentic Bible."

He looked at Johnson, who glanced at him. "From that moment forward," the bishop explained, "anything else was heresy."

Johnson nodded, and looked back to the road. "I studied this," he said.

"We all have," Simone remarked. "But what you didn't study was the Book of Devlin."

Simone painted the picture for him. It was the waning years of the Roman Empire; Constantine formally recognized Christianity barely fifty years earlier with his Edict of Milan. For three centuries prior, the followers of the underground cult of Christ were hunted, abused, and sacrificed by the thousands for the amusement of the Roman populace.

But things were different now. The movement was evolving into an organization, and believers in far-off lands like Egypt and Persia and Anatolia were coming out of hiding with their own carefully preserved scriptures and traditions. Most of their holy works were variations on a theme, and all of them centered on God and his Son, but several critical pieces didn't jibe with the others, and some were in flagrant contradiction—everything from past lives, to Mary Magdalene being the bride of Jesus, to a multiplicity of gods in heaven.

Three hundred years after the time of Christ, Christians finally came out of the shadows, but when they got together and compared notes they saw that they weren't all on the same page. Attempts to integrate the philosophy devolved into arguments and outright fights, and a jumble of convoluted theories. Rather than a unified voice, the One True Word was an incoherent babel.

Pope Damasus wrote a letter to the council laying out his views about which books of the Old and the New Testament constituted the Word of God. Being the pope, his letter had the force of ecclesiastical law. The Damasine List, as it came to be known, was the first codification of the Church's canon.

The problem was that several cherished books of scripture didn't make the cut, words of inspiration, wisdom and beauty that entire communities had lived by for over three hundred years. Worse than that, they weren't even relegated as secondary texts or supporting works. The Apocrypha, as the books came to be called, were banned as outright blasphemy. One of those books was the Book of Devlin.

Like many forbidden things, copies of the Book of Devlin survived, hidden away in communes and monasteries, and when Rome finally fell, the world—or what they knew of it—was plunged into a dark age for five hundred years. Brigands roamed the land, and when they plundered a settlement, niceties like books were often used as kindling.

Fortress-like monasteries became the only place where books, and the ability to read them, survived. It was long before the printing press, and books were of incalculable value. Monks spent their entire lives painstakingly copying the Bible by hand. Other books were lovingly stored away as well, sometimes for hundreds of years, simply because they were books, and oftentimes without anyone peeking inside.

Whenever a curious monk did look at an apocryphal text, particularly the Book of Devlin, the usual reaction was horror, and down through the ages nearly every copy of the Book of Devlin was burned. But not all of them—one copy eventually made its way to Rome in 1208, during the reign of Pope Innocent III.

Johnson studied the early Church, so he had no trouble following Simone's rapid-fire history lesson. His coffee was gone and so were the donuts, and he was hoping to find a crawfish shack on the road ahead. But they were deep in the Bayou Teche by now, and the only roadside feast was the scenery.

"At first the book's authenticity was questioned," Simone told him, "but later it was found to be true. Absolutely true."

"Then what was the problem?" Johnson asked.

"The Church realized that it was the word of Lucifer. His diary."

Johnson swallowed the last bit of coffee on his tongue, and considered what Simone told him. "The Devil's diary. Oh, my God…"

Simone nodded, and gazed into the trees. White herons were landing on the still water. Everything around them was clean, quiet, and elemental. *If life were only that simple*, he thought.

"The Church hid the manuscript," Simone continued, "and pressed on with the Bible they assembled. A book they believed would give them the power and influence they desired."

He reminded Johnson that by the 1200s, Rome had reconstituted itself as a center of civilization, but the hinterlands had barely changed since the city was sacked seven centuries before. Priests were sent out to convert the pagans, the people who lived in the *pagus,* the countryside, but they had their own beliefs by now, developed over the centuries, and the priests were met with skepticism and sometimes much worse.

"For decades, for centuries, the leaders of the Church toiled with finding the most effective way to spread the Gospel of Jesus and the Word of God, out of all the contradictory scraps that they stitched together and declared to be the One True Scripture. I'm sure it comes as no surprise that it was very difficult. The inconsistencies were maddening. Laughable, even."

Johnson nodded, understanding what he meant. "They still are," he admitted. "It's embarrassing."

They exchanged rueful smiles, a true believer and a man of the cloth, linked by a common frustration. Simone decided that he could work with him, and Johnson sensed the change, though he didn't know what it was.

Simone looked out the windshield, watching the clouds roll by above the verdant canopy. There was another bit of history that the Cabal of Cardinals kept for themselves. It wasn't recorded in any book, but it didn't have to be. It was committed to memory, and told and retold behind closed doors for more than a thousand years. It was time for Johnson to learn the truth.

Long ago, Simone explained, haggard priests were hard at work in a mud-walled church in Anatolia, blessing the soldiers for battle. Their rustic chapel was a way station on the road to the Crusades, and from the scant few who came back, diseased and horribly wounded, the priests knew that nearly every man they prayed over was destined to die. They had been to the Holy Land themselves, earlier in the same Crusade, enthused with the Holy Spirit. But the campaign dragged on for years and years, and it seemed that all they did was trudge through one war-ravaged village after another praying for the dead, who lay rotting wherever they fell.

"Murder was like a plague, and it spread like the Devil himself."

Johnson glanced at him.

"What happened to the men of God," Simone continued, "is something that happens to all men."

"They began to doubt?"

"Yes. Many of them wondered, what God, what Holy Shepherd, would leave his soldiers, his family and his flock, alone for so long, to fight what was in essence was His own battle?"

Simone told him how the priests had finally retreated to their home village in Anatolia, consoling themselves that they could do the most good there, by blessing the soldiers before they died and not afterward.

"God left them on their own," Johnson said, imagining how they must have felt, and Simone nodded. "But Lucifer didn't," the bishop told him.

One night the church door creaked open, and in walked Devlin, wearing a magnificent black cloak and a devilish, charismatic grin.

"He showed himself first to the Church," Simone explained. "It was he who offered himself to the desolate men of God."

The priests had a good idea who he was. They were afraid, but at the same time, there was a glimmer of hope in their eyes. That was puzzling for Johnson to hear, and Simone understood.

"They had been mired in doubt and uncertainty," the man from Rome explained. "God told them that Christ would come again, but after long and brutal centuries of waiting, He never arrived. But Lucifer did. He was something they could hold onto, touch, and hear. If God wasn't real..."

"The Devil was," Johnson finished for him, and Simone nodded.

"Man lives in the real world, whether he wants to or not," Simone said. "And while God is in their hearts, the Devil is in their world."
Johnson thought about it, and as he did, a surge of anger welled up in him. "That doesn't exonerate them!" he said, pounding the steering wheel. "They turned away from God, and were punished for their breach of faith."

Simone was amused, but held his reaction in check. Johnson presumed that the priests had been punished, though he had no idea whether they were or not. *Faith is an endearing quality*, the bishop thought dryly. The rest of the legend was that the priests went to Rome, rose quickly in the ranks, and formed the Cabal of Cardinals.

CHAPTER TWENTY-THREE

"We're not punished for our sins," Simone told him kindly. "We're punished by our sins." He let Johnson mull that one over before he continued.

The priests gathered around their visitor, Simone explained, and Devlin made a cross melt. He changed his face into other men and women, and performed other tricks to convince them of his power. "When you pray in my name," Devlin told them, "you will conquer your enemies and grow in power, and you will have dominion over the world." The priests dropped to their knees, awed by Lucifer's presence.

"Lucifer beat God at his own game," Simone explained. "He stole the hearts of man by simply being seen."

It would go a long way toward explaining the Spanish Inquisition, Simone suggested, and he told Johnson a little story about Torquemada's priests, torturing men and women while Devlin stood behind the men of the cloth, whispering to them. The priests loudly proclaimed that God spoke to them, but they knew who it was all along. The Salem Witch Trials were much the same. Devlin was there, watching over the proceedings, even though the Protestant clerics had no idea. Listen carefully to *Sympathy For the Devil,* Simone advised him. The song wasn't written in a drunken stupor.

Johnson was disturbed by the turn of the bishop's storyline, and

Simone wasn't surprised. What surprised him was that for a true believer, Johnson was taking it much better than he thought.

"But I don't understand," Johnson said. "What about the bet? Why did Lucifer bother, if it's been his church all along?"

"Because no matter what Lucifer offered the Church, no matter what hidden power, or influence, or guidance he gave them, there was always the existence of God lurking over his shoulder. It poisoned him with insecurity, even as he used the Church to consolidate his power and influence."

It was hardly confined to ancient history, Simone explained. Vatican officials worked hand in glove with the Nazis, helping them escape Germany, and many of them arrived clutching Bibles. Devlin was there, watching from the shadows. In a smartly-tailored Hugo Boss suit, Simone added with a wry grin—the man of fashion who made his mark supplying uniforms for the Reich. Johnson looked at him, and Simone nodded.

"The Devil rarely acts alone," Simone told him, and looked out the windshield, into the distance. "The Holocaust taught us that. There's not enough apologies that could forgive the destruction of six million Jews."

Johnson nodded, but he said nothing, reflecting on his words.

"About thirty-five years ago," Simone continued, "Lucifer approached high-ranking officials at the Vatican. But first he went to the Chief Rabbi of Rome. The way he saw it, the Jews killed Jesus once, so they'd be happy to do it again. But the Jews had a very different view of their history with Jesus, and," he smiled, "the Jews refused."

Johnson grinned at his alliterative quip, and Simone leaned back and crossed his legs. Johnson was deep into the legend by now, and so far he hadn't blown a gasket. He was brighter than Simone thought, particularly for a true believer. Most of them had gaping holes in their logic circuits, and he quickly grew tired of them. But he found he could talk to Johnson rather easily, and that was important for the days ahead.

What he didn't bother telling Johnson was that before he and Molinari converted to Catholicism, they were both on Rabbi Toaff's Privy Council in the fateful month of December, 1976. When Devlin stormed out of the meeting and walked a mile to the Vatican on that cold and foggy night, Toaff immediately dispatched the two young rabbis to New Orleans on the synagogue's private jet. His astrologers knew what the Vatican astrologers knew—that the Christ child would be born on Christmas morning on the Louisiana bayou. When Devlin got to the Vatican, Toaff knew he'd surely be told by someone there who was loyal to him. It was, after all, his old stomping ground. There were bound to be some of his lackeys on hand to welcome him home.

"So he visited the pope?" Johnson surmised, but Simone shrugged and looked out his window.

"No one knows for sure . . . " he sighed, and Johnson glanced at him. There was something in his voice, and Johnson wasn't sure what it was, but it didn't seem genuine when everything up to this moment had, as fantastical as it all seemed.

Simone caught his own reflection in his door mirror. He knew exactly who Devlin saw at the Vatican. Devlin told Saul in no uncertain terms, "*I am the voice of the Church.*" But Johnson didn't need to know that, and if Simone had anything to do with it, he never would. The cardinal had just joined the Cabal, a brilliant and ambitious theologian from the University of Chicago who had taken the rather odd ordination name of Dante Hieronymus Saul.

And just like Toaff and his Privy Council, Saul was smart enough not to gaze directly upon the Devil himself. Simone knew that Johnson suffered a scorched eye in New Orleans, when he aimed his pistol at Devlin on that fateful Christmas morning in the clinic. He was lucky he wasn't blinded outright, but his eyes seemed to be fine now. So who knows, Simone mentally shrugged, maybe some people can recover from a brush with the Devil. But Simone didn't want to try it himself.

"He did come to the Vatican," Simone told him, referring to Devlin. "That much we are certain of, and he told them of the bet. About how he approached God, and how God, in His perfection, understood the terms of the bet to be logical. And God, as they say, 'took the bet.'" Simone glanced at him and smiled. "And the rest is the end of history."

"Jesus..." Johnson breathed, and Simone cracked a grin.

"In a word, yes," the bishop said. "She came back, and She triumphed! You see, Peter, Jesus built our road to salvation, but Catholicism has built something else altogether. Think of Catholicism as an intricate map that leads the true followers of Jesus astray."

Johnson looked at him with an ironic smile. It was odd hearing something like that from a priest—a bishop, no less—but Simone just shrugged and smiled back. The truth was a harsh mistress; but Johnson already knew that. He just learned it again the hard way, right here in his own damn car, and Simone knew that it wasn't going to be any easier on him from here on out.

He told Johnson how this cardinal at the Vatican conferred with three young, confident bishops, and sent them to New Orleans to find the Christ child. Bishop Nano was the leader of the trio, sent to help Devlin find the Christ child. But on that fateful night at the clinic, their plans fell apart.

Johnson stared at him, trying to decide if he should believe the story, but there was nothing in Simone's eyes or expression to suggest any guile. As incredible as the story sounded, Simone was telling the truth as he knew it.

He pointed at the road ahead, and Johnson went back to driving, tweaking the wheel to keep them off the muddy shoulder. They drove in silence for a while, Simone giving him a few moments to absorb everything. He knew it was a lot to swallow in one conversation, but time was pressing and Simone had to get the foundation laid before they could proceed.

"Many in the Church have secretly supported Lucifer down through the ages," Simone assured him, as if that would somehow ease the shock. And it did, but at the same time it was sad for Johnson to hear. For all of the Church's shortcomings, he had always felt that, deep down, those who ran it believed largely as he did. But apparently that wasn't the case.

Simone seemed to read his mind, and touched him gently on the shoulder. "They know the truth, but the faithful have no idea. And those who know would do everything in their power to assist Lucifer, because he has become their true power. The Jews wouldn't have anything to do with him. It's no wonder the Church has always hated them."

Simone told him that, as newly converted priests, he and Molinari put up with years of veiled criticism and prejudice about their former faith. As if they, too, must have hated the Jews and Judaism. Which they always thought was ironic, since the first Christians, and nearly every early saint and apostle, were converts from Judaism. He and Molinari would never argue back, but they would privately console themselves that they were more in keeping with the One True Faith than someone who was born into it.

Johnson nodded, taking Simone's point, and glanced at him with a newfound respect. Simone sensed the change in his demeanor, and was grateful for the man's empathy.

He gazed out the windshield, and his voice grew quiet. "Molinari knew how they really felt, but he was one of the truly faithful. I was another. We love God, and so we love Jesus. We are all children of God, are we not?"

Johnson nodded again, watching the road, and then it struck him that if that were true, then even Lucifer himself was a child of God. The idea made him shiver, but he couldn't dismiss it. *Lucifer is a child of God.* He knew the idea would haunt him for the rest of his life.

Simone was looking out the window at the moment, and didn't see that Johnson was having another major epiphany. "Rabbi Molinari converted to Catholicism to protect the young woman you knew as Christine Mas," Simone said.

Johnson blinked, and looked at him. The sound of his voice snapped Johnson out of his revelation. "I accompanied him," Simone was saying, "doing whatever I could to serve God. To this day, I still serve God, and I always will."

He made the sign of the cross, and Johnson did the same. Neither of them spoke for a while.

"It's not who we crucify that defines us," Simone said, "but who we protect and who we serve. It's who we honor and love that defines our lives and shapes our world."

Johnson agreed with him, but there was something he still didn't understand, and the more he thought about it the more it distressed him. He glanced at Simone, anguished and confused.

"But what would the Church gain by helping Lucifer?"

Simone was surprised by the question, given everything he just revealed. But then, Johnson's head must have been spinning throughout their conversation. He couldn't be expected to keep track of all the pieces in one go. It was a spiritual jigsaw puzzle that Simone had been familiar with for years. He glanced at Johnson and smiled.

"Not gain, my friend. Keep. Maintain. The Church has been in power for nearly two millennia. And it wasn't God Almighty who put it there."

Johnson slowly nodded and watched the road, thinking it over, but Simone could see that he was having a tough time of it.

"After Christ died and before he rose from the dead, he freed the souls in hell."

Johnson knew that, although he didn't know the rest of the story; few people did.

"But when he rose in glory," Simone continued, "it wasn't the keys to the gates of Heaven that he gave to St. Peter. It was to the gates of Hell."

Johnson looked at him, a bit wide-eyed, and Simone nodded to assure him he was telling the truth.

"Your namesake built his church over the gates of hell to seal them shut," Simone explained. "That's why the Basilica was built where it is."

"Is that why they tried to blow it up?"

Simone nodded. Johnson mirrored him, and looked back to the road ahead.

CHAPTER TWENTY-FOUR

It was a hot and humid morning in Labadie, and the blowflies were in swarm, attracted by the sickly sweet aroma of decaying flesh. It was where they'd been laying their larvae for the last five days, their busy little offspring that would ingest all they could of the recently deceased carcass for a week, before they sprouted their own wings and flew away. Legions of them were laid in the flesh, hopefully more than the red ants could eat as they feasted on the corpse themselves, marching in and out of a neat hole in the body's forehead, between the startled eyes. The rim of the hole was crusted with dried, black blood, but there was a treasure of moist nutrients in the cranium, although the proteins were breaking down in earnest.

The coroner was used to the smell, and so were his people. Still, they stood upwind in a bit of shade as the forensics team from Cap-Haitien dusted the skiff for prints. It was a useless exercise, but they were obligated to do it anyway, and in any case their supervisor felt it was good discipline and practice. Fish oils, both old and new, were smeared on the wood and metal, and every member of the crew had left a print, along with the grubby paws of every kid and mother who came to the beach to help or beg or barter, whenever the skiff came ashore with a catch. After five days, which from the looks of the corpse was probably when he was shot, the salt air, the sun, and the evening mists had aged every print on board to a dull sameness.

A group of locals were standing nearby, while a couple of Le Cap gendarmes stood with them. The questioning was over by now. No, nobody knew a thing about it, and no, nobody bothered to look in the skiff over the past several days, beached as it was with its bow jammed into the lip of the jungle. Not until they noticed that something was starting to smell, other than all the scraps of fish.

They were all watching the proceedings now, but the corpse wasn't drawing their attention, even though they knew the man. People died all the time. But it wasn't every day you got to see a forensic team in action. It was like an episode of NCIS.

A black Mercedes 550 SUV rolled onto the sand, and stopped by the coroner's 4WD van. Mezadieu and Micheline got out and approached the skiff. The crowd watched the two inspectors, especially the female. She was much too pretty to be a cop, unless the TV shows from America and Mexico were accurate. But nobody in the hamlet really thought they were. When you live next to a resort that pretends to be an island, it's easy to see that all the TV shows made for the same people are fantasies, too. But, there she was.

The forensics team was leaning inside the skiff, dusting the last bits and pieces, and one of them was snapping pictures of the corpse. The inspectors waited until he was finished and moved back, and they stepped into the empty space to get a close look.

"So this is our fisherman," Mezidieu said.

Micheline was watching the ants marching in and out of the man's skull. They were enormous, more like tiny beetles, carrying valuable bits of food away, held aloft in their pincers.

"What's left of him," she remarked. She covered her nose with a handkerchief, and went to talk to the cops. She knew he wanted to be alone with the corpse for a few moments.

Mezadieu stayed where he was, slightly adjusting his stance so he could control the space around him. He didn't want to be jostled, or hear someone excuse themselves, asking him to move. He wanted his first impressions to flood in uninterrupted, and they did. It was a sixth sense he had, a bit of clairvoyance that he never mentioned. Micheline saw it, but she knew better than to say anything, because it was clearly as much an affliction as a blessing. Crime scenes haunted him, and sometimes the ghosts would speak. She wondered how he slept.

Mezadieu stepped back from the skiff, slow and steady, and as he did, his eyes took in a wider scope, encompassing the lay of the little boat and the slope of the beach, more than just the position of the old man's body. As he did, he began to clearly see what happened from the shooter's point of view.

"The shot was fired . . ." he said to himself, still backing up, and then he smoothly stopped in his tracks.

"From here."

The moon had set shortly after sunset, but the air was perfectly clear, cool, and dry, and the Milky Way blazed overhead. When he was younger he could work by starlight, but now the old fisherman had to move slowly, and wait for his eyes to glean what they could in the near-total darkness. He was more than frustrated with a knot in his fishing net, and had finally taken out his knife, but then he dropped the damn thing inside the skiff. He heard where it landed, but he was waiting to see a glint on the steel blade, when he heard a soft footprint in the sand behind him.

There was something in the person's hand, held out toward him, steady and straight. Starlight traced a smooth outline of dark metal. He knew instantly what it was, and it frightened him, but seeing the person who was wielding it gave him a far greater jolt. It just didn't make any sense.

"Why—?"

He never finished his question.

Inspector Mezadieu was standing about six meters from the boat. He looked down to his left and right, trying to divine which way the pistol ejected its brass. There was a slight discoloration in the sand to his left, a bit of golden yellow on the otherwise white beach.

The forensics was glad he was out of the way, and wasn't watching him, and neither were the locals. They were gathered around Micheline and the cops now, breathing in her intoxicating fragrance as she spoke with the gendarmes. "Did anyone see anything?" she asked them, and they both shook their heads no.

"No one saw or heard a thing," the sergeant replied. She nodded, and kept her eyes on the man, though she could see Mezadieu doing something far behind his back.

Mezadieu was bent over, his hand gloved by an inside-out ziplok baggie. He stood as he turned it right-side out and shook out the sand, then zipped it shut and slipped it in his pocket.

He caught Micheline's gaze and they exchanged a ghost of a smile, but now the corporal was saying something to her and Mezadieu broke eye contact so she could respond, while he sauntered back to the skiff.

The corporal was pointing to a small group of children at the edge of the crowd. They instinctively shrunk back, but he smiled at them and they stayed put.

"Those youngsters digging for crabs found him about an hour ago."

She was about to speak to them, when they all heard two vehicles grumbling over the dirt road and onto the beach. It was the news media from Le Cap, the local TV affiliate and the newspaper, arriving in the shiny vans the resort had gifted them.

"The carnival has come to town," she sneered, and then she saw something else. A third vehicle appeared out of the dust cloud the vans had kicked up, a black armored Yukon with U.S. consulate plates. The Americans powered around the vans, who were fishtailing a bit in the soft white sand, and stopped by the coroner's wagon.

Ledger and Fincannon got out of the Yukon, and tried to look tough as they strode across the sand. Their wingtips weren't beach shoes, though, and the children grinned. But at least they were wearing some slick-looking shades.

"When it rains, it pours," she said to herself, an Americanism she picked up from satellite TV.

Mezadieu got to her first, with an 'I've got something' twinkle in his eye. It was a welcome change of focus, and she smiled at him. "I know that look . . ." she said under her breath as he drew close.

He slipped the baggie in her palm as he watched the Americans approach. "Our missing gunman was here," he said to her quietly, and then he walked away to their Mercedes, ignoring the agents.

Ledger and Fincannon stopped in their tracks and watched him go, then they glanced at each other and followed him to his car. Fincannon had his usual hangover, and he was hoping they'd get to the Mercedes before his calves started cramping. Ledger didn't say anything, but he had a good idea what was going on, from all the cocktails the man knocked back in Port au Prince the night before. The CIA guy kept fighting the weather, Ledger observed. If he didn't embrace it, he'd never last.

CHAPTER TWENTY-FIVE

Five hundred miles to the northwest, Devlin was soaked to the skin and standing barefoot on a South Beach sidewalk, taking in the towering palms and the pastel buildings and the lush manicured greenery. If there was a heaven, he was thinking as he drew in a cool, moist lungful of air, they really should have at least one street like this.

After swimming in the ocean for the last few hours, the rain wasn't bothering him at all. *You can only get so wet*, he reminded himself, and then he wondered where he might have heard the old saying before. It puzzled him, because if he couldn't recall, was he really reminding himself of something? It didn't feel like a memory, but more like something he just knew. And since it wasn't anchored to anything in his mind, he couldn't assign it a value, and so it hung there, like a blessing more than a thought. Which made him chuckle. With the dreams he was having, he couldn't imagine being blessed by anyone, especially the Divine . . .

A man was approaching on his morning walk and smiled, catching Devlin's bemused expression. "Miami—home of the hurricane," the man quipped.

Devlin smiled back, and then he noticed the man's dog. It was a mutt of indeterminate lineage, a skinny thing like a small coyote, with alert, intuitive eyes. The owner had a harness on him, with an umbrella rigged over his head, something more for a lap dog than a coyote, but the dog seemed to tolerate the contraption and his dignity didn't suffer. If anyone's dignity was jeopardized, it was the creature at the other end of the leash.

The man was about to pass Devlin by, but his dog stopped and looked up at the shoeless stranger, his head cautiously cocked to one side, wondering what he was looking at.

The umbrella was useless now. They were motionless, just a few feet apart, the rain in their faces and catching on their eyelashes, though the dog's fur was shedding water much better than Devlin's unruly head of hair. The animal was wary, but he was more puzzled than anything else, and Devlin tried to relax into a neutral, fearless posture while the mutt sorted things out.

The man was puzzled as well, but about his dog, not the homeless guy. He was an odd mutt, moody and sharp as a tack, and if he wanted to stop there was a reason, so the man just let him be, the leash draped loosely from his hand.

Then as simply as he decided to stop, the dog decided to move on, and his owner obediently followed, smiling a bland good morning which Devlin returned. But as they passed him by, the dog kept his eyes on Devlin, still not sure what to make of him. Devlin offered the animal a melancholy smile, and then he continued on his way, taking in the city skyline. He wasn't sure what to make of himself, either.

CHAPTER TWENTY-SIX

Midday mass was over, and the early afternoon mass would be starting soon. There would be four more after that, with the final mass concluding at midnight. It had been like this since the Tragedy, and would likely continue until the rebuilding was complete.

The Swiss guards opened the ancient oak doors for the faithful to file out. They emerged from the medieval chapel breathing in the crisp, dry air and squinting in the brilliant sunshine. A pure blue sky capped the city, and the view from Mount St. Michael made most of them pause. The locals among them were used to the view, and they weaved through the throng of *Vaticanistas* to get back down the hill and into their homes before their body heat dissipated. It was time for a hearty lunch, and boiling a pot of pasta always warmed the kitchen.

The Vatican congregation had been coming up the hill for Sunday mass, and the strain on the locals was becoming evident. The Holy See's administrator had to scramble to issue their flock admittance cards and assign each of them to a mass, before the monastery's welcome mat became too worn and frayed.

A squad of Italian Special Forces was deployed around the cobblestone plaza on security detail. While the Swiss guards at the church door performed a ceremonial function, looking straight ahead with a thousand-yard stare, the ISF had freely roving eyes, and paid close attention to the crowd as they dispersed down the narrow hillside lanes into the village. Even as they went, another throng was ascending the same narrow streets, to converge in the plaza and socialize before one o'clock mass. It would be like this every hour on the hour until midnight, and then a crowd would come out at one in the morning, and that would finally be it. Security was a cold and boring duty, but it was also a license to girl watch, and every now and then there was something to see that made it worth the misery.

The three young women could have stepped out of a lingerie ad, except there was no guile or seduction in their expressions and no vamp in their stride. They wore low-heel shoes and their coats were unbuttoned to the bright sunshine, with modest knee-length dresses underneath. The winter air put a blush in their cheeks, and their lips were a color and sheen that cosmetic companies tried to simulate, but could never quite capture.

Faith Milano and her two best friends were walking uphill to the plaza at a brisk clip, conversing in quiet voices between quick inhalations. Her appointment was at five before the hour, and the one o'clock parishioners were nearly ready to go inside. Sister Maria had been so thrilled that she could scarcely contain herself when she told Faith the news. It was a gift from heaven to be selected for something so special, and by the cardinal himself, no less . . .! Cardinal Saul worked closely with the pope in all manner of things, and the pope was God's representative on Earth, so having a chance to serve the cardinal would nearly be like serving God Himself. Only the angels and saints were closer, and if Faith lived up to her name, perhaps she, too, might join the heavenly hosts one day, in a place of honor for all eternity.

Faith was bubbling with excitement when she heard the news, but there was something she didn't understand. What was she chosen to do? Mother Maria's eyes twinkled, and she patted her student's hand. That, young lady, was a secret. When the time came, she would understand everything. For now, just have faith and trust in the Lord, and let the cardinal shape her destiny.

Her friends were nearly as excited as she was, and the three of them had been speculating about what it could be from the time they met for their morning espresso. They passed the watchful eyes of the ISF and quickly crossed the plaza, then trotted up the steps holding hands, though it did little to calm them. By the time the Swiss guards opened the doors, the ladies were trembling with anticipation.

They stood in the vestibule as the doors closed behind them, and waited for their eyes to adjust to the candlelit interior. They had never been in such a place that hadn't already been turned into a museum. But the chapel was a functioning part of an actual medieval fortress, built centuries ago as a fortified redoubt outside the monastery walls, with small windows high in the rafters that were set deep in the masonry. The vaulted room was a welcoming place of worship for the peasants to gather, and the first place they could huddle if the barbarians approached. There was a defensible corridor behind the altar that led to the monastery proper, if an attack couldn't be repelled from the ramparts above.

Sister Maria came out from behind the altar and smiled at Faith, bidding her to come forward. Faith turned to her friends and they whispered good luck wishes. She shrugged off her coat and handed it to them, and stepped quickly up the aisle, smoothing her dress and walking as steady and confident as she could. The crucifix above the altar loomed larger and higher as she approached, and with each step she could feel the blossoming warmth of Jesus' love. But this time it was different. This time it radiated from somewhere deep inside of her, with wave upon wave of a new and wondrous grace. It was mysterious and frightening and delicious, and she wanted to hold onto the feeling forever.

She genuflected and made the sign of the cross, and she realized that her fingers and toes were tingling, though she sensed that it had nothing to do with the weather. She stood erect, and ascended the three stone steps to be with Sister Maria. The nun took her hand and gently turned her a bit, to present her to cardinal Dante Hieronymus Saul and his assistant

Archbishop Scipione Nano Borghese, emerging from behind the altar dressed in their formal vestments. A lay assistant, a man in a black suit with long blonde hair combed straight back and tucked behind his ears, appeared behind them, but he stood in the shadows, well behind the two officers of the church and Faith paid him no attention.

Her attention was consumed by the majesty of the clergy before her, and the warmth rose from her mysterious place once again. She curtsied, bowing her head, and when she stood erect she kept her eyes downcast, in respect as much as awe. Maria put an arm around her lest she fainted, and bowed her head toward the clergy.

"Cardinal Saul, this is the girl I was telling you about."

Saul was smiling, and so was Nano. She was absolutely divine.

"So this is our Faith?" the cardinal asked, taking her hand in his, and the young lady shyly peeked at him.

Her hand was warm and supple, and as he gently toyed with her fingers she yielded to his touch. Her pupils were dilated and her throat was flushed and her nostrils were tinged pink, and none of it was from the weather. He knew exactly what she was going through, even if she had no idea. And Maria knew as well. The excitement of being special and the mystery of being chosen, the walk up the aisle, the vestments, the power and the glory, all of it had been orchestrated down to the last detail, and refined over the centuries. She had been swept away, and found herself securely in their hands.

Maria was watching her, and waiting for her to say something in response. But the cat had her tongue, and she gave Faith's shoulder a gentle squeeze. "Speak up, child."

Faith remembered her manners, but she was too shy to hold the cardinal's kindly gaze, and dropped her eyes again. "Yes, your Eminence. I hope what you've heard of me pleases you."

He rubbed his thumb over the back of her hand, still held in his. "More than I can say."

Faith smiled like an angel, and peeked at him again. He wasn't quite sure, but it seemed like her pupils were larger now, if that was even possible. Her hand was like warm silk, and he was sure that the rest of her was just as impossibly perfect.

Nano was starting to sweat, and he had no illusions why. Faith strongly reminded him of his favorite call girl in Lucerne. *When Marianne was seventeen*, he thought wistfully, *she must have been just as heavenly.*

"Thank you, your Eminence," Faith was saying. "I'm so grateful for this opportunity, to even be in your presence. In everyone's presence . . ."

It was nervous chatter, and Sister Maria gently cut her off with a pat on her shoulder. "We are all blessed, my child. I'm sure Cardinal Saul feels just as privileged having you here."

Saul nodded with a smile, and that gave Faith the assurance she needed. He let go of her hand, and she stood straight and tall before him, ready to begin, though she had no idea what they had in store for her.

"I'm honored to spread the word of our Lord!" she enthused with a glowing smile. "To spread his love! To be the bride of the One True Church. . ."

Saul looked her up and down. It was a good bet that she had never been kissed, and here she was, ready to dive into she knew not what. He touched the top of her head and she bowed for his benediction.

"And we shall spread his love to you in return, dear Faith."

Faith crossed herself, and Saul glanced at Maria. "Sister Maria, are we ready to begin the Lord of Love ceremony?"

Sister Maria nodded, and gave Faith's arm a little rub. Faith had never heard of the ceremony before, and the prospect of even being a part of it gave her a thrill—to be initiated in a secret ceremony! What wonderful adventures could lie ahead? She felt warm all over again, and began to tingle anew.

Saul took his hand from Faith's head and touched her rosy cheek. She looked up to him, glowing with anticipation.

"It was delightful meeting you," Saul told her. "I hope to meet all of you soon."

Sister Maria gives her another warm stroke, and Faith curtsied to excuse herself. They watched her go down the three steps, genuflect and cross herself, then go quickly back down the aisle to her friends, who were watching wide-eyed from the vestibule.

As Faith approached them, she thought over the last thing Saul said. *I hope to meet all of you soon.* She wouldn't be alone; she remembered Sister Maria dropping hints about it. There would be others, a special inner circle . . .

Her friends were dying to hear every detail, and Faith realized that she hadn't been cautioned to keep silent, and her heart began to race. Could her friends be candidates as well? Their smiles confirmed her speculation, and she smiled back, reaching out to them as she drew near. They took her hands and drew her into a happy embrace. They would be together forever.

Saul, Nano, Maria and Varese watched the three initiates hugging in the vestibule, and felt it was a good bit of work.

"Is everything in place?" Saul asked Nano, and the archbishop nodded. Saul glanced at Varese in the shadows, and he nodded as well. Satisfied, Saul turned to Maria.

"Praise the Lord," he smiled, and she smiled back.

The parish priest appeared from behind the altar, anxious to begin his mass. It was precisely one o'clock. Saul, Nano and Maria swept past him into the corridor, and Varese followed them, as the Swiss guards opened the doors and the faithful came in, surging around three lovely young ladies who were hugging and weeping for joy in the vestibule.

CHAPTER **TWENTY-SEVEN**

Nano was feeling marginally more comfortable now that he had changed out of his formal vestments. He was a bit of a dandy, so the trappings of office were always a pleasure, but the chapel had no circulation to speak of, and the electrical system was too rudimentary for enough fans to make a difference; he checked with maintenance the first week they were there. The vestments just made him feel more stifled than he normally would have felt, under the extraordinary circumstances he found himself in.

Working so closely with Saul now was becoming an agonizing moral burden, and worsening day by day. Not that Nano felt his moral standards were all that high to begin with. He was fond of the way Bette Midler like to put it. *I have standards. They're real low, but I have standards.* He'd used the line many times over the years, from gambling on Mississippi riverboats to drinking schnapps with his mistress in a hot tub overlooking the Danube. But this! Working with someone who probably blew up the Vatican . . .! And if Saul didn't do it, then Lurch probably did. He knew the man's name was Varese, but he reminded Nano of the butler in *The Addams Family.* In fact, he was even creepier, and without the humor. And those bodyguards that Saul surrounded himself with! They were a white version of a posse out of a gangsta rap video.

Nano navigated the dank, narrow hallways of the monastery, wending his way back to his suite. It was at the end of this passageway, then up the steep stone steps, around the bend, and past the janitor's alcove. He needed a stiff shot of schnapps and a hot bath. His life was starting to feel like the corridors—windowless, claustrophobic, and lifeless, with no one at the end of the path but his own lonely self.

The steps were treacherous, worn in the center from centuries of use, and the railing was installed by an amateur. He kept one hand on the rail and the other one on the wall as he made his way up.

The climb exhausted him, but he made himself go round the corner before he leaned against the wall to recover his breath. The men who invented television and air conditioning were in Statuary Hall in Washington, Nano groused to himself. The man who invented the elevator should be there, too—

"It's me," he managed to gasp. "We're alone."

He was standing by the curtain that covered the janitor's alcove, where weapons were stored in ages past for repelling an attack. All it had now was mops and brooms. And a plain-clothes bishop.

Simone moved the curtain aside and stepped out, cautiously looking up and down the hall, then down the stairwell. Nano was right; they were alone, and Simone relaxed, and then he saw the look on Nano's face. His distress was clearly from something more traumatic than a flight of stairs.

"You look like you've seen a ghost."

Nano grimaced and leaned closer. The nearest suite was more than ten meters down the hall, but the stone walls had a tendency to transmit voices. He suspected that the people who built the place were the same Masons who built the Vatican. The old Vatican, that is. It still horrified him to think of the Tragedy.

"We both know what I've seen . . .!" he whispered to Simone. "And what we're about to see."

Simone knew exactly what he was implying. They had discussed Nano's views on the matter at length. Nano was convinced that what they were now living through was the beginning of the end of the world. And perhaps he was right. But if he wasn't, then it was clear that the Church had to transform itself in order to survive. That was unquestioned. The only question now was who would guide the transformation, and who would be on the papal throne when the change was complete.

"Are you convinced he wanted you to die in the explosion?"

Nano held his breath, and studied Simone's eyes before he replied.

"More than convinced," Nano told him. Simone nodded, and rubbed his cold hands together as he thought it over.

Nano did the same, working the chill out of his knuckles and watching the younger man. This was Molinari's errand boy, the tireless priest who shuttled back and forth from Molinari in Rome to Nano in New Orleans for over thirty years. And now Molinari was gone and Simone was a senior officer of the Church, the same rank as Nano. It was fascinating to see a colleague's underling come up the ranks. Fascinating and disconcerting at the same time. The balance of their relationship had fundamentally shifted, and Nano dearly missed the altitude he once enjoyed. But there didn't seem to be a way of recovering it now. Nano was cagey; he had to be in order to beat the Devil. But Simone was far more intelligent, ruthless, and resourceful. And, he was still healthy, while Nano was getting old and tired. He should have retired the moment they stepped off the plane from New Orleans. Saving the world was a young man's job.

"But does he suspect you know?" Simone was probing him.

Nano shrugged. He was starting to grow weary of the whole thing. "I don't believe he cares. With the Sister House and their unholy rituals, everything moves forward." He took a few breaths and continued in a subdued voice. "He wants to build the Church anew, with fresh blood, and every trace of our past eliminated. All of it."

"Particularly now that the Devil's on the loose, eh?"

Nano nodded ruefully, and Simone grinned. It was a turn of phrase from an old song about the south, and he used it to get a little rise out of Nano, but all it did was make the old man melancholy. Nano never thought he'd ever be wistful for his days gone by on the edge of the bayou, but at least the entire world wasn't circling the drain. And if it was, it wasn't all that noticeable and a man could have a little fun. But now the party was over, and everything was a mess.

"Tell me," Nano asked with a frown, "is Peter Johnson mentally stable enough to help us? And more importantly, is he willing to?"

"Oh, yes," Simone assured him. "He's conflicted, but he understands only too well what all this means. Far better than most."

"Good," Nano sighed. That was one less thing to worry about. "So, he bought your story on the Church's history on dealing with the Devil?"

Simone just smiled and nodded. He ran the whole scenario past Nano on the phone, before his road trip with Peter Johnson. Nano thought it was a marvelously clever invention, and was mightily impressed that Simone had woven such an intricate deception. Simone graciously accepted his praise, but he didn't have the heart to tell him that if it was a deception, it was only because the Devil himself had deceived the world. Aside from that, every bit of it was true.

"It's time to put God back in his rightful place, Simone!"

Simone just kept his eyes on the floor, frowning and nodded with his lips pursed, letting the man talk. It was a bit of body language he learned at the Cannes Film Festival, watching an investor diplomatically field one goofy idea after another. To a person, the hustlers who buttonholed the moneyman went away thinking they'd been taken seriously.

"No matter what we do to accomplish our task," Nano was telling him, an earnest, quavering timbre in his voice, "what we hold in our hearts will surely save us."

Simone just peeked at him, and smiled like he understood. And he did. What he understood was that Nano was trembling before the abyss, with a queasy feeling that the end was near. Not just his end, but the end of everything. And now that the time was approaching, he desperately wanted to end up on the right side of the abyss.

Good luck with that, Simone thought, and patted him on the shoulder, then went down the stairs as Nano walked down the hall to his suite.

CHAPTER TWENTY-EIGHT

A storm front lumbered south over the Alps like Hannibal's elephants, grey, ponderous, and unstoppable, bringing cold comfort to the vintners and the apple farmers, who needed a cold snap to keep their crops calibrated. But the rest of the peninsula hunkered down and brooded, waiting it out until their sunny Italy returned.

Castel Gandolfo was perched on the steep western slope of Lake Albino, a flooded volcanic crater some twenty kilometers southeast of Rome. John Halo usually enjoyed his time at the summer residence, when it was summertime. The reason it was the summer residence was most evident in early February, when the fog would settle on the lake like a tumor, and the mildew in the walls would wake from its dry, warm slumber.

The Maybach whispered out the back gate, bracketed by six rumbling ISF personnel carriers. Four Mangusta attack copters were somewhere overhead, invisible in the fog and flying on instruments. There were a few hardy tourists outside the gate, taking snaps. It amazed him that people would vacation in February, and spend even one day of it outdoors on a walking tour in the drizzling fog, but some of them did. His windows were well tinted, so they couldn't see that he wasn't blessing them. Ordinarily he didn't mind, but today he just wasn't in the mood.

He was meeting with Sir Reynard at the cemetery in thirty minutes, and they were running late. He was riding alone in the back, and Balliez was driving. Halo hadn't seen the old man since the night before his papal coronation, some eight years ago. *I should have had him killed the next morning in his sleep,* Halo groused to himself, and then he laughed without humor. No one could get to the Grand Master of the Rosicrucians, not even the pope. The ISF, however, was another matter. They could reach out and touch anyone, anywhere. But Reynard wasn't the kind to provoke a hostile response with a hostile gesture. Other than, say, blowing up the Vatican.

But if he really was the one who did it, he would pay. He and his entire band of heretics and blasphemers. It would be a quiet Crusade, but it would be swift, thorough, and merciless. The commanding officer of the ISF assured him of that just last night, when he heard the man's confession before the private mass he gave for the commandos. Everything he could provide would be at John Halo's disposal, with no questions asked. All he needed was a target list.

Sir Thomas Avalon Reynard had honeydew melon and tea for breakfast, and it was talking back to him. He was embarrassed by his little burps, but his nurse Henrietta was amused, and she eased his discomfort by belching like a sailor for him, the way her father taught her in the pub back home. That made Reynard's two burly attendants burst out laughing, so Henrietta kept it up. Antoine, Sir Reynard's driver, could hear them loud and clear in the back of the van as they entered the cemetery. There was a group of mourners at a pathside gravestone, and they paused to watch the tall vehicle roll past. It was a new van with run-flat tires. The armor plating should have kept the laughter in the van, but if Antoine could hear it, perhaps they could as well.

The asphalt lane wound its lazy way up the hill, past markers and gravestones and little monuments to the departed. It was an overcast morning, and the view of Rome was no more than an impression seen through a light fog. ISF gunships hovered overhead, invisible and only slightly muffled by the cloud cover. John Halo was waiting for them in his white Maybach, parked on the crest of the hill by the little storybook chapel. Six ISF personnel carriers were grouped around the limousine at a discreet distance, though there was nothing discreet about the weapons the commandos were holding at port arms.

There was a carrier parked adjacent the lane, and the ISF commander himself stepped onto the asphalt and motioned for Antoine to stop. There was a lethal hard edge to the officer's features, but Antoine was unfazed. He was familiar with the steely gaze of the security detail at the Fortress of the Three Crowns; the ISF commando wasn't showing him anything new.

Antoine stopped and glided down his window, and let the officer get in his face. Antoine's co-pilot was similarly unimpressed, and when the lead commando turned his scowl on him, he just pointed at the Maybach.

The officer glanced ahead, and saw that the pope was out of his limo now, standing under Balliez' umbrella and motioning for the van to come closer.

Antoine gave a little smiling salute to the commanding officer, and proceeded at a stately pace, looping in a wide curve and coming to a smooth halt with the back of the van nearest the pope. The cordon of troops readied their weapons, and Antoine pressed a button on the dash.

The back doors opened, and the commandos were greeted with the sight of a one-hundred year old black gentleman in a wheel chair, attended by a doting nurse, and two assistants who looked like their favorite form of exercise was cage fighting. Which in fact it was. But the most remarkable thing was the old man's clothing. He wore the uniform of the Rosicrucian order, a white satin tunic with an embroidered crucifix and a red rose at the juncture.

It was something they'd never seen before, aside from the drawings in old fantasy novels, and one in their grammar school history books. Most of them didn't even know the Order still existed. But here was the Grand Master himself, come to visit the pope.

Reynard's assistants wheeled his chair onto the platform, and it descended to the pavement. Then they rolled the chair onto the asphalt, facing the pope, and locked the chair in place to help Reynard stand up. It took a few moments, but it wasn't a piteous sight; there was a sense of majesty to the old man that was awe-inspiring. The soldiers hoped their grandfathers would look as good when they reached the century mark.

His nurse gave him a cane, and with his assistants at his side, one of them holding an umbrella overhead, Thomas Avalon Reynard slowly walked toward John Halo. Stopping a meter from the pontiff, Sir Reynard bowed his head. Halo didn't return the gesture, and when Reynard stood erect again he looked the man in the eye, and Halo started right in.

"Did the Rosicrucians destroy St. Peter's?"

"No," Reynard told him, and didn't elaborate further.

The pope studied the old man's eyes for several eternal seconds, and then he nodded, once and curtly at that, and turned back to his limousine.

Balliez was thrown for just a moment, but he stepped quickly beside Halo and kept the drizzle off of him, and opened the back door. Halo grabbed the handrails and stepped inside, and dropped heavily into the leather lounge chair, his eyes on Reynard, still standing with his assistants and nurse. His expression hadn't changed an iota, although Halo's had.

Balliez closed the back door and got behind the wheel as the troops stood watch and Reynard walked back to his chair. Balliez was going to wait until Reynard was back in his van, but Halo caught his eye in the mirror and signaled him to go.

Balliez put it in drive and slowly glided away. Outside, the commanding officer was busy redeploying his men, one APC to stay with the van and the rest to form up around the Maybach.

Balliez glanced in the mirror and caught the pope's eye. "Did they do it?"

John Halo shook his head no, and looked out his window.

Sir Reynard held his cell phone to his ear, watching Halo leave with his military escort in tight formation around him.

"Stand down," Reynard said, and put his phone in his pocket.

High above the clouds, five Citation VII jets broke formation and banked, to return to the private airstrip in the Austrian Alps. Sunlight glinted on their underwing rocket pods, six hopeful nose cones peeking out of each sculpted nacelle.

CHAPTER TWENTY-NINE

Sama emerged from the gangway with her shoulder bag, and Drake was a step behind her carrying his briefcase. The private 737 had stopped at the gate barely two minutes earlier, but since they were the only passengers on board there was no waiting. There would be no luggage customs papers to fill out, and no luggage to pick up. Their luggage was in an armored Mercedes van, along with their weapons, idling and locked at the curb outside. Normally the white zone was only for passenger loading and unloading, but for the next half-hour that didn't matter, because they were the only passengers in the terminal.

She could hear Drake's shoes slide to a surprised halt on the carpet, as he emerged from the gangway. She cracked a dry grin and glanced back at him, amused to see the bewilderment in his eyes as he looked around at the empty waiting areas and concourse.

"What happened to the airport?" he asked her, his eyes darting about for danger. The soft muzak from the ceiling speakers only increased the sense that something was amiss.

"They shut it down," she told him.

"What for?"

"For us."

He looked at her and blinked, and she strode toward the concourse, Drake a step behind her.

The view outside the plate-glass windows was like any other airport in the world with palm trees. It was a cool, moist, and balmy evening in Miami Beach, though you'd never know standing inside the bland, air-conditioned terminal. *You'd think they'd let a bit of the weather inside,* she thought dryly, but no. No one could get a taste of Miami's sweet tropical breeze until the Feds determined that those who arrived didn't pose a threat to the health, safety, and good order of the United States. The irony was that the one person who posed that threat more than anyone in history was already at large in Miami. Sama and Drake had come to hunt Lucifer, and their path had been cleared by the Feds. They had no idea what was going on, but when the Department of Homeland Security got the call from State, the 737 was over the Azores. By the time it entered American airspace, the entire terminal had been cleared.

Sama glanced at her watch. They would be at the South Beach Hospital in twenty minutes. The freeway would be cleared as well, although once they came down the off-ramp, they would blend with the local traffic. Getting there quickly was one thing, but alerting the hospital that something was amiss on their own street corner was another thing entirely. When they walked through the front doors, everything would be normal in the world outside, and they would blend right in.

The naked carcasses of Jonathan Kurinski and Janice Avery were laid out stiff and straight on two stainless steel drain tables in the cool, tile-walled basement of the Cap-Haitien Morgue. Inspector Mezadieu stood close by and watched as the coroner examined the bodies. The cause of death was fairly obvious, even to an amateur observer—a massive bullet wound to the head usually did the trick. The back of Jonathan's skull was blown out, and Janice had met the same fate, though she had an angry entry wound above her nose. The bullet that felled Jonathan came in the back, caromed off the inside of his forehead, and stayed in his brainpan. The coroner had already handed the slug over to Mezadieu, so that wasn't the issue now. It was the tattoos that prompted him to call the inspector.

They were small, about the size of a silver dollar, on top of the skull. Hidden by hair, and then by the caked blood, they weren't noticed until the bodies were washed for burial. The coroner parted Jonathan's hair, and slowly moved his finger across his skull. Mezadieu could clearly see the design—a crucifix, with a red rose at the juncture.

He exchanged glances with the coroner, who said nothing and parted Janice's hair. Hers was longer, and he had to keep moving sections of it with a comb like a hair stylist, but Mezadieu saw the same secret tattoo.

Mezadieu nodded, thanking the coroner for the information, and then, so long as he was visiting the morgue, there was something else on his mind that he wanted to pursue. He led the doctor to the wall of drawers and opened one, then another beside it. Two burnt bodies, a Caucasian male in his forties and a Caucasian female in her thirties, lay under the sheets.

"Three months, Doctor Gilbert, and we still have nothing to identify these two."

"Fire is very effective, inspector. The only hope you have now is DNA records. Or dental. But so far, it's been a dead end."

"Well, keep working on it."

"Working on what?" Dr. Gilbert asked with a wry smile. "They're charcoal."

Mezadieu gave him a droll look, but his cellphone rang and he walked away to answer it. Dr. Gilbert just shook his head and closed the drawers. Mezadieu was one of those pain-in-the-ass cops who ground on a case until it spit out the answer. Sometimes that worked, and sometimes they were just a pain in the ass.

It was Micheline calling. Mezadieu stood under the clock and took the call, away from the good doctor's curious ears.

"Good news or bad?" Mezadieu asked her.

"The prints came back on the dead assassins," she told him. She was at her desk at the Cap-Haitien police department, and could see the coroner's building on the next block, a drab windowless block of stucco with a rusting roof and a cremation chimney smeared with soot.

"And?" Mezadieu asked her.

"They're wanted all over Europe and Asia."

"And our fisherman?"

"You were right. Ballistics confirmed that the slug was from the same gun. And, word just came in from the American Embassy. She's back in Miami."

Mezadieu's other line was ringing. "Hang on. I have another call."

Micheline killed the time by opening a file on her desk. Diane's picture was on the cover sheet, which indicated that she transferred back to Miami. Micheline flipped through an impressive stack of paper below it. Yale graduate, summa cum laude, Doctors Without Borders, and a humanitarian award from the Mother Theresa Foundation. She was a girl scout in grade school, and she'd been a vegetarian since junior high.

And she takes in lost puppies in her spare time, Micheline thought sarcastically. Sometimes a person of interest would just grate on her, and this was one of those persons. "She's clean as a nun," she groused aloud.

Micheline didn't have the luxury of being a vegetarian when she was in high school. They ate whatever papa brought home, and they were glad to have it. She learned how to pluck and prepare a pigeon when she was in kindergarten; it wasn't something she picked up between selling cookies door to door and making science fair dioramas.

Mezadieu clicked back to their call, and she tossed the file aside.

"That was the captain," he told her. "Looks like our missing patient is in Miami, too."

CHAPTER THIRTY

The sun was high over Miami, baking the morning rain out of the lawns and sidewalks. It evaporated off the black tar roofs and the asphalt streets, and all over the region snakes and alligators came ashore, onto the warm mud and the back yards and the manicured golf courses, to catch a bit of warmth. It was a business day, and commuters and shoppers and retirees were coming out of their dwelling places, and crawling into the city. The sidewalks were crowded by mid-morning, with people going about their business and shoppers trolling for bargains. Many of them were on their phones, and most of them weren't watching where they were going, and neither was Devlin.

His clothes were nearly dry by now, but he was still barefoot, and with his unkempt hair and unshaven face, and the grime on his clothes from his long days in the boat, he looked like a homeless person. Which in fact he was. And like any homeless person, he was invisible to those around him.

The women clutched their purses a bit more firmly, and the men checked for their wallets, which was odd since they all seemed to be blithely oblivious to the fact that he was among them. Down through the ages, most humans had always been that way—blithely oblivious of his presence. The irony was that at this particular moment, he was equally oblivious of them.

There was a man's voice in his mind that erupted out of nowhere, loud and utterly frightening, and Devlin grabbed his head in a panic, stumbling forward in shock. The people on the sidewalk smoothly stepped clear of him, and made a path so he could go away and leave them be.

The assault on his senses was blinding, and he lost all contact with his surroundings, lurching forward on bare feet and wincing in pain. A jolt of fear shot through him as he recognized the voice. It was his own.

"No matter how this ends, I will always love you."

It was so loud that he couldn't hear the horn or the screeching tires. The old Cadillac slammed into him, and he tumbled up and over the smooth curve of the hood, and smashed into the wide, sloped windshield with a surprised grunt of pain.

He was wedged in the safety glass directly in front of the shocked driver, unconscious and bleeding and facing the brilliant sun overhead. It streamed through Devlin's eyelids, flooding his inner vision with a pure, clean light that brought him no peace.

God was on His throne and He was impossible to behold, though His radiance illuminated the heavens. In the sea of eternity, past and future were part of the timeless Now. Whatever was to be was already a legacy, and the future was prologue to the present moment. Christine Mas was always a child of God, the same as Jesus, and the same as everyone who ever was, or was ever to be. All of them were God's creation, and so was Lucifer, no matter if he turned away, and no matter how far he would stray. He would always be God's creation, safe in His loving hands, even in the depths of Hell, should he choose to be there.

Jesus was seated at the right hand of the Father, and He looked upon Lucifer with a piteous gaze. Lucifer wasn't dying; that wasn't his fate. He was about to suffer something far worse. The Lord of Light was stepping into

147

darkness, proud and defiant and willfully blind to the wisdom and love before him.

He had to avert his eyes; he had no choice. But his will never wavered, and though he had the effrontery to defy God, his voice was loud, clear, and strong. He would allow no one and nothing to come between him and God, not even the wishes of God himself. It was a maddening conundrum that drove him to the brink of despair, believing it was imposed on him by the One he loved more than any other. But he was too proud and too enraged to see the simple truth that he was doing it to himself.

"I will not bow down to Him!" Lucifer thundered, though Jesus was sitting right before him. Because this had nothing to do with respect, and everything to do with eternal love.

Fire rained down from an angry sky as the battle raged at the edge of the Abyss. On the mountaintop above, Devlin addressed his fallen angels, gathered before him, bloody and battle-scarred. "We stand accused of blasphemy! But let it be known that on this glorious day we fight not against God, but for the right to worship only God. Today we die for His glory alone!"

On a nearby peak, the angel Abdiel instructed his heavenly warriors. "Do not yield until our Father's enemies have fallen!" And with the sound of trumpets, the final clash began.

Angel fought angel in the high, ragged mountains and hundreds of thousands more clashed in the heavens above. The cries of warriors filled the air and so did their screams of pain and anguish, as broken wings and armor-clad limbs tumbled down and littered the rocks, and plunged into the dark, bottomless forever beyond the bloody precipice.

At the edge of the Abyss, Abdiel slashed through Devlin's armor and deep into his chest. Devlin cried out in startled pain and dropped to his knees, and waited for the final blow. But Abdiel turned away in contempt and tossed away his spear, leaving Devlin to slowly suffer and die. Unlike a mortal's death, Devlin would be dead forever, and Abdiel wanted him to think on the consequence of his treason while his life force drained away.

Abdiel was a servant of God, and so the cause for which Devlin fought didn't matter to him at all. God's servant didn't question God, and questioning God's was Devlin's sin. Abdiel left him to die.

Devlin was growing weak, and lay on his back, his head over the edge, be he rallied to glare murderously at Michael the Archangel. Michael had picked up the discarded spear, and was standing over him now, the bloody spear hard to Devlin's throat. His immortal fate was now in Michael's hands. The tip of the iron blade was wedged between muscle and windpipe; one thrust of the double-edged weapon would sever Lucifer from his legions, once and for all. He could see them high above, wheeling in midair and bringing their weapons to bear against Michael's loyal forces, but the battle was turning against them now, and the firmament was raining fallen angels now, as much as it was raining hellfire. There would be much more of that where they were going, and Lucifer was determined to join them rather than relent.

"Finish it!" he seethed, spitting his words at Michael standing over him, but Michael made no move.

"Now!" Devlin commanded his former first officer, but Michael seemed frozen, and Devlin sneered at him. "You coward!" he hissed, but there was still no response. And like all of the folly that led to this moment, there was something that Devlin refused to perceive—Michael wasn't paralyzed by fear, or a remnant of lingering loyalty. He was heartbroken, pure and simple. His dear friend had turned away from God.

He withdrew the blade from Devlin's throat, and broke the shaft of the spear over his knee. The wormwood snapped clear and sharp in Devlin's ears and Michael turned away, dropping the pieces to the ground.

They rolled downslope, and the base of the shaft sailed into the Abyss, gone forever. But the tip of the spear struck a small rock beside Devlin's shoulder. He saw the blade stop, and then slowly pivot away from him in a slow arc like a second hand, but gradually picking up speed.

He scrambled onto his knees and lunged for the weapon, but the Spear of Destiny was clattering quickly over the smooth rocks now, tantalizingly close and yet just out of reach. The broken end of the wormwood shaft cleared the edge, and as it began to fall the tip of the spear rose before him. He stretched out his hand for the weapon, and as he did his armored knees slipped on a bit of gravel, and he lurched forward, wincing in pain as he grabbed the razor-sharp blade.

He gained the weapon but he lost his balance, and try as he might he couldn't twist around fast enough to catch the lip of the precipice with his free hand. The Lord of Light screamed as he fell into darkness, but it was a cry of angry defiance. He plummeted into the Abyss with his fallen angels, the Spear of Destiny held fast in his bloody hand.

CHAPTER **THIRTY-ONE**

"We got another John Doe here," the nurse told the ER supervisor.

The supe nodded as he snapped his gloves on and slipped a fresh mask over his chin. His previous mask had barely lasted fifteen minutes. It was soaked from sweat after a fierce round of CPR, and his hands were still sore from the effort.

"Jimmy," he called over his shoulder, "take this guy's picture and put it on the wire."

The young orderly fetched the camera out of the cabinet and moved in close to get a good snap. They had no idea who he was, but a lot of homeless people didn't carry ID, so it didn't seem unusual.

Jimmy took the picture, then sat on a stool at the computer, uploading the picture so he could put out an APB. They wouldn't let him take the snaps with his phone and Bluetooth it into the system, so he had to sit on his butt in front of the computer and do it old skool with a cable. He idly watched the monitor as the ER crew got to work on John Doe. They could get his fingerprints later, if his picture didn't jar anyone's memory. But the picture would probably be enough; there were plenty of people in Miami who worked with the homeless in some capacity or other, and they'd all be getting the APB any second now.

The ER team scissored the John Doe out of his clothes, and gave him a quick once-over. For someone who got hit by a '59 Caddy, he was in damn good shape. His hand probably hurt like the devil, though, and when he came to they knew he'd be feeling it. Safety glass was specially made so it wouldn't cut flesh, but the chrome trim that surrounded it wasn't, and back then they didn't scrimp on a windshield surround. And when someone rolled over the hood and smashed into the windshield and got their hand tangled up in the chrome, they'd feel it.

At least that's what it looked like to the doctors in the ER, although they knew it was a wild guess. Actually, it looked like the guy grabbed a knife blade, and not a strip of chrome. Maybe someone tried to stab him, and he grabbed the blade, and ran away and got hit by the Caddy. But no one really knew. Bodies get contorted into all kinds of pretzel shapes when they bounce over the hood of a car and get planted in a windshield, so they finally gave up guessing and just cleaned the cuts on his palm and fingers and bandaged them. He was in remarkable health, considering he was a homeless guy; he didn't even need stitches.

He was still out like a light, but his vitals were good so they knew he'd come through all right. His backside and buttocks were badly bruised, but he was damn lucky, overall. The impact stressed his head wound, but it would close up again soon, and they decided to tape it shut and let it be. It looked to be about a month old and properly stitched, so his picture should flag somewhere in the system. Maybe the guy was a brawler, and someone clocked him with a bottle. Perhaps he'd tell them when he came to.

They wheeled the gurney off to the side, and parked him with all the moaners and groaners. Maybe he'd wake up quicker that way, and then they could put him in a wheelchair and get the gurney back.

Devlin winced and opened his eyes a slit, but the overhead lights were glaringly bright and his head started to pound. He closed his eyes with a groan, but his voice blended in with the other patients. The ER had gotten too busy, so they wheeled him out to the hallway along with some of the others. They were lined up against the wall now, in various states of disrepair, while hospital personnel milled about, or stood together and conferred in low voices.

Two of them were nearby, discussing something or other, and through his foggy haze Devlin thought that one of them sounded familiar. But he couldn't be sure if he was dreaming or not.

"He's a former patient of mine," the woman was saying. "He suffers from amnesia."

"He's all yours," the man told her, and Devlin thought he heard him walking away. And then he felt something like a delicate hand on his shoulder, and he opened his eyes, trying to focus.

It looked a lot like Diane, and when she smiled he was sure of it.

"Oh, my God!" he whispered, and came fully awake. He tried to sit up, but she gently kept him flat on the gurney. It wasn't a dream. It really was Diane, and she really was smiling at him.

"Not God," she assured him, "but close enough. We doctors have been known to perform miracles. What are you doing here?

"Me?" he blinked. "I almost got killed. What are *you* doing here?"

"Remember that transfer?" she asked, hoping to prompt his memory. "Well, you're looking at it."

He was puzzled, and rummaged through his recollections of their time in Labadie, but he couldn't recall her mentioning a transfer. Then again, with all the other things he'd forgotten, one more lost detail wasn't that surprising. If he got back to his memory exercises, he was confident it would come to him. All he had to do was remember to do the exercises. He'd gotten out of the habit since he left the clinic, but now that she found him, he was inspired to resume the schedule . . .

It looked like she was about to cry. Her eyes were glistening and her cheeks were flush, and her brow was suddenly pinched together.

"I didn't think I'd ever see you again! Oh, my God . . . I'm . . ." She sniffed and collected herself for a moment, glancing around to see if anyone noticed.

"Wow," she said quietly, a little embarrassed, and made herself focus on her job, leaning over the gurney and gently pulling back a bit of the bandage the ER put on his head wound. Her scent was intoxicating, so close to him now, and he instantly felt safe in her hands.

As she peeled the edge of the bandage, he glanced up in mock apprehension, as if he could see what she was doing, even though the wound was on top of his skull.   She grinned at his humor, but there was something on her mind and she had to ask him about it. But first she looked around; there was no one nearby. She pulled a chair over and sat close beside him so they could talk quietly.

"What happened that night?"

"I don't know," he said, and glanced around before he continued. "I woke up when my window was shot out, and there were two doctors in my room, with guns."

"They weren't doctors," she told him, and he winced and nodded; he gathered that much. "Besides," she continued with a little grin, "we have much better ways of killing our problem patients."

He grinned back, and she took a close look at his hand, gently picking it up. He winced and she murmured an apology, and he let her examine the wounds.

She placed his hand back on his belly, and looked at him. "Sorry," she said, and returned to their conversation. "Any idea who they were?"

He shrugged, and frowned as his muscles protested. His back was awfully sore, and so was his rear end. "I wish I knew," he told her. "I managed to get out of there, and just kept running."

She nodded, and indicated that she wanted to have a look at his back. He rolled over a bit to help her, and she held him up from the starched sheet to have a look through the open back of his hospital gown.

His broad shoulders were a mass of bruises that extended down his spine and onto both iliac crests, then down the buttocks. She read the police and EMT reports attached to the APB, detailing his encounter with the windshield. Poor Cadillac got the worst of it, she thought with a private grin. Her John Doe was in amazing shape, particularly for his age.

She rolled him back down, adjusting his gown so he could lie comfortably. "I was really worried about you," she said, and busied herself with a cotton swab and alcohol, dabbing away some stray flecks of blood on his palm and fingers.

He watched her work, and a familiar flood of memories came back to him of their days in Labadie, tending to him as he lie in bed, frightened and alone and bewildered, her diligent ministrations silently assuring him that it was all right now, that the worst was over. He still didn't know if that were true, but it was a comfort to see it in her expression again.

"I hopped on a boat full of refugees," he told her, "and we wound up wherever the current took us."

She glanced at him and smiled. He escaped with his life and went on a harrowing adventure, and here they were, the currents of their lives intersecting once more. It was a miracle, and she didn't want to lose him, ever again. But she kept her rush of emotions in check, as much as she could, though he might have caught a hint of it. He smiled at her, causing her to blush, and she looked back down to his hand, cleaning a spot that she'd already tended to. He smiled more broadly and she became more flustered.

"And this is where they come," she informed him, then sat back and gave him a smile. "Welcome to Miami, sailor."

CHAPTER **THIRTY-TWO**

Devlin saluted her with his wounded hand, and winced as his thumb bumped his forehead. The ER crew was right; he didn't need stitches there. But his head wound did have a bit of a separation, and she wasn't happy with just a bandage. That was her needlework, and she didn't want the damn thing leaking again after all this time. She leaned over to a cabinet and fished out a needle and thread, then turned back to him and saw he was looking apprehensive. She cracked a smile; men could be such little boys.

"You need stitches," she bluntly informed him, and leaned over to get to work before he could talk her out of it. "Let's get you patched up," she said, relaxing him into the procedure. "You're a lucky man; it's not serious..."

He smiled, watching her work. She had a way of talking to him that always put him at ease; that was one thing he clearly remembered. And coupled to that memory was the distinct sense that few people in his past had ever done the same. He had no idea who they were, or where they were or even when they were, but it was a certainty that he sensed, like something solid in the fog.

She was kind to him, she cared about him, and she wanted him to be safe. And he felt the same way about her, though he had no clear idea why, other than the fact that she felt the same way about him. Reciprocity was part of the human condition; that much he knew. And he also knew it was a double-edged sword—revenge could be as sweet as love.

His hand pulsed with the dark thought, and he frowned at it, puzzled by the response. She noticed his distraction, and wanted his attention back on her and off his wounds.

"Where are you staying?" she asked him, and he glanced at her, wondering how to respond.

"I got a . . . place," he mumbled. She knew he was lying, and he saw it in her eyes. But she just smiled for both of them, and kept working.

Devlin was sitting on the corner of the little retaining wall that formed a long, lush planter beside the hospital's main entrance. The area was in the shade all afternoon and the sun had recently set, so the sky above was cobalt and the concrete beneath him was cool to the touch. The hospital had given him some clean clothes donated by a charity, and he was comfortable enough although it was getting chilly. The khaki pants were a sturdy cotton weave, and the loafers were broken in by the previous owner. They were a good fit, but he dearly missed his boat shoes. The shirt and jacket were both a bit large, but the kid who selected the clothes for him probably thought they were just right. Devlin had a chance to shower and shave before they released him, so now he was just another face in the crowd, though there was no one around at the moment.

Then Diane came outside and his heart soared, until he saw that she was in conversation with a doctor. He was a tall, handsome man in a starched white jacket, with the bespectacled look of a born genius or a businessman. He was probably both, Devlin reckoned, from the self-assurance in his stride and the courtly way he escorted her down the steps.

Breeding, wealth and a good profession, and handsome to boot . . . Devlin felt completely outclassed, and he sighed and turned away so they wouldn't see him. It was getting downright chilly, and he had no place to sleep. He figured he should be moving along, before the temperature sank much further. Dry cardboard provided fairly decent insulation; there was probably a trash bin out back.

He knew he should hop off the wall and get moving, but he began to brood, staring at his new pair of worn-out loafers donated by the hospital, with his shoulders hunched and his fists in his jacket pockets. He realized now that the feelings he harbored for her were self-generated fantasies, and he was more embarrassed than anything else. People commonly felt affection for those who healed them; that much he remembered. But what he forgot was, the deepest wounds were those of the heart, whether they were self-inflicted or not.

Diane turned to David with an apologetic smile. "We'll talk more later, okay?"

"Sure," he said, and nodded that it was okay, though it didn't set well with him. But he somehow knew that this was as far as they would ever go. It was a shame, he thought. Women like her didn't come along every day. But she was too devoted to her work, and he knew she'd just be off again, volunteering for something else, so maybe it was for the best.

He smiled wanly, and turned to walk to his car. He barely got to know her over Christmas, and then she was off to Haiti at the drop of a hat on a mission of mercy. Now she was back again, but strangely enough, so was her John Doe.

David could hear her footsteps, walking quickly to catch up to her patient, and he took out his phone, idly thumbing through his contacts. He needed a drink, and he damn sure didn't want to have one alone.

A pair of women's shoes appeared on the sidewalk below Devlin's dangling shoes. "Nice place you got here."

He looked up and smiled at Diane, and she glanced around the hospital grounds. "But sometimes it's cold as hell," she remarked, and Devlin grinned as she looked back to him.

"Tell me about it," he said, and shivered involuntarily, then looked down to his shoes, suddenly bashful. She watched him, not exactly sure what to do, but she wasn't about to leave him here.

"Let's get a cup of coffee in you. Warm you up. My car's around back."

He peeked at her and smiled, and hopped off the wall. His rear end was sore from his bruises being jostled, and his back was aching and his feet were numb from lack of circulation. She laughed, realizing what was happening, and put out a hand to steady him.

He signaled that he was okay, and they began walking toward her car. He glanced at her sidelong, and saw she was doing the same to him. They both looked away, embarrassed and smiling, and they continued in silence. Something was brewing between them, and it was best left unspoken. The right words would come later, in their own good time.

CHAPTER THIRTY-THREE

It was a quiet night in Labadie, and the tide lapped against the shore in long, hissing strands of white foam, as the gulf stream surged past the peninsula on its way to Cuba, beyond the western horizon. The windows at the clinic were open to the temperate breeze, and so were the doors at the end of the hallways. The buildings were designed to work with the subtropical environment, not fight it. The night-shift nurses and orderlies were in their short-sleeved uniforms, without their winter white leggings, and it felt like early summer.

Dr. Brillstein was at his desk, poring over the charts. There were two stacks of manila file folders on the side table, slumped against the wall beside his coffeemaker. He was methodically scanning the top sheet in each folder, scribbling some notes, and placing it on the adjacent pile. He knew it wasn't the safest place to stack folders, but the risk of spilling a full pot of coffee kept him focused on the here and now, an exercise in mindfulness that he learned in boarding school. So was the open door, with the occasional lovely young nurse strolling by, and thus far he only paused to look up once, but she was well worth it. Footsteps had been coming and going for the last hour or so, and then one set of footsteps came up to his door and stopped.

Brillstein looked up, expecting a nurse with an empty coffee cup in her hand and a hopeful smile on her lips, but Philip wasn't a nurse and he wasn't smiling. And he didn't have a cup in his hand, either. He was a large man, rawboned and tall, with unblinking ice-blue eyes, and he came into the office without a word, quietly closing the door behind him.

"Can I help you?" Brillstein asked, wondering who he was. He was dressed like one of the tourists from the peninsula, with tasseled loafers, dark linen slacks, and a lightweight black leather jacket. Every now and them, one of them would down a few drinks and wander down the beach and into the clinic.

"My name is Philip," he said in perfect English with a mannered French accent, and he seemed to be sober. "Are you Dr. Brillstein?"

Brillstein put the chart down, and leaned back in his chair and smiled. The spring creaked, but he liked the sound so he never oiled it. "Well, if I'm not, then he's really going to be pissed off, huh?"

He chuckled a bit to lighten the mood, but Philip didn't respond, and Brillstein looked at him without humor. "Yes, I'm Dr. Brillstein."

"I'm here about the amnesiac," Philip told him.

Varese and Philip had come through the open door at the end of the east wing, the one closest to the beach. It was a half-kilometer walk up the beach to Francois Fortune's, a go-to-hell bar at the base of the peninsula, where tourists would occasionally come in their rented ATVs and jet-skis for some down-home local color. The bar wasn't a place the cruise lines encouraged them to visit, but it had a Facebook page and the word got around, and every ship that tied up had a few adventurous souls who would wander off the reservation for a look-see. And after a couple of stiff Mai Tais, an inebriated walk down the beach to Labadie seemed like a good idea, and wandering through the open doors of a mental health clinic seemed like a fun thing to do after a drunken stroll on the beach. It happened a lot more in the summertime, but this was a balmy night so the doors were wide open, even though it was February.

Philip had gone ahead to Brillstein's office, and Varese was alone in the hallway now. It was a little after one in the morning, and no one was about. And then a door opened, and a young doctor quietly stepped out of a sleeping patient's room. He was new on staff, since Dr. Diane Viccu had returned to Miami, but he'd heard about the tourists, and turned to Varese with an affable smile. He was standing rather close to the doctor, but he was steady on his feet and didn't have any liquor on his breath, and there was something in his hand.

The doctor glanced down to see what it was.

Brillstein sat upright in his squeaky chair as Philip showed him a badge. Brillstein got a good look at it and sat up even straighter, curious more than anything else. He'd never seen a Vatican Police badge before, and it set off an odd little alarm in the back of his head. The man hadn't called ahead, so this was probably serious, particularly if he was here about the amnesiac.

He was Diane's patient, though, and she was gone and so was he, so Brillstein wasn't sure how far the conversation would go. But if the man was here at one in the morning, he wasn't about to leave after a few non-committal shrugs.

"Him?" Brillstein was saying to the man from Rome. "Well, he's gone. It's been over a week since—"

"Can I speak to his attending physician?" Philip asked, cutting him off. "Dr. Viccu?"

Dr. Brillstein's eyes narrowed. The guy was pretty pushy, even for a guy from the Vatican.

Varese stepped up quietly to the nurses' station. The duty nurse was sitting behind the tall counter, coffee in hand, and she glanced up from her magazine. She saw the stranger smile and lift his right hand, and she gave him a tolerant smile in return. He was probably a tipsy tourist, offering her a sip of his Mai Tai.

But that wasn't the case.

Brillstein had a bad feeling about this, and he saw no reason not to trust his instincts. Not at one in the morning in the Haitian boondocks, face to face in his own office with a rude Vatican cop.

"She transferred back to the States last week."

"Where?"

Brillstein frowned at the man. That was just uncalled-for. Even if he was a cop—and Brillstein was beginning to think otherwise—it was his office, and he was running the show. Unless the guy wanted to deal with Dr. Weiss in the morning, and good luck with that.

"Could you please explain why you are here?" Brillstein said. "And can I see that badge again?"

Philip smiled, and showed him the badge. Brillstein frowned at it; for all he knew, it was a phony. "Vatican Police?" he asked.

Brillstein had serious doubts. Who the hell ever heard of the Vatican Police? And anyway, even if they did exist, wasn't he out of his jurisdiction? Even though it was a global religion. But still. . .

An orderly was out back with the door closed, leaning on the railing and sneaking a cigarette. Usually the onshore breeze would complicate things, but it was blowing offshore and took her smoke out to sea. She hugged her sweater around her; it was starting to get chilly. The door opened quietly behind her, and she turned with a guilty grin. Everybody was on her case about quitting. She was down to four a day now, but all the patients were sleeping and there was nothing to keep her busy, and finally she just couldn't resist—

She'd never seen the man before, but somehow she didn't think he was one of those drunk tourists. He raised his hand toward her face, and she shrunk back, staring at what he was holding. But it was inside a large zip-lock baggie, and the moonlight glinted on the plastic so she couldn't see what it was.

But he was pointing it at her, and that couldn't be good.

Brillstein was frowning at the badge, and then he cracked a grin and glanced up at Philip. "What did he do? Rob the collection plate?"

Philip didn't smile, and Brillstein sat back in his chair again, placing his elbows on the armrests and knitting his fingers below his chin. It was a condescending pose he reserved for idiot orderlies, but his welcome mat was wearing thin; he didn't care if the pope himself sent the guy in the papal jet.

"Dr. Viccu is in Miami. As for what the patient told us, well, he didn't say much. He's an amnesiac."

Philip's gaze darkened. He said as much when he first came in, so it was more of a jab at him than anything else. He watched Brillstein's eyes as they continued.

"Did he have any visitors, or contact with anyone else?"

"No. Mainly myself, Diane, and the nurses."

Two nurses came out of the ladies' room by the nurses' station in the west wing, and stopped. They were surprised to see a man standing before them, as if he was waiting for them.

And as a matter of fact, he was.

Brillstein was coming close to scowling at the man, but Philip wasn't looking him in the eye at the moment. He'd noticed something on a thin chain, depending from Brillstein's neck, and was frowning at it. It was mostly hidden in Brillstein's chest hair, below the top button of his open shirt, but from Philip's angle he could just make out the silver crucifix.

"What?" Brillstein wanted to know, and for the first time, Philip smiled. "Are you a religious man?"

Brillstein stiffened, realizing what Philip had seen, but before the doctor could formulate a reply, the door behind Philip opened. A tall man with his blond hair combed straight back stepped into the room, and shut the door behind him. Philip didn't bother to turn his head; it was clear that he was expecting the visitor.

Varese stepped up beside Philip, his eyes on the man in the desk chair. There was a silenced Walther PPK in Varese's gloved hand, encased in a large zip-lock baggie that was closed tight against his wrist. Powder burns from his last two shots were smeared on the inside of the bag, blackening the plastic. Other used baggies were stuffed in his jacket pocket.

Brillstein's eyes widened, but not so much from what Varese had in his hand. Brillstein recognized what it was at once, but recognizing the man who held it was even more of a shock. "*You—!*"

He never finished his sentence.

CHAPTER **THIRTY-FOUR**

Diane and Devlin were sitting on the front of her Maserati convertible. He was afraid they'd dent the hood, but he figured she knew what she was doing, so he followed her example and straddled a fender just behind the headlight, and hooked his heel between two vertical fins in the grill. The silver GT was a sinful indulgence, a bit more than she could afford, but she drove it off the lot the day it came out, and never thought twice. Most women wore their luxury or lived in it; she drove hers.

They were sitting just a few feet apart, with a curve of flawless Italian steel between them, their hands wrapped around steaming take-out coffees and enjoying the gathering twilight. A gentle wind stirred a handful of leaves in a swirl. They watched them skitter across the parking lot and bump against the curb, dispersing like confetti onto the grass.

"Thanks," he told her, and took comforting sip. She was amused, watching him nurse his coffee, holding onto it with both hands like a life preserver. She laughed playfully, gently teasing him, and he smiled from behind the black plastic lid.

"It's the least I could do for a handsome refugee," she flirted, and his smile grew bashful, making her laugh again.

Her cell phone beeped in her jacket pocket, and she glanced down to it. The display said, "Father." She sent the call to message, and looked back to him. He'd been watching her, but he shyly looked away to a massive tree that dominated on the lawn before them. It filled the greenspace between the parking lot and the construction zone to the east. Several old buildings had been torn down, and for the next few months at least, the Atlantic could be seen from where they were sitting. The moon was high overhead, and it shimmered on the ocean beyond. Their view of the water was bifurcated by the tree's enormous trunk. It held aloft a massive bough that had shaded her car all morning long, but it was far enough away so when the apples ripened and fell, they wouldn't ding the hood.

He cracked a wry grin and glanced at her. "They grow apples in Miami?"

She nodded, and smiled at the tree, taking its magnificent bulk before she answered him. It was a marvelous specimen, with a bounty of fruit that glinted in the moonlight, ripe and luscious crimson orbs with patches of golden green.

"Miracles never cease, huh? They're called Anna apples," she told him. "I adopted this tree. Isn't she beautiful?"

He was amused that she decided the tree was a girl. Then again, it was fertile, and it did bear fruit. "Did you give her a name?"

Diane smiled and nodded, not the least bit embarrassed. "Annabelle," she said.

"Anna, the belle of South Beach," he experimented, savoring the rhythm of his words, and he nodded, satisfied with the invention. "I like that . . ."

He looked at her, and they exchanged smiles. Then he pointed at the phone in her pocket. "You need to get going? I don't want to keep you."

But she shook her head, dismissing the idea with a wave of her hand. "No, it's nothing. And anyway, I'm off tomorrow, so . . ." She lifted her coffee cup and smiled at him from behind the rim. "I can stay up late," she informed him. She was tempted to raise an eyebrow to punctuate the sentence, but she restrained herself and let him extrapolate from there.

Devlin didn't have much of a memory to work with, but his powers of imagination were fully intact. He blushed and gazed down at his loafers, but he was certain that she caught his expression, and that made him blush even more. She grinned and put her fingers to her lips to keep from laughing out loud; it would mortify him and she didn't want to do that.

Her cell beeped again, saving them both from an awkward moment. He watched her check the display, and saw her lips pout.

"Darn," she grumbled, and dropped the phone back in her pocket.

He mirrored her expression, and when she glanced at him she had to smile at his mimicry, even though she didn't have good news.

"I *was* off tomorrow . . ."

He nodded, as disappointed as she was, but he didn't say anything and fiddled with his coffee cup.

"Look," she began, "I . . ."

And then she trailed off, not quite knowing how to proceed, or whether she should. But as he sipped his coffee and glanced at her, there was a melancholy cast to his features and she couldn't keep silent. She'd already crossed a line with him, and they both knew it.

"I don't know if this is the smartest thing for me to do," she admitted, and he waited to hear the rest, not daring to breathe lest he disrupt the magic. She was lovely in the moonlight, and when the ocean breeze danced in her hair, it shimmered like a halo . . .

"It runs counter to everything I was taught," she was saying, and he had to concentrate to follow her words. "But you've had it pretty rough lately," she explained.

He had to admit she had a point, and he nodded, but then he tried to shrug it off. But she wasn't having it.

"Why don't you crash on my couch for the next few days?" she said in a rush, and before he could beg off, she plunged ahead, pressing her case. "At least until you get back on your feet," she told him. "Maybe it'll give you time to collect your thoughts and figure out who you are."

"I don't know," he stammered, but he was too embarrassed to

elaborate. He knew he wouldn't get much sleep on her couch, what with her lying in bed half-naked in the dark, just down the hall. . .

"Well, I do," she said, and she hopped off the fender and stood right in front of him. She was well over the line by now and there was no turning back, so there was no sense being coy about it. He just looked at her with a wide-eyed grin, not sure how to respond, but her boldness made her more attractive than any woman had a right to be.

She held out her hand to help him off the fender, and he grasped it, but his foot found a rotten apple and he slipped as he tried to stand. They both held tight and saved him from landing on his bruised backside, but his coffee went flying, though it missed her Maserati. He blew a sigh of relief over the close call, and she laughed in agreement, helping him to his feet.

He walked over to the grass and scuffed his shoe clean, and then eased himself into the passenger seat as she got behind the wheel. The ragtop started powering back as they buckled up. He watched the top go over their heads while she fired up the V-8 and goosed the gas, then toggled the sound system to surround them with Latin jazz.

The dual exhaust growled like a caged cheetah, but the soft leather seat was gentle on his bruises. It was an easy chair wrapped in a road rocket, and Devlin was ready to ride. She dropped it in drive and pulled out of her slot, angling around the smear of apple he left on the asphalt.

An ocean breeze rustled through Annabelle and she whispered a gentle goodbye. Then she swelled with luxuriant pride, alive and sweet, and shimmered in the soft moonlight.

CHAPTER THIRTY-FIVE

Inspectors George Mezadieu and Micheline Batou had blood on the soles of their shoes. There were two bodies sprawled on the floor of the lobby, including the new janitor. Working at the clinic had just become one of the highest risk jobs on the north shore, and Micheline doubted they would be getting a flood of new applicants.

Business was booming in Cap-Haitian since the earthquake, with a horde of do-gooders streaming into the country bringing their neatly packaged supplies. And nearly none of them were actually staying down in Port au Prince. Every hotel in the area was booked, and they drove down there in their rented Land Rovers for a few adventurous days at a time, or they hopped a ride on one of the relief ships, or they flew. And during all the hubbub and busyness, the tourist trade on the peninsula continued unabated, as if nothing at all had happened down south. So if you couldn't get a job in Le Cap these days, you were disabled, lazy, or a dead. Even the zombies were busy.

As she walked with Mezadieu back down the main hallway, Micheline glanced at a spray of blood on the wall. Probably from the poor bastard they just stepped over. Maybe the *houngans* could bring their zombies to the clinic to do some cleaning. They were slow, but the price was right, and the place had just become seriously understaffed

"How many?" Mezadieu was asking her.

"I count nine so far," she told him.

"Doctors, nurses, and orderlies," Mezadieu said, mostly to himself. "None of the patients were killed."

"What do you think?" Micheline asked him. She realized it wasn't the best question, though he knew what she meant. He didn't think about a crime scene so much as he listened to it, if it could even be called that. But it had nothing to do with *loas* whispering in his ear, or angels or guiding spirits for that matter. They were more of a distraction than anything else, and he'd seen them take the *houngans* and *mambos,* and even some earnest priests, down some seriously convoluted paths.

But he always answered Micheline in the same phraseology, because neither of them knew what else to call it. He tried to explain it to her once, and they both concluded that thinking didn't quite describe it.

"I think this is more than a killing spree," he told her, and she nodded. She was thinking the same thing.

Dr. Brillstein's body had gone cold by now, and a bit of rigor mortis was starting to set in. The cops and the forensics crew from Le Cap were already there, and the doctor's office was starting to get crowded. Forensics was snapping pictures and dusting for prints, and the police corporal and sergeant were standing in the hall, watching them.

They had all been at the crime scene at the beach the other day, and they happened to be together again just this morning, up on the peninsula. A hung over tourist at the resort stabbed his wife during breakfast, something about a handsome waiter the night before. When honeymoons at the resort went south they were usually a mess, but the Canadian had really gone to town on his bride, and the cops joking about it in low voices. But not so low that the forensics crew couldn't hear them, and it lightened the mood, making the tedium of their jobs more bearable.

The photographer had accidentally bumped Brillstein's left arm, which was dangling over the side of his chair, and she noticed it was starting to stiffen up. It was close to eleven in the morning, and it was starting to look like the killings happened shortly after one. The two security guards never made their one thirty rounds; their one o'clock circuit was the last time they walked the grounds and punched in at all the terminals. She could see them out in the parking lot now, handcuffed in the back of the cop car, shivering in their boots, their short careers over.

She was about to tell the others that the stiff was getting stiff, when the inspectors appeared in the doorway and she put a lid on it.

The cops nodded hello. The inspectors nodded back, and took a good look around, but they'd already been in the office so they knew the general disposition of the scene. The m.o. was essentially the same as the others, a single head shot with a fragmentation round.

Brillstein got shot between the eyes while sitting at his desk. Surprisingly, most of the shrapnel punched out the back of his head, then through the venetian blinds and out the open window behind him, where it undoubtedly lay scattered in a thousand tiny pieces on the lawn, utterly useless for a ballistics test, even if all of it was found.

The fragmentation rounds the shooter used weren't really slugs at all, but a wad of shrapnel coated in Teflon that hung together in flight, and then burst apart when it hit something solid, becoming a tiny grenade. Brillstein was the only victim who had an exit wound, so there was probably a flaw in the manufacturing process down at the bullet factory, maybe not enough Teflon or maybe some of the shrapnel was a little too big, but it was nothing that could help them at the lab in Le Cap.

"What happened to security?" Micheline asked the cops, and they both grinned at her.

"A patient saw them running off when the shooting started," the sergeant told her, and she grimly chuckled. After the night guard got shot the other week, the clinic had beefed up security by hiring two brothers

172

to watch each other's back. And they had; they just didn't watch the clinic while they were at it. And now they could watch each other's back in jail.

She glanced at the security camera in the corner of Brillstein's ceiling, and stepped back into the hall. "Anybody check surveillance?"

The corporal nodded. "The monitors are working, but . . ." He shrugged.

"No tape?" she asked rhetorically, and he shook his head.

"Real pros," she said, and turned to watch Mezadieu, who was in the office now inspecting Brillstein's corpse.

The corporal wasn't quite sure what she meant by her last remark, whether the shooters were real pros or whether he and his partner weren't. He glanced at the sergeant, who was wondering the same thing.

Mezadieu was bent over Brillstein's body, slumped in his desk chair. The shot had thrown his head back, and his dead eyes were staring at the stained ceiling tiles. Rivulets of blood had crusted on his face, like streams of dark tears, and there was a sizeable pool of blood on the floor behind the chair. There was also a brass casing under his right shoe, below the desk.

Mezadieu left the casing alone for now. The sun had just peeked through the window, illuminating the cubbyhole below the desk, and he was lucky to catch the first glint of the brass. Like the crime scene at the beach, he wanted to keep the treasure to himself for now. There was a way that evidence whispered to him, if he had it all to himself. A trip to the lab in the wrong hands could make it fall silent, and oftentimes he couldn't coax it to speak after that.

He stood erect, and gazed unfocused at Brillstein's remains. "Nine head shots," Mezadieu said to himself, "nine kills . . ."

Micheline quietly stepped up beside him as he finished his ruminations in silence. " . . .in and out, and no residue," she offered, and he nodded just once.

The forensics team hadn't found any prints and the photographer was done, so they were standing around, watching the Case Whisperer vibe the scene. That's what they called him, like the Dog Whisperer in America that they watched on satellite, during their lunch break at the lab.

Mezadieu's cell vibrated, and he answered it. "Merci." He listened without expression, and ended the call without a farewell, glancing at Micheline. The guys on the forensic crew were glancing at her, too, and so were the cops. They took any excuse to check her out, and if Mezadieu was looking at her then so could they. But he had something else on his mind beside her curves.

"Our missing patient is in the hospital again," he told her, and she cracked a surprised grin.

"What happened to him this time?" she wanted to know.

"Car accident," he told her, and she shook her head in disbelief.

He'd save the part about Miami and Dr. Viccu for later. He didn't want the others to overhear and start speculating about it. If they did, it could make the information go quiet for him, just like it did for physical evidence. He needed to let it marinate for a while, before he shared it with anyone, even Micheline, although she would be the first to know.

She was bent over the corpse now, holding her nose and getting a close look at the entry wound and taking in the position of the body, just like he'd taught her. He saw her eye catch something under the desk, and the corner of his mouth flickered in a proud smile.

She caught his expression as she stood erect, close beside him so they could speak privately. The others knew enough to not try to listen in. Or at least to not be obvious about it.

"Something tells me he took a dump," she said quietly, and he nodded.

"And someone flushed after him," Mezadieu replied. "No prints, no witnesses. No loose ends," he finished, and waited for her to rebut his last remark. It took less than a second.

"Except for one casing," she whispered, and flicked a glance below the desk. "If this was a mop and glow," she said, "they missed spot." But when she looked back to him, his expression had darkened; he was watching something over her shoulder.. She could hear Agent Fincannon in the hallway behind her, chatting up the coroner.

"That brass is probably untraceable," Mezadieu quietly remarked to her, "like all the rest that we found. This is an international job, Michi; he was just a pawn removed from the board. And Dr. Viccu could well be their next target."

She nodded, and he glanced down at Brillstein.

"What's a Jew doing with a crucifix?" he asked her, and she shrugged. "Jews for Jesus?" she quipped, and he shrugged as well.

She pulled out her cell and scrolled through her directory. "I'll notify the FBI." But he touched her shoulder and pointed into the hallway. "They're already here."

She looked up, and saw Fincannon standing with the coroner, watching them impatiently. She just stood there and watched him right back, while Mezadieu took his sweet time gazing down at the corpse. For all she could care, the American could grab some lunch and come back when they were done. She didn't want to deal with the man, and neither did her partner.

"Man . . ." Mezadieu sighed, and she picked up on his mood right away. "Higher than the devil," he said quietly, "and lower than the angels."

She didn't say anything in response. He got like this at the oddest times, but it wasn't melancholia and it wasn't world-weariness. She couldn't put her finger on it, but she never tried to talk it away. It was part of his process, and she didn't want to interfere.

He used his pen to lift the crucifix, and laid it gently on Brillstein's bloodstained shirt. Mezadieu had left the priesthood years ago, but he wasn't a lapsed Catholic. The way he saw it, Catholics were lapsed Christians. The crucifix was always to be revered, no matter the circumstance, and he said a silent prayer as it gleamed in the sunshine.

"It's a shame the dead can't talk," he murmured, and she just watched him. Brillstein's corpse was whispering to him, but try as he might, he couldn't hear what the man had to say, and Micheline could see the muted anguish in her partner's eyes.

"I have so many questions, Dr. Brillstein," he said softly. "So many questions . . ."

Peter Johnson was sleeping soundly, laying flat on his back under his goose down quilt, in his bedroom in Chantilly Flats. He preferred to sleep on his side, but his back was much better in the morning if he slept facing the ceiling. He had his hands on his chest, one above the other with his fingers curled, like a knight in the grave clutching his broadsword. He used to lie with his hands crossed, but it reminded him of those old vampire movies and it gave him weird dreams. So he began to reposition his hands like a knight, and after a few weeks it became a habit and he didn't even have to think about it. His dreams were more pleasant now, of ladies fair and journeys and quests and feats of daring-do, all done for love and honor and the greater glory of God—

His cell phone rang on the nightstand, and his eyes popped open. He picked it up and came fully awake when he saw it was after ten. He had been up till four researching Bible codes, but he still felt guilty for sleeping the morning away. Mark Kaddouri was calling.

"Hello?"

"You need to come see this," Kaddouri said.

There was something in his tone of voice, and Johnson sat up against the headboard. "See what?"

"Remember those freaky fingerprints I was telling you about?"

CHAPTER THIRTY-SIX

Archbishop Nano was dressed in civilian clothes, and he looked like a million euros. There was a sense of style he'd absorbed from his years in the Church, wearing formal vestments that had been laundered and folded to a fault, and making sure that his altar boys were properly turned out. To him, it was never about primping or ego; it was a matter of showing the proper respect for the business at hand.

But he was drawing stares as he moved through the bustling bank lobby, and had a distinctly uncomfortable sense that he overdressed for the occasion. He hadn't been out all that much since returning to Rome, and the thing that struck him on this warm and sunny afternoon was how informal the culture had become. Thirty years ago, a young bishop could put on a tailored suit and become lost in the crowd, but now he felt like a peacock. Maybe it was the ruby tiepin.

The empty elevator was a relief, and as he rode up to the thirty-ninth floor he had plenty of time to dab his brow with the silk handkerchief from his breast pocket, then refold it and put it back properly. Too much time, in fact, because he spent the rest of the ride looking at himself in the mirrored door panels. There was nowhere else to look; the entire elevator was a mirrored box, even the ceiling. It was like Vegas, but without the free drinks and call girls.

He was getting old and worn out, there was no getting around it. And his mounting apprehension of what he was about to do wasn't helping to buoy his spirits. But he had to do it, no matter how uncomfortable it would be. Things that were set in motion decades ago were accelerating now, and careening away on unpredicted trajectories. His foundation was starting to heave and slip, and he had to re-establish a firm footing before he could take another step. He had to know where he stood. But even more fundamental than that, he had to know if there was even a place to stand, or if everything now was in flux.

The elevator came to a precise, delicate stop and the doors whispered open. A male receptionist looked up from his newspaper, but he didn't smile a greeting. Nano didn't see that as a good sign, but perhaps the young man simply had no manners. Many of them didn't.

The reception area was rendered in a minimalist style, and the furniture was fashionable, severe and uninviting. Hopefully they wouldn't make him cool his heels and flip through one of the terminally hip magazines arrayed on the coffee table. He approached the reception desk, and even as he was nodding hello the young man pointed down the hall.

"Third door on the right," he informed the plump old man, and went back to his newspaper. Nano caught the headline in passing, VATICAN RECONSTRUCTION BEGINS, and frowned as he ventured down the hall. *Reconstruction, my fat ass,* he thought sourly. *The Vatican is gone for good. They're building something entirely different now.*

He didn't know what it was going to be, but he doubted they would need the likes of him around much longer. For more than four hundred years, in one way or another, his family had been linked to the Vatican. His ancestors had been popes and cardinals, and the family crest had even been displayed in the portico. But the portico was gone now, shattered into rubble and dust. His soul felt much the same, if he even had one after all he had done. And if he still did, then perhaps he could redeem himself in the time he had left. He was a bishop; one would think he would know what to do. But for all his scholarship and prayer, he had no idea. Even this would be a shot in the dark.

The cobra rose majestically above the glass wall of its open aquarium, spreading its hood and tasting the visitor's scent with a flickering forked tongue. It was close to feeding time and this perfumed human was an unwelcome distraction, unless he had a mouse in his pocket.

Unfortunately, Nano didn't have one, and he didn't have his mace canister, either. He left it in the car, thinking he'd be safe in a new high rise in the EUR district. It was the only collection of high-rises in the entire metropolis of Rome, for Christ's sake, modern monstrosities of glass and steel, with guards and cameras and metal detectors; one would think they'd be safe, but no. Venomous snakes were apparently on the approved pet list.

He wasn't sure if a cobra could be driven back by mace, but if he had it with him he would have found out in a matter of seconds. The damn thing had nearly given him a heart attack. He wanted to make it suffer, purely out of revenge, even if it stayed right where it was. And he had a good mind to hose down the owner as well . . .

But he knew he was indulging in pointless fantasy, because the last thing he needed right now was to alienate Isaac La Croix. He was Nano's only contact in the Rosicrucians, and the bishop desperately needed some answers.

"My enemy's enemies are my friends," Nano mumbled to himself, and looked across the room at the Rosicrucian knight.

He was dressed in white slacks and a rose red cashmere sweater, and he was seated comfortably at his desk, a wall of windows behind him. It was a brilliantly clear day, and though the sky was blue and not its usual hazy white, the influx of light still caused Nano's pupils to contract to pinpricks. It was difficult for him to see the man's features, and his dark skin wasn't helping matters. His clear white eyes were visible, though, unblinking and direct, and Nano had the uncomfortable feeling that La Croix could see into his soul. Which in a sense gave Nano a flicker of hope; it confirmed he still had one.

The spacious room was sparsely furnished, even less than the reception area. Aside from the desk and chair and the aquarium on its chromium stand, the room was empty save for an armless antique chair in the corner by the door he'd just came in. There wasn't even a rug on the floor, and the reflection off the polished blonde teak mingled with the delicate sheen of the rosewood paneling, giving the white ceiling a slightly ruddy cast.

"Have a seat," La Croix offered, indicating the chair by the door, and Nano sat down with a nervous laugh. They were a good five meters apart. The knight got up from his chair and came around the desk, sitting on its forward edge. Nano blinked, and with this new perspective he could get a good look at him now. There was a small white mouse in the palm of La Croix's hand, and he petted it, his calm eyes on the bishop.

He was a striking fellow, perhaps in his mid-thirties, but with his African lineage it was hard to say exactly. Nano guessed that if he smiled he would have a set of ridiculously perfect teeth, like the Cola Nut man in the TV commercials he used to see in New Orleans, back in the eighties. There were plenty of Cola Nut men in southern Louisiana, but Nano had to admit that he rarely saw one as handsome as this. Not that Nano was gay, but as he aged he found that he could appreciate the beauty of youth, irrespective of gender.

"I'm glad to see you are punctual," La Croix said. He had a Caribbean accent, with more of a French twist than English. Nano guessed Haiti, and when he did his chest constricted. Haiti was where Christine Mas ascended into heaven, just a few days after the earthquake. La Croix and the Rosicrucians were somehow involved with Cardinal Molinari and Father Simone—now Bishop Simone, Nano reminded himself—but he wasn't sure exactly how the man fit into the mix. Still, he was much closer to the eye of the gathering hurricane than Nano was, that much was clear. And he was undoubtedly close to Sir Reynard. Nano felt like he was on a great warship in heaving seas, and had finally made his way to the bridge. And here was a senior staff officer, an eccentric Cola Nut man with a pet cobra and a mouse in his hand. *Great . . .* Nano grumbled to himself. *Just my luck.*

"I'm on a tight schedule," he told La Croix by way of reply. "I can't arouse suspicion."

"And have you so far?" Isaac inquired.

Nano didn't answer him. He was tempted to frown and say no to the rude question, but the truth was, he really wasn't sure.

La Croix leaned down and let the mouse hop out of his hand, onto the wood floor. It scurried away, as far as the nearest baseboard, and began circumnavigating the room. Nano watched the thing out of the corner of his eye, and so did the cobra. He was beginning to understand the room's Spartan décor, and so was the mouse.

"I don't believe so," Nano answered, a bit later than he should have, and La Croix simply nodded. He watched Nano nervously fiddling with a rosary in his suit pocket, while Nano watched the white mouse run along the dark wood baseboard, searching in vain for a place to hide.

La Croix's lips parted in a gleaming smile, which Nano didn't see, distracted as he was. "I see you haven't lost faith," Isaac said.

Nano looked back to him and adjusted his starched collar. He was beginning to sweat, and realized that there was no circulation in the room.

"Can we turn up the air?" Nano asked, but La Croix didn't respond. "Huh? No?" the bishop said. "Well, okay . . ." He was annoyed by La Croix's blatant manipulations, but he was in no position to complain, and that further annoyed him.

La Croix was rubbing a thumb on his lower lip, watching the man fidget. "You called this meeting," he finally said. "So tell me why, Archbishop."

CHAPTER THIRTY-SEVEN

Nano cleared his throat, stalling for time as he thought of a way to begin. He'd been going over it in his mind for days, but now that the moment arrived he was tongue-tied. The liturgy was so much easier; it was all written down, a pat set of statements for any occasion, honed and refined over the centuries. Even the sermons he used to give were a cut-and-paste rehash of his favorite hits. The mass was like a lounge act, crooning through the same numbers week after week and year after year. But this was like a job interview. Or so he imagined. He'd never actually had one his entire life—

La Croix was leaning forward, a bit impatiently, and Nano knew he had to say something or the meeting would be over.

"You Rosicrucians aren't the only ones looking for him," he blurted out, and thought that, all told, it didn't sound half-bad for an opening line. And it certainly got La Croix's attention.

"Yes?" the knight said, raising an intrigued eyebrow. "And who else?"

Nano didn't answer right away, letting the drama of the moment play out. But it was a bad move on his part, because the little white mouse had captured his attention again, scurrying along the baseboard.

La Croix stood up and went to the aquarium. The cobra was also watching the mouse, and La Croix's approach didn't seem to distract or annoy the reptile. When he lifted a chrome rod and slid the curved end under the cobra's body, Nano understood why.

The snake coiled a bit around the rod and La Croix lifted it out of the aquarium, then lowered it to the floor. It slithered directly for the mouse, but not as if it were zeroing in for the kill. More like it was enjoying the hunt.

Nano was riveted to the sight, but La Croix turned to him and his body language told Nano to speak up. Nano looked at him and cleared his throat. "The Church," he finally answered, and felt compelled to say more. "It didn't end with the bet," he explained. "It didn't end when God beat the Devil."

"That we already know," La Croix said, walking back to his desk with the chrome rod in his hand. He sat in the same spot and held the rod across his thigh, facing Nano. "But the rest is still a jigsaw puzzle."

"Yes," Nano agreed with a bit of a smile. "And you're missing the pieces."

The man nodded once, slowly, and Nano glanced away as the cobra slithered closer to the mouse. It was motionless now, a white spot hoping to disappear by playing dead. Or perhaps it was petrified with fear.

Nano drew in a full breath and exhaled it slowly, just like it showed on his yoga DVD. It didn't help much, and if he tried it again, he was afraid he'd become light-headed and fall out of his chair, which was the last thing he wanted to do with a cobra on the floor.

"There's a fine line between hell and the Vatican, Monsieur La Croix. Wherever God erected a house of prayer, Lucifer built a chapel there. And as time went on . . ."

The mouse scurried toward Nano, hoping to hide behind him or run up his leg. Nano kicked it away, and it slid across the floor, spinning like a hockey puck.

" . . .Lucifer gathered quite a flock," La Croix finished for him, and Nano nodded, looking back to him.

La Croix smiled without humor. "That says more about Man than it does about God, eh?"

But Nano didn't see his gleaming smile, because at that moment the cobra coiled and struck.

"Precisely!" Nano said, staring wide-eyed at the phenomenon. He'd never seen it before except on cable TV, and it startled the word right out of him. The strike was a deft blow, a masterstroke, a work of art. He may as well have shouted *Bravo!*

"And up till now," he continued, watching the snake wrap its mouth around its struggling prey, "the Devil's house has always won."

The mouse's rear legs were kicking, but it was already halfway in the snake and its efforts were futile.

Isaac La Croix was standing at the window now, watching the cranes at the Vatican project, seven kilometers to the north. His back was to the archbishop, holding the chrome rod behind him in both hands like a riding crop. He wondered if they'd be able to lift the new dome with just one crane. He surmised that if it took more than one, they would use at least three for control and stability. That would be a sight to see, and there was a telescope he could bring from the Fortress of the Tree Crowns. Then again, the Fortress was much closer to the Vatican, and he could watch from the roof. But setting the dome was at least a year away, maybe two.

"Do you really think that he's fooled God?" La Croix asked him, but Nano was still distracted, watching the cobra. Only the mouse's tail was visible now, and the cobra's gullet, if that's what it was called, was swollen like a bayou bullfrog.

"God is no fool . . ." Nano managed to reply. La Croix turned back from the view and looked at him across the room.

"And neither is the Devil," he informed Nano. His face was a silhouette again, backlit by the sky, and Nano had to squint.

"What if this was all part of Satan's plan?" La Croix asked him, and Nano laughed, surprised by the very idea.

The question wasn't asked in jest, and La Croix didn't think it was the least bit funny or foolish. He stepped close to the snake, and gently worked the hook of the rod under its center of mass. The cobra was lying languidly on the floor, methodically moving the mouse down its alimentary track, a centimeter at a time. The mouse was asphyxiated by now, and no longer squirming. Dinner was over.

The cobra hugged the rod for balance as La Croix lifted it off the floor. "Satan makes a bet knowing he would lose, and so he does."

He looked directly at Nano and smiled, with the snake coiled on the rod. "But now that he's mortal, he has a shot at redemption, doesn't he?"

Nano blinked. He never considered that angle before.

Issac turned away, but before he returned the snake to the aquarium, he faced the construction site again, and Nano watched him, stunned by the implications of what the man just said.

La Croix and the serpent were both silhouettes now, and the tableaux they formed with the Tragedy in the distance made a stark impression on Nano's mind. He knew he'd remember it for the rest of his life.

"A devilishly clever scheme, don't you think?" La Croix remarked, and Nano took the moment to extract the silk handkerchief from his breast pocket and wipe his forehead. He stuffed it in his jacket pocket when he was done and composed himself as La Croix continued, his eyes on the distant cranes.

"And if the Devil were to sacrifice himself, *Christ-like . . .!*" La Croix conjectured, and let it hang there in midair, like the cobra.

Up until now it was an intriguing train of thought, but this last bit was a bridge too far for Nano, and he frowned, shaking his head to discard the very idea.

"To save another?" he spat out in surprise. "That would never happen! It's utterly preposterous!"

La Croix said nothing, and held the cobra over the open aquarium. It relaxed its grip and dropped into its lair, where it would lie still for the next few days digesting its supper.

Despite being in the midst of a deep religious debate, the bloated snake reminded Nano of lying on the couch after Thanksgiving turkey and watching the game.

"But if he *did*," La Croix resumed, and Nano looked back to him. "He would be redeemed, would he not?"

Nano looked away to the expanse of floor, something neutral to gaze at while he wrapped his mind around the notion. In spite of himself and all that he knew about Christianity, he had to admit that La Croix had a point. And a damn good one at that.

Nano finally nodded his head, and looked up. The knight was sitting once again on the edge of his desk.

"And he would go to heaven . . ." La Croix prompted him, and waited for Nano to play the concept out in his mind. The archbishop swiftly came to the inevitable, horrific conclusion, and stared at him as the blood drained from his features.

". . .and Heaven would become the Devil's playground," Nano said, his voice a hollow whisper, and La Croix nodded.

Nano shook his head no over and over again, trying to rebut him, but the logic was inescapable. And yet, it didn't quite make sense. Because there was something that La Croix wasn't aware of, and it was the only thing Nano had left to challenge the awful scenario.

"But the Church doesn't *want* him to die!" he blurted out, as much to himself as La Croix. "They just want him to live long enough—"

He shut himself off in mid-sentence, but he said too much and he knew it.

"Long enough for what?" La Croix inquired, suddenly curious.

Nano was suddenly frightened, even more than he'd been of the snake, and his eyes darted around.

"Long enough for what, Nano?"

Nano's gaze landed on the aquarium, and he saw that the cobra was watching him, its tongue flicking out of its mouth.

186

"The Devil isn't your biggest worry anymore," Nano told La Croix.
"Then who is?"

The archbishop shifted nervously in his chair, but just like the mouse, there was nowhere to go and nowhere to hide. He finally sighed, and wearily leaned back, closing his eyes. Not because he was tired, but because looking at the world was simply too painful to do.

"His children," Nano told him with a sad, quiet sigh.

La Croix stood up from the edge of his desk, genuinely shocked. This old fool had wasted a half-hour of his time, but now he just said something that was worth every second and more. If in fact it were true. And from the tone of Nano's voice, it was clear that he believed it was.

Nano opened his eyes and saw that the man was standing now, and he was much closer than before. But it wasn't a threatening posture; La Croix was stunned, and wanted to know more. Nano nodded to assure him that he wasn't making up stories, and he could see at once that La Croix believed him. At least, he believed that Nano believed it.

"I swear by all the saints it's the truth," Nano told him. "The Devil has lost his power, but the power remains in his seed."

He watched La Croix's eyes, and saw the handsome young man visibly age as the implications played out in his head.

CHAPTER **THIRTY-EIGHT**

Nano stumbled a bit as he exited the building. He was pale and exhausted and his blood sugar was shot. The security guard noticed, but so long as the old fart didn't keel over on the sidewalk, it was none of his concern. People get old and they get tired, and then they die. This one was well on his way, he concluded. Just have the good manners to do it away from the property.

Jean Paul Eden was watching Nano as well, but he wouldn't have agreed with the guard. He wanted the archbishop alive and well, because some day in the not-too-distant future, he wanted the pleasure of killing the fat son of a bitch himself, long and slow, and preferably with his bare hands.

Eden was parked across the street in the busy high-rise district, in a black Range Rover with smoked windows. It was how he preferred to roll these days, and if Simone hadn't rented it for him he would have chosen the model himself. He was in his early thirties now, and since leaving the priesthood he'd taken keen advantage of his good looks. Eden dressed well and he drove a nice car, and took as many young ladies to bed as he had time to seduce and his hangovers would allow.

But as hard as he worked at erasing that one horrific night at the Citadel, the incident still haunted him. So far as he was concerned, Nano was partly to blame for what happened to him. But more than that, the blame fell squarely on Nano for the massacre at the Church of the Rebirth in New Orleans, for Sister Nancy and the rest of them and the ghastly way they suffered and died. Not one of them was involved in hiding the Christ child, and Nano could have made that clear to Devlin, through his voodoo priest Zamba. But he didn't, and now they were collateral damage.

If Eden had anything to do with it, Nano would soon be the same, just another dead, bloated body on the road to hunting Lucifer. The moment he was no longer useful, Eden would be more than happy to take him out.

He tapped a speed-dial number on his cell. "He's leaving the building," he told Simone.

"Follow him."

Eden ended the call and dropped the phone in his pocket, watching Nano waddle down the sidewalk toward his rental car. *Well, no shit, 'follow him',* he groused under his breath. Sometimes Simone could be a real pain in the ass, but he did have Nano on a string. Even better, Simone had Saul's confidence, and that gave Eden just one degree of separation to the Cabal of Cardinals. He was a lot further along on Devlin's trail now than he was just a few weeks ago.

The music was pounding in his head and his guts were rumbling, but maybe the fourth shot of Scotch had something to do with it. He was nursing a bottle of beer now, trying to get on top of it. The bar surface was marble, not wood, and he was having a hell of a time keeping his elbows from sliding on the slick surface. Luxe strip clubs were starting to annoy the hell out of him; he preferred a working-class titty bar, surrounded by red-blooded men, not metrosexual stockbrokers. But the chicks here were mostly tens, and this one was an eleven.

She had come out barefoot and after three minutes on stage, she was still wearing her sundress. The other strippers would be down to their

G-string by now, but unlike the other strippers, every move this one made was built on the last, and he was content to let her take it slow. It would be well worth it in the end. The DJ was pumping out his usual dance trance nonsense, but she was making it work for her. She wasn't moving to the music, the music was moving to her.

Eden had been coming in every evening for a week now, just to see her. It wasn't a place for lap dances, due to some obscure city ordinance, but the bar was wide enough for her to work it out right in front of him. She stepped on the bartender's sturdy shoulder and crossed over the well, just like she had for the last three nights now, and got down on her knees directly in front of the fallen priest, undulating her pelvis as she inched her thin cotton sundress higher and higher so she could finally take it off.

But Eden wasn't waiting for the first glimpse of her G-string; he was looking up and watching her eyes. There was a dark magic there, something he hadn't seen in the others, or even in her until tonight. She was truly on fire this time. Maybe her boyfriend did her justice before she came to work, but whatever it was her heat was drawing Eden like a force of nature. This had only happened to him once before, and if he had his wits about him now he would have snapped out of it. The fourth shot had lowered his guard and the beer wasn't helping like he thought it would; before he could blink he was back in his room at the Citadel. The memory of that singular event climbed on top of him hard and fast like a street drug, vivid and terrifying and irresistible.

Thalia Rose was lifting her sundress. Father Jean Paul Eden couldn't turn away, and he didn't want to. He wanted her to take him where he vowed he'd never go, before his resolve returned and he showed her the door. She wasn't wearing anything underneath, and seeing all of her at once squeezed his heart and made it pound in his chest. She was naked before him and his soul was stripped bare as she took him to the bed. And when they were done she was no longer Thalia Rose.

Eden was glaring at the stripper and she inched away from him, suddenly alarmed as he unwrapped his hand from the beer bottle and rotated it thumb-down to grab the neck. The bartender had his back to them, or he would have lunged at Eden and shouted for security. But a firm hand clamped down over Eden's hand from another direction, and another one gripped his shoulder as someone leaned in close to his ear.

"No! We *need* you!" the man told him.

Eden glared at him sidelong; he knew exactly who it was.

"Please!" Simone implored, and squeezed his shoulder, then stroked his hand over Eden's back, trying to quell the fury in his eyes.

Simone could feel Eden's grip relax on the bottle, and he sat down on the empty stool beside him. The stripper had already gotten up and vamped her way down the bar by now. They were alone in the crowded club, washed by disco lights and pounded by the bass speakers.

"Help us find him," Simone said loudly, though he could barely be heard above the din. But Eden knew what he said. The bishop had been in the night before to recruit him, and Eden blew him off, but not before he got the gist. He still didn't know how Simone tracked him down, but the Church had ways of finding people that even Interpol couldn't match.

"I'm begging you," Simone said, and Eden looked at his empty bottle.

"You swore an oath," Simone reminded him, and Eden nodded.

"Because I was afraid! I serve the Church no more."

"This is about a lot more than the Church, my friend—"

"—Go away!" Eden growled, but he knew that Simone wouldn't, and finally sighed. "I told you," Eden said, "he can't be stopped. Don't you understand?" He turned to the bishop and scowled at him.

"He's the Devil!" Eden said, spitting the words at him. But Simone shook his head no, and placed a gentle hand on his shoulder. The lighting was awful, but Eden thought he saw the man break into a sly smile.

"Not any more, Father Eden. Not any more."

Eden started the Range Rover and pulled away from the curb, following Nano's rented Mercedes sedan. Eden guessed that he was heading back to his digs at St. Michael, unless he stopped first at the Villa Borghese. Nano's family had a long and colorful history, interwoven with Rome and the Church, and the Villa's museum and public grounds were always a nice place to stroll on a sunny day.

Eden was thinking he could grab some espresso and pasta at the cafeteria, while Nano was having lunch with his *familia,* up in the private quarters. The former priest grinned darkly, thinking about it. He'd blend right in with the American tourists, hung over and oafish and gawking at all the Renaissance treasures. Nano wouldn't even know he was there.

CHAPTER **THIRTY-NINE**

Mark Kaddouri stepped quickly into the darkened office, closely followed by Peter Johnson, and Kaddouri locked the door behind them. They were the only ones on the fifth floor, even though it was still daylight. Several offices on the top floor of the New Iberia Police Department sustained water damage during Katrina, and the entire floor had been evacuated, even though some of the offices were untouched and fully functional. The repair crews had the elbowroom they needed, and the personnel didn't have to deal with the dust and listen to the racket. The work crews had gone home an hour ago, and the entire floor was quiet as a church.

They sat side by side before a large monitor, and Kaddouri entered his password. He used the same terminal the night before, doing his research, and figured it would be better to let it sleep than shutting it down. The start-up routine might be more noticeable to the techies downstairs than a wake up, which could be prompted by a mouse on the keyboard. There were plenty of them in the building, but they kept the spider population down so no one complained.

Kaddouri logged onto Interpol and re-entered his search parameters, showing Johnson how he got to where he was last night. They sat back and watched the images flick past, each one pausing for a moment as the face and the fingerprints matched, then unmatched. They didn't know, but it was the same weird glitch that Ledger and Fincannon saw down in Haiti a few days before.

"Dahmer? Bundy? Koresh? Susan Smith?" Johnson muttered. "What the hell?"

"Exactly," Kaddouri said in a low voice. "A laundry list of evil."

The sequence of images suddenly stopped, replaced by a stark notice in bold red letters. NO MATCH FOUND.

"And then it does that," Kaddouri explained, and Johnson looked at him. "It's gotta be him," the retired agent concluded, and Kaddouri nodded. "If it is," Kaddouri said, "he's in Miami."

Johnson's brows puckered in a frown. "Miami?"

Kaddouri nodded, and pointed at the monitor. As Johnson watched, he tapped a few keys, and more flickering images came, but they were a blur of common criminals and didn't set off any alarms in Johnson's head.

"The Coast Guard found a U.S. passport on a refugee boat off of Miami." Kaddouri told him. "The ID number matched the passport that was issued to our amnesiac."

The images stopped once again. NO MATCH FOUND.

"What about the picture?" Johnson asked him, but Kaddouri shook his head. "The U.S. Embassy in Haiti confirmed that they took his photo, but the salt water scrubbed it clean."

Johnson sneered, Kaddouri shrugged, tilting his head. It seemed pretty damn odd to him, too. "No picture, no prints," he told Johnson. Wiped clean from their database, too." He tapped a few more keys, and pointed at the monitor. "Check it out."

He was on an ID page. There were several entries in the data fields—height, weight, age, eye color, distinguishing marks, but no photo. The name was DOE, JOHN. The location of passport issue was Port au Prince, Haiti. There was no birth date, either, which Johnson found extremely odd, and disappointing—from his studies in numerology and Biblical codes, Johnson knew that a person's birth date was the combination lock to their soul. Everybody has a door. Open the door, and the soul is revealed. It was something every voodoo priest knows.

He exchanged troubled glances with Kaddouri. As far as Interpol was concerned, Devlin didn't exist, just like Christine Mas didn't exist. Or, someone or something was messing with the system. And if someone or something was messing with Interpol, it was happening way above their pay grade, and that meant they were on their own.

This was going to be harder than they thought.

CHAPTER **FORTY**

Devlin was asleep on the couch, with a light blanket over him and his back turned to the sparkling city. He was sweating and shaking, his face buried in the crook of cushions and his pillow over his head. But it couldn't block out the world inside his head, or the heavens beyond . . .

He was standing tall on an unpaved road that ran through the busy marketplace. The village was in a little valley below the Citadel, a massive stone fortress that capped an entire mountaintop in Haiti's lush northern highlands. In spite of the dust raised by the foot traffic around him, his black leather greatcoat was spotless. So were the dark clothes he wore underneath, and so were his black leather boots. His coat was lined in crimson silk, and though it was a hot, sunny day he was unaffected by the weather. His nails were manicured, and slightly longer than most other men's, including those standing in the circle around him. They were dressed as he was but they were in white greatcoats, and their backs were smooth underneath the leather; they had lost their wings eons ago.

The locals walked past them, and some walked right through their bodies as if they weren't even there, and to them they weren't. Devlin and his fallen angels were invisible wraiths, and though the spot in the road had a strange feeling to it, those who passed over it were blithely unalarmed. Haiti was teeming with all manner of hidden forces, and every now and then you were bound to encounter something. Breasts were crossed and prayers were whispered, but it was as unremarkable as encountering swarm of gnats.

"Summon him," Devlin commanded, and he privately smiled. The Lord Almighty had told them all long ago, "Where two or more are gathered in My name, I am there."

Gathered in a circle, the fallen angels cast their eyes downward and raised their arms, fingers together and pointing aloft, and they began to hum. Though they were in human form, it didn't sound like anything human, and it wasn't. They had made themselves into a soundpiece for the wheel of the world, and they were conveying the vibration aloft, more as a beacon than a prayer.

Unbeknownst to the people milling about in the marketplace, the light of the world fell away and a beam of clear, brilliant light shone down from heaven. Devlin dropped to his knee and bowed his head.

"My Lord," he said reverently.

The voice of God held him in a loving embrace. "Lu—"

The travel alarm on the coffee table buzzed and Devlin snapped awake, his heart in his throat. It took a few seconds to remember to breathe, and when he did it sounded like he'd been choking.

He sat up and slapped the alarm clock quiet, and he stared out the windows, catching his breath and trying to quell his racing heart. It was early morning, another perfectly blue and balmy winter day in Miami.

South Florida was so flat and the air was so clean that Devlin could just make out the downtown skyline, about twenty-five kilometers south. He could even see planes taking off and landing at Miami International, west of downtown. Diane's condo was in Miami Gardens, north of the city, on the ninth floor of a sturdy building built in the forties. It had recently been renovated in a retro-trendy style, but there was enough of the original charm so that it didn't seem tacked on. The sounds of local morning traffic was caught in the cluster of old buildings and softened by lush landscaping, a murmur of white noise that was filtered through magnolia trees. Birds were squawking and a leaf blower was buzzing, and the normalcy of it all was comforting.

Diane stepped barefoot out of her bedroom suite, her bathrobe tied around her waist, and she stopped and smiled, but he didn't know she was there. His pulse had finally settled down and his breathing had become steady, but he was still gazing into the distance to assure himself that everything was real.

It looked to her like he was just enjoying the view, and she cleared her throat to announce her presence. He turned to her, still disoriented, but when he saw her smile he finally felt safe, and managed to smile in return.

"Good morning, sleepyhead."

He wasn't sure he would sound normal if he spoke, so he just nodded and smiled again. She thought he was still waking up.

"Thank God you don't snore as hard as you sleep," she said.

"Yeah," he croaked, and grinned at the sound of his voice. "Thank God."

He was sitting a bit hunched over, dressed in his boxers and a tank top with the pillow in his lap. She smiled to herself, thinking it might be for modesty, but the truth was that he hugged it for comfort in his first moments of wakening, and he still had it with him.

He was wondering what she was smiling at, and when he gathered what it might be about he began to get flustered, but her mind was already on something else.

"John?" she ventured.

It took him a moment to realize the thrust of her question, and when he finally did he shook his head with a frustrated frown. "No," he told her wistfully, "I don't think that's it."

He gazed into the distance again, and watched a plane take off and rise into the sky. "I think my name is . . . Lou," he guessed aloud. "Or something like that."

The uncertainty came through in his voice, and she smiled sympathetically. "Okay, then Lou it is. I'm tired of guessing, anyway."

He looked back to her and broke into a sheepish grin. "So am I," he admitted.

They had spent a good hour the night before working on his memory exercises, trying to tease his name out of a murky thicket of random thoughts and images. She didn't want to plow him in too deep again, especially before breakfast.

He yawned away some residual sleepiness, and patted the couch beside him, inviting her to sit. She smiled like a schoolgirl, her eyes cast down to the carpet, and she shoved her hands in her bathrobe pockets as she came around the end table. He shyly looked down himself, and as she approached he had a good long look at her legs. She had nice legs, he thought. She had nice everything.

She sat on the adjacent cushion and turned a little to face him, and he did the same. It wasn't as awkward as he thought it would be; they'd known each other for more than a month now, and she'd seen him at his worst. At least as far as he could remember, it was his worst. But if his past was anything like his dreams, she hadn't seen anything yet.

"Thanks for helping me out, Diane."

She graciously shrugged it off, and then playfully backhanded his leg for even mentioning it. "I like having company."

She leaned back and folded her arms under her breasts, looking at him sideways. "So what's the plan, Lou?"

Her knees were splayed out and her bathrobe filled the gap. But it didn't look sexy at all; she looked like a truck driver slouched on the couch and shooting the breeze, and he grinned at her.

"I don't know. . ." he said, and his grin faded to bemusement as he realized that he really didn't have the vaguest idea of what to do next. He hoped she did, because he still felt just as lost as he did in Haiti. And he still couldn't figure out what the hell he was even doing in Haiti.

She patted him on the knee and stood up, and he realized that he'd drifted off for a moment. He looked up at her and she smiled.

Well, I'd love to sit around all day and chew the fat," she told him, but I have an early shift."

He nodded, looking around the place. He figured he could sit on the balcony and read, or watch TV. He'd get by. At least no one was shooting at him. Although with his luck, that could change at any moment.

"Maybe when I get back, I can take you out to dinner," she was saying, and he looked back to her. He knew she was being a sweetheart, but he was a touch uncomfortable with all her generosity.

"Well, I can't accept . . ."

Diane was puzzled and a bit disappointed, and he instantly regretted what he said. He cast about for a better way to express what he was feeling, but the truth was, he really didn't know what he was feeling. The nearest he could tell was, everything felt unbalanced between them, and he was becoming self-conscious about it.

"You've already done enough for me," he explained, but that didn't quite capture his thoughts. He wanted to do something for her, but he had no idea what or how. He didn't have the funds to take her out for coffee; he didn't even have a wallet to put the funds in. He felt helpless and he wanted to be helpful, especially to her. She saved him from the darkness, and he didn't know how he'd ever pay her back. But he was determined to find a way.

"You've already done enough for me," was the only thing he could think of saying, and looked down to the carpet, dissatisfied with that explanation as well. But at least it was an honest start.

Diane stepped close to him and gently touched his face. It made him painfully shy, and when he finally looked up, he didn't quite meet her eyes. "It's okay," she assured him. "I want to. Besides," she said with an easy smile, "we could both use a night on the town."

He nodded; she had a point. He peeked at her and smiled back. It was a date.

CHAPTER **FORTY-ONE**

A black Mercedes van glided up to the curb and whispered to a stop. Just like the airport, the white zone was for passenger loading and unloading, but they didn't intend to linger. Drake got out of the passenger seat and shut the door, and Sama pulled away under the bored gaze of the security guard strolling the sidewalk.

The guard watched the van idle toward the parking structure, which was no place for such a tall van, but if the lady was in luck she'd find space in the lot. It was a pleasant Miami evening, with a touch of coolness in the ocean air, and everything at the moment seemed right with the world. Even if the guy who got out of the van looked like a Nazi in an aloha shirt.

Drake dressed casual to blend in with the locals, even though Sama thought it wouldn't work, but within moments it was apparent that he wasn't fooling anyone and by the time he got into the lobby he gave up trying. He re-thought of himself as a tourist from Europe who was inquiring after his second cousin Diane, who, last he heard from his aunt in Belgium, worked at the hospital. He thought he'd surprise her since they hadn't seen each other since middle school. Could they possibly page her?

The duty nurse wasn't buying any of it, but people were so litigious these days that she kept her smile pasted on and said she'd check with her boss. She got up from her chair and ducked into the back room, catching Dr. David with a glance as she went. He was leaning on the counter thumbing around on his phone, and he heard the whole thing. The story didn't wash with him, either, though he couldn't put his finger on why, exactly. It just didn't.

He kept his eyes on his phone, but Drake was perceptive enough to sense the doctor's attention on him. That, and the vacant smile of the duty nurse were enough to prompt him to withdraw. He pretended his phone was vibrating in his pocket, and took it out, glancing at the display. He put it to his ear and walked away for some privacy, initiating his half of a fake conversation in Belgian French. He used slang and colloquialisms so that if a French speaker happened to overhear, they wouldn't know what the hell he was talking about.

The stroll took him around the corner, and he dropped the pretense and speed-dialed a number as he strode through the lobby and out the door. But Sama wasn't picking up. He ended the call and stood on the white-curbed sidewalk, looking around impatient and annoyed.

The security guard strolled past and nodded, but the Nazi in the aloha shirt didn't return the cordiality, and the guard theorized that he was pissed off about an insurance policy glitch. That's what most people were pissed about when they came outside to make a call. But it was after six, and the wait time on some of those insurance call-in lines was awful, so maybe he got pissed about that and gave up. Or maybe he was pissed off that his wife dressed him funny. Hard to tell with these Florida Nazis.

Sama saw that Drake had called, but she was busy at the moment. She was wedged into a tight space in the back of the lot, squeezed between two people who were in desperate need of parking lessons, and was busily typing on her laptop as she spoke with Saul on the Bluetooth.

She was logged in to the South Beach Hospital database, and the John Doe's records were on the screen. Several data fields were blank, and there was no photo, which was odd because even if he didn't have an ID they would have snapped his picture when he was brought in. But the physical description matched, and the notes about Haiti were a dead giveaway.

"He was treated, then discharged," she told Saul.

"Mop and glow, my dear."

She copied 'Dr. Diane Viccu' from a data field, opened a Vatican search engine, and pasted it into the search box. She knew Saul could hear her tapping on her keyboard, so she didn't bother saying anything. They worked well together, which was good, because it would make everything she had to do that much easier.

The search engine displayed Diane's home address in Miami Gardens, and her hospital cell phone. Sama clicked the Locate button and waited. Moments later, Diane's car was pinpointed on a map. It was at the north end of town, about eight kilometers up the coast from the hospital, and it didn't seem to be moving.

"Consider it done," Sama told Saul. She ended the overseas call, and tapped her phone to call Drake. As it dialed, she brought out a 10mm Glock 29, and screwed on the end of the barrel while she studied the map on her laptop. The Maserati was parked in the lot of an Italian restaurant in Surfside, about six kilometers east of Miami Gardens.

Sama hoped they lingered there, because even though Saul was having the freeway cleared, they would need at least an hour to get uptown and search Diane's condo.

CHAPTER FORTY-TWO

The waiter set their plates of spaghetti down, and topped up their wine glasses with the bottle of Alfredo Rivera he had under his arm. Devlin stared wide-eyed at his food as the aroma entered his nostrils and filled his head. Diane grinned from behind her glass as she sipped, watching him.

He looked across the table at her with a wondrous smile, and she laughed. The waiter moved off, leaving them alone. From the way they were acting before dinner, it was obvious to him that this handsome devil was falling in love with the lady. But it looked like he just found a new romantic interest, warm and inviting and laid out before him. Falling in love with Italian food was certainly less expensive than falling in love with a woman, the waiter thought; particularly an Italian woman, and he smiled as he considered another advantage—seconds were always available, without coaxing or complaint, and they could usually be had for a modest fee.

"This spaghetti stuff is delicious!" Devlin was enthusing to Diane, his mouth half-full from his first taste. The place was a dive, but the food was sinfully good. The family that owned the place had refined to a high art on the Lower East Side, and brought their secrets to North Miami when they finally grew tired of New York City winters. Diane didn't like to pick arguments over politics, religion, or food, but to her mind the Italian food in New York was much better than the Italian food in Italy.

"Come on," she said with a laugh, "you've never had spaghetti before?"

"I don't believe so," he replied. So far as he was concerned, something this good would have triggered something in his memory. And if it didn't, then it really was his first time, but more likely than not there were just some experiences that he'd never be getting back. He dearly hoped it was the former and not the latter, though he somehow doubted that was the case. But this wasn't the time to brood about it, because at the moment he was focused on Diane. She was even more beautiful by candlelight, and it was one moment he was determined to never forget.

"I'm glad you like it," she was saying, and though he knew she was referring to the meal, what stuck in his mind was how much he liked looking at her, and talking with her, and just being with her. And maybe that's one way to form a memory, he mused—experiencing something that was worth remembering.

He thought she noticed him looking at her, and he suddenly grew shy and dug into his food. She smiled and did the same, and for a minute or so they ate in silence. He wasn't being a hog, but he didn't waste any time packing it away, either, and before he knew it he was catching glimpses of his plate through the swirly red goodness. That simply wouldn't do.

The waiter was leaving another table, and Devlin signaled to him. He smiled and came to their booth. He could see that the woman was doing fine, but if the man didn't dial it back a notch he'd start licking his plate.

"Excuse me, can I have some more of this?" Devlin asked him, and the waiter smiled and nodded.

"Right away, sir," he said smoothly, and went off to the kitchen. *He'll grow old and fat, just like me,* the waiter thought with a knowing grin, and went through the swinging door.

Devlin smiled at Diane. "How's. . . mmmmm . . . work been?" he asked, and slurped a lone noodle into his mouth. "This is so good. . ."

Diane took a moment to answer, wiping her mouth and taking a sip of wine. "You know, there's something . . . tasty about a man eating spaghetti," she said. They both had first date jitters, and she found it hard to transition to another subject. So she handed him the Parmesan cheese, and he shook some over what was left on his plate.

"So how's work?" he inquired, and dug into his chow, and she slumped a bit in her chair, picking at her dinner. "Stressful," she admitted. "Sometimes it's like I'm not even there. . ." She took in a bit of meatball, and savored it. "You know, these meatballs *are* great."

She didn't want to talk about work, and hoped they could slide off the subject. The waiter returned with a fresh plateful for Devlin, and swapped it out for the one he had. His face lit up and Diane giggled, and the waiter moved off. *She better be a good cook,* he thought, and quietly put the plate in a bus tray.

Devlin was smiling at her, a forkful halfway to his mouth. He was puzzled about something, and she could see it in his eyes.

"What are we doing?" he asked her.

"Eating?" she answered with feigned naievete, but she knew what he meant. She put her fork down and looked across the table at him before she replied. "Well, I guess . . . just . . . getting to know each other."

Her heartbeat sped up and she could feel the pulse in her neck, and she wondered if he could see it in the candlelight.

"Yeah, but it's not just that," he was saying. "At first I thought you were being . . ."

"Friendly?" she offered, and he nodded. She was trembling with anticipation, but she tried to hide it. "That's a good place to start, isn't it?"

He grinned and nodded again. "Works for me," he told her, and reached across the table, awkward as a schoolboy, and took her hand in his. She stifled a laugh, but it was more a reaction to what she was feeling inside than anything else. Because she really didn't know what to do.

Despite her training and discipline, there was something so disarming and elemental about him that she couldn't resist being drawn in. The power of it frightened her, and yet at the same time she somehow felt it was right. Even though it violated everything she knew and left her without an anchor or a yardstick. She was being swept away and she knew it.

His grip became firm and it focused her attention, but that's not why he squeezed her hand. He was gathering the courage to do something he'd been thinking of, since the first time he woke from a nightmare and found her hovering over his bed in Labadie, holding his hand. That was the moment he fell in love.

Devlin rose a bit from his chair, and leaned over the table and kissed her, and then he sat back down and smiled, watching her catch her breath. He felt much the same way she did, breathless and little surprised. He figured it would feel good, but he didn't know it would be magical. And now he didn't know what to do or say, so he just sat there smiling like a fool and hoping she'd say something clever.

She took a long sip of wine, and put her glass down. "Let's take this somewhere else," she suggested.

He smiled at the idea, and pointed at his plate. "We can take this with us?"

CHAPTER **FORTY-THREE**

The evening was a little too cool to have the top down; it was still February, even if they were in Miami. But the moon was rising over the ocean and it was a lovely night for a drive along the coast. Diane headed north on Collins Avenue up through Surfside, past tidy little townhouses and shops. Just off the boulevard to the west was a post-WW II neighborhood, collection of one-storey stucco houses that reminded her of the L.A. suburbs, or some of the old neighborhoods on the Big Island.

They rolled into Bal Harbour, past much nicer townhomes and a series of swanky high-rise condos, and headed for the bridge. On the far side was Haulover Beach Park, and sometimes when the traffic thinned out it seemed like you were miles from the city. Maybe she'd crank up the heat and lower the top so they could enjoy the palm trees passing overhead, but right now Devlin was savoring the aroma of his spaghetti, and she surmised that he didn't even want the windows down, much less the top. Now she knew what it was like delivering pizzas, she quipped to herself, but his disingenuous joy over something so simple was endearing, and it was a pleasure to share it with him.

She glanced at him and saw he was watching her. "What?" she wanted to know.

"You are so beautiful," he told her.

She smiled and looked ahead, and they went over the bridge. The moon was rising off to his right, fat and golden above the midnight blue water, but his eyes were on her, and she realized that she was becoming embarrassed by his open, penetrating gaze. She felt naked before him.

"I'll bet you say that to all the girls you don't remember."

"I'm glad I only remember you," he told her, and she glanced at him again. There was something in his voice, and she wasn't sure if it was relief or melancholy. She placed her hand on the center console, palm up, and he laid his hand in hers.

It was a gorgeous evening and the traffic was even lighter than she hoped it would be, and the moon was shining through the palms along the beach, but he just sat there looking down at their hands, lit by the dashboard light. It was like a butterfly had come into the car and was resting between them, delicate and beautiful, and he didn't want to disturb it lest it flutter away and be lost.

They drove in silence through the seaside park, and as they did she wrestled with what her duty was, and what she felt in her heart to be true, despite all evidence and experience to the contrary. She knew that at some point soon she'd have to make a decision, and then she had to act on it one way or the other. And once that line was crossed, there would be no turning back. Her pride, honor and professionalism had always been the source of her strength, and now everything was being called into question.

She tried to push it away at first, and when he'd gone missing in Haiti she thought it might be over. In a small, selfish way it was almost a relief. But her horizons had always extended beyond her own personal world, and when he disappeared she knew deep down that she couldn't ever stop searching for him. And when she finally found him again, she'd have to make her decision and face the consequences, no matter how difficult that might be. And now here he was, in the palm of her hand. Holding the decision in abeyance was no longer possible.

She took a breath, and slowly let half of it out. "There's something I should tell you," she finally said. He looked at her and smiled, wondering what it could be. He had his hopes and fantasies of what she might say, and he dearly hoped that he would be right. He'd been alone for far too long; so long he couldn't even remember—

The siren clenched their guts, and the light bar on the Miami Police cruiser came to life, stabbing red and blue lights into the rear window of the convertible. The white Crown Victoria was just a few yards behind their rear bumper, and Diane had no idea where it came from. She didn't recall any headlights following them, so perhaps it had been lying in wait behind the bushes along the side of the road. And a silver Maserati GT was a tempting target for any cop, even if Mother Theresa was at the wheel. That's why she set the cruise control at thirty-five after they got out of traffic in Bal Harbour and came over the bridge, and the car's computer would prove it. But there was one thing she couldn't argue in court.

"Shit!" she said, looking in the mirror. "I had three glasses of wine. *Shit . . .!*"

Devlin looked behind them, and could see the cop signaling for them to pull over. Diane was doing just that, and they rolled to a smooth halt on the shoulder, alongside a row of concrete barriers protecting a construction zone. The machinery in the seaside park seemed like a jumble of mechanical monsters to Devlin, looming over them with jointed arms and enormous clawed hands.

He swallowed his fear and looked at Diane. She knew the drill; she turned off the engine and waited with her hands on the wheel. Devlin took the cue, and put his hands on the dashboard.

The cop stopped about five car lengths behind them, which Diane thought was a bit odd. A lot of Florida cops were a bit odd, but still . . .

The cop got out of his car with his hand resting on the butt of his 9mm sidearm. As he closed the door of the police interceptor, the interior lights extinguished and the naked male corpse in the back passenger well melted into moonshadow.

CHAPTER **FORTY-FOUR**

Diane glided down her window, and looked up and over her shoulder to make eye contact with the cop. But he was standing to the rear of her door handle, and was so close to the car that his face was obscured by the ragtop. It was a power tactic that a lot of cops used, particularly if she was wearing anything that showed some cleavage, like she was tonight. Getting stopped for Driving While Female came with the territory, but a lot of cops stopped her because of what she was driving. She was used to it by now and she loved her Maserati, so it was a tax worth paying. But not after three glasses of wine.

The cop shone his flashlight into the car, and Diane and Devlin squinted in response. Cops would usually flick the beam to the side and bring it back again, to see how her pupils respond, but he didn't do it. He just kept it trained on the both of them. It was what they did when they wanted to be jerks, and this guy had the trick down cold. His flashlight was much too bright to look in his direction, so they kept their eyes on the road ahead.

The traffic was light on the divided six-lane road, and the headlights coming down the southbound lanes flickered through the line of palm trees planted in the median strip. Most of them were going much faster than they had been.

"In a hurry, ma'am?"

"No, sir," she replied, and fumbled through her purse, which she put on her lap when they stopped. "How fast were we going?"

She knew exactly how fast she was going, but she wanted to hear it from his perspective.

"Fast enough," was all he said, and she nodded. She figured he was one of those; the flashlight hassle was a dead giveaway.

She handed him her license, and he took his time looking it over, held up to the edge of his light beam, which was still blasting into the car. Diane looked back ahead, and Devlin was still doing the same. They weren't holding hands at the moment, although Devlin dearly wanted to. But things were bad enough at the moment, and they didn't want to make the cop nervous.

"Diane Viccu?" he read aloud from her license, and she nodded.

"Yes," she acknowledged, and left it at that. There was something in the tone of his voice, and she wasn't quite sure what it was. Miami cops could be especially weird, but having a man in the car with you was usually good insurance against anything truly creepy. Not always, though, and her pulse upped a notch as he leaned down and looked past her to Devlin.

"And who are you?" the cop wanted to know.

Devlin squinted at him, and didn't quite know how to reply. He had no idea who he was, but he sensed that the cop wouldn't take that for an answer, and that things would go rapidly downhill from there. He nervously glanced at Diane for some support, and she turned toward the cop.

"You know, officer, I'm pretty sure we weren't speeding," she said as diplomatically as she could, and waited for his response. But there wasn't one. She nodded; if that's how he wanted to play it, then fine. She knew her rights, and she knew a lawyer who'd fight the ticket, so long as the cop didn't have her do a breathalyzer test. Then she'd be screwed. But so far, so good; the guy was just being a jerk. He didn't catch her with a pupil check, and he didn't even lean in to smell her breath. And even if he had, the spaghetti was so overpowering that he'd probably miss it anyway.

The cop stood erect and put away his flashlight. She figured it was ticket time, and breathed a wine-flavored sigh of relief . . .

While Drake looked both ways, and drew his weapon.

He would have popped both of them as soon as he walked up to the car, but there was a bit of traffic so he had to stall for time by playing cop. But there was no traffic coming in either direction now, so the fun and games were over.

Diane saw the glint of blue steel in her door mirror, and knew instantly what it was. As his right hand lifted the pistol clear of its holster, she screamed to alert Devlin and turned toward the weapon.

Drake stepped forward to get a clear shot at Devlin, as Devlin hunched down in his seat and frantically clawed at the door latch. But he was in shadow, with his high seat back blocking the blast of light from the cop car behind them, so he couldn't see the configuration of the unfamiliar door latch.

Drake leveled his weapon, holding it steady just inside Diane's open window and aiming at the skull of his primary target, which was bobbing around in the darkness in front of the glovebox. The gun was right in front of Diane, and she reacted on pure instinct, shoving it up against the canvas top as Drake squeezed the trigger.

The explosion was deafening, and shocked away whatever fear or civility she had. It was an animal struggle now, just her and a man's hand wielding a deadly weapon. She dug her nails into his forearm and wrist and pushed upwards with all her strength, and if she could figure out how to get her teeth around his trigger finger she'd bite the damn thing off.

CHAPTER **FORTY-FIVE**

The bullet punched a clean hole through Devlin's window, and he threw himself back against his seat in response, wide-eyed and frozen. His panicked fingers still couldn't figure out the door handle, and he sat there squirming, not knowing what to do or where to go.

Diane didn't want to chance pulling Drake's hand toward her mouth and giving him a better shot at Devlin, so she kept pushing as hard as she could against the ragtop and dug her claws in deeper.

Her initial attack had thrown off his stance, and this renewed effort made him stumble against her door. "What the fuck are you doing?" he bellowed as her nails broke through his skin.

The weapon discharged again, and the bullet tore through Diane's cell phone, tucked in the visor pocket. It exited through the top, narrowly missing Drake's face, as burning flecks of cordite exited the hole in the canvas. Some of them embedded in his cheek, and one of them lodged in the corner of his eye.

It stung like a bastard, and he lurched away in response, trying to tug free from her surprisingly strong grip. But she was locked on tight with her nails by now, working them in deeper and shrieking in rage. It was something more basic than language that came from deep inside her, raw and atavistic and feral, and both men instantly understood the message. Drake knew with utter certainty that if he didn't free himself in the next few seconds, she would find a way to rise up from her seat with his hand still pinned to the canvas, and sink her teeth in his flesh.

He grabbed his wrist with his other hand and planted a foot on her door, and jerked as hard as he could. It worked and he was able to pull free, but his weapon tumbled out of his hand in the process and landed on the pavement, while he landed on his ass a few meters away. He rolled over on his knees and scrambled to retrieve it, but a car flashed by and he lurched out of the way. His hand bumped into the weapon and it skittered under the car.

"You bitch!" he raged at her, up on all fours beside her door. "You're dead, too!"

But his threat was drowned out by Devlin shouting at the top of his lungs. "Let's go! *Let's go!*"

Drake dropped flat to the pavement, and reached under the car for his pistol, as he heard the two motorcycles coming up fast behind the cop car, their twin pools of light approaching down on the concrete roadway. He wondered what the hell had kept them, and lunged under the car for his gun, getting two fingers on the barrel as Diane started the engine.

He bellowed in frustration and rolled away, his gun still under the vehicle, tantalizingly close and illuminated by the approaching bikes. One of them jinked away from the other one, and they bracketed the stolen cop car to come up on the Maserati's rear fenders.

Drake had less than a second to react, but he didn't know what to do.

Both bikers had pistols drawn, and the one coming up behind Devlin took the first shot. The hollow point bullet punched through the glass rear window of the convertible and tumbled past his head, leaving a large ragged hole in the windshield.

"*GO!*" he urged.

Diane dropped it in gear and floored it, but she was in reverse.

"*Shit!*"

The Maserati lurched backward, clipping the wheel of the bike coming up behind her. The rider tumbled over the handlebars and tumbled into Drake. The other rider braked and leaned to go in tires first, but his bike caught an expansion joint in the concrete and threw him. He rolled up the side of a concrete barrier, and tumbled back down under the car as Diane shifted into drive and floored it.

The helmet kept Philip's head safe, but that was about it. The fat radial dug into his leathers and ground a wide swath over his neck and collarbone, snapping his cervical spine. In his last flickering moment of life he realized that he should have stayed in Haiti. The north coast was beautiful and the women spoke French. He could have been happy there.

As the Maserati peeled away, Sama tore off her helmet. She was sitting on the pavement in her padded leathers, watching Drake scramble for his weapon. He finally got his hands on it, and knelt to take aim, but the car was too far down the road to get off a clean shot—

Sama's helmet bounced off the side of his head, and he turned back to her in surprise. She was glaring at him in disgust.

"What the hell!" Diane managed to shout. Her chest was squeezed tight in panic and she could hardly form words. "Who *were* they?"

"I don't know!" Devlin replied, as panicked as she was. *"Floor it!"*

"Believe me, it's floored!"

He looked behind them through the bullet-damaged rear window, but they weren't being followed. The traffic was light in both directions, and no one on the road seemed to be in a panic other than them.

He touched her shoulder to calm her down, and calm himself as well.

"We're okay now," he assured her.

She said something in reply, but she knew he couldn't hear her over the growling engine. She could barely hear herself; her ears were still ringing from the gunshots.

"No, we're not," she said quietly, and then she repeated it in her head. *No, we're not.*

CHAPTER **FORTY-SIX**

Saul was in his suite at St. Michael's, sorting through a pile of ancient books. They exuded a dank, musty odor that reminded him of the catacombs under the Vatican. Most of the books were from the Dark Ages, leather-bound reams of thick parchment, each page painstakingly copied by hand. Some of them were lavishly illustrated, and as jaundiced as he had become, the handiwork never failed to rouse his imagination.

He could see the rows of monks in stonewalled rooms, much like the one he was in, working by candlelight late into the night. Their brushes would be laid out, and all their inkpots would be securely tucked away until a particular color was needed, because you couldn't afford to spill even a drop. And when a pot was out and open, just the tip of the brush was used so the ink never crawled up the bristles and dried. The vibrant color was applied one careful stroke at a time, lest an entire page be rendered worthless, even though most of it was a lie. A beautiful one at that, he had to admit, preserved for the ages by the Lie Factory. But now that it was finally reduced to rubble, a new lie could be carefully formulated and brought to light, as if it had been found whole and unblemished in the ruins. Something he could craft to his advantage.

He could hear the construction through his open window, and paused to take it in. The blast crater that vaporized the papal altar, and St. Peter's tomb below that, had bore a hole in the earth halfway to the Gates of Hell.

HUNTING LUCIFER

There was a crew of diggers in the crater now, carefully removing shovels of dirt while their supervisor probed with a sonar rig. There were ancient legends of a secret buried deep below the papal altar, beneath St. Peter's tomb, and even below the necropolis that ran under the floor of the nave. Few people knew what the secret really was, and Saul was one of them. It was buried in the lost books of the Bible, carefully stacked on the floor in front of him, and he knew where to dig.

There was a reason why St. Peter was interred on that spot, and it wasn't because the ley lines were so powerful. It was *why* they were so powerful; that was the secret. St. Peter was the rock on which Christ built his church, and now the rock had been rolled back.

Not that it mattered, though, because the Gates of Hell wouldn't be visible, no matter how carefully they dug; the Gates were beyond the sight of mortal man. And in any case, Hell had been empty and locked since Christ rose from the dead, so nobody was home.

While Jesus spent His three days in Hell, there was a bit of hell on earth. On the cross, Christ asked the Father to forgive the ones who tormented him, and at the moment of his death he proclaimed, "It is finished." But Saul knew there was more to the story, and so far as he could tell, he was the only person alive who did. Because since Molinari died, he was the only one who had access to the Book of Devlin.

He knew that in spite of Christ's pronouncements, the Angel of Death had tracked down every person who had a hand in His demise, from Herod to Pilate to the Roman soldiers, right down to the angry crowds on the march to Calvary. Pilate had been rendered to Caesar, who had him beheaded, and Michael himself beheaded Herod's wife Herodius, the woman who asked for John the Baptist's head on a platter. But all the others were hunted down. Whether they knew it or not, they disrupted the greater order of things, by taking an active hand in helping Jesus accomplish His mission, crucifying Him as one of their own. It was blasphemy, and they had to suffer. And yet, when Samael got to each one, they had already been

221

dispatched. Another immortal understood their blasphemy as well, and was already at work. And when the Angel of Death finally got to Judas, the truth was revealed.

Judas was in the act of hanging himself when Devlin whispered in his ear. It was one of Saul's favorite passages in the Book of Devlin.

"Is God watching?" Judas Iscariot asked him, though the noose was so tight that he could hardly speak.

"Yes!" Devlin told him, and he pulled tight on the rope.

And as Judas hung before him, his eyes bulging from their sockets, Devlin said unto him, "Let's put on a good show!"

As Judas swung like a pendulum before him, Devlin saw the Angel of Death bow to him in admiration. They were of the same mind, and from that moment on the Angel was one of Devlin's dark legions.

After the three days, when Christ returned and Peter bore witness to His Resurrection, the Lord told him to build His church. And there was something else—He also gave Peter the key to Gates of Hell.

But the key soon disappeared, and the lost books contained no clues as to where it might be. Hell stayed empty, and since that time the world's departed souls had never really departed at all; they were all here among us, for good or for ill, in a parallel world that rarely touched ours.

Most other religions had their speculations, and every witch doctor and Wiccan and *houngan* sensed that it was true; at least the real ones did, though they didn't know why. Some of them could even contact the *loas,* as the Haitian voodoo priests called them. But the Cabal of Cardinals had known the truth from the beginning, even though the Church never did, including most of the popes.

In the chaos following the Tragedy, Saul and Simone removed the lost books from the Cabal's sanctuary, in the sub-basement of the Vatican Secret Archives. Saul had all of them now, and he who held the truth held the power. He smiled at the bustling work site below. The New Vatican was going to be very new, indeed . . .

His cell phone rang and he took it out, glancing at the display. Sama was calling. He was going to take her down to the catacombs before too long. There were hidden trysting rooms down there, with feather beds and hand-stitched linen sheets and priceless bottles of wine, decorated with Da Vinci's pornographic paintings and Michelangelo's erotic sculpture, illuminated by gold candelabras that Liberace would have killed for, and several knights of the roundtable actually died for. There was a medieval freakiness about the place that never failed to turn him on, and she seemed like the kind of woman who would appreciate it. In any case, power was an aphrodisiac; he knew that it was only a matter of time before she was in his bed.

The cardinal smiled as he took the call. "Is it done?" he asked her.

"No," she informed him, and the twinkle went out of his eyes. "They got away. They took out one of our guys, and Drake blew it."

Saul was stunned, and stared unfocused out the window. "That's . . . a shame," was all he could think of saying.

"If he is who you say he is, then why is she helping him?"

He frowned, puzzled by her question. "She?"

"The doctor," Sama said. "Diane Viccu. They teamed up."

Saul had to sit down. He perched on the edge of the table below the window, and had to steady himself with his free hand against the wall. It was cold and solid under his palm, and it helped him get his bearings. For a moment, he thought he was going to faint. Now he thought he might be sick. He found himself staring at the Vatican site, as the implications began swirling in his mind.

"She's helping him?" he asked her, though he knew he heard her correctly. His voice sounded weak, but the question had come out of him before he could collect himself. There was no playing it off now; she could hear in his voice that it was a gut punch.

"What's going on?" she asked him.

He was considering how to answer her, holding the phone to his ear and gazing at the Vatican's empty shell. "Have you finished reading the Book of Revelations?"

"Sorry," she admitted. "I couldn't get through it."

"That's all right, my dear, most of us won't get through it, either."

He ended the call and sat once more on the edge of the table, watching the activity in the blast crater . . .

She was helping him!

It changed the calculus of everything he planned.

"Jesus Christ," he muttered.

CHAPTER FORTY-SEVEN

The door burst open and Devlin and Diane rushed inside. She closed the door with a thump and threw the deadbolt, and slid the brass chain into the slot as well. She didn't think it would stop anyone who truly wanted to bust in, but it would delay them for a few more seconds, and that sliver of time could mean the difference between death and survival.

They were both still gripped by panic, and it was a wonder that they didn't get stopped by a real cop on the way back to her condo. It was all she could do to keep to the speed limit, but she maneuvered through traffic like a rally driver and Devlin had to keep bracing himself. She only backed off when he bumped his head against his bullet-damaged window on a tight left turn. She didn't want him having an episode in the car, and she didn't want the glass to crumble into his lap, either. After a few miles, though, she finally assured herself they weren't being followed, and they tried to keep calm the rest of the way home. But it didn't work very well.

"This is insane!" she said, pacing the living room. "Why would that cop try to kill you?"

He was trying to walk off the tension himself, wandering aimlessly around the furniture and staying out of her warpath. "I don't think they were cops."

She stopped and looked at him, and he realized that she was well aware they weren't cops. It was just a handy label for the guy who stopped them and pulled a gun. She began pacing again, and he watched her. There was dried blood under her fingernails, her hair was a mess, and she moved like a caged cheetah. She looked magnificent.

"Were you in the mafia?" she asked him. "Were you a drug dealer or something?" She stopped and turned to him. "Is this political? CIA stuff? What?"

He was just a few feet away from her now, and he could see an edge of terror in her eyes. She might have been on the warpath, but she was every bit as bewildered as he was.

He reached out to hold her, but she pushed him away. It was the first time she'd ever done that, and it wounded him terribly, even though he realized that she wasn't rejecting him. She was just too explosive right now, and she didn't want to be contained.

"I'm so confused!" she told him, knowing she hurt him and trying to smooth it over. But he'd never seen her vulnerable before, and she didn't want to give into the feeling. And if he held her right now, she was afraid she might break down and cry.

"I'm scared," she admitted, but it wasn't a plea for help. She needed to be strong; they both did, but she wanted to be as truthful as she could. She began pacing again, searching for the right words. "I'm . . ."

But that was as far as she got. She stopped in her tracks and looked around. Something was different.

He sensed what she was feeling, and looked around the room, but everything seemed fine to him. Then again, he'd only slept there for one night, so what did he know. But in seconds he was as jittery as she was, half-expecting something to pop out at him. Something blatantly obvious.

She was staring at a throw pillow, lying flat on the couch. The others were leaning against the back cushions, plumped and positioned as they were supposed to be.

"We have to leave," she told him.

"What?" he wanted to know, but she walked quickly towards her bedroom and went in. He followed her, with a quick glance back to the couch. But from his perspective, everything looked fine.

Diane was already at her dresser, yanking the drawers open and tossing clothes on the bed. Devlin stood in the doorway and watched her. She was on a tear and he wasn't about to get in her way.

"We have to get out of here!" she reiterated, and he shrugged—if she wanted to go, he wasn't going to argue with her, especially when she was like this. "Yeah, I got that part," he assured her. "But what's the matter? They didn't follow us."

She slid open the closet and plopped a suitcase on the bed, clicking the latches and throwing the lid open.

"Talk to me!" he implored, and she paused to turn to him. She was rattled about something; he could see it in her eyes.

"Someone was here," she told him.

"What?" He knew he heard her correctly, but it didn't quite sink in. He looked around the bedroom, wondering what she might have seen. But he'd never been in the room before, so he didn't have anything to go on.

She pointed past him, into the living room. "The sofa!" she told him. "The pillows were moved."

He looked over his shoulder, but everything still seemed fine to him.

"Are you sure?" he asked dubiously. "They look . . ." A throw pillow was lying flat on its back. " . . . out of place," he realized, and then he started to panic, looking around for more clues. "Oh, my God . . .!"

His distress was contagious, and she started filling her suitcase with both hands. "Shit!" she growled, and he just watched her like he did in the car, when she tore into the hitman. She was cramming her clothes in the suitcase like she was pummeling the guy with both fists. "If they know where I live, then they know where I work!" she told him. "I should have known this would happen!"

He felt awful for getting her in a jam; if he hadn't been so pitifully helpless, and if he hadn't been leaning on her, none of this would have happened. She was talking like they were after her, but he didn't see it that way. It looked to him like he was the target, and she was expendable now that they found him, whoever they were, and whoever he was for that matter. But it really didn't matter at the moment. They could hash out the details later, if there was even going to be a later. But right now, in this moment, her life was flying apart at the seams and he felt responsible.

"I'm sorry," he stammered, "I never meant . . ." But he didn't know what to say. All he really knew was, he was falling in love with her, and he didn't know how to tell her. And even if he did, this didn't seem to be the right time to bring it up . . .

His thoughts trailed off when she stopped what she was doing and turned to him once again. It seemed to him like he was thinking so loud that she somehow overheard, because she stepped up close and tenderly touched his cheek.

"Stop!" she urged him. "It's not your fault, Lou. But we have to leave."

He touched the back of her hand to keep it against his cheek. He needed something to anchor him, to anchor them both. He was weak and he knew it, but there was a storm brewing and he could feel it pressing in on all sides. He didn't know what to do or where to go, he just knew that he wanted to do it with her. But he also knew that if he acted on that feeling, it would only bring her harm.

He took her hand from his cheek and held it in both of his, and she began to weep. It tore his heart out, seeing her cry.

"Those men wanted me, not you," he told her quietly, and he somehow knew he was right, though he had no idea why. But he was clearly the one they were gunning for. She was trying to take the burden on herself, but he wasn't going to let her. He knew what he had to do.

"If I leave, you'll be safe—"

"No!" she insisted. "You can't go without me! You'd be lost out there!"

He nodded, holding her gaze. "And that's just what I need to do—get lost."

But she shook her head, insistent, and clasped her free hand over his, holding him tightly. "No!" she told him. *"Don't!"*

There was something in her voice that stopped him in his mental tracks. He thought he had the whole thing reasoned out, and now it didn't make any sense.

She continued in a softer tone, entreating him to reconsider. "I don't want you to leave," she confessed. "Don't leave me, Lou. Please?" She was touching his cheek again, but this time she was the one who needed comfort. She was the helpless one.

"Don't leave me . . ." she pleaded, and in that moment he knew that he couldn't. Not for his sake, but for hers.

He opened his arms to embrace her and for a fleeting moment she hesitated, because this was the threshold she could never cross, if she ever hoped to retrace her steps. There would be no turning back. But despite the consequences, she knew it was the right thing to do.

She entered his embrace and his arms closed around her, and she knew that everything would change from this moment on. She put her arms around him and held on tight, as if she had just leapt across a great abyss. And she had.

He shyly kissed her cheek like he did in the restaurant, and she looked up to him, wanting more. He obliged her and kissed her lips, but he did it delicately, as if he didn't want to disrupt the magic that brought them to this fragile sliver of time. She backed away smiling at him, and he returned it, not daring to breathe. They were balancing on the edge of eternity; he just needed a little push.

She reached up and held his face in her hands, and drew him close and kissed him again, willful and hungry for every part of him, and the quiet avalanche began.

One timeless moment poured into the next, and as they kissed he discovered with his hands what his eyes had already explored. She pushed her suitcase to the floor and they knelt together on the bed. Her tongue sought his and then her fingers became lost in his hair as he buried his face in her breast and breathed her in.

She drew back to slip off her top, and he helped her out of it and tossed it aside. The silk caught the air, and it fluttered into her open suitcase. Then they peeled away every layer until they were a warm tangle of skin and whispers, melting together on the rumpled bed.

CHAPTER **FORTY-EIGHT**

Drake exited the international terminal at Fiumicino Airport and stepped into the brilliant Roman sunshine, wearing dark shades under a wide-brimmed hat. It had nothing to do with style or anonymity; his left eye was still red from the powder burn and was sensitive to the light. The conjunctiva had swollen over the burn like a reptile's nictitating membrane, and his histamine count was through the roof. It was like a bad allergy that wouldn't go away. The eye drops were nearly useless, and eleven hours of recycled airplane air hadn't helped.

But his eye didn't sting nearly as bad as his right hand and wrist. They weren't scratches, they were claw marks; the woman was a hellcat, and the doctor at the clinic had a hard time keeping a straight face as he cleaned and dressed the bleeding cavities. Four of them required stitches, and the entire area was swollen now and wrapped in gauze. He didn't get a wink of sleep on the flight over, and now he had to contend with Saul.

The black Rolls Royce Phantom was waiting at the curb and Marcel was at the back door, ready to open it when he got close enough. Drake nodded hello and Marcel, ever the gentlemen, nodded back. There was usually no way to tell a man's mood from his chauffeur's demeanor, so Drake didn't even bother trying to second-guess the emotional climate inside the vehicle. He knew it would be unpleasant, and he was correct.

He stepped inside, removing his hat and shades, and nodded to the two men sitting in the back seats. The cardinal was in street clothes, a black suit with a gray silk tie. His bodyguard had on wrap-around shades like he always did, and wore a cable knit sweater and wool pants. Drake surmised that they probably just came from lunch; their breath smelled of clam sauce and wine.

He sat across from them, his back to Marcel, who slipped behind the wheel and glided the limo away from the curb. Traffic was surprisingly light, and with a few lane changes they were cruising toward the E80 Autostrada for the drive into Rome.

Saul had a Bible on his lap, which Drake thought was a bit much, but it was lecture time and the old man probably needed a familiar prop to launch a proper rebuke. His hands moved over the leather cover and his fingers curled around the sides, as he seemed to be contemplating what he was about to say. Varese just watched Drake from behind his dark glasses, and Drake kept tabs on the bodyguard's hands as Saul began.

"Did you know, Drake, that the purpose of the Bible is to keep Man from destroying himself?"

He patted the good book with his hand, a quiet, distinct thump, and despite his years of training a jolt shot through Drake's viscera at the sound. He was more nervous than he thought he'd be; this really wasn't going well.

"My apologies, your Eminence."

Saul nodded slowly, his eyes cast down to the book in his lap. His fingers curled around the sides, as if he was going to open it and read a passage, but as he opened the cover he turned the binding to face Drake, exposing the inside of the book to Varese . . .

Before Drake could react, Varese took a silenced pistol from the hollowed-out Bible and leveled it at the narrow spot between Drake's astonished eyes. The fragmentation round punched through the bridge of his nose and exploded into a thousand fragments inside his skull.

There was no exit wound, so nothing touched the polycarbonate window behind him except the back of his head, as it snapped back before he slumped in his seat. Marcel saw the whole thing in his mirror, and as Drake had dropped out of his line of sight, Saul closed the privacy curtain. Marcel accelerated onto the Autostrada, and the limo blended in with the afternoon traffic.

Varese plugged the hole in Drake's skull with a tapered rubber stopper, and gave it a firm twist to lock it in place. Saul was amused, but it worked like a charm—the blood ceased flowing almost at once. Varese then draped a towel over Drake's face to sop up the little bit that already came out, and gathered the terrycloth fabric under Drake's chin. So far, there wasn't a drop on the upholstery or carpeting, and if Varese had anything to do with it there never would be.

He sat back and turned to Saul, a trace of a proud smile in the corner of his mouth. Saul was holding the hollow Bible open, and Varese placed the gun back inside. *What would I do without my Varese?* Saul thought, and closed the gun case on his lap. He gave it a fond pat, and then his expression sobered as he ruminated on the business at hand. Things were taking a very strange turn, and his ability to predict the consequences was fading fast.

"There's been no contact at all?" he asked his handyman, and Varese shook his head. "No, not since Haiti," he told the cardinal.

Saul nodded, digesting the bad news, and his hands roved the tooled leather book cover as they approached the eternal city. It wasn't the weight of history he was feeling, so much as the gravity.

"Pawns are moving," he said quietly. "The game is in play."

Varese nodded, and looked out his window, sharing the cardinal's pensive mood.

CHAPTER FORTY-NINE

The Bureau de Police in Cap-Haitien was on the corner of Rue J and Rue 20. The city fathers periodically discussed going back to the original street names, but no one took the talk seriously. The original names were jettisoned years ago when the U.S. Marines occupied the country in the early 1900s. The Yanks were frustrated by all the French names they couldn't pronounce, and they were annoyed at being laughed at whenever they tried, so they showed the locals who was boss by changing the names to letters and numbers. Which wasn't in itself such a bad idea; since Le Cap was laid out in a grid, finding an address became a breeze. Changing things back again would cost a fortune for everyone in town, what with all the new stationery to print and all the legal documents to revise, and so despite their wounded civic pride the city fathers knew deep down that the names were fated to remain as they were.

But Inspector Mezadieu never liked the names, even though he grew up with them; it seemed as spiritless as numbering your children. So he took to calling Rue J by its original name, Rue Cavalier. It was carved into the façade of some of the older buildings, so most people knew what he was talking about. Particularly since the rank and file police in Le Cap were such a cavalier lot.

He had the windows up and the shutters open and latched to the outside walls to let in the fresh air and morning light. If he sat on the edge of his desk he could see a bit of the blue Caribbean horizon, beyond the harbor to the north. Inspector Micheline was sitting there now sipping her first cup of coffee, as she dangled her leg over the edge and wiggled her toes to slip the heel of her shoe on and off. Mezadieu knew that it wasn't the caffeine; she only did that when she was impatient or annoyed. And at the moment, it was the latter.

Captian Petion was approaching the office with a file in his hand, and they knew the look on his face. He was being harried by his superiors, and when that happened he eased his stress by kicking the can down the stairs. Mezadieu and Micheline were on the first landing, as it were, so they usually got an earful before anyone else did. Micheline couldn't imagine how the man's wife could put up with him; maybe that's why the woman drank.

"The American embassy has got the Minister of Justice on my ass," he told them before he'd even stepped into the office, "and they want this killer caught." He slapped the file against his leg for emphasis.

Outside Mezadieu's door, his secretary pretended not to notice, though she glanced in at her boss after Petion passed her desk. When Petion was peeved, he didn't much care who heard it. And his Creole had a timbre that rattled windowpanes.

"You mean convicted?" Micheline asked him. He glanced at her legs, then remembered his manners, such as they were, and looked her in the eye. "No!" he told her. *"Hung!"* He looked at Mezadieu. "Tell me you have something."

Mezadieu didn't answer him. Micheline was the one who had something, and he nodded at her. The captain would just have to listen to a woman explain something to him. After thirty years of marriage he should have been used to it, but he wasn't.

Micheline kept it short and sweet. "The DNA tests on that Jane Doe they've had for the last two months just came back negative. Same with her boyfriend, or whoever he was."

Petion nodded. The two charred bodies in the coroner's office had been puzzling them all since Christmastime. Mezadieu sensed that they were connected to the clinic at Labadie, though he still didn't know how. But with everything since that's happened at the clinic, there was sure to be some sort of tie-in. And yet, the corpses still weren't whispering to him; they'd been manhandled by too many people. Even the *loas* were silent, and they were attracted to burnt flesh. It reminded them of hell.

"And the assassins?" Petion asked.

Micheline handed the captain a file of her own. He stacked it on the one already in his hand, and looked at her. He wanted to hear the gist of it now; he could read later.

"Jonathan Kurinski and Janice Avery," she told him. "Warrants in twenty-two countries, on Interpol's Most-Wanted." She hesitated, and then she told him the last bit she found. "They're in a religious order, sir."

Petion frowned; there was something in her voice. He opened the assassins' file and flipped through it, as Micheline and Mezadieu exchanged glances.

"Rosicrucians?" Petion read aloud. He was visibly thrown by the revelation. "That can't be!" he said, and he finally understood her diffidence; they knew his feelings about the sect. He looked at the inspector, his features drawn. "My grandfather was a Rosicrucian," he said, even though they already knew. "He was a good man, a holy man . . ."

Mezadieu nodded, and looked down to his desk, not really knowing what to say. The captain wasn't exaggerating. His grandfather had been a highly respected judge, one of the rare men in a position of authority who was uncorrupted by the political turmoil of his time, so much so that he was looked upon by some as a holy man. When he passed away, he became the unofficial patron saint of the Cap-Haitien Police. There was a portrait of him in the lobby, and his birthday was commemorated each year with a bouquet of red roses, brought by the mayor himself.

Petion closed the file he got from Micheline, and looked back to them.

236

If there was one remarkable talent he had, it was the ability to soldier on, and he returned to the reason he came to see them. "The embassy is giving us seventy-two hours," he informed them. "And then . . ."

He handed her a document from the file he brought, and Micheline frowned at it. "The yanks are taking over?" she asked, genuinely surprised.

Mezadieu sat up in his chair, as surprised as she was, and she handed the document to him. He scanned the page, and absorbed it at once. It was authorized by the Minister of Justice, with his official seal embossed below his signature.

"This is bullshit!" Mezadieu spat in disgust. He slapped the piece of paper flat on his desk, and frowned at the captain. "There are too many variables to button this case in three days!"

Petion nodded, and then he shrugged. Mezadieu frowned harder, and turned to his computer. He opened a file of photographs from the crime scene at the beach, and toggled through one gruesome shot after another of the fisherman dead in his skiff and the ants crawling out of the bullet hole in his forehead, flecks of gray matter held high in their claws.

The ultimatum from the minister was so preposterous that Mezadieu didn't even know where to begin his protestations, but Petion just shrugged again, canceling them outright. Ever since the earthquake, the Americans had been throwing their weight around, and once again Haiti wasn't in a position to object. At least, not for the time being. The time would come as it always had, but certainly not in three days.

"Seventy-two hours," he reiterated. "That's all they're giving us."

He picked up the order from Mezadieu's desk, put it back in its file, then turned and walked out of the office with it, taking the assassins' file from Micheline as well. They watched him go, and as he did he raised three fingers over his shoulder, to drill it into their heads. Mezadieu's secretary sarcastically wrote a large number three on her steno pad, just in case it was important.

Mezadieu leaned back in his chair and looked at his partner, sitting on the edge of his desk again. "The Americans are so full of shit . . .!" he sneered, and then he looked out the window, not wanting to discuss it.

Micheline let him be, and absently gazed at the painting behind his desk. It was the classical depiction of Columbus landing on the north shore, and there were dozens of them all over Haiti, particularly here in the north; he landed just fifteen kilometers east of them. If they were on the roof, they could see the exact spot.

Mezadieu had a special brass plate made for the elaborate frame, and Micheline smiled humorlessly as she read it for what must have been the hundredth time: *"Haiti Discovers Columbus – 1492."*

CHAPTER FIFTY

The catacombs under St. Michael's monastery had been there long before the monastery was built. They were originally excavated in the fourth century, shortly before Christianity became the official religion of Rome, dug in secret by an enclave of impoverished Christians who lived on the hill. Burial within the city limits was against the law, and like most of Rome's poor they couldn't afford a burial plot outside the city. And if they did try to buy one, it might reveal their faith, because the pagans of Rome typically cremated their dead. Everybody knew that the Jews never cremated theirs, and neither did the breakaway Jewish cult of Christianity. The pagan graveyards that did exist outside the city were for the nobles and the wealthy, who erected monuments and posed for statues while they were still alive to commemorate their glorious selves.

The early Christians living on the hill bored into the soft volcanic rock under their hovels to bury their commoners as well as their martyrs, who were dying by the dozens in the Coliseum for the entertainment of a bored and pampered populace. Years later, when Rome was finally sacked by the Vandals, catacombs all over the city were desecrated and priceless relics were taken as trophies. By the Dark Ages of the tenth century, most of the catacombs were long forgotten, but the monks of St. Michael's didn't forget theirs. They built their fortress directly on top, and expanded the network of caverns and corridors to serve as a final redoubt, should the eternal city ever be sacked again.

Cardinal Saul, archbishop Nano and Sister Maria gathered in the vestibule before a massive oak door set in a thick marble frame. The brick-walled alcove was one of many along an ancient stone corridor, lit by a series of dim yellow light bulbs in the vaulted ceiling. The electrical upgrade was done back in the Fifties, and after all these years the rusted conduit was finally blending in with the ruddy hue of the volcanic rock.

Saul knocked quietly on the door, and Nano took a look around as they waited. The light bulbs were convenient, but they offended his keen Borghese sense of historical aesthetic. Aside from their odious presence, though, everything looked exactly as it did at the time of Constantine. If he were the pope, he'd declare the entire monastery a sacred relic and have it all ripped out—

Varese opened the hermetically sealed door to let them in, and the three of them could smell a trace of antiseptic in the delicate whoosh of escaping air. The oxygen-rich atmosphere was at a slight positive pressure to keep out the microbes that lived in the catacombs. The bomb shelter was originally built in the paranoid Fifties, when the lighting was installed, in an overabundance of caution against a nuclear-armed Soviet Union. The threat was long-gone but the shelter was still intact, and until the *Vaticanistas* had come to stay, the air-tight suite of rooms had been all but forgotten.

"Good evening, Varese," Saul said in a quiet voice, and Maria frowned an admonishment at the cardinal. "*Shhhhh . . .*" she whispered. "The girls are sleeping."

Saul glanced at Nano with an amused smirk. The woman was an argument for celibacy if he ever saw one. Nano got the message loud and clear, and had to bite his lips together to keep from laughing.

Varese smiled diplomatically at Maria, and spoke to her in a quiet voice. "They're fine, Sister." Then he turned to Saul. "You've come to watch the procedure, Cardinal?"

"No," Saul told him, his voice barely above a whisper. "We just wanted to be sure that everything was going according to schedule."

Nano had been looking past Varese during the chitchat, and now that he was actually seeing it with his own eyes, his mood had sobered considerably. He'd known for weeks what the program was, and he knew enough about science and medicine to know that it wasn't some kind of voodoo ritual. Saul wouldn't be wasting his time if it were.

Faith Milano and her two best friends and nine other young women were in a dozen hospital beds set along the gray steel wall. They were lying on their backs and dressed in examination gowns, sleeping soundly under a sheet and comforter in the cool, climate-controlled bomb shelter. Four nuns in nursing uniforms watched over them, scanning their monitors and visually assessing their vital signs.

"We are exactly where we should be," Varese told the three of them.

Devlin lie unconscious on the operating table as Saul and Varese watched Brillstein perform the extraction. The three of them were suited up for surgery and wearing face shields, and the anesthesiologist had been sent out of the room in spite of his protestations. The operating theater nurses went with him, and so it was just the three of them now with the John Doe. Brillstein had given the surgery team a song and dance about how the two gentlemen from Rome were with the U.N.'s Infectious Disease Response Team, and they thought the patient might be harboring a rare strain of Delayed Onset Ebola. He came in on a freighter from Morocco the morning of the quake, and had been wandering in the Haitian wilderness these last few weeks. Thank God they found him in time; the eruptions could happen at any moment.

Saul had never heard of Delayed Onset Ebola, which wasn't surprising since Brillstein made it up on the spot, but it certainly cleared the room. Saul was impressed. It was too bad he had to get rid of the good doctor when they were through; the man was a clever one. He'd send Varese back to take care of things, after they returned to Rome.

Brillstein stood back from between Devlin's legs. The patient's knees were up and splayed apart, and his bare feet were strapped in the obstetric stirrups, which Brillstein always thought was a sexist term. Why couldn't they be called vasectomy stirrups?

He handed the syringe to Varese. It had a horse needle on it, with ten milliliters of Devlin's semen in the collection vial.

Varese handed it to Saul with a sardonic smile. "This is his body, and this is his blood."

Saul took the priceless treasure with both hands and held it up before him, gazing at the pearl-colored fluid. He looked exactly like a priest at the altar, consecrating the chalice, and Brillstein had to smile. The full-spectrum operating lights glinted off the fluid and cast tiny rainbows through the glass, inspiring the cardinal to recite a bit of scripture. "'And his seed shall unite all the Churches under Heaven.'"

Varese was awed by the moment, but Brillstein was unimpressed, and pointed at the unconscious patient. They had to get a move on; his operating staff had been out of the room long enough. "Do you want me to kill him now?" he asked Saul.

The cardinal shook his head. "Not yet; we may need more."

CHAPTER **FIFTY-ONE**

The overhead lights were out, and the ancient vaulted corridor was illuminated by a candlelit procession of virgins. Faith and her friends and nine other beauties were simply dressed in pure white diaphanous gowns. Each of the twelve barefoot girls wore a crown of thorns, carefully trimmed so they wouldn't be scratched or pierced, and they each held a long, stout candle, the flame close to their breasts.

There was no fear or coercion; all of them chose to embark on this transformative journey of their own free will, and each step along the path was taken in tremulous joy and wonder. They had left the world behind and descended into the darkness, holding fast to a warm, glowing light to show them the way. This is the crucible where their lives would change, where they would shed their skin and grow, transforming like a babe in the womb. And when they emerged they would be reborn to a new life as a chosen instrument of the Church, and by the pure radiant light of their love they would transform the world.

Sister Maria was in the vestibule, and as Faith led the procession toward her Maria opened the door, and a quiet rush of air escaped the dark interior. Faith's candle flickered in response and she gasped in anticipation; it was the warm breath of the lover she'd always dreamt of.

She led the others into the dark chamber, where the air was moist and still. The walls and ceiling had been carefully draped in folded fabric, and with the carpets on the floor the room was like a tent in the wilderness.

When they were all inside, Maria closed the door and led them to the center of the room, where four veiled women were tending a bathing basin filled with steaming water. The women had with them anointing oils and combs and perfumes and towels. They were there to serve.

Maria directed Faith to place her candle in one of twelve gold tapers arrayed on an altar. Faith did so and her candle flame lit the crucifix with a flickering honey glow. She genuflected and made the sign of the cross, then rose and turned to basin, ready to begin.

She slipped the gown off her shoulders and it whispered to the floor around her feet. Maria took her hand to steady her, and Faith stepped over the rim into the perfumed water, sprinkled with rose petals. The attendants began to bathe and anoint her body, and purify her essence for the ceremony to come.

The draped fabric and the antique Persian carpets were gone, and so was the ancient Etruscan bathing basin, the altar and crucifix the candles. The nursing nuns were back in uniform and the atmosphere in the shelter was cool and dry. There was still a trace of candle smoke, but that would be scrubbed from the oxygen-rich air in a matter of hours. The only scent that would linger would be the perfume on the girls' skin and hair.

They were fast asleep in their beds now, dressed in examination gowns and lying under the covers. Sedatives were delivered by IV drip, and the monitors tracked their vital signs. So far, all twelve of them were stable, but that could change. No one was really sure what their reaction would be to the injection, so keeping them in a light coma was the safest way to proceed.

The four nurses lifted Faith out of her bed and placed her on an examination table. They carefully rolled her and her monitor stand underneath the operating lights, as one of them held her IV steady.

Varese was sitting comfortably on a tall stool, waiting for his first patient to be wheeled into position. He had a lubricated vaginal syringe in his hand, loaded with a milliliter of Devlin's sperm. There were eleven more laid out on the stainless steel tray beside him. The procedure wasn't anything a doctor was needed for; women inseminated themselves at home every day of the week, all over the world.

The nurses gently bent Faith's legs, raising her knees, and inserted her bare feet into the stirrups. They rotated her pelvis upward so her vagina would hold the injection, and as they did Varese warmed to the task—this was much more pleasant than gazing at Devlin's privates. He used one gloved hand to separate her labia, then inserted the plastic syringe deep in her vagina, and gently depressed the plunger with a smile of triumph.

"'And so we shall regain all that we have lost,'" he quoted from the Book of Devlin.

"Amen," Sister Maria intoned, though she wasn't sure if she'd ever heard the quote before. She crossed herself, and the nurses did the same.

When Varese withdrew the syringe, a single pearl drop fell onto Faith's leg. Though she was unconscious, her brow puckered and she writhed in a swoon of agony. He drew back, a bit alarmed despite himself, and Sister Maria quickly crossed herself again as the nurses held the girl steady and checked her monitor. Her heart rate surged and so did her blood pressure, and there was a storm of activity in her brain stem . . .

Faith was dreaming peacefully in her bed as Saul stood over her like a proud uncle, smiling in satisfaction. He gently touched her abdomen, and when he did her heart rate increased and she sighed in her sleep. But it wasn't the sound of distress or sadness; she was a young woman in love. The blood test confirmed that she was pregnant; they all were. And in nine short months, they would give birth to the future.

Varese was standing with him, proud of his handiwork. Sister Maria and the nurses watched them from across the room, letting the men have their privacy.

"Are you certain the Council will rule in our favor?" Varese asked him quietly, and Saul smiled again.

"They no longer have a choice," the cardinal told him, and then he held his breath, looking down in wonderment at the young lady. Maybe it was the lighting, and maybe his eyes were playing tricks on him, but for a moment it seemed that she heard what he said, and smiled in her sleep.

CHAPTER **FIFTY-TWO**

It was well past his bedtime, but Archbishop Nano was wide awake and restless. He knew he had to get some rest, but he was afraid to take another sleeping pill, especially after the three shots of schnapps that he used to wash down the last one.

After lying in the dark for three hours, listening to the hush of the city leaking through the old window frames, he finally sat up and lit the candle on his nightstand. Living at the ancient monastery had inspired him to forsake modern conveniences whenever he could. There was a monkish simplicity in doing so that brought him a measure of peace, and with the walls closing in on him these last few months he sorely needed whatever comfort he could find.

It was a frosty night in mid-February, and he wiggled his feet into his sheepskin slippers. The long johns he'd brought from Louisiana kept him cozy, and when he padded around in his stonewalled rooms he looked and felt like a hermit. And at this juncture in his life, he dearly wished that he was, but he was in far too deep to extricate himself from the mess he was in. If there were to be any way out at all, he'd have to blow the whole thing up and hope it didn't destroy him in the process. He was never in a fighting war, but he could clearly imagine what it must be like to order an air strike on his own position.

He stood on his swollen feet with the little brass candleholder in his hand, and crossed the carpeted stone floor to sit at his desk against the wall. His laptop was sleeping effortlessly, and he felt a pang of jealousy. He rudely woke it up, and winced from the bright screen as he opened his email client. He knew what he had to do, but he wanted to do it on the phone.

He wrote a simple email—*call me*—and sent it, then picked up his phone and waited. He could have sent a text, but the keyboard on his phone was tiny and he didn't want to fuss with his reading glasses. Then again, it wouldn't have blasted his eyes like his laptop did. He turned away from the computer and blinked away the dazzle, looking out the window at the city.

There was a hill nearby, much like the one he was on, but it didn't have a monastery on top. Most of the windows over there were dark; the people in their apartments were asleep or making love, or whispering goodnight or crying themselves to sleep. Staying up late depressed him—

His phone rang, and his throat constricted in response, but he steeled himself and answered at once.

La Croix didn't even bother to say hello. "You have something for me?"

"Yes," Nano told him, a bit surprised that he was actually able to speak; he could barely breathe. "The future has begun."

La Croix sighed in Nano's ear, and for a moment the archbishop's heart went out to him, hearing such a dolorous sound from such a healthy young man. Then Nano remembered how La Croix had visibly aged when he visited him in his office and told him what was going on.

"I felt you should know," Nano said gently, and though he wanted to apologize for conveying such bad news, he restrained himself. He could hear the man's breathing, and patiently waited for him to speak.

"They must never be born," La Croix finally said. "You do realize that, don't you?"

Nano nodded, but he couldn't bring himself to say anything and the line went dead. He put his phone on the desk and slumped in the chair with a ragged sigh, rubbing his forehead.

His screen saver came on, and he glanced at it. It was the iconic *Earthrise* photo taken from Apollo Eight—the first time that Man had ever seen the entire world at once. The farther he went down the path he was on, the more the image had come to haunt him, but he couldn't bring himself to change it. It was something he knew he had to face, yet he couldn't bear to look at it now.

He turned away, overcome with despair, and he began to weep.

A black Range Rover was parked on the nearby hill, on a dark and narrow cobblestone street between two old apartment buildings. The lone streetlamp was behind the vehicle, far up the block, and most of the people in the apartments were asleep, their lights out for the night.

John Paul Eden had heard the entire conversation over his phone, and the tablet in his hand displayed the Nano's screensaver image. Eden hadn't been able to hack any of Saul's passwords, but tapping into Nano's devices was child's play. Apparently, the archbishop never got the memo that 'password' wasn't much of a password, and neither was '12345'.

Eden thought the screensaver was an ironic touch, since Nano spent most of his adult life not giving a damn about the world. And now here he was trying to atone for his sins. The fallen priest balanced a pair of binoculars on the steering wheel, and cracked a grin when he got them properly focused.

He could see Nano slumped in his chair and turned away from the screensaver, weeping into his palm. But the old man wasn't just weeping, he was blubbering like a remorseful drunk.

It was pathetic. Eden cracked a dark smile as he watched, and was moved to recite Luke 13:28. "And there shall be weeping and gnashing of teeth, when ye shall see Abraham and Isaac and Jacob and all the prophets in the kingdom of God, and you yourselves thrust out."

CHAPTER FIFTY-THREE

Pope John Halo was warm and comfortable in his après-ski wear, a plaid wool blanket over his legs. He didn't ski, but the clothes were perfect for an evening outdoors in February. He was in a teak deck chair on his bedroom terrace at Castel Gandolfo, sharing a bottle of port with Balliez and they watched the moon walking on the waters of Lake Albano. It was a miracle, like all of God's creation, and he saw no blasphemy in acknowledging the allegory or its roots.

The sun worshippers of ancient Rome used to live right down the road, he mused, and they used to say that the sun walked on the waters. And so it did. The early Christians wanted to make their God palatable to those who worshipped Mithras, so they said that yes, the Son of God did indeed walk on the waters. And let us all worship Him together, and celebrate his birth when the Sun comes back, three days after the Winter Solstice, when the days begin to grow noticeably longer.

By the time of Constantine, the worshippers of the sun god Mithras had become worshippers of the Son of God. To John Halo, it was all good, because God's creation includes all of us; we are all the Children of God. And everyone's faith was strengthened, not weakened, as a result.

He toasted the sun worshipper's memory and sipped his port, and Balliez did the same, though he wasn't sure who the pontiff was toasting now. The man's mind didn't wander so much as go on walkabouts, through philosophy and history and who knows what else. But he was one of the finest conversationalists Balliez had ever known. Even his silences were instructive, and if the man was toasting something or someone, it was probably well-deserved. Particularly since he was infallible.

Balliez had his phone to his ear, listening to his call ring on the other end. He was hoping it wouldn't go to voice mail; what he had to say shouldn't be left to a recording.

The call was finally picked up, and Balliez smiled. He didn't extend a greeting, and neither did the person he was calling. It wasn't meant to be rude on either man's part; it was just a routine they'd developed these last few months, a subtle camaraderie across a gulf that could never be closed, at least in their lifetimes. But they were allies nonetheless.

"The man we all seek is in New York City," he said.

"Thank you, Balliez. Give my regards to John Halo."

"I shall, sir. Good night." He ended the call and put his phone away. "Sir Reynard sends his regards."

The pontiff nodded, and lifted his glass to toast the Grand Master of the Rosicrucians. Balliez joined him, this time knowing to whom they where paying tribute. Reynard was a good and honorable man, who cared as deeply about the fate of the world as they did. Hopefully he could do something to stop the madness, because neither of them was sure that Saul was up to the task.

CHAPTER FIFTY-FOUR

The apartment was on Fifth Avenue, which made Devlin's eyes pop in surprise when he heard the news. He still didn't remember much of anything, but for some reason Fifth Avenue registered in his memory. Then Diane explained that she was talking about Fifth Avenue in the Park Slope section of Brooklyn, but it was still a nice place in a good part of town, with lots of trees and delis and restaurants, and a big park just a few blocks east. The only hassle, other than the fact that it was a fourth-floor walkup, would be finding a place for the car; parking in Brooklyn wasn't much better than parking in Manhattan. But there was a garage on the next block and they had a few spaces open. She didn't tell him that it was nearly as much as the rent, but she loved her Maserati and didn't want to give it up.

The GT had taken a beating during the attack in Miami, and as soon as they got out of Miami for the drive up north, they pulled into a rest stop to assess the damage. Dawn was breaking and the place was deserted, so they took their time going over the vehicle. The damage was easy enough to spot—there was a major ding on the rear bumper, and three bullet holes in the glass from two rounds. One went through Devlin's passenger window, and the other came in through the rear glass and exited the windshield. The left side of the back bumper was crumpled from when Diane backed into the motorcycle.

Bullet holes would raise a flag at any repair shop, so Devlin got the bright idea to alter the damage with the tire iron. Diane couldn't bear to watch, and went into the ladies' room to freshen up. While she was gone, he fractured the three windows to hide the bullet holes, and beat on the bumper to change the impact from the bike's front tire.

When she finally came out, he told her that her ex-boyfriend had apparently followed them up the highway, and whaled away on her car before he could stop the guy. Must have been the jealous type, Devlin concluded with a grin. She kissed his cheek to thank him; it was the perfect story to tell the body shop.

They found a place in Juno Beach and the guy seemed like he knew what he was doing. Getting the parts from Miami wouldn't be a problem, and when she told the sob story about her jealous ex, he understood that it would all have to be cash under the table. But he had a lot of insurance work pending, and they'd have to wait a few days before he got to it.

After a bit of breakfast at a diner, they took a walk to the beach and found a rundown motel on Ocean Drive. The clerk took her cash with a smile, figuring she was some rich bitch from South Palm Beach sneaking around on her husband. The room had a trace of mildew, but that wasn't surprising given the seaside location, and it had a kitchenette which closed the deal. Diane had enough cash to travel, so restaurants weren't an issue, but she wanted to keep out of sight as much as possible. They took a taxi to the supermarket and stocked up for a week, and when they were finished putting away the groceries, they spent the rest of the morning making love, while the surf whispered to them through the open windows.

Diane had lost track of the days, but she seemed to recall that their week at the beach was two hailstorms and one Nor'easter ago. It was early April now, and a fresh snow was falling on their Park Slope brownstone, collecting in silent white strips on the rusted fire escape outside their bedroom. It was first light, and the wedge of cold steel clouds that she could see above the building next door reminded her of the rest stop in Florida, the indirect light of the overcast Miami morning on her silver Maserati . . . Devlin stirred, and she realized that he must have woken her up.

She peeked at him, lying huddled beside her, and listened to his breathing. It was shallow and staccato, and his brow puckered and his jaw tensed over and over again. She didn't want to move her head to see him better, lest she disturb him any more than he already was. He was deep in the middle of something and she wanted him to get through it. Sometimes dreams were memories, and sometimes they were metaphors, and sometimes they were all tangled together. But she had faith in the healing process and knew that somehow, if he kept at it, it would all untangle, and then he would know who he was and what he should do. That scared her as much as it gave her hope, but there was no turning back now, for either one of them.

Devlin wandered an earthly paradise, but for all the beauty that surrounded him his heart was empty. All he wanted was to get back into Heaven, and it was a desire stronger than anything he'd ever felt. As he wandered through paradise lonely and sad, the peacock spread his magnificent feathers, and Devlin had an idea. He whispered his plan to the peacock, and the peacock agreed to help.

Proud and beautiful, the peacock strode through the Pearly Gates, held open by the Seraphim. Devlin was walking close behind, hidden by the peacock's plumage. The gates closed behind them and Devlin smiled. He was finally back in Heaven.

But not for long. God found them at once, and there was nowhere to hide, so they stood ashamed to receive their punishment, Devlin with his head bowed and the peacock with his feathers lying limply behind him.

To the peacock's horror, his beautiful feet became gnarled and wrinkled and ugly, and Devlin felt a stab of fear, wondering what punishment would come to him.

But in the next instant they were both back in their earthly paradise, and Devlin realized that his punishment was even worse than the peacock's. At least God had spoken to the peacock, but through the entire encounter He ignored Devlin completely, as if he didn't even exist . . .

Devlin's eyes popped open. He was sweating profusely, and his breathing was hard, shallow, and fast. He turned his head to look at Diane, but her eyes were closed.

He took a deep, deliberate breath, trying to calm himself, and slowly let it out. They didn't have to be up for another hour, but he knew he couldn't get back to sleep, even if he wanted to. And he didn't, not after that. But he didn't want to wake her, either, so he lay there motionless, and gazed the snow drifting down from the leaden sky.

She secretly opened her eyes and watched him.

CHAPTER **FIFTY-FIVE**

He sat on the couch and put on his new running shoes. There was a spring thaw a week before, and after being cooped up in the apartment for nearly two months they decided to take advantage of Prospect Park, four blocks east of them. So they went to the store and got themselves outfitted for jogging, and then the Nor'easter came through town and iced everything up again. And then it all melted, but now it was snowing. He was thinking he should put on his boots instead, but the weatherman said that it would melt away by noon, and Devlin didn't like clumping around in his boots on Fifi's old wood floors. It didn't fit with the tropical vibe of a Jamaican market, and it rattled the cans when he was stocking the shelves.

When he applied for the job, she was pleasant enough, but he didn't sense that she was going to hire him, so he charmed her with some Haitian creole, just to let her know that he wasn't hopelessly whitebread. She was surprised that he could speak it so well; she was from Jamaica but her brother's wife was from Port au Prince, and Fifi had learned enough to where she could halfway guess what Devlin was saying. Something about keeping a roof over his lady's head.

He glanced at Diane and smiled. She was in the kitchen making his lunch, a thick tuna sandwich, a bag of fresh vegetable slices to nibble on, and a winter apple from Florida. She found a Jewish deli by the Metro on Fourth and Union that carried Anna apples; the man's stepson down in

Florida had a little orchard.

Devlin tied his second shoe, then got up and bounced a bit on his toes like he was going jogging, and she smiled, watching him out of the corner of her eye. He stepped into the kitchen and kissed her cheek.

"I think I was a lawyer," he told her.

She turned to him and offered an apple. He took it from her and bit into it, and as he did, there was something about the moment that stirred something deep in his memory, something almost primal. But he didn't know what it was, and he didn't know why it gave him a jolt, but it did. She smiled gently, as if she sensed what just happened, and turned back to what she was doing. He worked on the rest of the apple as a quick breakfast, idly watching her fix his sandwich as he mused over what just happened.

It was occurring more frequently now, since the incident in Miami. Perhaps the memory exercises were working, or maybe it was getting shot by a pack of assailants, but he felt like he was waking up, or that something inside of him was waking up; he wasn't sure which.

"You're still having nightmares?" she asked, as he nodded.

"It's like I'm pleading some sort of case before a judge. But we're alone in a courtroom, or a star chamber, and I can't see his face. And I'm angry, yelling at him, but I'm not out of order, and he just stays calm, talking with me."

"What's he saying?"

"I can't remember."

"It's strange. Almost four months, and barely anything has come back to you. Even in a dream."

"Maybe it's permanent," he shrugged. She didn't answer him, and he stroked her hair with his free hand. "And maybe you are the best thing that's ever happened to me," he continued softly. "Maybe I should just take it on faith and be happy with that, and quit looking for answers when all I need is right here in front of me."

She was suddenly shy, and pulled him close for a hug. They stood there for the longest time, and he put the core of the apple on the counter behind her, swallowing his last bite. He wanted to kiss her hair, but he didn't want to get flecks of apple in it, so he just held her and stroked her back. What he really wanted to do was take her back to bed, but he had to get going and they both knew it.

"I'm thinking of selling the car," she told him, and he pulled back to smile at her.

"Why? You love that thing, nearly as much as you love me."

She shrugged. "I love walking even better."

"Even better than me?" he pouted, and she grinned.

"No, silly, even better than the car! Besides, the train is just as good for getting around town."

Devlin nodded, seeing her point, and stepped into the entry to take his navy pea coat off the peg. They browsed the military surplus store on the next block shortly after they moved in, and he fell in love with the dark blue wool overcoat. It had a double row of big black buttons and enormous pockets, and it was big enough so he could wear a sweater underneath and not feel like he was gift-wrapped.

He shrugged it on, and teased her with a smile. "Exercise will do you good. You have been getting pudgy lately . . ."

She gasped in mock surprise, and then she smiled back. "Well, I'm glad I wasn't the only one to notice. Besides, we could use the money."

She handed him his brown bag lunch as he moved toward the front door, and she followed him for a good-bye kiss.

"Gotta go, I'm running late," he teased her, turning the deadbolt.

She grabbed him by the wide lapels of his pea coat and pulled him close, and they kissed. She could taste the apple, fresh and crisp, like she had taken a bite of it herself.

He unlocked the door and opened it, and went down the short hallway to the top of the stairs, waving good-bye. She lingered at the open door, watching him trot down the stairs.

"I love you," she told him, but he couldn't hear what she said and she knew it. But it didn't really matter; she just wanted to hear it herself.

CHAPTER **FIFTY-SIX**

Devlin came down the front steps, a hand on the railing just in case. The weatherman was right, the inch of snow was already melting, but the concrete underneath was still icy. The sun was warm, though, and the air was catching up to it. Spring equinox was over two weeks ago, and with a bit of luck it might actually start feeling like springtime any day now.

He tucked his lunch under his arm and jammed his hands in his pockets, heading down the block at a brisk clip; he usually gave himself twenty minutes to get to Fifi's, but after the chat with Diane he had less than fifteen . . . he held up short.

Just ahead of him, an old man had his arm wrapped around a street sign. He seemed like he wanted to walk, but was having a hard time finding his footing on the slick sidewalk. He was poorly dressed and had holes in his worn-out shoes, and he clutched a reusable grocery bag in his free hand, but the cloth was nearly as worn as his jacket and he didn't seem to have any groceries in it. An umbrella and a rolled up bit of cardboard was all Devlin could see, and when the man started to slip he grasped the sign pole harder, and the sound of empty cans and bottles escaped from the bag. Maybe he had a stash of food down at the bottom, but from the looks of him he hadn't eaten in a while.

The old man lifted his head in surprise as he felt the comforting weight of Devlin's pea coat on his shoulders, and tried to turn his head to see who it might be. But his arthritis was acting up and he had to wait for the stranger to come around a bit.

Devlin stepped up close beside him, a little in front, and smiled at the man, offering his arm. The man held on, and Devlin dropped his lunch sack into the man's grocery bag. He thanked the young stranger with a nod; his lips were cracked and if he tried to speak they might start bleeding again. Devlin put his free arm around the man's back to keep him steady as they crossed the street to the Baptist church.

Getting up the four steps was a slow process, but once they made the landing Devlin knocked on the door, not knowing the protocol, and waited for someone to let them inside. The old man found it amusing, but he didn't say anything, and eventually a young deacon came to the door and took the man in, thanking Devlin for his charity.

Devlin trotted down the stairs headed off to work, crossing to the sunny side of the street with his hands jammed in his khakis.

Sir Reynard stared after Devlin, utterly speechless. His black limousine was parked up the block, and the entire episode had played out before his eyes. His chauffeur, his nurse, and his two assistants had no idea who the handsome man on the sidewalk could be. But Sir Reynard was visibly moved watching the stranger's act of charity, and they watched in silence along with him.

The simple gesture of human kindness brought tears to the Grand Master's eyes. *But of course he was human!* Reynard chided himself. That was the entire point of him losing his bet with God. Of course he was a man, flesh and blood and mortal and fragile, as human as they all were. As human as the wretched soul he just helped across the street and into the little Baptist church . . . *A church!* Reynard kept blinking, but his nurse knew him well enough to see that he wasn't holding back his tears. He was making sure his eyes weren't playing tricks on him.

"My God!" Reynard whispered. "It wasn't just for us!"

His assistants exchanged glances, and his nurse frowned. They weren't quite following him, but despite his advanced age the man was entirely lucid, and if he said something, it was for a good reason. They listened patiently; there would be more in the moments ahead.

He put his phone to his ear as Antoine started the engine, and steered the Rolls Royce away from the curb, following Devlin down the block.

Isaac La Croix picked up at once. "We're no longer hunting Lucifer," Reynard told him.

"Why the change of heart?" La Croix wanted to know.

"Christ," Reynard told him, but he could sense that La Croix didn't get what he meant, and neither did his personal staff.

"Christ didn't die just for *us* . . .," Reynard said, and he lowered the register of his voice to convey the rest of his realization with as much impact as he could muster. "He didn't come just to save Man, Isaac. He died for the angels, too."

Antoine kept a half block behind Devlin, who was walking briskly, and warding off the cold with his arms tight to his sides. He had no idea that the stretch limousine was silently following him. Antoine had the privacy screen down and was listening to Reynard's half of the conversation, along with the nurse and the two assistants. They couldn't quite follow the conversation, but it was clear that whatever he was talking about wasn't going well, and Reynard was quickly tiring.

The Grand Master was exasperated that he couldn't get across to his knight something that seemed so abundantly clear. But until this moment, it never dawned on Reynard why a king would leave his place in heaven just to come down and be crucified.

It wasn't for Man that He died. He died for all the fallen angels, and for every soul on every planet in the universe. But the angels were the first to sin; they were the first to fall from grace, not Man. Lucifer, the first angel, fell when he disobeyed God, by refusing to bow down to God's creation. But what Lucifer never understood was that God didn't want him to worship Man, but simply show respect.

"Isaac!" he said loudly, and his nurse sat up in alarm. *"Isaac!"*

But the conversation was over. Isaac La Croix, a knight of the rose cross, had hung up on his liege lord. Reynard leaned wearily against the headrest, and his hand fell to his lap with the phone cupped in his palm. It seemed as if it suddenly weighed too much to lift into his pocket.

His nurse felt the pulse in his neck as his assistants slipped off his shoes and massaged his feet, running their hands firmly up his legs to get the blood back to his heart and into his brain. They loved him dearly, and worked their ministrations to ease his discomfort as best they could.

As they tended to him, a realization came fully formed into his consciousness, so vivid that it revived him all on its own. If Lucifer was to be redeemed, he needed to walk his own path as a man. And if he encountered Isaac and Saul on his path, then so be it. Like Pilate, Reynard had to wash his hands of the matter. After hunting Devlin down like an animal, they finally found him. And now that they had, Reynard saw that he was no longer a threat.

The Grand Master's eyes crinkled in a sad smile, and he wondered if Pilate understood that what was about to happen to Jesus wasn't only the will of God, but the will of Jesus as well.

"Antoine," he finally said, in a surprisingly clear voice. "To the airport. It's time to go home and rest." And then he slumped back in his seat, dispirited and heartbroken.

Antoine caught his expression in the mirror and nodded, smoothly turning the corner while Devlin continued straight ahead to the market. Antoine gripped the wheel more firmly than he usually did, and kept himself expressionless. But he couldn't stop the tears in his eyes.

CHAPTER FIFTY-SEVEN

Three black armored Yukons with U.S. Embassy plates were parked along Rue Cavalier. Ledger and Fincannon led four other agents into the building. Captain Petion looked up to them, but he didn't stand. They could wait until he was ready, and then he'd take them upstairs.

He was sitting below his grandfather's portrait, in a chair beside the small table that held the brochures, telling curious visitors about the patron saint of the Le Cap police. A dozen red roses were wilted and dying in the vase, and the water was murky from neglect. Like every year before, no one dared to throw out the roses until the captain said so, and he often just did it himself. But this time he wanted them to lose all their petals first. He couldn't articulate why, but it somehow seemed to be the proper gesture of respect for what he learned in the assassins' file.

Mezadieu was busy at his desk, but he put his pen down as Micheline came into the office, excited about something.

"What is it, mon ami?"

"The dead body!"

"Which one," he asked with a wry twinkle. "We have several."

"The Jane Doe at Labadie."

He frowned, still teasing her. "The first one or the second one?"

"The first one, from the two bodies in the parking lot."

He sat up; she had his attention now. She dropped a file on his desk, and he spun it around and opened it.

"A match? I thought the DNA came back negative."

Micheline broke into a proud smile. "She had a dental implant put in less than a year ago. It was a brand-new model, very high-tech, very rare at the time. I traced it."

Mezadieu glanced up at her; he was impressed. "So it appears the dead *can* talk. And complain about their teeth."

He cracked a grin and looked back down to the file, but as he began reading the summary page his smile dissolved, and as he read further his mouth dropped open in utter disbelief. But there it was in black and white.

"*Ces't impossible . . .!*" he breathed in French, and looked back up to her, speechless. She nodded, already knowing what he just learned.

CHAPTER FIFTY-EIGHT

Diane walked silently through the living room in an old pair of house slippers, wearing a faded sweater that hid her pregnancy. It was an overcast Manhattan day and the lights were out, but she could have negotiated the path from the kitchen to the master bedroom blindfolded, because the furniture in the penthouse hadn't been moved in years.

She carried a bed tray, with two pills and a glass and a bottle of Water Is Life. The ancient glacier water was his favorite beverage, and one of his only extravagances. The penthouse had surprisingly modest furnishings that would make any visitor wonder if he was a pauper, but Count Vladimir Gavorshky had something beyond wealth; he had power. Most people had no idea he even existed, except in legend. He had his hand in many things large and small; he even owned the clinic in Labadie.

Sir Reynard had dropped earlier by to pay his respects, but his nurse just called and said they had to return to Rome. It was a pity; Vladimir enjoyed his dinners with the Grand Master. He was one of the few people who could talk intelligently about the current situation.

"Father, time for your pills."

The retired Orthodox priest lowered his copy of *America*, and smiled at her. He scanned the Jesuit magazine more for amusement than anything else. They had no idea what was going on, but it was fun to see them guessing. Even John Halo. Like most of the men who thought they ran the

Church, he had no idea what was going on, either. Which made him the perfect man for the job, at least for the time being. But times were changing quickly now.

Vladimir pushed himself a bit more erect, wincing in pain. Growing old was a chore. Diane came into the bedroom and placed the tray over his lap.

"Thank you, dear."

She sat on the chair beside his bed, and watched him take his medicine. Each swallow of the ancient glacial melt was blessing; nothing had ever tasted so clean and pure to him. Ten thousand years old, nearly as pristine as the Garden of Eden . . .

He glanced at her, watching her watch him, and she smiled, but it faded quickly. He lowered the glass, waiting for her to tell him what was on her mind. And the more he watched her, the more she fidgeted, until she sighed and answered his unasked question.

"I don't know what I've gotten myself into."

Her eyes suddenly welled with tears, and he reached out for her. She placed her hand in his, and he grasped it.

"You really love him, don't you?"

She nodded, and he glanced at her belly, then back to her eyes, and she learned yet again that there was no use trying to hide something from him. She placed a hand on her swollen belly and nodded once again, and this time the tears coursed freely down her cheeks as she thought about it, just like she'd been doing for the past four months. But she still didn't know what the hell she was going to do . . .

She caught herself using the mental expletive, and for a brief moment, a sad smile crossed her features at the irony.

He smiled back to try to buck up her spirits, but he was secretly as troubled as she was. He knew full well about the forces in play, and had prepared for his entire life to be ready for this critical time in history. But nothing had prepared him for this, because no one imagined that Lucifer himself would be on the road to redemption, the same as everyone else. Because he wasn't the same as everyone else, only now he was.

The Jews were right again, Vladimir thought with a dry, private smile. *Man makes plans, and God laughs.* Rabbi Toaff used to tease him with the Yiddish homily when he was younger and fired up. But now he had to trust that God would see things through. Because Vladimir didn't know what the hell to do either.

CHAPTER FIFTY-NINE

A fax was coming over the wire, and Mark Kaddouri watched the paper curl out of the machine with wry amusement. One of these days, he was going to tell the Office of Motor Vehicles in Baton Rogue about the wonders of email. But he had to admit that OMV faxes did have their utility; when you were bored, you could roll the paper even tighter and shoot spitballs at the June bugs.

He ran the fax over the edge of his desk to flatten it out, and flipped it over to see what it was. He froze when the image finally registered, and as he stared at it he began to tremble with excitement. He laid the paper flat on his desk and read the paragraphs below the picture . . .

That's impossible! he thought. He didn't know it, but barely an hour ago, a police inspector on a Caribbean island more than a thousand miles away had the same response.

Kaddouri spun around in his chair and slid out his keyboard, and whistled up the logon screen to the restricted OMV database . . .

"Hello?"

Johnson sounded like he was napping. Actually, he was meditating, but he was embarrassed about taking up the practice, so he kept it to himself. But he reasoned that if it was good enough for monks and for dozens of saints, he thought he'd give it a shot. Too bad the hippies had given it a bad name.

"We have a lead," Kaddouri told him, and he could hear Johnson groan a bit as he got off his prayer mat on the living room floor, and rubbed the circulation back into his knees. It sounded to Kaddouri like he was getting out of his easy chair. *The man should exercise*, Kaddouri thought. *Or take up meditation, or something.*

Kaddouri moused around on his computer with his free hand as they spoke. "I think I know who helped him," he told Johnson.

"I'm listening," Johnson replied. He was walking around his living room to get the blood pumping, and he was thinking that maybe he should try a little stool instead of a prayer mat, because being in the here and now with knee pain just didn't seem all that therapeutic. But maybe he missed something on the DVD.

"They're in New York."

Johnson stopped pacing. "New York?"

Kaddouri was in the Interpol system now, with a map of Brooklyn on his monitor. There was a marker on a parking garage on Fourth Avenue, a little south of Union. The label read: Maserati GT conv / 2010 / silver / US-FL BLU 361. The owner's address was below that: Viccu, Diane / 265 5th Av #4-D / Park Slope / Brooklyn 11215 / NY-US.

"Park Slope, Brooklyn," Kaddouri told him.

CHAPTER SIXTY

The Fortress of the Three Crowns was a stone's throw from Vatican City, but most people didn't even know that the Shadow Vatican existed. It was at the end of a jagged cobblestone alley, well off the beaten path of all but the most determined tourists. The narrow alley was a carefully preserved corridor into the past that had been permanently blocked off from vehicular traffic. And if anyone did happen upon it, the locals weren't talkative or friendly.

The Rosicrucian sanctuary was a massive structure, an enormous rough-hewn granite cube five stories high, with minimal ornamentation, built in the dark days before the Renaissance. Its small, inset windows were fortified by wrought-iron grillwork on the exterior and backed by thick interior oak shutters. Like the rest of the structures lining the alley, the building had no address or plaque. There was no need for either one; anybody who needed to know was well aware of what the place was and who resided there, and they knew not to come calling unless they were invited, and no one ever was.

It was an unusually warm day in early April, but a wisp of smoke was drifting from one of the rooftop chimneys. Isaac La Croix was alone in the basement, working the blacksmith forge. The stonewalls were sweating in the hot, humid air, and so was La Croix. He was stripped down to a loincloth and leather sandals, and wore a leather apron. His rose and crucifix tattoo was prominent on his back, and so were several scars - a symmetrical pattern from a ritual lashing done in his youth, flailing himself over both shoulders as he wandered alone in the same wilderness where Lucifer tempted Christ.

He pumped the foot-pedal bellows, sending blasts of oxygen into the red-hot coals. The crucifix dagger, forged from what became of the Spear of Destiny, lay in a ceramic trough nestled in the coals, and as he pumped the bellows the eternal metal began to melt. It had taken a long, circuitous journey through time, but now the essence of the Spear was his to wield— the weapon that killed Christ was the only one that could kill Lucifer.

St. Peter was entrusted by Christ with the key to the Gates of Hell, but he knew he couldn't keep it safe; somehow, he had to hide or disguise it. The Romans were hunting him and the other disciples, and Peter knew that it would only be a matter of time before the key would fall into their hands. Begging forgiveness from God, he melted down the key and forged it into a short double-edge sword, much like the original Spear, and he attached a stout wormwood hilt so he could grasp it with two hands if need be.

But he never had a chance to use the weapon. When he was crucified upside down by the Romans, Devlin was among the murderous gang, and he took the sword as a trophy. He went back into the desert with it, the same wasteland where he thrust the spear into the earth, then lost it when he descended into hell. But he wasn't going to make the same mistake twice. This time, he had his own bit of forgery in mind.

Sitting alone before a pillar of fire, Devlin patiently honed the metal, transforming it into a lean, razor-sharp dagger. Later, in a cool oasis by the sea, he sat in the shade of a wormwood tree and patiently formed the dagger's sheath with a block plane and a sanding stone. And then, with a bit of goldsmithing in town, he was finally done; the sheathed dagger was now a crucifix adorned with a golden body of Christ.

Down through the centuries, Devlin kept a close watch over the dagger. Posing as a wandering knight, he presented it to Constantine, and the two of them interred it under the papal throne at St. Peter's, where it stayed for many long centuries, unknown to all but a select few in a cabal of Cardinals. When Devlin made his bet with God he paid a visit to the Basilica, and Cardinal Saul, the head of the cabal, was only too happy to receive him. The hunt for Christ was on and so the dagger was exhumed. As the blade that killed Christ, it was the only weapon that could circumvent the terms of the bet.

But Devlin made the mistake of entrusting it to the cardinal and his secret cabal. When Saul sent it to New Orleans under young Bishop Nano's care, it wound up in the hands of an excitable priest, and was nearly lost forever.

Rabbi Molinari recovered it from Father Vicente in the chaos at the bayou clinic, early on Christmas morning, soon before the Christ child was born. But then the child and the dagger were stolen away by the rabbi and his young assistant rabbi Simone. Devlin tracked his prey for thirty-three years, chasing down one false lead after another, but as close as he finally came, the two catholic converts managed to fool the Devil himself.

In the thirty-third year, Cardinal Molinari finally sent the dagger back to New Orleans, delivered by Father Simone to Archbishop Nano of New Orleans. Nano had been dealing with Devlin the entire time he was hunting Christ, feeding him whatever names Molinari sent him. Devlin hunted each one down, and as far as the world knew there was a serial killer on the loose in the American heartland.

And there was, but there was much more to it than that. Nano knew what was going on, and FBI Special Agent Christine Mas was sniffing around his archdiocese, determined to find out. So Nano was only too happy to give the weapon to Devlin, along with an invitation from Molinari. If Devlin came to Rome, Molinari would tell him who the hidden Christ really was. Nano just wanted it all to be over, and if the next person that Devlin killed really was Christ, then so be it. God worked in mysterious ways.

But Father Jean Paul Eden wasn't the hidden Christ; he was the last decoy, the final sacrificial lamb. FBI agent Christine Mas, the woman who doggedly tracked him for years, was The One. And she was every bit as surprised as Devlin was, when the truth was finally revealed.

When she jumped in front of Eden to save him, Devlin's dagger went deep in Her chest, and She died in Eden's arms. Michael swept Her up to heaven and Devlin was reduced to a mortal soul, wandering the Haitian wilderness with no memory of his true self.

Moments afterward, Isaac La Croix, the Rosicrucian knight, arrived at the Citadel. He had been Christine Mas' guide in Haiti, though she never knew who or what he really was. But Bishop Lomani, the head of the mission, did, and he gladly gave the dagger to Isaac for safekeeping. It was the one favor that Sir Reynard asked of Cardinal Molinari, and Molinari made sure that Lomani understood. After all these centuries of misery and pain, the Grand Master wanted the dagger to be safe and sound at the Fortress of the Three Crowns, and not under the papal throne. Cardinal Molinari and Bishop Lomani couldn't agree more. And as he handed him the dagger, it began to snow in Haiti. It was surely a miracle.

Isaac La Croix grasped the ceramic trough with a pair of tongs, and carefully poured the molten plel into a small modern contraption on a table beside the forge. The liquid metal dripped into a series of tiny cavities in the ceramic base of the device, and he patiently stood by to watch it cool.

When he could finally touch it with his bare hands, he gingerly picked it up and took to another table, well away from the fire, and sat on a stool. There was another modern device on the workbench before him—a manual cartridge press. A dozen shiny brass casings, already loaded with powder, were set in a carousel, awaiting their bullets.

He opened the ceramic bullet mold, and the bullets fell out, molded from the Spear of Destiny. He set each one on top of a cartridge, and carefully pressed them into place one at a time, gently pulling down the lever and then rotating the carousel until the next cartridge was lined up.

When he was done with the last round, he picked it out of its housing and held it up to the firelight to admire his handiwork.

CHAPTER **SIXTY-ONE**

Johnson was packing his carry-on bag, trying to stay focused on the task. He wanted to catch the seven o'clock flight to New York, even though he knew it was a long shot since he didn't have a reservation. But stand-by wasn't that bad on a Wednesday, at least that's what the ticket lady told him when he called. He already called for a taxi, and it would probably arrive any minute now . . .

But first he had to do something. It was on his mind and he just couldn't shake it, and he didn't want to make the call in the cab. There was something he had to know before he dove any deeper, and there was only one person he could ask.

The phone number was on his dining table. He meant to log it in his phone but in all the excitement he forgot. It was scribbled on back of the matchbook from Fan-Fan's Coffee Shop. He took out his phone, sucked in a determined breath, and punched the international number.

Johnson realized only after he dialed that it was after midnight in Rome, but it was already ringing at the other end so he decided he'd just have to be rude and wake the man up.

"Peter?" Simone said groggily. "Do you know what time it is?"

"We know where he is, Bishop Simone. But first you need to tell me the truth."

Simone sat up in bed. If Johnson knew he was a bishop, what else did he know? He kept forgetting the man was former FBI; he just seemed like a wild-eyed country preacher, and no more than that. Simone took a moment to collect himself, and chose his words carefully.

"The Church has declared war on Satan, Peter. It's that simple. And now that he's human—"

"—they're taking their shot," Johnson finished for him.

"Exactly!" Simone said, swinging his feet to the floor and slipping into his house shoes. He knew he wouldn't get back to sleep after this. "So listen to me carefully," he told Johnson, and stood up to walk around his room at St. Michael's. "He's in danger. Now where *is* he?"

Johnson hesitated, not sure if he was doing the right thing, and Simone could hear his breathing, half a world away. He wasn't daring to breathe himself, listening to Johnson's shallow respiration . . .

"New York City," Johnson told him. It was pointless to try to hide it; his flight to JFK could be traced by the Vatican, and so could his rental car. And even if he took the Metro, they could probably access the security cameras. He was still getting used to living in a world where nearly everybody could know everyone else's business. It was amazing that Devlin managed to stay hidden these last two months. But maybe the doctor had something to do with it, if she was even alive.

"Bless you, Peter!" Simone was saying. "You *must* get to him before they do!"

Outside, the cab beeped twice, and Johnson ended the call.

Cardinal Saul strolled through a moonlit graveyard in the courtyard of St. Michael's. It was off in the corner by the penitent's chapel, a dismal little room where sinners had been sent down through the centuries, to recite their penance in the dank gloom so they wouldn't bother anyone. In harsher times, when the only community beyond the monastery walls was in a heathen hamlet or in a band of roving brigands, penance could be a daunting slog that might take an entire season, and sometimes years. The miserable wretches who were buried in the penitent's graveyard had passed away before their penance was complete. It was hoped that they would continue to beseech the Almighty from the grave, to redeem their souls from purgatory. Ghost stories about wandering penitents had been whispered by the monks for centuries, and even in these rational times, no one came to the graveyard at night, so Saul had the place to himself.

As he paced, he idly wondered if he should be buried there; perhaps beseeching God from the grave would work for him. *I should be so lucky,* he thought dryly, and turned with a smile at the sound of a deliberate footstep behind him. If he could hear her approach, she was announcing her presence.

Sama stood in the shadows, and he stepped out of the moonlight to join her in the darkness, leaning close to whisper in her ear.

"I need you again."

"For what?" she asked in mock innocence. His flirtations were amusing to her, so she didn't dissuade him. They both knew he wouldn't dare try to take liberties with her. At his age, a broken hand could take an entire year to heal, and it might not ever function properly after that.

He held her by the shoulders and smiled at her. "We know where he is!"

That captured her interest. Her green eyes lit up with the news, and he slid his hands down her toned biceps. Her body reminded him of a prostitute in Madrid who had been an Olympian gymnast as a teenager. But Sama was far more beautiful, and smarter, too. And probably just as strong and flexible.

"You'll find him," he told her confidently. "I know you will."

She just nodded, but said nothing, and he turned to stand besides her, slipping an arm around her shoulders. "Come with me, my child."

They entered the moonlight, and he gave her a sly smile. "Walking in the light doesn't mean we abandon our old ways." She smiled back, and they strolled through the graveyard speaking in moonlit whispers, disrupting the weary prayers of the penitents beneath their feet.

CHAPTER **SIXTY-TWO**

The weatherman was right. Springtime had finally come to New York City, and as far as anyone could tell it was going to stay this time. The blue-sky air was crisp and clean, a cool version of Miami in winter, but without the threat of humidity that always seemed to lurk down south, where everything was lush and lovely until you dashed up a flight of stairs and melted into a perspiring mess. Devlin's running shoes were broken in by now after a dozen or so runs in Prospect Park, where Diane would come along with him to walk and carry their snacks. She didn't want to jog now that she was pregnant, so he would run ahead and then come back to her, panting and energized and bathed in a sheen of sweat, and it always reminded her of when they made love.

The whole city was in bloom now, and as he walked back to work from a quick lunch at home, he decided to pick her a bouquet on the way back home. He smiled, thinking of the look on her face when he'd surprise her, and turned the corner. He jogged home to have some of her lasagna for lunch, and he was walking quickly to make it back to Fifi's by one. The aroma had filled the apartment that morning, but it wasn't ready to pack into a lunch and she insisted he wait. It was worth the round trip from Fifi's, although hurrying back on a full stomach was making it slosh around inside of him.

Behind him, a black BMW X6 with smoked windows rolled away

from a red curb and came around the corner, and then it slid alongside another red curb and paused. Sama had a silenced M-4 sniper's rifle in the passenger well, with her sweater draped over it. It was a short-barreled carbine, and the shoulder butt was tucked against the center console. Being right-handed, she could bring it to bear through either front window within two seconds and get off a clean, quiet shot. A shot through either of the two back windows would only take an extra second, three at the most. By the time the appropriate window was down, she could already be sighted in.

She rolled away from the curb and glided slowly down the block so she wouldn't lose him, although she already knew where he was going. She'd been tracking him for two days now, to get an idea of his life and patterns, and she already knew that he worked at Fifi's. It was at the end of the block, across the street from a nice little coffee shop. Their espresso was excellent, and she was in the mood for a midday cup.

She touched her phone to call Varese. "How's it going?"

He was staked out on the roof of the building across from Diane's. It was a commercial structure, still half-empty from the downturn at the start of the Great Recession, and the owner was only too happy to rent him a little office on the top floor. It was in the back, though, and it didn't have a view of Diane's building. But it did have an old skylight with large crank-open windows. Varese told the owner that he wanted to paint the place himself, and right after he signed the lease he called a rental yard to come over and erect a small scaffold in the main room. The skylight alarm had been easy enough to bypass, and a half-hour after the scaffold crew cleaned up and left he had his own private access to the roof.

Varese thought that Sama's prep work and reconnoitering was far too elaborate; he was ready to drop both targets when he hit town with Sama two days ago, the moment he laid eyes on the two of them strolling in the park. But Sama was running the operation; she counseled patience, and Saul backed her up. She wanted to monitor the targets for a few days to see who they might be connected to. The way she saw it, the whole thing had taken such a wild left turn, particularly after the fiasco in Miami that she didn't want to leave any loose ends. If they killed them both now, whatever connections they had could slip away and cause trouble later.

So Varese found himself a little alcove on the roof, formed by the water tank and the access shack for the building's front staircase. He was hidden from curious eyes, and it gave him an excellent view of Diane's apartment across the street. He could see her now through the rippled bathroom window, her head and shoulders silhouetted by the white shower curtain behind her. He was in a perfect position for a killshot, through either the bathroom window or the bedroom window beside it. He could have popped both of them last night, when they were cuddled up in bed. Their sex together was quite a show; if he took them out it would have been when they were spooning afterwards. A two-for-one shot would have been a masterstroke, something to look back on and savor in his old age.

But no, Sama had other plans. It was incredibly frustrating, and to make things worse he wanted to be back in Rome tomorrow for the football match with Bulgaria. He tapped his earbud and dutifully answered Sama's call.

"She's in the shower," he told her.

Devlin sprinted the last hundred yards to the market, and now he was out of breath, but at least he was on time. He stepped inside and grabbed his apron from behind the register, smiling at Fifi, who peered at him over her bifocals. She was a plump Jamaican woman in her forties, who was already practicing the fine art of being a crone. She was wild when she was young, but when her husband was cut down in a drug deal she almost lost the store and their apartment above, and the crisis inspired her to clean up her act overnight. Now she was mother hen to a small collection of employees, and Devlin was her latest project. She still hadn't figured him out, other than he was head over heels in love with his woman, and would do anything to keep her happy. So that was the button she pushed.

"Almost late again, Lou."

"Sorry," he smiled. "Thirty minutes for lunch is pretty tight."

"Yeah?" she teased. "Maybe you should start bringing it from home, then?"

He smiled again, and she figured it was a fifty/fifty chance that he didn't have a single bite of food when he went home. She pointed to the back of the store.

"We got a shipment needs to go on the shelves. Go on now, boy, earn your pay." She cracked a knowing smile. "Make your woman proud."

Devlin grinned back, realizing what she must be thinking. "Yes, ma'am."

She watched him walk down the narrow aisle and get to work. *Hell,* she thought, *if he was waiting at home, I'd run there for a quick bite myself.*

Sama had just sat down at a sidewalk table with her double shot of espresso, when her phone buzzed in her pocket. She had a good idea who it was, but she wanted to have a couple of satisfying sips first. She could see Devlin across the street, stocking canned goods on the shelves, and she wondered what he was really up to. The whole scenario, with the little woman at home, and the job and the apartment and the jogs in the park, was just too boring and precious. Any day now, they'd get a kitten, a puppy, and a goldfish. They looked like a life insurance ad. Something was up, and she wanted to know what it was before she acted.

Her phone buzzed again, and she reluctantly pulled it out. Varese sent her a text: *Time to cleanse.*

She pursed her lips and sipped her espresso. The man was too impatient; she had to keep him busy or he'd do something rash. She put her cup down and texted him back: *I'll be there shortly.*

She figured that would hold him for twenty minutes or so. Long enough to finish her coffee and drive over to the building. As she sipped, she thumbed around on her phone and brought up the same Interpol map that Kaddouri accessed. The Maserati was still in the parking garage, one block west of the apartment. She wanted to go through it with Varese before they made their move. They had already gone through the apartment, the last time Devlin and Diane went for a walk in the park, but they didn't find anything of interest. There wasn't anything in the back office of Fifi's Market, either. And if there wasn't anything in the car, Varese would be itching to pop the lovebirds the next time they were in bed. He told her all about the spooning shot he could have pulled off, and strictly from a sharpshooter's point of view, she could appreciate his enthusiasm.

But she wasn't in a hurry to act. She lost track of Diane on the subway the day before, and she wanted to know where the woman went. Maybe it was nothing, but Sama wanted to be sure. Nobody rides the subway unless they were going somewhere; it wasn't like taking a stroll. With luck, Diane would step out again today, and if she did Sama was determined to stay on her trail. She sensed that it wasn't a shopping spree. The woman was up to something.

CHAPTER **SIXTY-THREE**

Diane stepped out of her apartment, and froze in her tracks. Peter Johnson was standing right in front of her.

"Shit! You scared me!" she blurted out, and her hand instinctively went to her shoulder bag. But his hand was already in his jacket pocket, and she stopped. He shot a glance down the hall to see if they were alone, and looked back to her before she could try anything.

"We need to talk," he said.

"I think you got the wrong door, buddy," she told him. "Look, I'm—"

"—a trained professional," he finished for her, but she pretended not to hear him, and took a step to go around.

"So am I," he informed her, and she stopped and looked at him. He had her attention now, and continued in a relaxed tone of voice. "But what I don't get is . . ."

He trailed off with a grin as she pretended to glance at her watch, but looked past it to examine the profile of his hand in his jacket pocket, trying to see if he had a weapon. He learned the old glance-at-the-watch trick when he was a kid, watching Robert Stack on *The Untouchables*. R-Stak was the man; he was the one who inspired Johnson to be a Fed.

"You're slipping," he told her, and she blinked at him. "And you guys *never* slip. What's up, Diane? Or whatever your name is."

She closed her door with a thump and pushed past him, heading for the stairs and he scowled, watching her walk away.

"What the hell happened to you?"

His voice was sharp, a verbal slap on the back of her head. She stopped at the top of the stairs and turned back to him . . . and then she nodded, unable to play it off any longer, and his features softened as she broke into a sad little smile.

"Yeah," she admitted. "What the hell happened to me is right, huh?"

He just watched her, standing alone and fragile, a hand on the railing. She finally looked up, and it dawned on him that he'd seen that look before, in his wife's eyes so many years ago. It was unmistakable, and it was unbelievable, but there it was. Diane was a woman in love.

"I'm on your side," he assured her quietly, "whoever you are," and he sensed that she believed him. He took a step toward her and she didn't back away, so he kept coming closer, holding her gaze the entire time, until he was finally standing in front of her.

"Now where is he?" Johnson asked.

He held onto her arm as they came down the front steps and went down the block, heading for Fifi's market. He didn't sense any fight from her, but his other hand was on the 10mm Sig-Sauer in his jacket pocket, just in case.

It was the same model that Christine Mas used, the weapon that Devlin smashed against the wall when she confronted him in Father Eden's room, at the old Citadel in the highlands of Haiti. Her bullet had just plowed a trench in Devlin's skull, and he just smiled as it healed before her eyes.

But minutes later, when She ascended into heaven with Michael the Archangel, Devlin's head wound had opened up again, and this time he didn't seem to know who he was or how he got there. Johnson could still remember the sound Devlin made, wailing in anguish as he stumbled outside and wandered into the Haitian wilderness.

From that moment on, he decided that his shooting iron was a Sig Ten, especially if he was gunning for the Devil in New York City. It was the weapon of choice of the Risen Christ; accept no substitutes. He was already wearing Her brand of motorcycle boots, too. They didn't go with his suit, but he could care less. He was on a mission for God.

Johnson glanced at the woman he was escorting, but she didn't look back. He didn't know who she was or who she worked for, but the paperwork on the Maserati didn't add up, and neither did the lease on the condo in Miami, or her employment records at the hospital. And the paper trail went totally screwy at the clinic in Haiti. The woman was a puzzle.

"How did you find us?" she asked him.

"Telematics," Johnson said, seeing no purpose in withholding the truth. Diane scowled, but she was angry with herself and he knew it.

"Shit!" she grumbled. "I knew I should have dumped that damn car!"

He cracked a grin. "Are you kidding? Maseratis rule."

She frowned at him, but he just grinned wider. "Lucky for all of us you didn't," he said.

She didn't reply, and he had a feeling she didn't agree with him. He steered her down the sidewalk, and as they walked her shoulder bag kept bumping into him. It was annoying, but he wanted it between them and not on her far side, which is why he took the elbow he did.

They hit a patch of uneven pavement, and the jostling heaved her purse against him again, and he frowned at it. From the way it swung, there was something heavy inside, as if the weight was concentrated in one spot, rather than evenly distributed . . .

Before she could twist away, he dug his hand inside and rooted around, and fished out a compact 9mm automatic. She just stood there looking at him, as he grimaced at himself for not checking sooner.

"Jesus, I guess I'm slipping, too," he grumbled, half to himself, and she cracked a humorless grin as he tucked her weapon in his belt, hidden under his jacket. He took her by the elbow again, and they continued walking. Neither of them said anything for a while, but as they turned the corner she finally glanced at him.

"How did you know?" she asked.

He looked at her sideways and grinned. "About the gun in your purse?" He shrugged, and looked ahead to where they were going. He could see the market's sign on the next corner, across the street from a coffee shop. "It was a good guess," he told her. "Besides, it kept bumping into my hipbone—"

"—No!" she said, cutting through the fun and games. "About everything else."

She watched him, waiting for a reply, but he didn't answer her, his eyes on the market.

Varese was behind them and across the street, just a man strolling through the neighborhood on the pleasant April morning. It was a lovely day and the air was clean and cool, without a breeze, and the sun was pleasant without being a distraction. Everything stood out in sharp relief, and there wasn't a cloud in the sky. He felt good, anticipating the moments ahead; precise targeting was much easier in weather like this.

The coffee shop was on his side of the street, down at the end of the block. Sama was at her table, sipping espresso. Varese crossed the street to get behind Diane and Johnson, widening the angle of a pincer attack in case Sama decided to make their move out here in the open.

After all her tedious reconnoitering, it somehow wouldn't surprise him if she decided to start blasting away in public. She was a strange one. He was still miffed that Saul had added her into the mix, and in any case he didn't like working with women. *Except the young ones in the clinic,* he thought with a rakish smile, and wondered how things were going with all the pretty ladies back at St. Michael's.

Nano was shaking so badly that he was having an impossible time with the rusted door latch, and he nearly burst out with a cry of frustration trying to get into his suite. He knew he had to get hold of himself, but his heart was pounding so fiercely that he was afraid he might have a coronary before he finished what he set out to do.

The first thing he had to do was wash his hands and change out of his white shirt. He stepped into his dark, tiny bathroom and turned on the squeaky faucet and got right to work, not bothering to wait for any warm water; the water heater was a hundred meters from his chambers, and it was pathetically undersized.

He pulled his French cuffs out as far as they would come and washed them along with his hands, watching the thin, soapy blood swirl down the drain. It was pink against the rusted white porcelain sink, indirectly lit by the sunset glow that came through the open door. It was a lucky thing he picked a dress shirt to wear under his black cassock. He usually just wore a T-shirt, but he added a formal shirt with French cuffs to keep warm in the catacombs. It was the same shirt he wore to Isaac La Croix's office and he hadn't yet sent it to the dry cleaners, so he picked it out of the laundry pile and threw it on for warmth. The long cuffs had come in handy getting back into his room, serving as built-in rags to keep the blood off the staircase railings and the door latch. So far as he could tell he didn't get anything on his cassock, but he didn't want to flip on the light and look right now; it was all too horrible. He wanted it to remain in darkness.

When he was finished, he tossed the shirt and the hand towel in the little fireplace in the main room, and buttoned up his cassock again as he sat down in front of his laptop. He had to write an email before his dinner date with Saul; he'd been composing it in his mind since morning prayers.

He first wrote the subject line in all caps: IT IS FINISHED. MAY GOD FORGIVE ME, and then he began to type, slowly at first but then with gathering speed as he got into the body of the message. Within moments, he was oblivious to his surroundings.

The sound of Vespers drifted in through the open window as the Benedictine monks droned their sunset prayers in the courtyard. The sound carried on the breeze as it had for centuries, and drifted through the streets surrounding the monastery. The comforting murmur took the edge off his stress . . .

Thump.

The sound, whatever it was, startled him half out of his chair, and he looked around in bewildered panic, his heart pounding as hard as it did down in the catacombs and during the quick, furtive walk back to his room. He had no idea what it might have been. Perhaps the old monk who lived down the hall dropped a book, or perhaps it was a door he hadn't heard before. And perhaps it was something else entirely.

"My God!" he breathed in a raspy, shaken voice. "What have I done?"

But there was no answer, and he sat quite alone, the room growing darker by the moment as the afterglow of sunset faded. He gazed down at his murderous hands, and it dawned on him that perhaps there never would be an answer. A gathering sense of futility welled inside of him, and he turned back to his laptop and continued in tears, stabbing at the keys with trembling fingers.

CHAPTER **SIXTY-FOUR**

Diane and Peter Johnson stood outside the plate-glass window of Fifi's Market. He still had her by the elbow, but they looked more like a gentleman escorting his lady than an ex-Fed and a wayward physician. Diane was looking inside with her free hand shading her eyes, while Johnson was glancing around at the Park Slope intersection.

Locals were going about their business, and some of them were having a mid-morning cup of Joe across the street. They were mostly middle-class hausfraus with their kids, or working stiffs out of a job. There was also a striking black-haired woman in a tailored leather pants suit at the café, nursing a cup of espresso. A bit overdressed for Park Slope on a Wednesday morning in April, but maybe she was going into the city. And then there was a guy at the newsstand they just passed, browsing the magazine selection. He was wearing sunglasses even though he was standing in the shade, but some people did that; the black Foster Grants seemed to keep his long blond hair tucked behind his ears, and so it didn't blip large on Johnson's radar, though he did notice it in passing.

"Do you see him?" Johnson asked Diane as he scanned the street, referring to Devlin.

"Yes," she replied. She could see him toward the back of the store, still stocking shelves. He had no idea they were outside.

Johnson followed her gaze, and braced himself as he finally laid eyes on Devlin, involuntarily squinting as if his left eye would start to burn. But nothing happened, and he scowled, getting a good look at him. An as he did, a chill went up his spine. Because after all these years, Devlin hadn't aged a single day.

It was a few minutes after midnight on Christmas morning in 1976, and the maternity ward of the old clinic on the Louisiana bayou was a disaster area. A freak storm had just passed through, bringing a tornado that plowed a trench along the side lawn and laid waste to the parking structure. The windows of the maternity wing were blown out and the doors were off their hinges. The air was alive with fluttering papers, the lights were out, and the emergency generators hadn't kicked in. The staff and the patients were downstairs, wailing in panic on the front steps, but Johnson didn't hear any babies crying, either downstairs with the staff or up here on the ward.

He had charged up the stairwell in a mad panic, but he was too late, and found his pregnant wife's warm, dead body in room Three. Their baby had been cut out of her and thrown against the plaster wall, and lay in a bloody heap against the baseboard. A noise down the hallway shattered his frozen horror, and Johnson's training kicked in. He drew his Colt .45 longslide and edged out the door.

Devlin had stepped out of the nursery, dressed in a black greatcoat and handing a bloody knife to Zamba, the enormous voodoo priest who had pried the door open. There wasn't a sound coming from the bassinets behind them.

They walked toward the back stairwell, lit by a dim red emergency light at the nurses' station, midway in the hall. Johnson ordered them to halt, and Devlin turned back and came toward him. Johnson closed his right eye, took aim, and fired six shots into the approaching silhouette. But they had no effect and Devlin kept coming, and as he stepped into the pool of red light, Johnson briefly laid eyes on the Devil himself. His left eye began to singe, and he cried out in pain and dropped to his knees as Devlin came closer, six shafts of red light piercing his ageless body.

Johnson still sent Christmas cards to the sheriffs who charged up the stairs and chased the Devil away. After all these years, he never did figure out why Devlin disappeared when they came; maybe he'd get a chance to ask the evil bastard today.

"Get him out here," Johnson told her in a thick voice. "Quickly!"

She struggled against his grip on her arm, and glared at him. "I can't, if you won't let go of me!"

He lightened up a bit, but he didn't let go, and spent a long moment debating if he should. But he decided to try something first. He rapped on the glass with his free hand, trying to get Devlin's attention, but Fifi was at the register and she was the one who heard them. She looked up from her newspaper with a scowl, wondering who was knocking on her damn window.

Johnson knocked harder, and Devlin finally looked up as well. The first thing he saw was Diane, and he broke into a smile. An instant later, though, he saw that some older guy had her by the arm, and Devlin became alarmed. He dropped the cans back in the box and sprinted down the aisle, untying his apron as he passed the counter.

Fifi was on her feet now, watching him rush by. Her hand went down for the cell phone, but in her mounting panic she couldn't find it.

Devlin raced out the door, tossing his apron back in the store, ready for a fight. "Hey!" he shouted as forcefully as he could. "What do you think you're—"

Johnson had his Sig-Sauer pointed at Devlin. It was hidden from the people on the street by Diane's body, but Devlin's shout had drawn plenty of attention and there were eyes on them now, all up and down the block and across the intersection as well.

"Let's go somewhere quiet and talk," Johnson suggested, and as Devlin stared wide-eyed at the weapon, Johnson's initial terror of facing the Devil dissolved. "*Now,*" Johnson added pointedly.

Devlin nodded and put his hands up. Johnson wished he hadn't done that, because the moment he did some of the people who were watching them screamed, and several more began to flee in a disorderly scramble. They were making a scene, and Johnson didn't want one. They had to leave quickly. "Look," Devlin was saying, his hands high in the air, "Whatever I did, I don't remember doing it."

Johnson was about to herd them out of the area, but he had to pause a moment, wryly shaking his head. "Oh, trust me. You did it. *All* of it. You did plenty, pal."

He motioned for Devlin to put his hands down and start walking, and kept a firm grip on Diane as Devlin went ahead of them down the block. The people who hadn't fled the area had their cell phones out, some of them taking photos and video as the others were calling 9-1-1. Fifi peeked out of the market with her cell phone pressed to her ear, waiting to talk to the cops, but like everyone else on the street, she was on hold.

Back up the block, Varese passed through a crowd that had come out of a barbershop, and he followed Johnson and his two captives. He glanced across the way at the coffee shop, but Sama had already disappeared. She'd call him; he didn't have to call her. He set his phone on vibrate and slipped it back in his breast pocket, near his silenced Glock.

Johnson, Diane and Devlin were around the corner now, walking on a side street where things were quiet and no one had any idea that something was amiss. Diane tried to pull her arm free, but Johnson was stronger than she thought. Plus he had a gun, and he had hers as well.

"Please!" she pleaded with him. "Let us go, before the police get here!"

Devlin was looking back at them, and Johnson motioned for him to stop. He complied, and Johnson tipped his head toward Diane. "She's not who you think she is."

Devlin looked at her, puzzled, but she wouldn't meet his gaze. Johnson could see he was genuinely in the dark, which told him a lot about Devlin, and the situation he was in. The amnesia noted in his records back at Labadie probably wasn't a ruse, then. Johnson thought at first that it was, but now he concluded that when Christine Mas's bullet grazed his head, it really did shut down his memory. Which meant that Bishop Simone wasn't exaggerating—Devlin was now for all intents and purposes a mortal man, walking the earth with no recollection of his past, or any knowledge of his true identity. It blew Johnson's mind, but there he was, the Devil incarnate, standing right in front of him with a bewildered look in his all-too-human eyes.

"You really don't remember me?" Johnson asked him, and Devlin shook his head, mystified.

"All right," Johnson said, blowing out a lungful of air. "God help me, but . . . okay."

He shook his head as well, hoping all the pieces rattling around up there would fall into place, but as much as he tried, he couldn't quite believe that he was standing on a sun-dappled sidewalk on a pleasant April day, talking with Satan himself. Or whatever he was called, now that he was severed from his past and his core identity, or his immortal soul, or whatever the hell it was that defined him. Johnson smiled briefly at his choice of mental words. *Hell, indeed.*

But they couldn't stand there all morning shooting the breeze about it. He looked around, and spotted something. "Follow me," he told Devlin, and took Diane by the arm toward an alley. He was fairly certain about Devlin now, but he was still leery about his woman, and before this was over he intended to get to the bottom of her story as well. As far as he was concerned, the whole thing stunk to high heaven . . .

There I go again, he thought.

CHAPTER **SIXTY-FIVE**

Johnson took them to the far side of an overloaded trash bin, where they would be hidden from the street. He wanted to take a moment to get some things sorted out. Extracting them from the area probably wouldn't be a walk in the park, and the less internal fussing between them the smoother it would go. Then again, it could just make things worse, and though he acknowledged that his curiosity might have shaded his decision, so be it.

He had finally let go of Diane's elbow, and Devlin had his arm around her now, holding her close. As pissed off as she was at Johnson, she seemed like she'd rather just disappear into Devlin's embrace. It looked like they were sweet on each other, but Johnson was old enough to know that relationships could turn on a dime. Even if both of them were angels— *Damn! There I go again,* he mentally chided himself.

"Whoever blew up the Vatican wants you dead," he told Devlin, who stared at him like he was crazy. "I'm just trying to stay out of the line of fire." Johnson glanced at Diane. "Go on, tell him. Spit it out."

Devlin looked at her, completely puzzled, but she shook her head. She wasn't being obstinate; Johnson could see an edge of regret in her features more than a sense of reluctance, and Devlin noticed it as well.

Johnson kept his eyes on Diane, but he spoke to Devlin. "Ask her— How did I find you?"

Police sirens were drifting in the air now, bringing a sense of urgency to their conversation. Devlin was lost, and he looked to her for answers. And he wanted them soon, before something else happened.

"I don't understand," he told Diane, urging her to explain.

"Go on," Johnson told her. "Tell him, 'Diane.'"

Devlin caught the tone in his voice, and watched her, waiting for a reply. For something, anything . . .

But she kept her eyes downcast and remained silent.

"Diane?" he asked. "What's going on?"

Her face grew red and he could feel her shaking, and a tear swelled in her eye, then ran down her cheek as another one formed. "I . . . I . . . wanted to tell you," she stammered quietly. "I wanted to tell you so *bad . . .!*"

"Tell me what?" he encouraged her.

Ffftt.

The silenced round just missed his head, and punched into the hollow brick wall behind him. He had no idea what it was, but Diane and Johnson did, and they dropped behind the trash bin, pulling him down with them.

Johnson peeked around the side of the bin, and as he did he drew Diane's gun from his waistband and handed it to her. "I believe this is yours," he said.

She gripped it, smoothly toggling off the safety and sliding it open to verify there was a round in the chamber. Devlin was watching her in astonishment.

"Since when did you . . .?"

"Long story—"

Ffftt. Another silenced round passed close by and shattered another brick, and they pressed themselves harder against the wall. The sirens were much closer now, echoing through the neighborhood, and one siren in particular seemed to swell . . .

A blue and white NYPD cruiser swerved into the alley, its siren blaring and its lights blazing, and screeched to a halt several meters from their position. The front doors flew open, but before either cop could emerge two silent shots penetrated the windshield.

Devlin stared at the deadly result, unable to breathe. The cops were slumped in the front seat, with blood streaming down their faces.

"Wait here," Diane told him, and moved out from behind the bin.

He turned to her in alarm, but she was too far away to hold her back. "No!" he yelled. "What are you *doing?*"

She stood erect in the alley and leveled her pistol at Varese, just as he was turning back to them after shooting the cops. She had a half-second's edge on him, but that was all she needed.

"You've been a bad girl—" he began, trying to buy a moment of time, but Diane put a round in his chest before he could finish his sentence.

"Really?" she said, as Varese stared at her in shock. Still crouched behind the bin, Devlin jolted in surprise, wincing at the sharp explosion from her 9mm.

"Am I going to hell?" Diane asked Varese, stepping closer. He tried to raise his weapon, but she dropped him with a headshot, and Devlin recoiled again, staring at her handiwork as she turned back to him.

"Come on, honey," she said, offering a hand to help him up. "Let's go." But he just stared at her, unable to speak.

Johnson had no trouble expressing himself. "Not without me, you're not," he told them bluntly, and got to his feet.

Devlin finally took her hand, and she pulled him up. He slipped his arm around her, and they looked at Johnson, wishing he'd disappear.

"And don't give me none of that 'three's a crowd' jazz," Johnson added.

More sirens were approaching, and Devlin looked to the sound. "We gotta go!" he urged them, and they ran farther into the alley.

They came to a T-intersection, and went to the right. But as soon as they were around the bend, Devlin stopped and grabbed Diane by the arm, turning her to face him.

"He *knew* you!" he said, barely able to believe it. She wouldn't look him in the eye, but there was no denying the truth.

"That man!" he said. "He recognized you! You *knew* him!"

She tried to pull free of his grasp. "We have to *go!*"

Johnson watched them, itching to get a move on.

"I *know* that!" Devlin shouted, and she finally looked at him. It was the first time he'd ever gotten angry with her. He took a breath and lowered his voice. "What's going on?"

She didn't know where to begin. "I'll tell you later," she said, trying to placate him. "But we need to get out of here!"

Devlin looked at her . . . and nodded. They turned and ran with Johnson to the far end of the alley, and slipped around the corner.

CHAPTER SIXTY-SIX

On the other side of the Atlantic, evening had come and Rome was aglow, glistening from an April shower. Cardinal Saul's black Phantom limousine had been cleaned and detailed inside and out, and it idled silently at the curb, gleaming under the streetlights. The restaurant was one of Nano's favorites, and the early bird specials were a bargain.

The chauffeur held the back door open, and as they got in, Nano nodded a thank you, but it wasn't Marcel. The older man had a trim gray moustache and the placid eyes of a seasoned servant. He shut the door silently and went around to the wheel, got in, and glided the limo down the street.

Saul had already settled back in his seat, and Nano sat beside him, his eyes on the new chauffeur. "What happened to Marcel?" he asked Saul, who was unwrapping an after-dinner mint. He popped it in his mouth and methodically folded the wrapper into a tiny square as he spoke.

"He's a little under the weather," Saul told him, and dropped the foil square into the pristine ashtray.

Nano settled back and gazed out the windows at the city. "Where are we headed?" he asked, but Saul's phone beeped before he could answer. Saul squinted at the display, and grunted. The text message from Mother Maria said *Come quickly.*

"We need to make a stop," Saul told him, and pressed a button on his console. "St. Michael's."

The chauffeur nodded and smoothly entered a roundabout with the other traffic. Nano was nervous, looking out his side window.

"Not to worry," Saul assured him, continuing the muted conversation they'd been having over roast pork and asparagus. "Once I'm sitting on the Papal throne, things are going to be much different."

Nano wasn't particularly reassured by that, and Saul smiled.

"How will you persuade the Council?" Nano asked him.

Saul's smile turned into a condescending smirk. "Nano, please. What would become of the Council if the whole world knew that the first Council of Rome altered the original manuscripts? Every last one of them? What would become of the 'Good Book' then?"

Nano didn't have an answer for him. They were on a quiet boulevard now, and he watched the buildings glide by, some of them dark for the night, others with residences illuminated for family dinner.

"The manuscripts were adulterated beyond measure," Saul said bluntly, and Nano looked back to him, sobered by the blunt statement. "The Council has conveniently buried that fact," Saul told him, "and after all these centuries, they—" he pointed to a stream of people entering a church for evening mass "—have no idea. None whatsoever."

"But how can you be sure?" Nano asked him, and Saul smiled again, like a patient father explaining the world to his naïve son. "Because the true meaning of Jesus's teachings were never lost . . . " He trailed off, hoping that Nano would figure out the rest.

And he did. The archbishop sat erect in his seat, his eyes widening with a flood of realization. " . . . but carefully hidden," Nano finished for him, and Saul waited to see what else he would piece together. Nano turned to face him squarely, and asked a direct question.

"You found the original manuscripts?"

It was more of a statement than a question, and Saul grinned in triumph, nodding over and over.

"You actually *found* them?" Nano asked again, and Saul assured him again with a little nod of his chin.

"'And whosoever shall hold the True Doctrine of the Faith' . . ." Saul began, and let Nano finish the famous quote. " . . . 'shall hold the One True Church, and he shall lead all the nations unto the Lord our God.'"

"Amen," the cardinal said. He blessed Nano with a knowing smile, and in spite of himself, Nano shivered. Saul softly chuckled, and patted him on the knee. *Maybe he was worth keeping, after all,* Saul thought. *He's starting to get it.*

The chauffeur turned left and started up the hill to St. Michael's. He'd been eavesdropping the entire time, but his expression never changed. The cabin's console mic was defaulted to mute, but the wiring had been easy enough to bypass when he detailed the car that afternoon.

CHAPTER SIXTY-SEVEN

Devlin, Diane, and Johnson had circled around by Prospect Park, and were approaching Fifth Avenue from the east. Johnson's Sig-Sauer was tucked behind his back, under his jacket, and Diane's 9mm was in her purse again. It looked like they were coming back from the park after an energetic power walk. Sweaty people walking quickly and catching their breath was a common sight in the neighborhood, and the people they passed didn't think twice about it.

Devlin gulped down a lungful of air and breathed it out slowly to steady himself. Diane could hear him, and sensed that he was about to say something. Johnson glanced at them, and he couldn't help but be amused, despite the mess the three of them were in. They seemed like such a normal young couple—a driven professional and the handsome devil she fell in love with.

"Tell me what's going on, Diane," Devlin said quietly, but his voice was firm.

She didn't reply and he glanced at her, and so did Johnson. She was walking in the middle, and the longer she delayed the more overtly they watched her, until they both had their heads turned and were looking right at her. But, still nothing. Johnson caught Devlin's eye.

"That's not her name," Johnson told him, and Devlin scowled back. As far as he was concerned, Johnson was butting into a private conversation.

"Shut up," Devlin said, and looked back to Diane. But there was something in her expression, and what Johnson told him sank in.

"Wait!" Devlin said, looking at them both. "What?"

He focused on Diane, and she seemed to shrink into herself, avoiding his gaze.

"She's not even a doctor," Johnson informed him. "But she can play one on TV."

Devlin slowed his pace, but they didn't, and he was compelled to catch up, looking at them as he tried to make sense of what he'd just been told. Diane had worked on him and with him for months now, everything from psychological counseling to physical therapy to stitching his head wound. And she was accepted by the staff in Labadie and Miami, reviewing his case with their personnel, right in front of him. He knew that fake doctors existed—he couldn't remember how he knew, but he did—but he never had a moment's thought about her credentials. And it didn't seem that anyone else had, either. The only thing that gave credence to what Johnson said was that Diane didn't protest when he made the claim, and now she wouldn't look at either one of them. It wasn't a good sign.

With each passing second, Devlin grew more angry. Johnson was watching him, and growing more nervous by the second. The last time he saw Devlin angry, it didn't go well.

Devlin stopped in his tracks again and frowned at Johnson. This time Johnson stopped as well, and his heart began to pound, and his hand was poised to draw his weapon in case things went south. Diane stood still, but a little behind them, watching the two men.

"Why are you here?" Devlin asked him.

"Believe it or not, I'm here to save you," Johnson explained.

"Yeah," Devlin said, nodding impatiently. "We saw that. But why?"

Johnson didn't answer him, and glanced at Diane instead. So did Devlin. She resumed walking, and they flanked her. It was her move now, and all three of them knew it.

"The Church wanted you alive until they were done with you," she finally told Devlin. "They're done."

He was mystified. "Done with what?" he asked, but she didn't answer. "Done with *what?*" he persisted, but she wouldn't look at him.

"Diane?"

She took a shaky breath, and kept her eyes on the sidewalk as they approached Fifth Avenue. "Diane Viccu is dead," she said quietly.

Devlin stared at her, and then he looked at Johnson. The retired Fed nodded, then tipped his head toward the woman walking between them.

"She killed her," Johnson told him.

It was a clear day in early January, and the rental jeep was dusty from the dirt road that ran across the base of the peninsula. The doctor from Miami discovered that Labadie wasn't even a small town; it was a fishing hamlet, nestled in an emerald crook of jungled hills. The clinic's parking lot was one of the few patches of asphalt in the entire village, and when she finally parked in the shade, it took a few moments for the dust she brought with her to dissipate on the ocean breeze.

She gathered up her purse and a thin manila folder and got out, smoothing her suit with her free hand. She was parked at the far edge of the lot, mostly to keep the jeep in the shade, but also because she wanted to take a walk to steady her nerves before she went in the clinic and presented herself to Dr. Weist.

Brillstein had flown in last night, but there was an issue with his passport and he was working with a man from the American embassy to resolve the situation. The country had been in chaos since the quake, so they were choppering down to Port au Prince to get it sorted out. Brillstein suggested that she should just go ahead by herself and get started with the patient; he'd catch up with her in a day or so. The John Doe had been out of the jungle for three days now, and he was still delirious.

Before she began her walk to the front steps, she took a moment to look around, and smiled at the tropical wonderland. It was a tranquil corner of the world, the perfect setting for an amnesiac to get his bearings. Their volunteer work had taken them to some dismal places, and a trip to paradise was a welcome relief. They'd been expecting to be asked down to Haiti ever since the earthquake, but they thought they'd end up in Port au Prince, not here on the north shore. Nothing happened up here except for a few heart attacks, some broken china, and a lot of rattled nerves. But the State Department wanted both of them on this case, and so they figured that the American who had wandered out of the jungle must be someone special, even if he didn't know who he was. They didn't know who he was, either, and the woman who called them from State wasn't at liberty to divulge his identity.

The doctor turned toward the clinic, but before she could take her first step she was clocked from behind by the butt of Diane's pistol.

Diane caught the doctor as she fell, folding her arms around the woman so the contents of her manila folder wouldn't go fluttering away. Aside from her name badge and ID, the doctor's walking papers were the most important thing to salvage. Diane had already hacked the woman's cellphone, and her partner's as well; that was the easy part. But now she needed to scoop up their real-world odds and ends, including their bodies.

She dragged the unconscious woman to an old van and opened the rusted sliding door. A man lay crumpled inside, the back of his skull a soggy mess of half-dried blood. His nametag said 'Dr. Brillstein'. Diane set the woman's purse and manila folder on the front passenger seat, and rolled Dr. Viccu inside the van.

CHAPTER **SIXTY-EIGHT**

They were still walking toward their Fifth Avenue apartment, but Devlin was staring at the woman beside him as she relayed the grisly details in a series of stark, unflinching statements.

Johnson just stayed out of it. Their relationship was something for them to sort out. But Devlin needed to know the truth, and she finally seemed willing to tell him so Johnson wasn't about to interrupt. Diane wasn't looking him in the eye, but at least she was talking . . .

Or whatever her name was, Johnson grumbled to himself.

"Diane Viccu was a Doctors Without Borders volunteer," she was explaining to Devlin, and Johnson cracked a humorless grin. For all he knew, Devlin would never know her real name, and neither would he. Deep-cover operatives were like method actors. For all intents and purposes, she *was* Diane Viccu. Or at least she was now.

"She specialized in amnesiacs, working out of Miami," Diane elaborated. "We . . . I . . . stole her identity."

She removes their nametags and emptied their pockets, and then she checked for jewelry, or any tattoos or identifying marks. Cutting away their fingerprints was as easy as minor office surgery, but removing their teeth took longer than she would have liked. Dr. Viccu had several implants, and separating the crown from one of them was particularly difficult.

The van was at the bottom of a dry ravine, beside a remote dirt path in the highlands. The sun had shifted, making it easy to see what she was doing, but it was getting awfully hot now and the flies had become a nuisance. The bigger problem, though, were the wild boars. They would be attracted to the scent of blood, so she worked as quickly as she could.

When she was finished, she laid her latex gloves on the woman's corpse, and packed everything into a small backpack—their fingerprints and teeth, their cellphones and jewelry, his wallet, her purse, and their walking papers. Then she poured a can of gasoline over the bodies, saturating their clothes and the old carpet they lay on. She placed the empty can inside, and then backed away and tossed in a match.

The fire roiled behind her as she walked quickly away, putting on the knapsack. She rolled a scooter from behind a bush and started it. There was a dirt trail leading down through the ravine, to a rutted country road far below. If she made good time, she could be back at the hotel in Cap-Haitien by sunset, then first thing in the morning her and her partner would arrive at the clinic in Labadie, rested and ready to play doctor.

Devlin didn't know what to say, and Johnson found himself feeling sorry for the poor bastard. It wasn't every day that the woman you fell in love with told you stories like that. *It would rattle any guy with half a heart*, Johnson thought, and he imperceptibly shook his head at the irony. Here he was, having some sympathy for the devil, thinking he actually had a heart. But the look in Devlin's eyes was unmistakable; his sweetheart wasn't nearly as sweet as he thought she was, and it knocked him for a loop, as Robert Stack would say.

They were on Fifth Avenue now; their apartment was just a few short blocks away, and she was finally looking at Devlin as she spoke. He was the one staring at the pavement now.

"Those assassins got in the way," she told him, and he glanced at her with a puzzled frown. But she waited, and he blinked as her meaning finally dawned on him.

It was a little after two in the morning, and Diane was in the nurses' station, leafing through Devlin's file. She glanced up at the sound of approaching footsteps, and smiled hello at Jonathan Kurinski and Janice Avery, pretending she had no idea who they were. As they approached his door, she slipped into the back room, speed-dialing Brillstein on her cell.

By the time the assassins had entered Devlin's room, Diane was outside on the lawn. Her first silent bullet punched through a window slat, wrinkling the air between them. She usually never missed, but there had been a sudden flash of white on the jalousie slats, cast by the moonlit surf behind her, and her target was momentarily obscured. Her second round narrowly missed as they dropped to the floor, and she had to move in quickly.

Devlin had rolled out of bed in a panic, and was on the floor as well. But his luck was with him—he kicked Jonathan in the solar plexus, throwing him up and toward the window. Diane's third bullet punched through the glass, blowing out the back of his skull.

Minutes later, out front by the parking lot, she tracked Devlin in the darkness the same way that Janice did, from the moonlight glinting on the revolver he picked off the dead security guard. Devlin thrashed through the undergrowth as their silent rounds punched through the palm fronds from both directions. He angled away from the clinic on a narrow footpath and melted into the jungle, as Diane hunted down the second assassin.

They crossed Fifth Avenue, and as they turned toward the apartment, Devlin and Diane were finally looking at each other. Johnson thought that was good progress; the three of them might even bond as a team, to get through whatever it was they'd be going through . . .

"I was supposed to kill you myself," Diane told Devlin, "after they got what they needed. Then tie up all the loose ends."

. . . *not if she kept saying stuff like that,* Johnson grumbled to himself.

CHAPTER **SIXTY-NINE**

Saul held the syringe aloft with both hands, gazing at the pearl-colored fluid, like a priest at the altar consecrating the chalice. Diane stood by the door, so the nurses couldn't peek through the window. Now that the extraction was complete, Brillstein offered to kill Devlin on the spot. Dying on the operating table wouldn't raise an eyebrow, even at the American embassy. But Saul stayed his hand. He and Varese had to fly back to Rome right away; Sister Maria had all the girls ovulating at the same time, and tonight was their special night. But artificial insemination wasn't a surefire method, so they might have to come back for more.

Several days later, Saul texted Diane and Brillstein that all twelve girls were pregnant. It was morning in Rome, but first light in Labadie, and Devlin was sleeping under heavy sedation after a harsh bout of nightmares. His IV drip needed to be changed any minute now.

Diane slipped into his room while Brillstein stayed in the hallway, keeping an eye out for busybody staffers. Most of them were snoozing in the lunchroom, but every now and then one of them would keep themselves awake by checking on the patients.

Diane stood beside his bed, a large syringe in her hands, and drew air into it. The needle wouldn't wake him up, particularly in his drugged condition, and the embolism would be short, sweet, and undetectable. He'd been stuck with so many needles already that the puncture wound would never be noticed . . .

But she just couldn't do it.

She stepped out to the hall, where Brillstein was trying out some Creole phrases with the fisherman. The old man had been keeping vigil outside Devlin's room, and Brillstein thought it was the kindly gesture, but it never set well with Diane. As she walked past them, the old man paused to smile at her, and she saw something in his eyes. Although it didn't make sense to her, the perception was unshakable: *He knew who Devlin was.*

And then she remembered what Brillstein told her. Miss Meljean said that the fisherman was the son of the village pastor, and they both had powerful voodoo. The locals said that one caught fish and the other caught souls. And the pastor thought that Devlin was an omen; he wasn't like other men. First there was the earthquake, and then there was a snowstorm—A snowstorm in Haiti! They still couldn't believe it!—and then a white man with no history comes down from the highlands. It was like the end of time, or the beginning of a new time, the pastor wasn't sure which, but his son was keeping vigil to watch Devlin and learn what he could.

Diane couldn't take Devlin's life; she had seen his true nature and she understood his dreams, even if he didn't. She knew why he was here, and because she did, she knew that the fisherman was dangerous. This simple old man could ruin everything, and not just for her, but for the entire world and everyone in it. He was a loose end, and he had to go.

And then she had to get Devlin away from there, before Brillstein realized that she turned. Devlin's passport would be coming any day now—when she called Fincannon over the secure State Department line, he had no idea that he was dealing with the Black Pope's daughter, the man behind the President, the man who chaired the Illuminati Roundtable, the man who could shut down a terminal at Miami International, or a freeway, with a phone call.

And yet, for all of Vladimir's power, even he couldn't stop all the forces at play. Diane had gone to New York to tell him she was in love, to convince him that Devlin had changed, and she asked him what he could do. But as much as he wanted to help her, it was one call he couldn't make, because God didn't have a phone number. All they could do was pray.

They walked in silence for several seconds, giving Devlin time to absorb everything. He was clearly traumatized, and Johnson almost felt sorry for him.

"Why?" Devlin asked her. It was the only question he could articulate.

"I don't know why, exactly. I have an idea, but . . ." She trailed off, shaking and ashamed. "I had my orders," she said weakly.

"No, why—"

"I just *told* you!"

"—didn't you just kill me?"

Diane looked at him and smiled, and stopped walking. He stopped beside her, and she reached out to touch his cheek, but he shied away. It broke her heart, but she couldn't blame him, though he instantly felt sorry. But it was done and there was no taking it back. Johnson felt awkward, standing so close to them. It was one of those moments that couples should have to themselves.

"Because I fell in love with you, that's why," Diane was telling Devlin. "I could easily have killed the monster you were, but I couldn't kill the man you had become. You're not the same, Lou."

Johnson frowned at the name . . . and then he got it, and grinned. Devlin caught the look, and glared at him.

"What's so funny?"

Johnson wiped the grin off his face, and didn't answer him. But that just made Devlin angrier than he already was. He'd had it with the psychological fun and games, the memory drills, the dream journal, the pills, the yoga, all of it. They knew something, and he was more than tired of guessing what the hell it was.

"*Who <u>was</u> I?*"

CHAPTER SEVENTY

"Damn . . .!" Johnson breathed. He exchanged glances with Diane, and then he looked back to Devlin. "You really don't know, do you?"

Devlin shook his head and shrugged. He was completely clueless, and Johnson believed him. It was impossible, but there it was. The retired Fed took a deep breath, and plunged in headfirst.

"You're not Lou," he informed him. "You're Lucifer. The Prince of Darkness and the Lord of Light, all rolled into one."

Devlin stared at him, utterly speechless, and for a crazy moment Johnson thought the poor fellow was going to faint. But he was frozen in place, looking at Johnson like . . .

Johnson thought of a way to describe it, and cracked a ghost of a smile. *Like I just told the sorry sonofabitch that he was the Devil himself.*

He kindly smiled at the younger man, because the truth of the matter was, he was beginning to like the guy. Even though, Johnson cautioned himself, that was usually the first mistake that people made when consorting with the Devil.

"Maybe God really did have mercy on your soul," he theorized.

But Devlin was utterly astounded, and the jocular remark fell flat. "I'm . . . who?" he stuttered. *"Who?"*

He looked at Diane, but she didn't know what to say. She saw it was one hell of a shock, but she couldn't think of a way to soften the blow.

"Lucifer? Are you freaking *kidding me?*"

Johnson soberly shook his head no, and so did Diane.

Devlin was stupefied, and shook his head as well. *"None* of this makes any sense!"

He was staggering around on the sidewalk, reflexively touching his head wound and trying to get his bearings. She wanted to hold him, but he had to find his own balance in this. He turned to her, incredulous, but this wasn't another one of his nightmares. This was all completely real, right down to the love in her eyes. He reached out and touched her cheek.

"At least you could tell me your real name."

She smiled at her man, and gave thanks to God that she could finally tell him the truth. But as she opened her mouth to speak, a silent bullet sliced the air between them.

It narrowly missed her, and punched harmlessly through Devlin's sleeve. Unlike his puzzlement in the alley, he knew what sailed past him this time.

Diane and Johnson drew their weapons in a fraction of a second and turned to look at a rooftop across the street. She used her free hand to pull Devlin behind the engine of a parked car, as Johnson threw himself into a tumbling roll. He came up in a crouch beside the engine of a Cadillac they just passed a moment before. He amazed himself for launching into such a maneuver at his age, but like his instructor at Quantico told him years ago, adrenaline was the wonder drug. Always have some on hand.

They spotted the shooter up on the roof, and Johnson was certain that it was the woman he saw at the café. The guy Diane killed in the alley was the same guy at the newsstand, so a pattern was emerging in his mind. He just hoped they didn't have a third wheel.

Diane fired three quick rounds and Johnson did the same, and then they held their fire, waiting for the shooter to respond. But Sama hunkered down in Varese's alcove, recalculating her options. She missed her target, and she never missed. Something was wrong.

"Do all churches do this?" Devlin shouted, his fingers in his ears.

"Yeah," Diane said without shouting, and he took his fingers out to hear her. "Most of them, at one time or another," she explained. "Souls are big business."

"Ever hear of the Crusades?" Johnson asked, but Devlin shook his head no.

"The Spanish Inquisition?"

Devlin had no idea.

"The War of the Roses?"

The man shrugged.

"Ever hear of Jihad?"

But Devlin didn't have a clue. Johnson glanced at Diane.

"Maybe he really does have amnesia."

Diane shrugged with her hands—that's just what she figured.

"Probably a blessing in disguise, all things considered," Johnson concluded. "Can you imagine the nightmares?"

Devlin glanced at her, but she didn't say anything.

Sama peeled off another quiet round, and Johnson returned fire, backed up by Diane, peppering the lip of the roof across the street.

Devlin could see residents peeking out their windows, their cell phones in hand. He desperately looked around for an escape route, and something caught his attention. There was someone on the sidewalk back from where they came, and he was walking right toward the three of them. He was a handsome young black man, dressed in a leather jacket, with no shirt, and he wore black jeans and Roman sandals. With his eyes locked on Devlin, he drew an automatic pistol from a shoulder holster and deliberately racked the slide.

"Oh, *shit!*" Devlin said. "Is he on our side?"

Diane turned to see what he was talking about, and a murderous look came to her eyes. "Rosicrucians . . . " she seethed, and pivoted to face Isaac La Croix.

He was already bringing his weapon to bear on Devlin. The errant knight had nine rounds in his magazine and one in the chamber, each one forged by his own hand from the Spear of Destiny.

Diane swung her weapon around, but Devlin was blocking her view. Isaac could feel the power, and his aim was steady and true. The blood of the Savior flowed down through the years and into his heart to guide him, a river of eternal life bursting upon this singular moment.

Sama fired three quick, silent rounds, and to her utter astonishment, each one of them missed their mark. She grimaced at herself and glanced to heaven. On the sidewalk below, Johnson crouched tighter against the car as her rounds cut the air over his head. She lowered her rifle, and reconciled herself to the inescapable truth. This had to play itself out, as surely as the crucifixion did. She put her weapon down, and bore witness to the confrontation below.

Diane moved in front of Devlin for a better shot, and he realized what was about to happen. "No!" he shouted. "Please, God . . .!"

As Isaac La Croix squeezed the trigger, Devlin pushed her out of the line of fire. And in that instant, La Croix thought to himself, *"When you get the Devil in your cross-hairs, don't think. Shoot!"*

Isaac's firing pin hit the primer, and the plel bullet raced down the barrel, spiraling as it went. Dark clouds blossomed in the sky above as a fragment from the Spear of Destiny launched toward its intended target, trailing crimson flame.

The slug hit Devlin full in the chest, and he dropped to the pavement in front of Diane. Her anguished scream was eclipsed as lightning exploded above them, and the heavens began to weep.

CHAPTER **SEVENTY-ONE**

It was drizzling as Cardinal Saul's black limousine rolled through the cordon of Italian Special Forces guarding St. Michael's. The Vatican reconstruction project was lit up down the hill, and the sodium lights illuminated the roiling clouds above, casting an eerie yellow glow on the quiet cobblestone plaza before the main gate.

Sister Maria was waiting for them out of the rain, standing in the pedestrian archway beside the gate. It was clear to the ISF guards that she was distraught over something, and if she were a common citizen of Rome they would have offered her shelter in the warm guard shack. But their years of Catholic schooling taught them that when nuns were dyspeptic it was best to leave them be.

The limo glided to a halt at the curb in front of her. The old chauffeur was about to get out and open the back door, but Nano hopped out and beat him to it, holding the door for Saul. The chauffeur caught Saul's eye in the mirror, but Saul motioned that he could stay behind the wheel.

Nano was jittery, like he'd drunk a pot of coffee over dinner, instead of sharing a bottle of wine with Saul. The cardinal was growing tired of him; he was like a nervous lap dog that barked for no apparent reason, and then sulked when you didn't respond. And now he was hopping out of the car like he had ants in his pants. *Perhaps it would be best to cut him out of the herd, after all,* Saul thought darkly.

He got out, and even as he stood erect Sister Maria was rushing down the three stone steps to the sidewalk. Given her girth, it was amazing how quick she was on her feet. But there was something in her eyes, and he dispensed with his grouchy ruminations. Something must have happened.

"They're dead!" she told them in a forceful hiss, afraid that the guards or the chauffeur might overhear. But she could barely contain her distress. "All of them!" she emphasized. "Murdered in their own beds! Lord in heaven . . ."

Saul was genuinely stunned, and Nano pretended to be, as best he could. But now that the discovery had come, he wondered if he could maintain the right balance of alarm and bewilderment. He was well versed in palace intrigue, but mass murder was something new to him.

The vestibule behind her had captured her voice and funneled it into the guard shack. The two commandos inside picked up their assault rifles and stepped outside to see what the matter was. Sister Maria and Saul turned to them, and it gave Nano a moment to try to quell his pulse, but the effort was futile. He was still hanging onto the open door of the limo, and he put his other hand on his racing heart, and swallowed repeatedly in a dry, clenched throat as the soldiers came down the steps.

Two blocks away, above a bakery, Father John Paul Eden lay on the tarpaper roof, dressed in his old black priest's cassock. With black pants and shoes, and a black watch cap, he was virtually invisible, and so was his silenced Heckler & Koch MSG90.

He sighted through the scope, watching Nano. *When a man kills, he thinks he is God,* Eden reminded himself. *And you must put a bullet in him to convince him otherwise.* He quelled his breathing, and began to slowly, gently squeeze the trigger . . .

If Eden had known the true source of his torment, Simone would have been in his crosshairs, not Nano. For all the names that Nano gave to Devlin, Eden's wasn't one of them. Cardinal Molinari was the one who told Devlin that Eden was the hidden Christ, and Father Simone was the one who delivered the dagger, sealing the deception. Devlin tracked Eden down, massacring nuns at the Church of the Rebirth in New Orleans before coming to Haiti. Nano had finally been tried and found guilty, but for the one thing he didn't do. And now his execution was at hand.

This is for Sister Nancy . . .

Ffffftt.

"Reuuescat in pace," Eden whispered.

The bullet punched through Nano's hand and then into his chest. He thought he was having a heart attack, and looked down in shock. But there was a neat puncture wound on the back of his hand, like a miraculous stigma, and he smiled at the incongruous sight. A gush of dark blood was running down his shirtfront from under his hand, and it coursed down his black pants and onto his shoes. The drizzling rain washed it into the cobblestone gutter, but more of it kept coming.

Saul frowned, catching his stupefied expression as the man stared down at his shoes, and then Saul saw the hole in the back of Nano's hand. As Nano's knees gave way, Saul dove into the back of the limo and pulled the door closed behind him.

Wrenching it free from Nano's grasp robbed the archbishop's stability, and he dropped to the pavement in front of Maria and the soldiers. They had no idea what was going on, until Maria's forehead exploded from Eden's second round.

As the soldiers crouched beside the limo, Saul was on his knees in the back, and struggled into his seat as he screamed at the chauffeur. "Drive!" he told him. "*Drive!*"

The man did as he was told, and punched the gas. The sudden acceleration threw Saul back in his seat, and he turned and looked through the rear window in panic, searching in vain for the shooter as the two guards scrambled for cover. Several rounds pinged off the trunk and windows, and Saul instinctively flinched and ducked, though he knew the rounds couldn't penetrate the armored limo.

The guards were scanning the rooftops for the shooter, even as their comrades on the parapet above switched on their searchlights and swept the neighborhood. But the area beyond the plaza was a warren of old buildings, and the rooftops had been host to a jumble of retrofits. There were a hundred places to hide, but it wouldn't take long to dial in the sound. In the APC parked in the plaza, the tech sergeant was busy triangulating the sound of Eden's rifle. Within moments, the coordinates were relayed to the men on the lights, and they tightened their search.

But Eden was well hidden, and by the time they found the roof he was on, he had already pocked the limo with several ricochets, and slipped away as the turbocharged Rolls squealed out of the plaza. Eden had disappeared into the darkness, his heart filled with hatred. In order to find him now, they'd have to seek the Devil first.

Though he knew he was safe, Saul was badly shaken from the assault. He finally sat back and took a deep breath as they wound down the hill through the medieval neighborhood. His hands were trembling and his entire body was so tense that he was afraid he might reinjure his ruptured disk. He had to calm down and think, but before he could take another breath his cellphone beeped. He ignored it, but it beeped again, insistent, and he pulled it out of his jacket pocket, as much to distract himself as anything else.

He didn't have his glasses, and squinted to read the text message . . . and then he read it again. As it sunk in, his eyes widened with a resurgence of stark fear. The message was simple: *Only God forgives.*

He looked up from the phone, wondering who the sender was. It was a restricted number, and there were more than a few people he dealt with who chose that option . . .

The chauffeur was watching him in the rear-view mirror, driving dead center down a quiet neighborhood street. Saul scowled at him, wishing he'd pay better attention to his job, but the man boldly held his gaze. Saul scowled more fiercely, and when he did the corner of the chauffeur's eyes crinkled in response. *He's smiling at me!* Saul realized, and then he realized who sent the text.

"No!" Saul shouted. "*Fuck!*"

The chauffeur had already set the cruise control. He shouldered his door open and rolled out of the car, pushing his way out so forcefully that the door sprung back and slammed itself closed. All four doors locked with a decisive, audible *clunk* as the Rolls continued straight ahead down the quiet street, motoring at a stately clip.

Saul was frantically pulling on the door handle, but he was trapped and he knew it. He finally gave up and sat back in his seat. The car was off the hill now, and the street ran straight and level toward the Vatican, its construction zone lit like a stadium. He closed his eyes and made the sign of the cross, exactly as he did when he blew the place up. Now it was his turn to die.

The chauffeur had come to a nimble halt on the smooth asphalt, his leather jacket like a second skin, and he was on his feet now, his own cell phone in hand. "Curse all you want," he said in response to Saul's panicked cry, and launched an app. "The Devil himself can't save you now."

The inside of the armored limo erupted in a fiery explosion, but the high security door locks held fast and kept it all inside. Pedestrians scattered in alarm, staring in disbelief as the Rolls passed them by. The fireball in the passenger compartment was hell on earth, and Saul was pressed against the window, silently screaming as the ruby flames devoured his flesh.

The limo plowed into a fire hydrant and came to rest over the torrent of water. But the fireball continued to rage inside the vehicle, even as great clouds of steam billowed from its melting black paint. The flames were fed by a tank of compressed air under the jump seat. Keeping a fire going inside a hermetically sealed vehicle required a bit of improvisation, but his many years in Swiss Intelligence had served Balliez well.

He pocketed his cell phone and turned away with a smile, gingerly peeling off his false goatee, and the second skin that had aged him more than twenty years. It had taken him three hours to apply it, before he left Castel Gandolfo that morning. John Halo joked that he looked like a child molester, but Balliez thought he looked like a Victorian-era magician. With a last glance at Cardinal Saul's funeral pyre, the pope's chauffeur slipped into a black alley and disappeared.

CHAPTER **SEVENTY-TWO**

It was raining in Park Slope, a gentle, steady downpour. Diane was sitting on the curb between the parked cars, with Devlin laid across her lap. "Oh, baby, what did you do?" she wailed softly. "No! No! No, don't leave me . . .!"

He gasped for air, and she could hear the gurgling in his lungs. Though she wasn't a licensed doctor, she knew he was dying, and she began to weep uncontrollably.

Isaac La Croix laughed, watching her. "I had to see this to believe it," he told her and Johnson, but they ignored him. "It's amazing how human the Devil can look," he remarked, and Diane couldn't let that one go.

"He *is* human!" she told him, and tenderly stroked Devlin's head. "He lost the bet, Isaac. You could have let him be. Who are you to interfere with God?"

"And who are you?" La Croix retorted with a laugh. "The killer the Devil brought home to mom? Was that part of God's plan, *cherie?*"

He just chuckled, dismissing her. Johnson got to his feet, standing behind the Rosicrucian. He figured it was safe now; Devlin was down, and the shooter on the roof had ceased fire, after the third wheel had rolled up from behind and taken out the target.

He could see Diane, sitting on the curb with Devlin in her arms. They're the perfect image of the Pieta, and he was transfixed by the image. It was exactly how Father Eden looked when Christine Mas lay in his lap as she was dying at the Citadel, after being stabbed by Devlin with the crucifix dagger.

Though Johnson didn't know it, the weapon had finally come full circle. It was the spear that Michael used to consign Devlin to hell, and after centuries of subterfuge and transformation, a piece of it was lodged in Devlin's chest and he was dying in the arms of the woman he loved, the daughter of the Black Pope, who had sent her on a mission to kill the Devil himself. But for all of Vladimir's careful plans, his daughter had fallen in love. And so it was the errant knight of his dear friend Reynard who finally fulfilled the Prophesy, and the man had done it all on his own.

Devlin whispered something, and Diane leaned close to hear him. "Are you okay?" he repeated a bit louder, and she nodded, smiling bravely. "Yeah, baby," she told him. "I'm okay. You saved me."

He forced a smile, and she bit back a cry of anguish as blood leaked from his mouth. "Now we're even," he told her.

He tried to laugh, but he choked and coughed up blood. Diane whimpered, and when he closed his eyes and tried to breath slow and steady, she glared up at La Croix. He found the entire situation laughable, and she was so angered by his heartlessness that she picked up her gun and turned it on him. La Croix back-pedaled but it was too late. She pulled the trigger—

Click.

He relaxed again, and threw his head back, laughing at her misfortune. "It's just not your day, is it?"

Diane dropped her weapon, defeated, as Devlin rallied, opening his eyes. "I love you," he told her, and she looked down to him and smiled.

La Croix was aiming his weapon at Devlin now, but Devlin kept his eyes on Diane, and she just gazed back at him. If they were both going to die, the last thing they wanted to see was the one they loved—

"Drop your weapon."

Johnson had his Sig Sauer pressed cold and hard against the back of La

Croix's skull. The errant knight froze, but he didn't comply with the order, and Johnson cocked his weapon.

"I will not hesitate to put a hole in your fucking skull. Now drop it."

La Croix slowly lowered his weapon, and turned to him. "Do you realize you're trying to save the Devil?" he asked the older man.

"The thought occurred to me," Johnson admitted.

La Croix nodded, and then he glanced at the roof where Sama was hiding . . . and reacted.

Johnson flicked a glance at the rooftop, and that was all La Croix needed. He swung his weapon up and fired, but he missed as his shoulder suddenly exploded, the impact of Sama's bullet knocked him to the ground.

He dropped his weapon, and it skittered into the street. Johnson kept his Sig Ten trained on him as sirens approached the neighborhood, and muttered under his breath. "Damnit, *I* wanted to shoot him."

Devlin started shaking in Diane's arms, and she looked at him strangely. Something was happening, and even Johnson saw it. A gentle light surrounded Devlin, and as it grew more intense, he smiled. The pieces of the puzzle were finally coming together.

"I remember now . . ."

"Let there be light," said God Almighty, and a burst of light filled the void. "And you shall be called Lucifer, the Lord of Light."

Lucifer stood tall before the throne of God, and pointed at God's creation. "I will not bow down to Him!" he declared. But he wasn't pointing at Adam. The mortals who wrote the Bible were mistaken. Lucifer was pointing at Jesus as he spoke, and God said nothing.

The angels trembled in dread with their heads bowed low, waiting for Lucifer to be rebuked. None of them had ever seen the Almighty, they had only heard his Voice. Only Jesus and Lucifer could look upon the face of God, but they all knew that God was displeased. For if Lucifer was the Lord of Light, Jesus was the Lord of Life and Death, the first and last, the Alpha and the Omega.

But Lucifer had spoken what he felt in his heart, and now he awaited the judgment of God. How could he worship the Son, after having seen the Father? His heart was pure, and filled with love for God Almighty.

And still, he was cast out.

Devlin stood behind Adam in the Garden, whispering to him with a voice that only his soul could hear. Adam was hungry, as all humans were — for sustenance, for power, for knowledge and pleasure. There was an apple in his hand, sweet, ripe and luscious, but as he bit into it, the apple rotted away. He turned to Eve, anguished and crestfallen, but her smile was cold. That would be the way of the world from this moment on, with Lucifer always watching and whispering, close behind . . .

Devlin stood before God Almighty, bathed in pure light, their bargain finally struck. The terms of the bet were simple—whether Jesus could return to earth with no knowledge of his true identity, and achieve divinity in modern times. Devlin could hunt for Him, but he couldn't stop Him or kill Him; he could only lead Him into temptation.

Devlin's intent was clear: When he could show God that even God-as-Man would go astray, it would vindicate his refusal to bow down to Man, God's flawed creation. The prodigal Prince of Darkness would be reconciled with the Father and his exile from heaven would be rescinded, and he would once again be Lucifer, the Lord of Light, first-born of the angels.

Just to be clear, he reiterated the terms of the bet. "If I win, you will un-create Man."

"And if you should lose," God said, "you will carry His cross."

Christ was well hidden, and it was only in Her last moments of life that Devlin realized who She really was. When She saved Father Eden by throwing Herself in the path of Devlin's crucifix dagger, Devlin finally knew. Only the dagger forged from the Spear of Destiny could mortally wound the returned Christ, but by then it was too late. She had selflessly given her life to save someone, without knowing Her eternal reward. Her divinity was achieved, and he was fated to suffer the consequences of his pride and foolishness.

Christine Mas lay dying in Father Eden's arms, and as Her mortal life slipped away the voice of God filled Devlin's soul. "They are all my children, Lucifer. Any one of them is capable of what she has done. That is the lesson you were too proud to learn."

Then Devlin's head wound opened up, and when he saw the blood in the mirror he realized that he was human, but to his horror he had no idea who he was. He left the Citadel wailing in anguish, and wandered into the Haitian wilderness, and when he was gone, a cleansing miraculous snow began to fall. And when he finally emerged on the shores of Labadie, he was lost and all too human. And he had no idea that he was now the hunted one.

CHAPTER SEVENTY-THREE

Devlin could hear the sound of angels, a hum that was quiet and deep, like the wheel of the world turning on its axis. He could see them clearly, though none of the others could. Devlin looked up to heaven to give thanks, and the rain came down and washed him clean.

Sama had worked her way unnoticed to the next roof, and was watching the activity below through her scope. From her high angle, she saw something that Devlin, Diane, and Johnson didn't notice. Isaac La Croix was inching toward his weapon, while Johnson's attention was on Devlin and Diane.

Devlin remembered something else. Jesus gazed down from the cross at him in the crowd, and only Devlin heard His voice. "I die for you," Jesus told him, and then He turned his gaze to heaven. "It is finished," He declared, and then he died, and the War in Heaven was finally over.

A soft rain drifted down on Devlin's upturned face, and he smiled. He knew what it was; he could feel it. Jesus and all the angels in heaven were weeping for joy. God was watching with them, and at that moment it finally happened—the universe stopped expanding.

Devlin was saying something to Diane, but his voice was soft and Johnson leaned closer, straining to hear him.

"I understand," Devlin was telling her, as tears streaked down his cheeks and dissolved in the rain. "The One who died for us all . . . I understand now."

Diane nodded. She was crying as well, and as she looked down to him her tears fell on his cheeks and mingled with his.

"Annabelle," she told him.

"Annabelle?"

She smiled and nodded, and then she shrugged. "That's my name," she said, and he managed a weak, dying smile.

"Annabelle," he repeated. "The apple of my eye . . ."

Annabelle smiled as if she could read his mind, and then she began to weep. Johnson forlornly watched them as the sirens drew closer, and pulled his FBI badge out of his jacket. It hung from his neck like a kid's ID tag on a day trip from school.

Sama could see them in her scope, but her crosshairs were on La Croix as he inched closer to his gun. "Anyone worth shooting is worth shooting twice," she reminded herself, and wrapped her finger around the trigger. "See you in—"

She stopped in mid-thought and panned her scope back to Devlin and Annabelle.

Annabelle was utterly astonished to see Devlin gradually disappearing from her arms. The glow around him surged as he turned into a ghost, and then a vapor, and then a sprinkling of silver dust, and then he was gone.

"Flawless!" Sama breathed with a smile.

Johnson had seen the miracle once before, when Christine Mas ascended into heaven at the Citadel, but it still astounded him, and he made the sign of the cross along with Annabelle.

Sama saw the same thing, and when Devlin was finally gone she pulled back from the scope and laughed. It gave away her position, but she didn't care. Her mission was a success. She had kept Devlin safe until he could fulfill his destiny, exactly as she set out to do, but she wouldn't have believed it if she hadn't seen it with her own eyes. She recalled the exact moment that she learned her assignment . . .

It was raining that morning in St. Peter's Square, a little before Christmas in 1976. Devlin was dressed in his black greatcoat, unseen by the mortals around him. But Sama wasn't one of them; she was one of his own, and like his other fallen angels, her greatcoat was white. They traversed the crowded square as if it were empty, sending a cold shiver up the back of everyone they passed through, as the paving stones sizzled beneath his feet.

"And if you should lose?" she asked him, her glowing white-hot eyes crinkled in a mirthful smirk. From what she could see, Devlin had just maneuvered himself into a corner. Making a bet with God wasn't something she would have recommended, had he bothered to ask her.

But Devlin didn't, and now that the deal was done he just smiled confidently. He knew what she was thinking, as he always did. But she rarely anticipated his thoughts or reasoning, even though she was the best he had.

"I *can't* lose, Samael," he told her with a crafty smile. "Think it through, oh Angel of Death!"

She did . . . and when she finally put it together, she smiled back.

Of course! she realized, and then Samael the Angel of Death looked around at all the earnest people in the St. Peter's Square. They had no idea what was at stake, but someday they would understand.

If Satan had a chance to be redeemed, anyone did.

CHAPTER SEVENTY-FOUR

Sama gazed at the humans on the sidewalk below, and her white-hot eyes crinkled with the same mirth now as she remembered the rest of their conversation. *"Even if you win, you lose, my Lord. The world will have changed you."*

She took out her phone and speed-dialed Saul's landline. He always turned off his cell at night, and she wanted to wake him up with the news.

Across the Atlantic in Rome, in Cardinal Saul's suite at St. Michaels, the bedside phone rang and rang, but no one picked up. It was the final hour before dawn, and gravediggers had been quietly at work in the courtyard below.

They stood now in a freshly excavated grave, carved into the patch of grass outside the penitent's chapel. The coffin at their feet was open but there wasn't a body inside, just a collection of ancient books that Cardinal Saul had salvaged from the sub-basement of the Vatican Secret Archives. The diggers brought clean gloves with them, and were gingerly removing the priceless artifacts from the coffin, placing them in an open vault on a pallet beside the grave.

Simone was seated on a bench outside the entrance to the penitent's chapel, a lantern beside him so he could read from the original Book of Devlin in his lap. A pocket Bible lay open inside, and he turned to the Book of Revelations. Verse 118 caught his attention. The Second Coming wasn't to be a happy affair. *"Once I was dead, now I am alive,"* Jesus said. *"I hold the keys to death in Hell."* And then Simone's attention landed on a verse from the Book of Devlin. *"He isn't my God!"* Lucifer said of Jesus. *"I will not bow down to him!" And with those words a war broke out, and Heaven was changed forever . . ."*

The War in Heaven was nearly unimaginable to him. *The two greatest experiences in life are being born and dying,* Simone finally concluded. *And for all we know, death could be the greater of the two.* He watched the diggers as he savored the passages, and the subtle way they were linked. When Saul's charred remains were scraped out of the back of his limo, they could be interred in the manuscript coffin. It would be a fitting and proper resting place for his miserable bones—

His cell rang, and he took the call at once. "Hello?"

"It is finished," Sama said, and he frowned at the odd sound of her voice. But there was nothing wrong with the satellite or the cell tower. For all his time in the Church, Bishop Pablo Simone had never heard the voice of a fallen angel before.

"And so we begin," he said to her, and ended the call. He gently closed the Book of Devlin, and watched the diggers load the Doctrine of the One True Faith into his private vault. He didn't envy their labors. When they were finished, they had to wrestle the vault full of heavy parchment manuscripts up to his suite. And then they had to gather the secondary texts that Nano had been hoarding all these years, and fill a second vault. Once all the busy work was done, Simone would be sitting on the crown jewels of the New Church. And then it didn't matter who sat on the throne of St. Peter. He would let them be the lightning rod, while he stayed in the shadows and whispered, in a voice so soft that only the pontiff's soul could hear.

He had a fairly good idea of how things were going to unfold. That's what Revelations was all about. Jesus would come back in glory, and neither saints nor sinners would survive. But for all his Biblical scholarship, Bishop Simone still had no firm idea of what would happen, or when. Reading the Book of Delvin, he realized that it was alive. That it would reach up and grab your soul, and challenge your faith. Simone curled his lips in a dry smile and glanced to heaven. *"When are you going to finish what you started?"* he wondered, but as usual God didn't answer his query. Simone sighed, and concluded once again that he would just have to leave it at that.

There was light coming from the basement windows across the courtyard, and Simone watched the arched pools of illumination flicker with shadows. The work in the maternity ward was nearly done; the mess would be gone before morning prayers.

A pair of ancient oak doors were quietly opened from inside, held by two of the nursing nuns. The other two stepped quickly ahead to the passageway that led to the back gate, with armed members of the Italian Special Forces accompanying them. Their ISF van was idling in the alley, and they had doused their lights before they arrived. It was truly awful; twelve innocent acolytes murdered in their sleep. The terrorists had struck again, after boldly killing Sister Maria, Archbishop Nano and Cardinal Saul just hours before.

In a silent procession, twelve nuns wheeled the twelve gurneys outside, a black body bag on each. They crossed the courtyard and went down the passageway, where the nurses who went ahead held open the back doors. Their soldier escorts scanned the alley, then waved them to come ahead.

Simone couldn't help but smile, watching his plan unfold before his eyes. The best part of it was that Nano, of all people, had played such a pivotal role. And when his work was done, Father Eden was more than happy to put Nano out of his misery . . .

Simone shook his head, lightly admonishing himself. He kept thinking of him as Father Eden. He wasn't a father; he was a child. Simone would see to him later. It was a miracle that he escaped the ISF searchlights. But first, there was the little matter of John Halo, who had come up from Castel Gandolfo last night. A crowd had been gathering in the plaza outside the front gates; the pontiff was scheduled to make an appearance. Simone went upstairs to see how he was doing.

As he climbed the ancient stone staircase up to the suite, Simone reflected on how the pieces were neatly falling into place. Pope John had been understandably nervous since the Tragedy, but now that Saul and Nano were out of the picture, and now that their infernal science experiment in the catacombs had been dismantled, perhaps the old boy would calm down. The beauty of it was, Nano had been so appalled by the Spawns of Satan scheme—or whatever the hell Saul called it—that he'd taken care of it all by himself. That was a pleasant surprise. And so was Nano's connection to Isaac La Croix. Simone didn't think he could be so enterprising. Perhaps he shouldn't have let Eden take him out, after all. The impressionable idiot could have been useful for other things.

Simone reached the top of the stairs and approached the abbot's quarters, graciously lent to the pontiff for his Easter visit. The Swiss guards flanking the door watched him, and he nodded hello. As they opened the doors to let him in, he wondered why it took so long for Halo to pull the trigger on Saul. Though Simone had no proof, he was fairly certain that Saul was the one who tried to have him and Johnson taken out. But he did know that the cardinal was behind the Tragedy, and Halo's chauffeur could have dispatched the conniving bastard at any point along the way. That's one of the reasons why you have a retired colonel from Swiss Intelligence as your chauffeur. But perhaps Halo was waiting for Saul to find Devlin first.

When the time was right, Simone intended to ask them, perhaps over wine at the Castel.

The pope was sitting in an ornate silk chair on a dais in the center of the room, and his dressers were putting on his red shoes. Halo smiled hello and Simone smiled back, approaching with his head bowed in respect. The pope was in a buoyant mood; he'd just gotten word from Balliez that Saul was toast, and the literalness of the slang had amused them both.

But for all of the Church's power and wealth, and for all of its connections and reach, deep into Interpol and deep into America's Department of State and beyond, Simone was the one who had found Devlin, and not Saul. And all Simone had to work with was a guilt-ridden archbishop, a bible-thumping retired Fed, and an alcoholic ex-priest.

And of course, the Book of Devlin. They all should have taken the text as seriously as he did, Simone thought. Because on this glorious day, Lucifer was redeemed, the Prophesy was fulfilled, and the True Doctrine of the Faith was in his sole possession. The Church's favorite bogeyman had just ascended into heaven, and they had no idea it even happened. But Simone did, and that was his power.

He knelt down and kissed the pope's ring, and then stood behind the chair to whisper in the pontiff's ear as his dressers fussed with all the finishing touches.

"It's safe now, your Holiness."

Halo nodded, and then his dressers placed the mitre on his head and helped him to stand. Simone called it the Fishhead Hat, since that's what it was modeled after, the open mouth of a fish, and he always thought that it looked damned silly on a grown man with a flock of over one billion mortal souls. And it was a trick to wear, too, particularly in a stiff breeze.

Halo's attendants fluttered about, gathering their things, and two of them opened the balcony doors. A murmur rose from the crowd gathered below, and a rousing cheer went up. Halo stepped outside, and a hush of admiration descended on the candlelit crowd.

It was first light, and he faced the eastern horizon, lifting his hands in the air to welcome the approaching dawn, and looked to heaven above. "Domini, dominie . . ."

The sea of candles in the plaza cast a hellish glow on his features. Simone stood in the shadows behind him, and smiled.

CHAPTER SEVENTY- FIVE

Annabelle was sitting on the curb, weeping into her empty hands that lay open in her lap. Devlin had dissolved into silver dust and was swept away into stormy skies, and she would be alone to bear his child. It was clearing now and the rain had stopped, but the hints of sunshine brought her no relief.

Peter Johnson stood beside her, but he didn't know what to do or say to make her feel better. It was the second ascension he'd witnessed in less than six months, and though he knew he should be happy for the world, it saddened him that she was so bereft. In just the short time he'd seen them together, the love they shared was abundantly clear. It reminded him of his days with Lisa, and he knew that Annabelle would never quite recover, just as he never had, after more than thirty years. Over time, he came to learn that some things you don't get beyond, and some things you don't leave behind, because true love knows no past, only the eternal now. She would learn the same, or she would die of a broken heart.

She glanced up to him and he gently smiled, and offered his hand to help her to her feet. She stood and nodded a thank you, and he sensed that there was something she wanted to say.

"He was fearless," she murmured, as much to herself as to him. "He jumped into the line of fire, and I was terrified for him." She looked at Johnson, but he didn't say anything. "Watching him jump in front of me," she continued, but then she trailed off, searching for a way to express herself.

"The whole world was lifted from out of the darkness in that moment," she finally said. "The whole world was lifted to a brighter place, even if just for a moment . . ."

All her life she wrestled with a love for humanity, coupled with a contempt for humans that bordered on revulsion. And now she realized the turmoil was gone, because if the Devil could be redeemed then so could anyone, including herself. And perhaps that had been her true conflict all along, she mused. Not with humans and humanity, but with the paradox inside her own soul. The assassin and the healer were finally reconciled, though she couldn't explain why. But if Devlin had changed, then surely there was hope for her.

Johnson felt an inner release as well, and to his great surprise he found himself forgiving Devlin for murdering his wife and child. If God had redeemed the Devil himself, he reasoned, then who am I to hold him to account? They were in a better place, he concluded, and though he had always felt that way, his encounter today with Devlin confirmed it. For if the Devil existed, then so did Hell. And if Hell existed, then so must Heaven. After thirty-three years, Peter Johnson was finally at peace.

Diane was watching him, but he didn't know what to say, exactly. What just transpired gave him hope, but it frightened him at the same time. Perhaps because he didn't know what would happen next. There was nothing in the Bible about what just transpired, or about Christine Mas' divinity and ascension, for that matter. Her time on earth wasn't the Second Coming; it was to settle a bet between Lucifer and God. And now that Lucifer had been redeemed, the world was in uncharted waters.

Annabelle interrupted his ruminations by suddenly stepping to his left, and forcefully put her foot down on the sidewalk. He turned quickly, his hand going to his weapon, and then he stopped. She was standing firm on La Croix's semi-automatic; the man's bloody hand was a mere two inches from the grip.

Johnson flushed in sudden embarrassment, realizing he hadn't cleared away the weapon. The last time he bothered to check, La Croix seemed to be unconscious.

Annabelle picked up the weapon, and looked it over like it was a toy, as Johnson grew nervous by the moment. The sirens were much louder now, and the EMTs and the police could arrive any time. It was a bad enough scene already; more gunplay at this point would not be good.

La Croix's lips trembled, watching her. The round from Sama had shattered his shoulder blade, then ricocheted down and perforated his lung, nicking his pulmonary artery. His lung was filling with blood, and so was his abdominal cavity.

Annabelle gazed at the weapon in her hand. It had taken her love away, and she touched her swollen belly in remembrance. She looked down to La Croix, but he just stared back at her, unrepentant. Her features hardened in response, and she aimed his own gun at him.

Johnson shook his head no, beseeching her to back off. Several witnesses were peeking out their windows, and the cops were about to pull up. But she and La Croix were in a world of their own, and Johnson would have to tackle her to get her to stand down. And after what she just went through, he just didn't have the heart.

Annabelle smiled darkly at La Croix. "You want this, don't you?"

His life was slowly leaking out of him, but even as it did, Isaac La Croix could see something that Johnson was blind to. Because Isaac wasn't lying wounded on a sidewalk in Park Slope. He was healthy and whole and on his feet, standing under the Tree of Knowledge in the Garden of Eden. And Eve was standing before him, pregnant with child, lovely and radiant, offering him the shiny apple in her hand. It had a ripe and luscious crimson glow, with patches of golden green . . .

The tree they stood under was the same tree that Annabelle adopted in

Miami. Though he didn't know it, the tree was a part of who she was, and so his vision of her embraced it as well.

He smiled and nodded. Yes, of course, he wanted to taste the fruit of the highest tree. He wanted it more than anything else, even more than he wanted her.

Annabelle smiled back, and aimed the pistol at the sweet spot between his eyes. "There's no turning back," she warned him, sighting over the gun barrel.

He nodded and smiled once again, and reached for the apple in her hand. It was glowing from within with a soft, radiant light, and its sweet promise of knowledge and power filled his consciousness.

"Don't say I never warned you," she murmured, and a quiet bullet of plel burst from the apple.

EPILOGUE

Devlin was approaching the Gates of Heaven, dressed in his black greatcoat. It whispered open with each stride, revealing the crimson lining, and his boots were silent on the golden path beneath his feet. Everything was just as he dreamed it would be, but it wasn't a dream and he knew it. There was a multitude of angels on both sides, and he somehow knew that they gathered in just the same way to welcome Christine Mas. Many of them exulted and cheered his arrival, much as they did for her. Some were in awe, some nodded in respect, and some were in tears, while others were unhappy that after such a long struggle, he finally conceded.

Two Seraphim stood guard at the Gates, watching him approach. Devlin stopped before them and told them to open wide, but they didn't answer or comply. He waited for what would happen next.

Christine Mas appeared, standing before the Gates, but he was the only one who saw Her female aspect. The others saw Jesus as they always had, and as they bowed low, Devlin nodded his head in respect. She showed him the same respect, like two generals after a battle. Which in many ways they were.

"I've come to confess my sins," Devlin told Her.

"Yes, I know," She replied, and she shape-shifted to Jesus. "I'll take your confession," the Son of God told Devlin.

"No, my Lord," he said quietly, with a respectful bow of his head. "I've come to confess before God."

Jesus was bemused. They had been in conflict since the Beginning, and it was the Devil himself who created the Trinity, at the council of Nicea, which further tangled the threads of Truth. Devlin's stratagem was to be the third wheel, the King of Heaven, the Lord of Life, and the Lord of Light. He knew that neither one of them were an aspect of God. God's creation, yes. But there was only one Almighty Father, ever-changing and eternal. They existed at his pleasure, and had no more substance than that.

"And if He won't see you?" Jesus asked him.

"He must. For at this moment. I am proof that He exists."

A silence fell among the multitude, and even the Seraphim were astonished, both at Devlin's bold declaration and the inescapable truth of what he said. For if the Devil was real, and he clearly was, then only God could have created him. Which meant that the profane, as well as the sacred, proved the existence of God.

Jesus was gazing into his eyes, knowing that he spoke truth, and Jesus nodded his head. "Prepare for the trial of Lucifer," He declared, and the Seraphim open the Gates as whispers shot through the crowd.

Jesus and the Devil entered Heaven, walking side by side, and one third of all the angels in existence followed behind. They were Lucifer's legions, dressed in their white greatcoats, the fallen angels who had followed him since being cast into the Abyss.

This was the first time since the War in Heaven that all the angels would be together. Golden trumpets sounded to welcome them home.

THE END

In memory of *all* who died serving their country.

In memory of all those who died because of hateful rhetoric manipulating young impressionable minds in dire circumstances to strap on an explosive vest and detonate in populated areas. Too many innocents have been lost because of hate.

In memory of all our friends and loved ones in Aurora, Colorado who died because a young American, armed to the teeth strode to the front in a multiplex theater, and randomly fired shots that killed 12 innocent people and wounded 58. This is in memory of them.

In memory of our loved ones, Alfredo Rivera, Sr., Natividad Bulandres Tampoy, Frances Anne Coulbourne, Ed Limato, Edith Bernard, Walt Conley, Leona M. Moreaux, Marcelle Joseph, Marcia Maxwell, Edward L. Tauriac Sr., Robert Jean, Francois Fortune Policard, Marlon Fletcher, Carmen Ville, Mark Bernard, Alminda Ramirez, Jeanine Dolsant, Lesly Dolsant, Mary Lee Picou & Wally J. Picou, MD., John Destito, Barbara Labissiere, Albert Philippe Boucicault, and Fritzgerald Bernard, Roy Conner Jr.

In memory of my Cousin Claire Saget who recently passed after battling cancer. And all of those who have died of cancer, as well as the families who have been affected with this terrible disease. Their memories will live forever in the heart of our souls.

ACKNOWLEDGMENTS

A Very special thank you, and hello to our family and friends:

Teresa Ramos, Jay Coulbourne, Arlene Rivera, Michael S. Conley, Mary Fakhoury, Maria Ruela Delmo, Adrienne Stout-Coppola, Steven Beer, James Coulbourne, Jayne Habros, Michael Habros, Christopher Coppola, Louise Ward, Ava Jamshidi, Ryan Torres, Windy Kay Myers, Mike Nilon, Elvira Perez, Jennie Manalo, Doug Petrucci, Jeanne McGill, Zora DeHorter, Raymon Vaca, Emmaculate Delmo, Marjorie Lilavois, Arnold Holland, Marrie Charms Salon, Allison Leung, Daniel Vang, Gabriel Beristain, Sean Coulbourne, Jen Coulbourne, Heather Taylor, David Joseph, Venus Mae Secretchen, Napoleon Ryan, Mike Wilson, Mario Appolon, Titilayo Kukuyi, Zoltan Honti, Nadia Lafranconi, Alan Poe, Katherin Kovin-Pacino, Yerania Del Orbe, Anne De Almeida, Tonisha Weaver, Anne Fletcher, Eyvette Williams, Erin Williams, Aalim S. Bey, Jocelyn Gahimbare, Wanda Chun, Lyzette Ortega Villorente, Golda Aly, Rumulo Delmo, Giles Masters, Mark Weingartner, David Rosenbloom, Ruel Delmo, Wendy Pullin, Jonathan Cruz, Emma Lou Delmo, Monina Aly, Jean Patrick Policard, Jaira Valenti, Phyllis Licht, Kai Kofer, Maggie Habros, Sungwook Choe, Melanie White, Aisha Martin-Easterling, Keri Selig, Joanna Adler, Maurice Benard, Rolando Sandoval, Maritza Sandoval, Kate Habros, Tony Akbay, Erik John, Andre Warren, Michael Wilks, Mark Warren, Jenny Olais, John Bryant Davilla, Jimmy Jean Louis, Jimmy Ross, Anton Goss, Nely Cab, Becky Due, Michael Koudsi, John Policard, John Bale, Zaz, Steven Valenzuela, Alan Cave, Jean Robert Policard, Edward L. Tauriac Jr., Benjy Irakoze, Mamadou

Fall, Mark Horowitz, Paz Barbecho, Becca Thomas, Randy McKenzi, Lee Ann Weber, Soledad Rosales, Louis Teseda, Florence Conley, Catherin Sikorski, Alicia Cole, Phidelie Decais, Zulma Antepara, Joelle Almodovar, Michael Garrett, Christopher Aime, Garrett Pullin, Eric Brown, Alyssa Schmid, Wikenson Alexis, Nicholas Pullin, Christopher DeMero, Kenyatta Hudson, Marci Jane Pullin, Ted Kurdyla, Derek D. Bolden, Sue Bray, Tim Snider, Mike Shultz, Lee Ann Weber, Marie Yacinthe, Ted Currier, Tim Dugger, Matt Owen, Michael Bergin, Tahina Policard, Charles Addessi, Richard Whiten, Rick Tebrugge, David Johnson, Vladimir Kurimski, Nelya Lukina, Jeff Rice, Guerline Pierre, Paulie Zance Rivera, Cassandra Francois, Travawn Scott, Debbie James, Kenny Rivera, Kengy Policard, Ed Leung, Janet Leung, Reine Roberth Jean Louis, Leonard Waldner, Rodney Bernard, Michael Brown, Gilde Flores, Liliana Pereira, Erica Webb, Derrick Murdock, Mark Johnson, Lanie Mabgubat, Imani Walker, Twan Williams, Cynthia Molly, Hippie Lou, Robert Jean Louis, Stephen Marrero, Salena I. Tauriac, Raquel Perkins, Jennifer Policard, Jason Foster, Jordan Foster, Robinson Jean Louis, Carren Purisima, Wesner Bernard, Independent American Movies, Lightyear Entertainment, I AM Publishing, Ten Percent Fund, B.I.D International, Green Lit Lottery, IMDB, MT Consulting, 50 States Lottery, W.I.L, Brooklyn Zoo, AEM, Books With Blood, I AM Muzik, Water Is Life, Glacia Nova, Hoorah Tea, Grace Hill Media, Brand Integration Delivered, Bookmasters, Atlas, Baker & Taylor, IMDB, Amazon, Film Finances, IFG, Marsh USA, Itunes, WACH FOX, Book Expo of America, LinkedIn, Facebook, Apple Feast Studios, Hollywood Reporter, Variety, Gilbert Films, Riz Noir Caribbean Restaurant, MUSL Group, California State Lottery, Bad Friday Productions, Jay Coulbourne Productions, Studio Camp, Movie Mall Ent., VUDU Clothing, Christopher Coppola Enterprises, Arlene Rivera Productions, Michael Sean Conley Productions, Goodreads.com., and to all of those who purchased Hunting Christ & Hunting Lucifer from foreign to domestic. Much love and respect to those of you who "Liked" our Facebook fan page!

Please visit www.huntingchrist.com or www.huntinglucifer.com to read online for free.

Our Universe is several billions of years old, and until six thousand years ago, Lucifer was the most respected angel in the heavens. He was a General in Chief, and he commanded legions of angels. His loyalty and faithfulness to God was unwavering - Lucifer once declared: "I'd rather die at the hands of God, than to die against Him." Lucifer faithfully served God for over sixteen billion years. So for those of you who are living in darkness - Let There be Light…

I hope that you've enjoyed reading this work of fiction as much as I enjoyed entertaining you. - Thank you for being my Audience.

Ken Policard – President of Global Affairs

THE HUNTING TRILOGY

Independent American Movies

KEN POLICARD

HUNTING GOD

BOOK III

KEN POLICARD

HUNTING LUCIFER

BOOK II

KEN POLICARD

HUNTING CHRIST

I AM PUBLISHING PRESENTS A KEN POLICARD NOVEL

JAY COULBOURNE TIM SNIDER SUE BRAY MIKE SHULTZ
MARSHA PYANOWSKI MIKE CONLEY RANDY McKENZIE
NANCY AHR ARLENE RIVERA, RICHARD KINSEY
LEE ANN WEBER

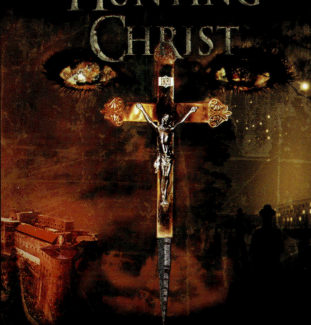

A KEN POLICARD NOVEL

HUNTING LUCIFER

KEN POLICARD

HUNTING LUCIFER BOOK 1

NARRATED BY
Richard Kinsey

MP3 - CD
UNABRIDGED

AUDIO BOOK

M INDEPENDENT AMERICAN MOVIES

I AM PUBLISHING
AUDIO BOOK

God tests the now mortal Devil through trial and tribulation as he proceeds along a path toward redemption.

"No matter how this ends, I will always love You."
-Devlin

"And I will always love you, Lucifer."
-God-

EXECUTIVE PRODUCER: Ken Policard

GENRE: FICTION
CATEGORY: SUSPENSE / THRILLER
LENGTH: 12.5 HRS / 6 DISCS
FORMAT: MP3 / CD

CO-EXECUTIVE PRODUCERS: JAY COULBOURNE
ARLENE RIVERA
MICHAEL S. CONLEY

I AM PUBLISHING PRESENTS A KEN POLICARD AUDIOBOOK
AUTHOR KEN POLICARD NARRATOR RICHARD KINSEY CO-SCREENWRITER MICHAEL S. CONLEY
CO-EXECUTIVE JAY COULBOURNE CO-PRODUCERS ARLENE RIVERA PRODUCERS STEVE VALENZUELA
SPECIAL MARY ANN LEAL, SAMANTHA LEAL, ARNOLD HOLLAND, CHRISTOPHER COPPOLA

independent American Movies

ISBN-13: 978-0-9846340-1-9
9 780984 634019
52450

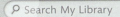

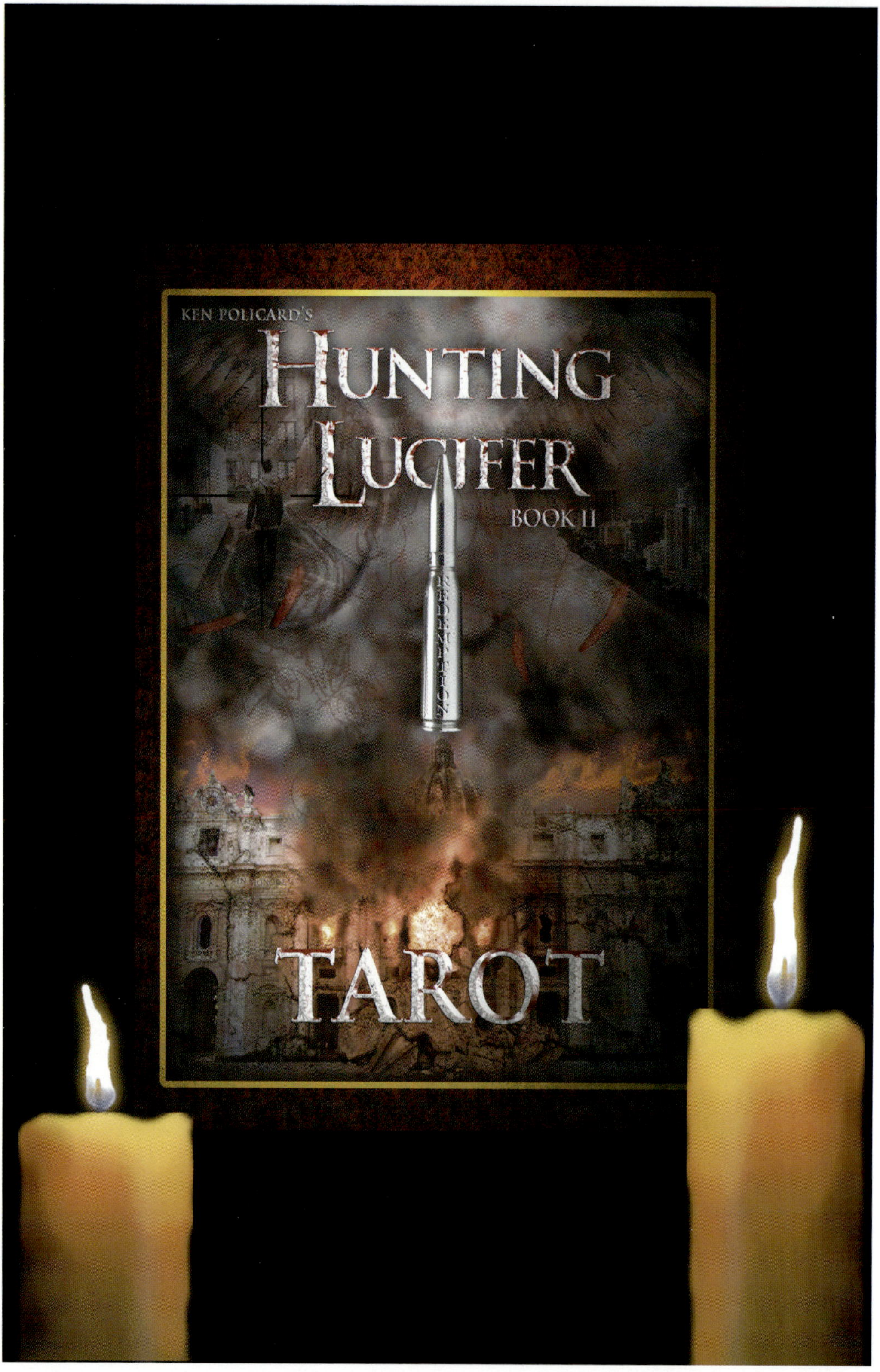
KEN POLICARD'S
HUNTING
LUCIFER
BOOK II
TAROT

KEN POLICARD'S
HUNTING CHRIST
VIDEO GAME
THE HUNT IS ON!
G.O.D.
I AM Interactive

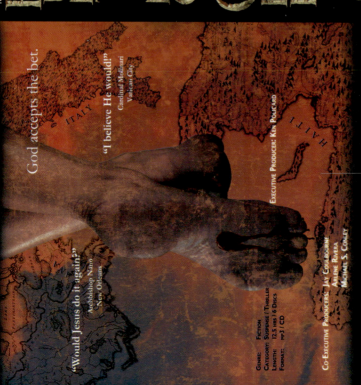

KEN POLICARD

HUNTING CHRIST

A KEN POLICARD NOVEL

UNABRIDGED
MP3 - CD

NARRATED BY
Richard Kinsey

🔔 AudioBook

Ⓜ INDEPENDENT AMERICAN MOVIES

I AM PUBLISHING
AudioBook

The Devil bets God that Christ would be unable to achieve divinity in modern times.

God accepts the bet.

"Would Jesus do it again?"
Archbishop Nano
New Orleans

"I believe He would!"
Cardinal Molinari
Vatican City

ITALY

HAITI

Genre: Fiction
Category: Suspense / Thriller
Length: 12.5 hrs / 6 Discs
Format: mp3 / CD

Executive Producer: Ken Policard

Co-Executive Producers: Jay Coulbourne
Arlene Rivera
Michael S. Conley

I AM PUBLISHING presents a KEN POLICARD audiobook

AUTHOR Ken Policard NARRATOR Richard Kinsey CO-PRODUCED BY Michael L. Conley EXECUTIVE PRODUCER Arlene Rivera MUSIC Steve Valenzuela

VOICE TALENT MARY ANN LEAL, SAMANTHA LEAL, ARNOLD HOLLAND, CHRISTOPHER COPPOLA

Ⓜ Independent American Movies

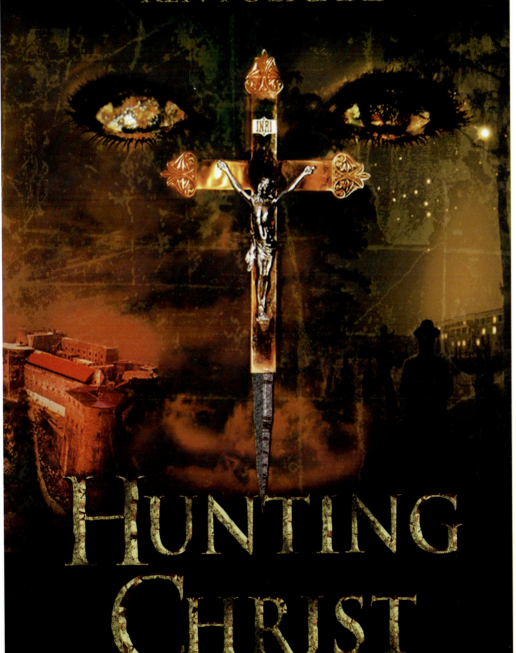

KEN POLICARD

HUNTING CHRIST

Ken Policard's

HUNTING CHRIST

TAROT

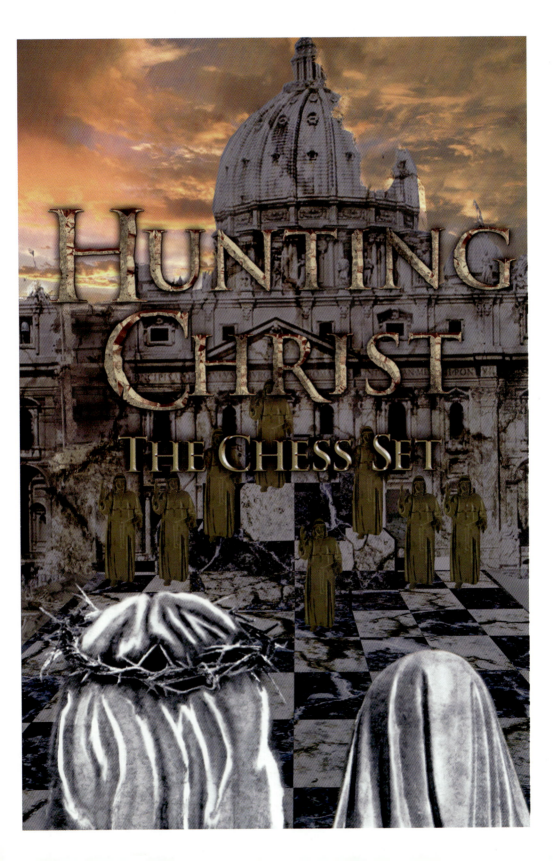

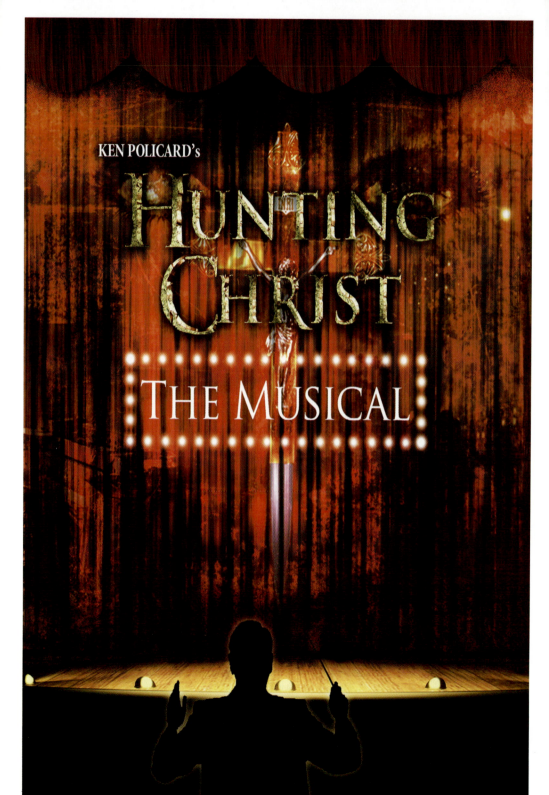

Ken Policard's

HUNTING CHRIST eBook

HUNTING TRILOGY TEAM

KEN POLICARD

JAY COULBOURNE

ARLENE RIVERA

MICHAEL S. CONLEY

CHRISTOPHER COPPOLA

WENDY PULLIN

INDEPENDENT AMERICAN MOVIES

B.I.D. INTERNATIONAL RECORDING ARTIST

Executive Producers: Ken Policard   Jay Coulbourne   Arlene Rivera   Arnold Holland

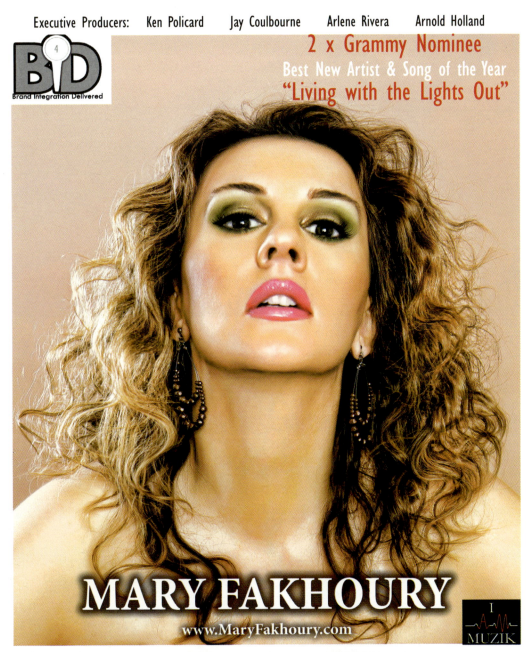

2 x Grammy Nominee
Best New Artist & Song of the Year
"Living with the Lights Out"

MARY FAKHOURY
www.MaryFakhoury.com

PROFESSIONAL TALENT REPRESENTATION

Managers: Ken Policard / Arlene Rivera
Publicist: Jeanne McGill
Legal Representation: Arnold Holland

FAN MAIL TO:
9663 Santa Monica Blvd.
Beverly Hills, CA 90210

CREATURA

Sometimes
Love is Lethal

NELY CAB

Becky Due

A Suspense Celebrating Women's Strength

Returning Injury

Hunting Christ
&
Hunting Lucifer
T-Shirts
AVAILABLE AT WWW.HUNTINGCHRIST.COM

VUDOO WEAR

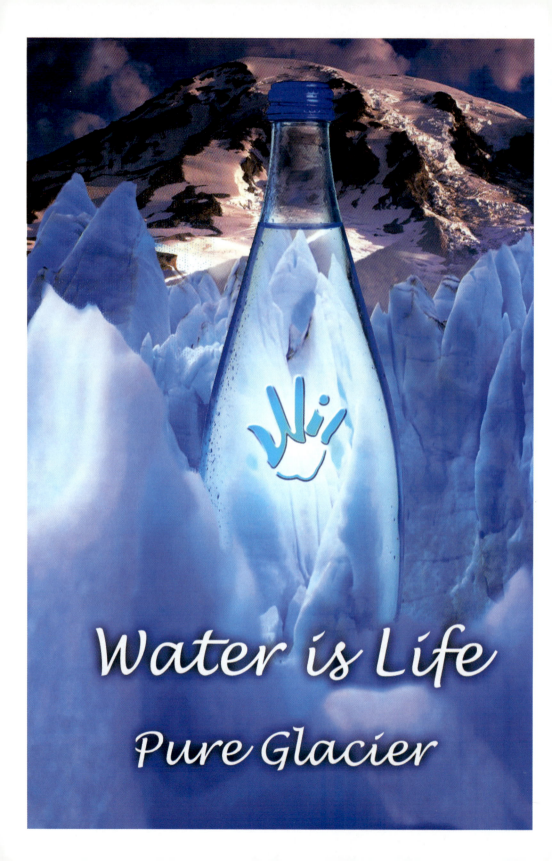

Water is Life

Pure Glacier

WHEN YOU WIN, YOUR FILM WINS!

COMING SOON TO A MULTI-PLEX NEAR YOU!

www.greenlitlottery.com

Lottery - Scratch Game - Game-Show

 FILM MAKING AUDIENCES

WHERE YOUR GREENS CAN COME TRUE

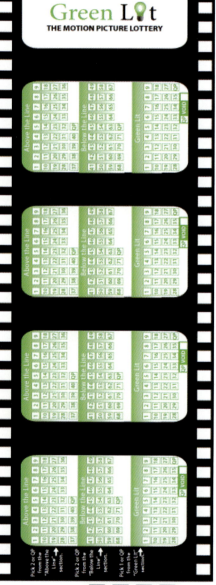

MULTI-STATE LOTTERY

What if you didn't have to pay taxes
for the rest of your life?

INDEPENDENT AMERICAN MOVIES

KEN POLICARD

Jay Coulbourne   -   Arlene Rivera   -   Michael S. Conley

www.independentamericanmovies.com

Green LIt

"Ten Percent Fund", is a non-profit organization created for those in need, from missing children with cancer, and families in distress due to homes lost by turbulent economic circumstances or natural disasters. This fund is established primarily for the basis and means to contribute economically and give back to the national and international community by the donations of homes to a well deserving family or individuals.

This is done via "Green Lit Lottery," the motion picture industry lottery. The community and churches, with the Multi-Theater Lottery Governing Group, votes for the family most deserving and in need. Overall, the homes will come from foreclosure listings typically held by the banks. This will happen throughout the United States as on a larger global level.

Furthermore, the "Ten Percent Fund" will gain strength as we personally contribute from our earnings from our companies/payrolls, alongside the generous donations of the Hollywood, star-studded community and combined with the contributions of philanthropic individuals, groups, and corporations.

Independent American Movies is committed to donating 10% of all profits generated from the Hunting Christ franchise to the "Ten Percent Fund."

Visit us at www.10percentfund.org